Jane Gardam has won two Whitbread awards (for *The Queen of the Tambourine* and *The Hollow Land*). She was also shortlisted for the Booker Prize with *God on the Rocks*, which was made into a much-praised TV film. She is the winner of the David Higham Award and the Royal Society of Literature's Winifred Holtby Prize for her short stories about Jamaica, *Black Faces, White Faces*. *The Pangs of Love*, another collection of short stories, won the Katherine Mansfield Award. *Going into a Dark House* won the Macmillan Silver Pen Award. In 1999 she was awarded the Heywood Hill Literary Prize for a lifetime's commitment to literature. Her most recent novel, *Old Filth*, was shortlisted for the Orange Prize in 2005.

Jane Gardam was born in Coatham, North Yorkshire. She lives in a cottage on the Pennines and in East Kent, near the sea.

'Funny and admirable . . . Jane Gardam writes with a dark and buoyant energy which continually challenges and provokes' *The Times*

'It is Gardam's particular skill to be able to lead us into profound psychological terrain yet at the same time offer up wonderful, at times gut-shaking, at times sly or vicious humour . . . I felt, by the end, that sense of doom you get on holidays when leaving friends whose lives have become so intimately known' *Literary Review*

'There are moments of absolute pleasure. The narrative voice is suave and subtle as an oboe, modulating effortlessly to the mood of her characters' *Independent Weekend*

Faith Fox

– A NATIVITY –

Jane Gardam

ABACUS

First published in Great Britain by Sinclair-Stevenson in 1996
First published by Abacus in 1997
This edition published by Abacus in 2008

A CIP catalogue record for this book
is available from the British Library.

ISBN 978-0-349-12101-7

Papers used by Abacus are natural, recyclable products made from
wood grown in sustainable forests and certified in accordance with
the rules of the Forest Stewardship Council.

Photoset in North Wales by
Derek Doyle & Associates, Mold, Clwyd.
Printed and bound in Great Britain by
Clays Ltd, St Ives plc
Paper supplied by Hellefoss AS, Norway

Abacus
An imprint of
Little, Brown Book Group
100 Victoria Embankment
London EC4Y 0DY

An Hachette Livre UK Company

www.littlebrown.co.uk

For Penelope Hoare

And who would rock the cradle
Wherein this infant lies
Must rock with easy motion
And watch with humble eyes.

Austrian carol, 1649

– Part One –

— Part One —

– 1 –

It was terrible when Holly Fox died. Terrible. Just awful. Pammie Jefford heard first, at the hospital, doing her voluntary work. At the sluice. In came a nun and hurtled by and out of the other door. Then after a minute another volunteer came in, looking white. It was a wonderful hospital. It had not lost a mother for years and years. Holly was only the third since the foundation of the place before the war, and the other two had been foreigners with queer blood groups. Holly Fox. Oh no, no – not *Holly Fox*! Oh God.

Pammie wouldn't dream of ringing anyone from the hospital and of course she couldn't stay on there today. 'You mean you *know* her?' they asked, not yet able to say *knew*; and Sister Mark said, 'God rest her. God rest her. Yes, away you go, dear,' and Pammie left, almost forgetting to take off her apron.

Outside in the drive she stood for minutes together beside her fast little Peugeot GTI, stood in the sunshine, not able to get in.

Holly Fox, *Holly Fox*!

Soon all round Surrey the telephones were ringing. Women were putting down receivers, covering their faces, putting fists to mouths, going

3

out into gardens and calling people in. Ringing up yet other people. Holly Fox's own generation mostly heard later because they were all at work. But these, Pammie's lot, friends of Holly's mother, were the women who had all lived at one time, thirty years ago, in the world of one another's children. Oh – *Holly Fox*!

'A blood clot. It could have happened at any time, apparently. Just a coincidence it was while she was in labour, though I don't suppose that helped. No, an easy time. A very *easy* time. No fuss. Just laughing and joking and deep breathing – well, you know how she was.'

'Was he there? Whatsisname? I never remember the husband's name. Pammie, Pammie – he was a *doctor*. And people don't die in childbirth now.'

'I don't know. It was early. Quite two weeks early. Maybe he was over in his own hospital. There was no sign of him at the nuns'. Well, there was no sign even of . . .'

Now they approached it.

'Even Thomasina wasn't there.'

'Whatever will happen? Oh, poor Thomasina.'

'Poor Thomasina.'

The news spread from Surrey into Hampshire and Sussex.

At a nice house in Liss four friends of Thomasina stopped their Bridge for nearly half an hour and picked up the cards again quite abstractedly. Somebody else near Petersfield was watching the six o'clock news, where a procession of skeletons straggled across a desert. Children's mouths in close-up were patrolled by flies. Starving madonnas, with lakes instead of eyes, rib-cages almost exposed through parchment skin, gazed uninterested at the cameras. 'Hello? No – perfectly good moment. Just the news. Ghastly – but what can one do? I'm waiting for the weather forecast: it's the Ladies' Cup tomorrow. What? *What*? Oh my God, no! Not Holly *Fox*? Oh, poor darling Thomasina! Who told her? Where is she? Where's her husband? Have you rung? I said *rung*? The house, of course. Oh, *course* go round there. Of course you must. If not, I'll go from over here. I'll get in the car now. Don't be *silly*, "butting in". She's somewhere, and the son-in-law's no earthly good. All his family live in Wigan or somewhere. Don't be so *wet*, Pammie. It's not like you. Go round.'

Others, nearer, had already gone round, but Thomasina's house in its large garden stood locked and silent. Florists' bunches were already gathering on the step. Pammie tramped round to the back. All was still and silent. Bulbs had been planted in hundreds under trees. Thomasina's gardening gloves lay together in prayer in the conservatory, beside a sheaf of carefully divided irises.

On the way home Pammie called on another woman, who answered the door, brick-red in the face with shock, glaring in outrage. 'She's at that health farm, Thomasina. That's where she is this week. To "get herself together for being a grandmother", she said, "in good time". It wasn't due, you know. "The first one's never early", she said. She said it here. This Thursday. Standing there where you are now. "May as well have a last fling de luxe", she said, "before my time stops being my own." She was going to be such a grandmother.'

'I know. We said, "She'll outclass Holly." '

'Not that she could have done. Holly was

unimprovable. It was all talk with Thomasina. "Taking over"! It wouldn't have happened. She's too erratic. But the help she would have been at first . . . ! Adored it, patronising Holly and saying, "How hopeless," and yet proud as hell that she was such a marvellous mother. Oh God – *would* have been such a marvellous mother. I don't believe it. *I do not believe it.* Holly. That bursting, bursting health.'

'I suppose that's what it was,' said Pammie. 'Yes, please, I'll have another.' She held up her glass. 'Yes, don't stop. It was *bursting* health and she burst.'

'What a foul thing to say.'

'Well, something burst. Gone. Bang. And things will go bang in Thomasina now. You'll see. At last.'

Jinny of the brick-red face whose house it was and who did not have to drive home and whose dinner was already in the Neff awaiting the husband's reliable seven-thirty return had a third whisky and soon began to weep.

'I must go,' said Pammie; 'I've a madrigal group.'

Jinny at the door, sniffing, said, 'Matter of fact, what we were talking about: "*would* have been" a good grandmother? . . . She *is* a grandmother.'

Pammie looked blank and then remembered. 'I never thought,' she said. 'Oh God! Is the child all right? They never said. Have you heard? What was it?'

'I don't know.'

'A boy, I think. Yes, I think now they were saying . . . Yes. A lovely child. Though it may be a girl. I don't know. I can't believe I never asked. One or the other, I suppose.'

Which is how Faith Braithwaite was heralded into the world.

– 2 –

Holly Fox had remained Holly Fox after marriage to
Andrew Braithwaite not because of the least breath
of feminism in her but because she had always been
such a vivid creature that nobody could think of her
with any other name.

She really was an extraordinarily nice girl. Well,
not nice so much as passionately loving and
infectiously happy. She adored people. She adored
places. She adored artefacts. At school she had
adored games and been wonderfully good at them.
She hadn't adored intellectual activities all that
much and had often been in tears over her work; but
after the tears, great big shiny ones, she had always
recovered quickly and was soon laughing. She
laughed beautifully – and she had always scraped
through her examinations somehow. Holly Fox got
by.

She was rather a noisy girl and you could pick out
her laughing voice a long way off, but then a lot of
girls are noisy, and at least she was tunefully noisy,
never strident. She was adored, doted upon by the
little girls at school, and to some of the big girls and
several members of staff she was the cause of pangs.
Her breeziness seemed to feed Sapphic passions

7

which she never reciprocated nor seemed to comprehend, for she sent off shameless little presents quite publicly to all and sundry and jolly birthday cards covered in kisses to home addresses.

Holly Fox was effective. She was never late for anything. She was clean and even in the hideous school uniform of the day she managed to look as if she knew how to wear clothes. She always carried an extra pair of tights about with her in case of ladders and at any time of any day she would have been confident enough to meet the Queen, never without handkerchief, comb, toothbrush, tampon, book of stamps.

She shone with health. Her teeth gleamed. Her strong clean nails were filed into nice white ovals. Her hair sprang up shinily from the scalp on either side of a quarter-inch-deep parting. She never looked weather-beaten or awry but always, even in deep November, bronzy and smooth. She tramped about in wellies and loved a rainy day. Such *fun*!

Her self-confidence was daunting and would have been loathsome had it not been obvious that it sprang from neither conceit nor self-awareness. She was so outgoing, so enthusiastic about her life, her friends, her family, her tennis, her Christianity (she ran astonishingly successful sponsored charities from the age of fourteen: 'Well, we just *know* so many *people* and they're all so *generous*'), that you could not really say that it sprang from self-absorption either.

It probably did spring from self-absorption, of course, for Holly Fox was not altogether a good listener. But how could you mind when the self she presented was so delightful? She never missed a birthday of the most long-ago family cleaning lady,

8

or au pair from earliest childhood, or teacher in her first primary school, or her mother's old, old friends, especially the hairy, warty ones. Her big joy, almost her passion, was the putting of people in touch with other people who were vaguely connected with one another by distant threads of blood, by godchildren of second and third cousins, by half-remembered funerals, the wedding parties of long-lost enemies and old and sometimes desperate-to-be-forgotten passions. Her bulky address book at the age of twenty or so was already like the Almanac de Gotha. Once inscribed in it you were hers for ever. Holly Fox never, never, dropped you.

And men? Sex? No great trouble there either. She *adored* men, and said so. Often. She had adored men since she was born, she said, calling out the information across rooms full of them, laughing not archly but, it has to be said, deliciously. Sometimes chin in hand, eyes large, she said it lovingly, longingly, introspectively, confidently, like an experienced old courtesan who had much that she might tell; or as if she were preparing for a maturity and old age when it would be said that Holly Fox in her prime had been a *femme fatale*, a raving beauty.

And this was untrue. Holly Fox was not beautiful at all, but behaved with a shining openness and an innocent heart so that when she looked at you with big clear eyes she seemed to expose a classic face. In fact it was broad, freckly, and the chin colossal.

At the time of her death at twenty-eight in the 1990s Holly Fox had settled deeply into the mores of an almost lost generation, her mother's. She wore pearls and good suits and a hat for lunch in London. Do you believe this? Well, it is true. I promise you that Holly Fox at twenty-eight in the early Nineties

9

would wear a hat for lunch in Fortnum & Mason, usually as the guest of older women, and sit there among the antiseptic Americans – who thought, mistakenly, how amazingly English she was – and all the old scrags with their painted faces and tortured voices that floated together, piercingly clear, high up among the pretty lights on the ceiling. So sweet, the old-fashioned voice, the little diamond brooch in the lapel (she loved a diamond). She smiled up at the deadpan waitresses who said to each other, 'Isn't she like *Brief Encounter*, and yet she can't be more than, say, thirty-five?' 'Or *Mrs Miniver*,' they said.

They knew their stuff, these old creaking Fortnum warriors, for Holly Fox was no better educated, no more politically, sociologically or sexually advanced, than either of these wartime film stars of nearly half a century before. Holly Fox was a throwback, a coelacanth. She aimed at being a thoroughly nice girl.

A fool and an idiot, then? A leech upon society? Not at all. Holly Fox before her marriage had been a nurse, a staff nurse in a great London hospital, and though she had had such trouble with her school examinations there was not a thing she balked at or mismanaged or mistook in her medical ones. She won distinctions. Before an examination she was still adept in fanning herself into the proper hysteria – 'I'll never do it, *never*' – but then she would pass out top.

'But I *meant* it!' she would cry. 'I thought I'd made a terrible *mess* of it! I swear. I can't believe it.'

Her nursing gifts, which unfolded naturally, were very thrilling to her. Her father had been a doctor, and his father before him, and instinctively she seemed to know the form, the jargon, the medical mythology. She seemed to comprehend the Hippocratic world so well that she even dared sometimes to send it up. As a first-year nurse she attended the hospital Christmas party dressed as a kissagram and embraced the Dean while ogresses in higher power stood dumbfounded. Sharp-faced, pock-marked authoritarians gaped, bewildered. The nerve of her with her pink glowing face – was it make-up or wasn't it? (It wasn't, it was health) – and her lah-di-dah vowels. 'What sort of example, Nurse Fox?' and so on.

But there was a certain steely authority about Holly Fox. Her credentials were impeccable. Her grandfather and father (and the man soon to be her husband) each had his name painted gold upon mahogany on the honours boards of the hospital Rugby XVs.

Cleverer girls than Holly Fox sometimes said that her confidence beneath the unrelenting sweetness made them sick. Ugly ones said she was over the top, snobbish, no beauty and a pain. But nobody could help liking her genuine good nature and her loving ways and lack of self-consciousness, and the fact that she was exactly the same with everybody, which, incidentally, is only nice if you are nice and not poisonous. Tamburlaine the Great was the same with everybody and so were Napoleon and Mussolini and Ivan the Terrible and Queen Elizabeth the First. But Holly Fox was not like them.

And she was not snobbish. No.

Or was she snobbish?

Oh, God, yes. Holly Fox actually, when you came down to it, was snobbish. Any political party not blue as the summer sky was in unthinkable shadow and she had never once been out with a man who hadn't been to an English public school, though she would have been *thrilled* with Harvard maybe, or Gordonstoun, which was OK because of the royal family.

During her nursing training, when Holly Fox met and worked with proles for the first time (and found them all perfectly sweet), she didn't know them socially. She would have been lost anywhere that her own language was not spoken, both metaphorically and actually, and before meeting her future husband she had never travelled north of the home counties of England except once by air to St Andrews for her mother's golf, and to Dublin for a ball given by a girl at school. She muddled up Westmorland and Wolverhampton.

But look – she was lovely. You could tick off a thousand shortcomings in Holly Fox, failures of imagination, limitations of everyday understanding, and you might not choose to go on holiday with her especially if you were of rather low vitality or cared for guidebooks or for reading on an empty beach in silence. You might not waste a ticket on her for a concert. You might get fed up that every theatre performance she ever went to was pronounced 'absolutely marvellous' and was the more marvellous the less she understood it. And you might not be inclined to tell her any secrets, because although they would be perfectly safe with her (she forgot them) you had to watch them bounce and slide like dandelion clocks off her hands, scarcely touching her consciousness.

All the same, Holly Fox wept with the bereaved, held the hands of the dying, and she was wonderful with patients in pain. Yet the knife-twist of failure or loss somehow you felt never came near her and 'tragedy', a word she used often, was never applied to anything large. She believed effortlessly in God, effortlessly in Christ, hazily in the Holy Spirit. She confused Bethlehem and the Gaza Strip and never thought which language Christ spoke in since what He said had always sounded so English. Eternal life presented no difficulties to Holly Fox for she knew that it must be so, and heaven somewhere or other, or why should such awful things happen to us here? There must be more to us than bodies that rotted and stank and broke apart and grew things both inside and out and looked worse as they aged and loathsome at the last. Children's bodies, too. All that she had had to see and face head-on in hospital, the facts that so often persuade better-educated, subtler people than Holly Fox against the existence of God, were for her simply proof that there must be something else to come or why should God have bothered? She had a point.

I tell you, everyone looked for the crumbled feet of clay on this shining girl and nobody found them. Certainly men never found them. Holly Fox was physically, uninhibitedly warm-blooded and determined on a lot of sexual love – in time. Not yet. What's more – and this was important to the medical students she usually went about with – she was pretty well-off and well-connected to the top medical mafia. Quite a few were stirred by the heart that beat so strongly beneath the starch that her hospital still insisted upon.

Oh Holly Fox, Holly Fox – she knew in her genes, as many don't, that what the sleazy, exhausted, nearly gutted soul of the young male hospital doctor wants is not femininity and softness, and someone

13

who won't bleat when he's never at home, so much as self-confidence; an effective, fearless sort of woman, preferably a wielder of some sort of power in the profession, who keeps cool, smiles at him when he comes home, ticks him off, keeps her (and his) love affairs to herself, is silent as the grave about gossip, doesn't get drunk at parties and has the making of a stupendous medically political hostess of the future.

Holly Fox, by the way, had not the least intention of going on with any work after marriage, even if she were to choose a penniless houseman. Her mother and grandmother had never worked; why should she? The penniless housemen in her life did not actually know this yet but, even if they had, it would have made little difference, for the choice – just look at that jaw, those blue eyes perhaps a little cold within the sparkle – the choice was going to be entirely hers. When Holly Fox fell matrimonially in love it was going to be with utter success, a full-scale operation.

'Andrew Braithwaite,' said Thomasina, her mother, to Pammie and Jinny and everyone. 'Poor lamb, she's begun to gaze at him. He hasn't a chance.'

He hadn't.

She got him.

Thomasina, Holly's mother, had been a widow for years and years without the slightest intention of remarriage. Her husband, a general surgeon in the home counties, had dropped down dead in the middle of an operation on a heart that was somehow kept beating while old Herbert's refused every sort of jump-start in the book. He had been dying for a cigarette at the time, and indeed did so. A good marriage really, very devoted, although there had always been a look, a world-weary, wary look, in Thomasina's eye that said she always steered clear of devotion.

Maybe she was a woman who did not really need a man all that much? Maybe a generation on she would have been a lesbian? Herbert and she had got out of the way of discussing their feelings, if they had ever done so, which is improbable. Herbert had been pretty bluff from the nursery, and not often at home in the evenings. Overworked, of course, and no hobbies except smoking. His adoring hospital entourage (he liked girls for suggestive, sexy conversations, no more) had made him as arrogant as the next man in a sycophantic profession, and in his social life at home he postured about, too proud to talk about his work to laymen, afraid at parties that someone would come and ask for free advice. He was a crashing social snob, very keen on his dead relations. His talkativeness at work and his amiability were the same as his daughter's and his laugh was famous. He went caroling through life, probably doing more good than harm.

Thomasina never let on about what had drawn her to him. She had the Surrey way of talking endlessly and objectively about her nearest without the least hint of them being also dear. First meeting, young love, marriage bed and the early years of Thomasina and Herbert Fox were unknown to all, and 'all' now included themselves. The world was kept in darkness. There were no photographs on display except for an unyielding bridal study on Thomasina's dressing table, Herbert blotchy with (perhaps) emotion and in RAMC uniform and Thomasina, twenty-five, looking elderly in a family wedding veil that hung down, all round as if there were lead weights in the hem, like a lace tablecloth at a Mrs Beeton dinner.

Poor Thomasina. You could see the awful honeymoon ahead. You could see the screwed-up damp handkerchiefs at Victoria Station. You could hear the sad boom of the guns, imagine the bomb-torn plain, the mountainous bandages, the terrible and wonderful heroism and patriotism. At home there would be Thomasina in a ghastly white hat and apron with a big red cross stitched on it, making field dressings, running tea stalls, being brave beneath the zeppelins.

Wrong. Wrong. Wrong war. Thomasina in that war was not even a child. It was the second war. Herbert only made RAMC officer because he was

16

doing some national service and Thomasina only looked like Edith Cavell because she had absorbed, as her daughter was to do later, so much of her mother's generation that she looked a generation older than she was. There was a very powerful gene in the female members of this family that held its generations in a vice.

But Thomasina, unlike Holly Fox, who was not given the opportunity, grew younger. If there had been later photographs of her you would have seen her grow clear of the lace and lilies and honeymoon tweeds of the times. In the coming years, with Herbert so often from home, her voice was to become deeper and more confident. Her golf began to be respectable and her tennis even better. The dark face of Thomasina glaring through the racket strings before a particularly devilish smash showed a depth of aggression you'd never have expected in her at a drinks party in her chintzy sitting room or her garden which overflowed with old-fashioned roses all tangled up with shrubs, sweet-smelling herbs, narcissi, dahlias in season, clouds of bluebells in spring, difficult trilliums and lilies and 'anything I feel like sticking in'. Green fingers? Not at all. 'I just buy and pray.'

But that was not altogether true, for in the garden – in dungarees, then tight pants, then jeans, then floppy trousers as the years rolled – Thomasina heaved and dug and slashed about by the hour, the day, the week, the season, clearing, sweeping, replenishing soil, feeding with rich black compost, adding most violent tonics ('chicken shit for choice'), plumping, slapping and puddling every-thing back in again. She opened for the National Gardens twice a year. It was an almost killing, numbing discipline; introverting, silencing, and bringing great comforts. Thomasina's garden rewarded her with richness: every leaf looked polished or silken, every rose was spotless, thripless, waiting to be photographed, waiting to be admired.

Oh, what was really going on inside Thomasina Fox?

As the marriage waned to a brother-and-sisterishness – except for occasional exercisings in the dark, which were forgotten by morning, never commented upon – brother-and-sisterish tracts of private territory were established. Thomasina became capable of cutting her losses as resolutely as she cut down her sweet peas. Her figure improved. The roundedness beneath the lace tablecloth that had threatened haunches turned to slimness and then to leanness and then to a lanky Sackville-Western ranginess that happened to be fashionable at the time. She flattened out above, which was also timely, for it was now the 1960s, when female beauty became anorexic and young girls yearned sometimes until teenage death for a breastless, stomachless torso. Other women of Thomasina's age responded rebelliously at this time with gathered, bunchy skirts, scooped necklines and beehive hair. Thomasina flaunted her independence by wearing short skirts even in the evening and cutting her hair to near baldness.

She never discussed it. Never said why, and Herbert never noticed. Her friends said things like, 'Oh my! Thomasina!' but she only smiled. To one another they said, 'She looks rather male. Can't say I like it,' or 'She's really far too thin. I hope she's not *got* something,' and 'It's a bit repulsive really, those hipbones sticking out at the front, like those awful dying cows in the East.' Men liked it, though. During the Sixties and Seventies Englishmen were learning rather guiltily to like women who could look like boys, who grew thinner and thinner, taller and taller, fiercer and fiercer. Their heels became four inches high, puncturing the wooden floors of Europe, the châteaux of the Loire, the assembly rooms at Bath, the little Surrey hospital where Holly Fox was born and where, twenty-eight years later, she was to die.

Thomasina became 'that woman with the marvellous figure' and even when one day it was noticed that her waistline was rather less defined and then a baggish thing emerged between the coat-hanger hip bones, and word went round, 'Good gracious – Thomasina, at last!', she still looked good. Through all the nine months she looked good, indeed wonderful, and felt it. Herbert was delighted and everyone most envious, after Holly was born on Christmas Day, to find Thomasina restored to her flatness and ranginess within days, as if the child had been lifted lightly out from inside some expensively invisible zip-fastener. The nuns all thought her a splendid woman and Herbert was so excited he nearly amputated somebody's good leg. Or said he did. They were being awfully funny and bright and not altogether truthful about this time, the Foxes. They joked and laughed at everything. Even when Herbert died a year or so later Thomasina kept her careful, mocking face in order magnificently. Extraordinary woman. Very brave. Scarcely spoke of him.

But oh, the difference in her.

The difference that followed. The difference centred itself in the intensity of her love for Holly.

19

From her daughter's birth Thomasina had been ahead of her time, skipping the feminism and going straight into the backlash. She had been an avid non-smoking, non-drinking breast-feeder. Now she became the impassioned mother, she and the baby inseparable. For years she gave up everything: childless friends (except Pammie), Bridge, golf, tennis. She spent her days at tots' dancing classes, music lessons, playgroups, junior-school swimming baths, nursery tea parties. She refused to consider employing a nanny or au pair. She refused drinks parties, fork suppers beloved of the region, men, offers of marriage. She never went on holiday. She and Holly lived intensely together in the black-and-white Thirties-Tudor house in its glossy-mag garden, now rather overgrown. On the telephone (when she couldn't avoid it: it was before answer-phones) she kept up an occasional contact, in a pleasant, shrieking old lingo, with friends – she had no relations to speak of – and she had people to the house only if they had babies. Babies for Holly. Holly must have her friends from the beginning, this only child. Thomasina read Dr Spock, Jung, John Bowlby, Fairbairn.

Yet beneath the ordered, almost ordained, rich, upper-class life of the day, for which everyone about her had fought and which they believed to be a true and gallant way of continuing the country's old validity (not for the money only – this was pre-Thatcher), Thomasina swam in a deep sea of love for her child, a gobbling love, an inordinate affection that blotted out all else and terrified her whenever she had to come up for a gasp of air. She never put into words, not even to herself, what the gasps of air disclosed: that Holly was her passion,

20

her lover, her life. If 'anything should happen' to Holly, Thomasina knew that she would die.

It was inexplicable. It was not what anyone was used to in Edgecombe Park, least of all Thomasina. For years, after all, the Foxes had made no secret of the fact that they didn't want children and with Thomasina growing so masculine and skinny and poor Herbert so glandular and fat – and silly – it had often been said that you only had to look at them to see that the poor things couldn't do it. Some said they never had, that Herbert was all bombast and smut and schoolboy jokes about sex and all his talk about it in the hospital was just talk. But there it was. Holly Fox arrived into Thomasina's world and Thomasina wrapped her now celibate elegant frame in ecstasy.

As Holly's childhood passed, Thomasina began to cope rather better with this secret life. A perfect mother was not obsessive, must learn to let her child go in order to develop her own relationships, have schoolgirl secrets, go off on school trips. The first of these, no further than the Kensington Science Museum when Holly was eight, marked a vital stage in Thomasina's journey. She spent the hours alone at home hallucinating the upturned coach, little bodies spilled about the road, the Irish bomb, the false step off the pavement. 'We're just going to buy a—' Screech! The ambulance siren, the police cars. The ring at the bell. The funeral procession.

Nobody, *nobody*, knew the immensity of these things, and Holly was greeted on her return by her mother's cool face and nice food waiting in the fridge. Holly overheard girls at school say, 'Holly's mother's *terrific*-looking but she's a bit hard somehow. D'you think she's horrible to Holly?' But how could she be, with Holly such an open, happy girl?

And still open and happy at nine, hugging and hugging her mother goodbye when she went off to boarding school in Kent, excited at all that was to come. Thomasina amazed the school staff that climactic day by her light-hearted adieux. Other mothers sniffled. This one hugged and kissed the child with the greatest good sense and looked understanding and amused as Holly vanished up some stairs, one sock higher than the other, arms full of teddies and a tin of home-made shortbread.

Thomasina left briskly, but as she turned out of the school gates she began to shake. Later she stopped the car in a lay-by on the Hog's Back. She did not weep there, but sat, and the landscape eventually became the landscape again and not the narrow beastly bed on which her daughter would at this minute be arranging her toys and photographs; or flinging herself down, sucking a handkerchief end, tears spilling. Holly was actually signing herself up for various clubs and had made an inseparable friend called Grizelda who the next day turned into another one called Persephone and then another called Emma.

That day it took an hour before Thomasina could restart the car and, driving carefully and slowly, somewhere on the road between Guildford and Liss, was able to take the decision that she would now change. She would never shake again, not even in private. *At this moment*, she thought, *Holly is probably signing herself up for various clubs and forming inseparable friendships*.

'Hello?' she cried on the telephone to Pammie – the car still warm outside in the drive, she still in her coat. 'Hello? Yes. She's *gone*! Oh ghastly, thanks. Ridiculous. I feel quite awful. She's at the South Pole at least. Can't go upstairs yet and pass the bedroom door. Yes, I'd love to. Six o'clock?'

She had declared herself, realigned herself. She would be welcomed back.

And I told the truth, she proudly thought. *I told the truth to them. I do feel awful. I don't want to look in the bedroom. I do think I'm being ridiculous. I'm being very wise and affectionate to them all to be sharing things with them again.*

But she knew that she hadn't shared them, had not even touched on the depth of her mania, the almost religious fervour of her devotion, the passionate pride in Holly – the Holly, Holly, Holly, that went on in her mind like a love affair that is incurable, that must take its course.

Sometimes, exhausted by the single train of her thought, the drum-beat rhythm of her love, Thomasina nearly screamed or wept. She knew that she ought 'to see someone about it', yet she hardly knew what this meant. Some psychiatrist, perhaps? But you had to be recommended to one by a GP and her GP was an old friend she and Herbert used to have to dinner and talk hospital politics. They'd even been on holidays with him. You couldn't possibly *talk* to him.

And I don't scream, she thought. *I am always only just on the point of screaming. I certainly never actually weep. I am in full control and I'm probably no different from thousands of others. Rich, idle, no job, one child, no husband. And* everyone *says that Holly is special. I can't be all that wrong, or dotty.*

I wish I could get interested in men again, she thought. *I'm too old now to stand love. Thank God that*

23

*sort of pain's over. Golf and Bridge and the old gang are
the answer. And Surrey's a lovely county to live in. Crazy
not to be happy.*

By the time Holly married, Thomasina had become a
very differently behaved woman. She seemed most
genuinely to welcome Holly's marriage and
believed that Andrew Braithwaite was 'perfectly all
right'. She laughed publicly and amusingly at
Holly's adoration of him and Holly laughed with
her. 'Ma, he's *wonderful*. I knew the very first
minute . . .'

'I can't say', Thomasina had said to Pammie and
Co. over the cards, 'that he exactly causes one to fall
back in *wonder*. I mean, of all the ones I've caught a
glimpse of this one has the least hair. He's
twenty-five, looks forty-three. They say he looked
forty-three even at school. Of course, bald men are
said to be the sexiest. Bald-*headed* of course. A lot of
bald men are like hearth mats underneath.'

'Is Andrew?'

'My *dear*, however should I know? I've not seen
him on a beach. It's winter. They only met six weeks
ago. He has a good figure, I'll say that for him. He
wears his clothes well. Nice long legs, so he can't be
Jewish. The stoop will be useful at the bedside. He
qualifies this summer.'

'GP?'

'No, no, he'll be a hospital doctor. He doesn't say
much about it to me, though he could. I'd like it if he
did. He knows I'm used to the vocab. I don't think
he even talks about work to Holly much, though I
suppose that's not surprising, she's not exactly
Alexander Fleming, bless her.' Thomasina had
learned the language of Edgecombe Park and led

the field now in sardonic depreciation of all that meant most to her. 'This *bloody* dog,' she would cry (she'd been given a dog by Holly for her birthday). 'Look at the parquet! I'll hang you. I'll string you up!' To Holly she would say, 'Your hair is like old hay today. I *loathe* you, darling.'

Andrew and Holly came to Spindleberries to announce their engagement and Thomasina made joyful noises and brought forth the champagne she had been putting in and taking out of the fridge for a month. She excelled herself with the wedding arrangements, looking younger and much more chic (apple-green silk) than the bride, and waved them off from the reception with a smiling face; off for a whole year, to California, where Andrew had been awarded a research fellowship. 'So *good* for them,' she thought. 'Nobody to tell them what to do or watch how things are going. And away from the dominating old mum.' Andrew's family were in the North; his parents, peculiarly old, had not come to the wedding. 'He won't have to be running up and down there to see them,' she said, 'thank goodness. Northern families can be very demanding. And he has a brother living near them, so he needn't worry. Rather ghastly distance for me, of course. California for a whole year. Boo hoo.'

She embarked on a full year for herself, captaining the Ladies' Golf team, taking herself off in a group organised by Abercrombie & Kent to India, where she stayed in palaces, shuddered at the beggars, suffered with the food and made a couple of thoroughly nice friends. Thanks to Herbert's nifty talent with investments the money was holding up well.

And the year passed and then some more years

back in the South of England, with Holly within reach again, and Thomasina's life went on. When at length, after rather a worryingly long time – some years – Holly became pregnant, Thomasina was to the world blasé yet comformingly ecstatic: a mixture of 'And about time too' and 'We don't know what she'll be like with a child, I'm afraid. It'll *wreck* her tennis.'

Away she went, Thomasina, to Challoners Health Farm for a week to prepare herself for the delights of grandmotherhood, full of good nature, good sense and sociability. She had won through. The obsession remained only in her memory of a long-gone shadowy time, a mad time that she could scarcely credit. Now she had at last filled the skin of the part she had played to rid her of it.

She had become the Thomasina that the world had always thought she was. She had been to Challoners before, and loved it. The weather was glorious, her room luxurious, the food – for she wasn't one of those who went there to be dieted – fresh and delicious, and everybody most amusing. At tea on the first day she overheard what she thought of as an 'old army voice' at another table saying, 'Just arrived. Anybody here famous this time? Apart from you and me, of course,' and thought, *What a very nice laugh*. When she turned from her silver tea pot to see who owned it, she thought, *And very nice teeth*.

He was all of seventy, long as a lamp post, moustached, blue-eyed and wearing corded clothes of ancient and superb design. They made the other men in the room, who were mostly young and beautiful and wearing dressing gowns and examining their fingernails, look like advertisements for something.

'But of course,' the general called across to her (he looked one, he was one), 'you must be famous. Let me think. Well, you're not a film star. I hear Joan Collins was here last week and she was a network of lines. So they tell me. I don't know who Joan Collins is but I suppose she's a film star because everyone was so surprised.' *No lines on you*, said his eyes; *you're an outdoor woman*.

She thought, *He's very attractive. He still likes women. It's not just that he knows what to say.*

Later they sat cross-legged side by side at an exercise class.

'To the left . . . *bend*. Now to the right . . . *bend*,' and the circle of the self-indulgent, the alcoholic, the arthritic, the over-tired, the lonely, the sad, and people on the run from things, leaned first one way and then the other. 'Stretch *up*. Good. Now *forward*.'

The general creaked to his feet. 'Sorry,' he said, 'no go. Too late. All over. Packing it in for now.'

Thomasina, still lithe as a tendril after the years of golf and gardening, smiled up at his cheerful and admiring face.

The class over, she went for a walk in the woods. In the evening there was Bridge. He played very well, rather noisily, wittily, like a young man, calling out, 'Well played,' to others. At bedtime they found that their doors were opposite each other on the main, the most expensive, corridor; and Thomasina, lying in her bed watching television – she seldom read and neither, he had said, did the general, except for the odd military biography – wondered insanely if she should have locked her door.

All of *seventy*, she thought, and considered what his naked body would look like. Thin, anyway, and he'd at least wear clothes over it. Silk pye-jams

27

probably, not those awful boxer-shorts things and certainly not sweaty and nude – like in television plays – with great tufts sprouting about. She thought that the general would have some tufts but they'd be clean and in the right places. He would smell of coal-tar soap, she thought, and brush his teeth with that lovely toothpaste you can get in the Burlington Arcade. She fell asleep smiling, wondering if she could bear it if the general's tufts turned out to be grey.

The general rose early next morning for a quick swim and a go on the exercise bikes in the gym. Thomasina was not at breakfast. He had his sauna and then his massage. He looked out for her over his mug of Bovril at twelve o'clock. He, too, had not been put on a diet but he had elected himself to one. Liked to feel he could still put himself through things a bit. Hard commons, early rising, never did anybody any harm. He realised after a few minutes that lean and slender Thomasina would not, of course, be on the diet either and would be eating in the dining room, so he swallowed the last of the Bovril and went to his room to change. No appearing in dressing gowns in the dining rooms for him.

But she was not there.

He walked to the after-lunch meditation class and she was not there either. He stayed for it, meditating on her, began to float, fell asleep.

Laughing at the end – 'I suppose I was snoring? Yes? Oh God, I *do* apologise' – he groaned to his feet and went in search of her again, finally deciding to knock on her door, though it was not the sort of thing he approved of. Not the way things should be done. God, she might be in her nightdress, resting.

But there was no answer.

The general made his way to the reception hall and front desk, where the big glass doors of the hydro stood open to the sunny park, and the professionally sunny receptionist in white starched overall told him that Mrs Fox had had to leave. She had been unexpectedly called away.

Turning, the general saw through the doorway a humped old woman being shepherded into a car in the drive by a bald young man. The car drove off very fast.

– 4 –

How wet in the heather. But Jack did not notice. He sat up by the Saxon cross. It was morning. Holly Fox had been dead twenty-four hours.

He had heard the phone ring as he was leaving his private chapel but had not hurried particularly across the courtyard. It had been ringing on and on. His brother's voice, so like his own. They had not spoken since last Christmas.

Andrew sounded unhurried too. Very, very slow, with long pauses. Would Jack please tell their parents?

Jack said at last, 'It's for you to do.'

'No. Better from you. I can't.'

'There's a neighbour,' said Jack. 'She's very good. I'll get the vicar to tell them, and then the neighbour – Middleditch – can go round, just to sit with them.'

'Can't you get there?'

'Yes. I'll go now. Directly.'

'Don't ring anybody up. Just go.'

Jack paused for so long Andrew thought he had hung up. Then Jack said, 'I'll see what's best. You can ring them yourself later – say, after midday. I'll stay with them, but . . .'

'What?'

He could not say the seed potatoes were critical. He said, 'I'll stay with them all afternoon. The child . . . ?'

'She's fine. Fine. Called Faith. I have to go. I'll ring them. Fuck you, Jack, I'll ring them.'

'That's all right. I'll see to it.'

'Is it so much to ask?' Andrew slammed down the phone.

Jack then had taken a piece of bread and gone, gnawing it as he walked from the house. He left by the doors of the Great Solar and crossed his courtyard of hollowed stones, went up through the tilting gravestones to the track, and climbed for a mile here until he reached the ridge road and could see the tides of the moors mounting, mounting on each other's backs, flowing always westward like the Vikings, the prows of crags probing up through the mists. Mounting and mounting, folding and folding. Even in the whitest, thickest, early mist, curlews were crying. Wobbling, liquid, long, long cries ripping the skin of the white lakes.

To Jack's left – he sat on a sopping lump of turf, his back resting against the stone cross – the three golf balls of the early warning system floated on smoke. To his right were the loops of the highest road westward. In front and below were the swooping valleys, the heather giving way to rough stone walls whose pattern thickened towards the valley bottoms. The sun came through with a flourish, lit the miles, lifted the mist, glittered on the waterfalls of ragged bracken and outcrops of stone.

A van came along the ridge, roaring out music like a circus. It stopped beside Jack and a window was wound down, making the circus wild. A package was handed out. The postman said, 'You'll get right wet sitting there, Jack, on that bank.'

'Good morning, Post. Thank you. No – quite all right.'

'Saving me a journey down, then?'

'Saving you a journey down.'

'Yer looked peaked, Jack. On a grand morning.'

Jack stood up, skinny as a monk, and watched the sun across the next valley-but-two switch on like a light across a pale, heaving ocean. 'Would you reckon rain, Jimmie?'

'I'd not think so. Not today.'

'Well. Beginning to come through again, the sun?'

'Aye. I'll be on my way, then. You don't want a lift back down?'

'No, thank you. God bless you.'

Before he turned down the track again, Jack felt in the little dip that lay high up above him on the top of the upright of the stone cross. Only your fingertips could tell if there was money there. If there was, you kept it. If there wasn't, you left some. There was a hazard in it. It was bad luck to find no money when you had no money on you, and Jack in his worn-out shirt and tattered trousers never had any money in his pockets – or anywhere else.

But superstition is not Christian. It is for the invaders, the ones of the high prows, and horned helmets, the tin eyes, the old beekeeping sea-rovers who despised Christ and roughed up his dwelling places. Louts from Teesside now did the same, but they were ugly and resentful: nothing splendid about them. Jack smiled, thinking of the sweet dead warrior Holly Fox, and felt high up in the stone, where he found a single gold pound coin. 'Well, well. American tourists.'

Down the track he went again. First he would pray for the child, then ask someone to help him start the car. Yes, he might ring his parents' vicar and that neighbour person if he could find the number, just in case Andrew did ring up when the two old people were alone. Of course, he'd go down himself. If he could. To his ma and pa. Faith's grandparents. His old saints. Yes.

The pound shall be for the child, he thought. *She shall have it when she arrives.*

– 5 –

'We should get ourselves down there,' old Braithwaite shouted, 'that's what we should do. What's the good of us up here? Get me my clothes.'

'What?'

'Get me my clothes. I'm getting up.'

Dolly Braithwaite came padding down the stairs and looked in the dining room, where her husband now slept with a night table beside him bearing reading lamp, urine bottle, gold watch, four pencils, a book of geometrical exercises and seven bottles of pills. The reading lamp was switched on. Old Braithwaite was lying looking at the ceiling. It was three o'clock in the morning.

'Get my clothes.'

'Don't be so silly.' She sat down beside the dead fire in the grate and leaned forward to switch on an electric heater standing near it. She wore floppy flat slippers with matted furry edging, and an old coat. 'Don't be so silly. You're an old man.'

'Haven't you a decent dressing gown?' He had not looked at her, but he knew. This was automatic conversation, a duet between long-mated and now-moulting birds.

'Of course I've a decent dressing gown. I just

picked up the first thing I found. You frightened me, bellowing like that. I thought something was wrong.'

'We ought to be down there. Down South.'

'However could we get there? We've never been there. Where would we stay?'

'Well, with Andrew. He's not too grand to give us a bed, is he? He'll have a spare room.'

'He'll be looking after her mother. He rang from her mother's. I wouldn't go and stay there.'

'I'd stay wherever. What's so wrong with her?'

'I don't know. We shouldn't judge. She's probably a nice enough woman, poor soul. But she couldn't take people like us dropping on her now. You couldn't expect it.'

'People like us. We're not "people like us", we're us. Just because she was got up in apple green.'

'Well, at her age.'

'She's a lot less than your age. She might just be in her fifties. She might be your age, mind you, though you'd never guess. It's being South.'

'Well, she's not had to put up with what I've had,' said Andrew's mother, 'and she's always had plenty of money.'

'Well, we've plenty of money. For what we want. And with the social services. They're marvellous. And you've got a better dressing gown than you make out. From Newhouses.'

'For goodness' sake, will you shut up about dressing gowns. You've a widowed son, and there's this baby . . .' Tears fell.

Soon Toots Braithwaite wept too. The tears wandered down his face to his neck and the pearl button that fastened the top of the Chilprufe vest he wore under his raspberry-striped winceyette pyjamas.

'I'll get a cup of tea,' she said. 'Give me your bottle

to empty,' and she went along the passage holding the brimming plastic urine conch and began to drop things on the kitchen floor, looking for matches.

'Take care what you're doing.'

'What?'

'You'll set us alight.'

'Of course I'm all right.'

She came back to the dining room. 'D'you want your wireless on? There's the World Service. You'll go back to sleep after your tea.'

'I'm not ill. For God's sake – I'm lame, that's all, and I'd not be lame if I could get out for a walk. I never get taken out, so I get no practice. That's all it is. Down to that ruddy seat by the churchyard and back again, waddling behind that frame.'

'Here's your tea.'

'Like a dying grasshopper.'

'You should be thankful for the frame. You were worse before you had it. You were impossible.'

'Saw a whole row of them the other day.'

'What, grasshoppers?'

'Old crocks like me. Going along in a row one behind the other off a bus. Ye gods! Like a centipede. A hiccupping centipede.'

'They couldn't all have come off a bus. How could they have got a busload of walking frames on a bus same time as a busload of people?'

'It was an outing. It'd be a special bus. A disabled bus. Built for it,' he said.

'Maybe we should go on outings.'

'We're not poor. Outings are for the poor. "Under-privileged", they call them now. And we're not old enough. What we should have is a taxi now and then to Scarborough. You see some things going on in Scarborough. We're not ninety. We've got money.'

Dolly sat, knees apart to the cold fireplace, the electric fire turned away from her towards Toots's bed, her head bowed.

'Now, there's no use,' he said. 'Don't upset yourself.'

'Oh, Toots. There's nothing to be done.'

'Stop crying. Stop saying there's nothing to be done. What time is it?'

'Four o'clock. It's getting light. The birds are started . . . Oh the poor thing. The poor things. That baby . . .'

'What they calling her, you say?' he asked, into a silence.

'Faith.'

'It's a plain sort of name. I'm not altogether taken with it.'

'It's some sort of joke business, apparently. They were all saying, "Holly had faith", "At least she had her faith" – that sort of business. So they called her Faith.'

'I'm not sure that's good taste. At a time like this. Puns.'

'Well, it's true. Holly was a good Christian girl and you don't expect that from down there somehow.'

'Aye. Mind, she let you know it,' said Toots.

'You shouldn't say that, Tom. And she didn't. She was a lovely . . . Oh Lord.'

'Hush, now. Hush, lassie. This what's-this – "Faith"? Did he say?'

'Of course he didn't say. It was all he could do to talk to us at all. Clipped like he is. Like a sneer when words did come out. Not crying. I'm glad Mrs Middleditch had told us first. She broke the back of it a bit. I think . . . It did . . . When it . . .'

37

'It didn't make it easier,' he said. 'Nothing makes it easier. And that woman – Middleditch. Where's she got it from? Who'd told her? I suppose the whole place knew it before us. She comes round here with that bowl of soup. *Middleditch.*'

'It was all kindness.'

'Kindness! All she fills her time with is kindness and ferreting things out. And that mouth of hers. Like a hen's bottom.'

'She can't help her appearance. And she's been a very good friend to us. Gets us our pensions and she ran the ruby wedding. Ran it single-handed.'

'Holly would have done that. Holly said she would have come all the way up here to run it if she'd only known. And she'd have given us a proper do, too, not tea and whisky and those sandwiches. We'd have had sherries and tartlets and guests of our own class and education.'

'Mrs Middleditch has had education. A lot of education. She was highly trained in a college.'

'Trained what in? College dinners, likely, judging from the look of that soup. Why have we got in with these kinds of people? We're sitting ducks for them, that's why. Told our own news like geriatrics. This ought to have been our affair. Private and personal. Sent in a letter as it was in times past, and we should have been allowed to keep it to ourselves for a bit. Half the parish arriving.'

'The vicar was very good,' she said. 'I'll think better of the vicar after this. I expect he let it out to Mrs Middleditch by accident and she got round here first, living just round the corner.'

'I'd guess it was she told him. She's ahead of the field of knowledge in that church. She'll be a woman priest next. She'll be handing us the cup. What's the matter? You're saying nothing.'

Dolly was getting slowly to her feet. She padded around the large pretty room overcrowded now with invalid furniture, the old family dining table, flaps down, under the window, a mighty sideboard laden with clean clothes, library books, unguents, ointments and sewing things that had wandered in among the decanters and candlesticks and fruit bowls that were still kept bravely about. She started drawing back curtains. She watched the black and white dawn garden, the wet grass. A bird or two hopped along the flower bed. One of them, a fat starling, watched her insolently between pecks at yesterday's dinner-time crumbs. There were no supper crumbs, for there had been no supper. The Middleditch soup still stood on the kitchen draining board. The bird marched up and down, not yet letting go of the night.

'I'd better get myself back to bed,' Dolly said, 'before the day starts up and they all come round again. Jack'll be down first thing.'

'Don't count on it. It's harvest time. And he's got the new intake.'

'I don't. I never count on Jack. He has his life to live.'

'Aye, and his wife and child,' said Toots. 'He's lucky.'

'They never got on, Andrew and Jack.'

'But he'll take the child, you know. You'll see.'

'What – *Jack*? *Jack* take the child? Don't be silly, it's its father's child,' said Dolly.

'And how does a hospital doctor working all hours God gave look after a new-born child?' said Toots. 'Unless they get a nanny. Or Mrs Fox could take over.'

'Over my dead body, she will,' said Dolly, rolling her eyes and looking as once she had done: effective, bellicose and certain.

'It's not up to you and it's not up to me what happens to this child. It's Andrew's and the other grandma's. It's a South-country child. You said yourself at the start, when you knew it was coming, not to get excited, because we'd never see it.'

'Andrew's not out of touch,' said Dolly. 'He still comes up here. He can't be out of touch, it's where he was born and grew up. He'll never get right out of touch from his home.'

'D'you see that Apple Green letting that baby be brought up here? "Talking North"? They think we all say ee bah goom and sit on doorsteps.'

'They know about the Duchess of Kent. She was brought up no distance off. She doesn't sit on doorsteps,' said Dolly.

'They think we either sit on doorsteps or we're the Duchess of Kent, that's the trouble. They don't know there's anything in between, and I'm not surprised if they go by the telly and the papers. "Up North", they call it.'

'Andrew knows,' said Dolly.

'No. No, I don't think Andrew does know any more. He's gone now, Andrew. He's forgotten it here. His home. He'll go right back into his shell again now, like he did at sixteen. He's got a whole world down there we've not a notion of. Go back to bed, Dolly. Go back to bed.'

– 6 –

Faith arrived at Ellerby Priors in a cocoon of shawls and pressed into a travel-cot wedged along the back seat of her father's Toyota. It was autumn and miles of stubble linseed shone dark gold. Well-kept metal field gates looked polished in the sun. Everywhere stood mountains of silage in black plastic rolls.

'Like liquorice,' said Pammie. 'Great fat black beetles. Aren't they horrible? What are they?' She sounded pleased to see some expected ugliness.

'It's a good system,' said Andrew. 'It's the harvest.'

'*Harvest*? In plastic bags?'

'Did you think it was haycocks and gleaning?'

'I don't believe I ever thought – I didn't know there were still any hedges, either. I thought they'd all been dug up and ruined our heritage. I read about it in *Country Life* every time I pick it up.'

'We've kept a few,' said Andrew. He was driving now between two long high ones, weaving across the plain. They delivered him out upon a village with a lawn-like green, duck pond, white posts, sheep wandering.

'It's really very pretty,' she said. 'It's as pretty as the Cotswolds without the coaches, though of course you don't get the wonderful golden stone.'

'You don't?'

'It's rough-looking somehow, isn't it, the stone up here? Very picturesque, though. Lovely churches and houses. They look occupied – I mean in one ownership. Oh, *this* is pretty! Is that a castle? Right in the village. That would be National Trust in Sussex. You'd have to pay to go over it. Where are we?'

Andrew didn't quite know and for the past half-hour had been wondering and wishing for a map. He had been born and bred not thirty miles off and for years before he married had come home for Christmas to his parents' house in Cleveland not more than an hour away. They lived by the sea on the estuary in the shadow of the chemical works. He had always taken the train and then a taxi from Darlington ('Must have cost him all of five pounds,' said Toots) and then another taxi on Boxing Day over to his brother's on the moors, where they were going now on side roads from the motorway. He knew every field and lane and tree round here, or so he had thought, and you only had to look around to see how unchanged these lanes must be. But he hadn't been concentrating, the past hour. Since they had swept off the A1 he had been trying not to hear Pammie's endless patronage of the terrain.

'Not far now,' he said.

'I'm fairly ravenous, Andrew dear. Shall we stop somewhere for lunch? She's being awfully good. We could leave her in the car.'

He set his face. It was a set face by nature. Now he clamped it. 'We are almost there,' he said. 'I think there'd be umbrage taken if we stopped off for lunch. There'll have been preparations. Anyway, there are no restaurants.'

'What – nowhere? Well, a pub, then.'

'I'm sorry, Pammie, I don't think we can leave her outside a pub.'

Pammie thought, *Since he's about to leave her for ever* – and began to seethe.

She had been seething for three months now over the arrangements for the child, Faith Fox: first at Andrew's careless handing over of her to a nanny he had found from somewhere or other, a girl who lumped her about all over Surrey, taking her along to her own friends, and God knows who *they* were. One had turned out to be a prison warder and some others a covey of homosexuals. Once she had disappeared with the baby overnight leaving no message and Andrew, telephoning home and getting no answer, had rung Pammie thinking she would know what had happened. Pammie had suggested the police. Andrew, on duty all night after working all day on the wards, had said it would probably be all right. The girl had good references and had most likely taken the baby to her mother's in Streatham.

'In *Streatham*!'

What's more he'd been right, and nanny and child had come drifting back about eleven o'clock the next morning, the nanny with a hangover and the baby stinking of cigarette smoke.

She'd had to go of course. Pammie had seen to that and Andrew had said yes, she was probably right, and with Pammie's help had engaged someone else, very highly qualified, from Oslo, beautiful and calm and an excellent safe driver. The baby's clothes were washed as white as snow by this paragon and she believed in regular bottles, an eventless day and no brand foods. For such a glowing, clean-looking girl, however, she left very dirty-looking knickers about the bathroom floor and wound herself daily for several hours around the telephone cord. Pammie saw her in this condition, her eyes dreaming, in the window of the front room of Andrew's house whenever she called in, and always talking in Norwegian. On making enquiries, naturally with Andrew's permission, Pammie had discovered that the nanny was ringing Oslo twice a day, the bill already touching three hundred pounds.

Also, she had broken down in the car one morning, flagged down another and asked the driver to take her and the baby to the supermarket, where she had left Faith with him in the car park while she shopped and then got him to drive them both home.

'But he was a *good* man,' she cried as Pammie drove her and her belongings relentlessly to Guildford station.

Pammie had then taken Faith home with her and had cancelled many appointments.

Exhausted Andrew, working a seventy-two-hour week in the hospital with sometimes three hours sleep a night, earning less money than many a nanny, living almost entirely on the wards or in his prison cell of a bedroom, widowed, wretched, had said, 'They must do their best. Whole gang of women with nothing else to do. Let them sort it out.'

From the beginning he had displayed not a suspicion of interest in Faith. The death of life-giving Holly had not so much frozen as embalmed him. For the first weeks he had walked in a dignified trance, inclining as usual graciously from his great height towards all his patients, who thought him a consultant at least. At the funeral he had taken the same stance outside the church door, exasperating, infuriating, the friends of his late wife's mother when they went back to the house afterwards for the wake. The house was (of course) Pammie's. All had talked of Andrew's stateliness and charm and all had said that no man should be able to behave like that, equally to all comers, at his young wife's funeral.

At least the baby hadn't been there. Pammie had seen to that. It would have been embarrassingly heart-rending. Faith had been taken that morning (by Pammie) back to the nuns for the day, though Andrew had not seen why nor appeared to be interested when told.

That had been the really terrible thing, said Pammie, and made you realise just how hard a doctor had to be.

'It is a front,' said Jinny, 'a con. It's against the invasion of privacy. It's called a bedside manner. They're disciplined. They have to be, doctors.'

'Doctors suffer underneath,' said Elaine (or Myra). 'Well, look how half of them are alcoholics.'

'And suicides,' said Viv.

It was Pammie and the nuns together who took Andrew in hand at last. Mother Clare asked to see him in the office when he was visiting the maternity hospital professionally, Faith under two months old. ('And how could he bear to do *that*?' asked Jilly, or Jinny. 'The very *premises*. He's a monster.') Mother Clare had Pammie in at the same time.

Together they confronted Andrew with Faith's future.

A brother? Andrew had a brother? Had Andrew thought –? The North-East was certainly a long way from the child's roots but blood is thicker than – etc. Were his family in the North not concerned? Surely somebody up there must be feeling they should help? Wasn't this family solidarity notable in the North?

Andrew said that he was of very old parents and his father bedridden.

'And the brother?' Mother Clare was not intimidated by young doctors.

Andrew had sat magisterially and made non-committal clearings of the throat.

'The *brother*, Dr Braithwaite?'

'He's nearly twenty years older than I am.'

When he had gone Mother Clare had said, 'God help that child,' and Pammie had exploded.

Yet somehow or other here was the Toyota winding its way across the Plain of York, and Faith lying large-eyed and composed on the back seat, watching the berries fly past her in the hedges.

– 7 –

And where was Thomasina, Thomasina last seen leaving the health farm, broken and finished? Nobody but the general, and Andrew who had not noticed, had seen the blinded old woman feeling out for the handle of the car door. When her friends had met her again later they had seen a new representation of her that had chilled their hearts. A terrible, terrifying, gruesome, sardonic Thomasina, talkative, blank-eyed, trilling with laughter. 'Oh, isn't it a *bore*?' She even said, '*Poor* Holly,' and, 'Funny little scrap. No, not a bit like her Ma. We're calling her *Faith* – awful name, isn't it? Vicar's idea, or the nuns' – Andrew doesn't seem to mind. Oh yes, dear little thing really. Very broad face. Square hands. Yeoman Yorkshire, darling, I'm afraid. Hope she doesn't come with a built-in accent.'

She missed the funeral. Yes – Thomasina missed the funeral. Everyone understood of course, as they looked for her about the crowded church. It would have been too much – too much for Thomasina. All those queer years when she and Holly had opted out together. Someone (Susan) had heard that morning that she had broken down. Someone else thought she had been taken to the Surrey Clinic and was under sedation. Pammie had moved heaven and earth to reach her and even Andrew had looked grave. But Thomasina was nowhere to be found. All that Andrew had said to Pammie about it, which was when he left to go back to the hospital for duty that same evening of the funeral, was that Thomasina's not having taken to the baby was a 'bit of a blow'.

For what everybody had assumed, of course, had scarcely needed to discuss, was that Thomasina would be scooping up Faith to rear her as her own. Thomasina so fit and young for her years. Thomasina so lovely and bereft. Thomasina had separated herself so extraordinarily from her own world for Holly, had dedicated herself utterly, utterly (and what a terrific job she had made of it), she would slip naturally (and therapeutically for all concerned), tenderly, into the new motherhood of Holly's child. They had all so much assumed it that they were already talking about how marvellous it was that it was so, and congratulating the ghost of Holly on the ready-made union. How *wonderful*, if this pointless disaster had had to occur, if fate had had to decide to remove from the world such a golden person, that here was Thomasina with her crooked smile continuing to fly her brave pennant. Well, she didn't.

She wouldn't.

She abandoned them all, the lot of them, Pammie and Jilly and Jinny and Susan and Elaine and the golf club and the NSPCC and her son-in-law Andrew with the great purple sleepless circles under his eyes. Faith Fox she did not look at when she went to say goodbye to Pammie and leave the dog with her – Pammie supervising the sterilisation of bottles, a washing machine nearby whirling with baby clothes. 'Not looked towards the cot, not *once*!'

Thomasina had laughed and kissed Pammie and said that she was off to Egypt. She was wearing a fuchsia-pink trouser suit and big jewellery and there was a man in a splendid old car at the gate who looked like a colonel. '*Very* nice-looking. Very nice car. This is *true*, Elaine.'

The fury of Surrey rang out round its Bridge tables, patios, clubs. Thomasina was now seen as traitor, as Quisling in their midst, for nearly thirty years ungenerous, secretive, across invisible tracts of uncharted snow. Her icy introversion, her uncaring selfishness? How they foamed, and spat, how they snarled, how they thundered. The defection of Thomasina filled their lives up to the end of the second month of Faith's life and died only to flare again more fiercely when picture postcards of the Sphinx began to arrive. These were objects calculated to dumbfound, condemned as in most evil taste.

'If she comes back – *if* she comes back –' they said (even Pammie), 'I'm afraid I can't know her any more.'

Only an Englishwoman, of course, would have behaved like Thomasina, and I mean English. A Scot might have suffered silently, would have most pointedly not removed herself. A Welshwoman would have wept and chattered but carried on. An Irishwoman would have brooded or keened, explained, referred the matter to higher authority and the world would have slowly healed a little. But an Englishwoman from either of the two main tribes, South and North, above and below the line from the Wash to the Severn, the language-line that

49

is still not quite broken to this day, would act the part of the unconquerable, camouflaging herself, her grief, her fear, behind a mask that can do nothing, is meant to do nothing, but antagonise. It is a mask slapped on out of consideration, out of a wish not to increase concern and also out of a genetic belief that our deepest feelings are diminished when we show them. The fearless, comic, incorruptible battle-axe Englishwoman is now almost gone. There don't seem to be many of the young shaping up in that mould.

And maybe good riddance but maybe more's the pity, for she'll be missed here and there and especially in fiction. But in great grief her ghost walks still, and very mysterious and insulting it seems to those who aren't of her cast of mind and who love her and wish to be near her. But those of her ilk comprehend and talk of her behind her back. They would mostly act the same way themselves.

So Thomasina went off with the general and Faith watched the red berries in the unknown lanes.

– 8 –

The day, then, that Pammie accompanied Andrew Braithwaite to Yorkshire to deposit his daughter Faith Fox (as everybody seemed to be calling her) with his brother Jack, her mind was executing something like a triple fugue. There was first the theme of the north, the foreign country and culture into which the little scrap was to be translated, 'The North' as Pammie imagined it. Then there was the factual 'north' as it was unfolded to her between London and their destination. Then there was the account of both norths that Pammie's mind was automatically preparing to take back to Surrey again. Pammie, whose life consisted of emotional thunderstorms and the describing of them, was as intensely involved in the rumblings and crashes and lightning flashes of this one, the Fox Saga, as an actress who has landed a plum role. Learning the book of all her adventures was as important to Pammie as experiencing them.

And so, when they reached after an hour or so the easeful George Inn at Stamford, she had been trying to square its style with the miners' roadside caffs she had expected and hearing her voice saying back home to Jilly *et al.*, 'I'll say one thing: Andrew didn't

51

stint. It wasn't a Happy Eater or a Little Chef, it was *perfectly* decent,' and wondering like a novelist whether to substitute 'civilised' or even 'marvellous' for 'decent'. And then wondering if Eileen and Nina and Josie and Lizzie perhaps knew this already. She had always rather prided herself on being narrow, and not a traveller. Maybe there were things about The North that were after all *known*?

They had left Surrey at six in the morning. At Stamford, pale stone sleeping in yellow sunshine, they were to stay an hour. In the coffee room of the George Inn the baby slept beside them on a sofa near the bedroom-sized fireplace and transparent sunshiny coal fire. The coffee was brought by a waitress, who set it between them and brought croissants and marmalade and a morning paper. All about the old coaching inn and then from all the town churches the clocks struck ten melodiously. Outside, down the cobbled yard, hanging baskets of autumn flowers glowed. Creepers were a polished dripping crimson over pale walls. The linings to bedroom curtains looked as rich as silk and the menus on the reception desk were expensive and delicious.

'D'you know, Andrew,' said Pammie, 'one could stay here.'

'If one had money.'

'Amazing. A hundred or so miles north of London. I thought this sort of thing didn't happen again until Scotland. I wouldn't at all say no to a weekend here. I'll tell Hugo.'

They were to arrive at Faith's new home at about one o'clock, Pammie imagined for a late lunch, if farmers had lunches. She tried to imagine a farmer's lunch and settled for something between wedges of bread and cheese eaten under a hawthorn bush and roast beef in a pine kitchen with vets rushing in and out to examine diseased livestock outside in a barnyard. Or maybe it would be a gentleman farmer who strolled about his land every other weekend and gave the rest of life to his investments. There would be dry sherry and then a vast dining room with windows looking at a park. Cold meat and mashed potatoes, rice pudding and stewed plums and everybody pretending to like it, because it was like school. Flagged floors and dogs. '*Ice* cold, my dear, and nobody speaking. Heathcliffe not in it.' Faith safely deposited, Pammie saw herself in tears as she said goodbye. There would be a wooden cradle on rockers, cobwebs, a family Bible and then the drive with perhaps a taciturn serf to Harrogate for the London train.

Andrew was to stay on at his brother's for a couple of days to see the poor child in, to see to the beginning of her life. (A little waif suddenly made its appearance to Pammie; aged eight or nine, she had strings of rain-sodden hair and was dashing across moorland.) Pammie had of course been invited to stay on at the farm too, for as long as she liked, but, 'No, no,' she had cried in Guildford, 'I have commitments. October is a frightful month for me. I couldn't possibly give the time.'

'It is very good of you to do this at all,' Andrew had said.

'Nonsense. As if I could do anything else.'

Thomasina's presence hung in the air.

But to the Bridge mob Pammie had said, 'I must say it does seem rather odd that the one to take her has to be a friend of her *grandmother*. You'd have thought there'd be some friend of his own. I know

53

Thomasina said Andrew was an odd fish and seemed to have no friends, though God knows if that was true, the things we now know about Thomasina. But you would think, wouldn't you, that he could have found some friend of Holly, or another doctor? A woman, of course; babies prefer the smell of a woman. But then I suppose he wouldn't want to turn up at his brother's a few weeks after his wife died with a young woman in the car.'

She didn't say, because she didn't have to as it was what everyone had been thinking since about five minutes after the disaster, that the sooner Andrew remarried, the better. Pammie had sung this little tune once, quietly, the day after the funeral when she had seen signs of June and Desiree and Philippa and Meg getting maudlin. She was a self-protecting woman, Pammie, and speaking out the cold-blooded thought had given her a pretty *frisson*. The 'Oh Pammie, shut up, don't *say* it' always produced the nourishment needed for her essential diet of self-love.

But how unfair. Pammie was a good woman. A healer. When she shocked or mocked, sinews were stiffened. Everyone knew that Pammie had true and deep affections. Pammie often said so herself and discussed them. And she had a huge sense of duty (likewise). She was a woman who had longed for children and they had been denied her and although she took great interest in the children of friends – a thing rare now in childless women – she had been left with a lot of passion going waste. Many love affairs and two engagements in youth had broken down on account of the emotionally exhausted withdrawal from the field of the nervous

54

men involved, and Pammie had been left, for years and years now, with a shadowy old husband who had once been something high up in the Coal Board and sat reading *The Times* all day in a pretty house on Coombe Hill. It had cedar trees and a triple garage.

She deserved much more. She deserved a position of power, did old Pammie. Because of a particularly strained childhood and girlhood – she was always abandoning things from flashy principles, for she had been much admired by indulgent over-serious parents – she had had no real career and had developed no real character. A hundred years before she would have run a household, written papers on women's shameful banishment from great causes. Even in her own time she might have risen high in the Civil Service if she had been more patient and less histrionic, less romantic. She had been too old to be part of the young feminism of the Sixties and Seventies, which she affected to despise as being *déjà vu*.

She was still, for her age, deeply romantic, seriously so. She had once been in love with a patrician who had known the Queen, which gave her a dreamy and knowing look whenever anyone got talking about the monarchy. A 'my lips are sealed' look. It was her one sweet memory, as if she and the Queen had hobnobbed together on dark afternoons at Balmoral over a dying fire.

Pammie was a fearful snob, keen on good taste, and the awful triple garage was the only sop she allowed her husband in this direction. She allowed it and the big Bentley and the other vehicles inside because he was a good man who had worked hard and it is nice to be rich and she felt he should be rewarded for it. The man who had been pally with the Queen had been poor.

'Your father's a schoolmaster, isn't he, Andrew?'

'Was. He retired long ago. He's old. And sick. He's disabled. MS.'

'Oh, I'm so sorry. How dreadful. Shall I meet him?'

'No, they live about fifteen miles away on the coast. I'll be going down to them tomorrow.'

'Oh, I'm so looking forward to seeing the farm,' she said, watching the motorway flip past. 'D'you know, I've never seen a farm. Just slow down and let me undo the strap a moment. I want to have a look at her. She's so quiet.'

'All right?'

'Yes. Adorable. Fast asleep. Is it an *arable* farm?'

'Pammie, I don't believe you've never seen a farm.'

'It's true. How could I?'

'Well, by looking out of the train windows on the way to London.'

'Don't be silly, all you see is motorway between me and Waterloo. Exactly like this. They're all the same. There's no view you can catch. I go by car anyway.'

'More fool you, Pammie. You sound like old Queen Mary who'd never seen a field of hay.'

'Ah, now Queen Mary . . .'

The motorway hours passed, then the hours eastward along the lanes. The Vale of York began. Andrew grew sleepy, grew bored, grew cantankerous with Pammie's pleasantness, then with her critical nothings; became lost in the lanes. Pammie went on discussing lunch.

She thought how good the baby was and how the baby's father did not know it. She talked more about lunch.

She abandoned all hope of lunch.

Faith slept on.

And Andrew cheered up because he had found a small crossroads that led to a side road to a village that led up a steep and swerving hill and shot out on a high and spectacular moor. The moor arrived suddenly and stretched to all horizons. The horizons were broad blue-black ink lines and between them and the car was a world of stormy purple heather. Sheep stood in the heather and other sheep wandered about the road. A few were seated on the road with folded arms, moving their jaws about. They rose resentfully on black feet and ambled to one side. Pammie said, 'They're very skinny, Andrew. More like goats.' ('Dear God, Jinny, it's pretty enough, but that *baby*! What *is* she in for?')

A mile or two along a road stretching along a high ridge, Andrew stopped the car and got out, leaving the door open and a clean wind blowing in on Pammie. He strode away over the grass at the roadside, jumped a ditch and was away into the heather. There he stood, with his back to the car. The sky was high and clear, autumnal light about him. For miles sun shone on heather and granite.

'Andrew? Andrew? Are you all right? What is it?' *How most peculiar*. He began to stride further away from her. *We can't be there yet*, she thought, *there's nothing to see*. 'Hello?' she called. 'Andrew?' He wandered further still. *He must want a pee*, she thought; *I know I do*.

He turned and began to walk, lunging and jumping, slowly back.

'Pammie. I was thinking. I'm not sure that we're not being silly going on to The Priors just now. I think what we might do instead is just drive on down to the coast, to my parents, and drop her off there for the night. They're dying to see her. I'm sorry.'

'But you say it's fifteen miles off.'

'Yes. But Jack goes down to see them a lot. He could come and get Faith from them tomorrow and I'd stay with her of course. I could actually drop you off at Harrogate during this afternoon. I could leave her with the grandparents for an hour or so. I'd ring The Priors from my parents' to say what we're doing, what has happened.'

'*Happened*? But what *has* happened? Harrogate's miles away south. And your father's ill and they're not expecting us. How could they cope all night with a baby with just you and them – you can't even make up a feed?'

'My mother—'

'She's old. You said so. She'll have quite forgotten. Don't be so silly. And you say there'll have been preparations made at the farm.'

'Well, not big preparations. They're not great on preparations.' He stood frowning, pondering the pattern of sheep droppings on the road.

'What you mean is,' said Pammie, 'you don't want me to see your brother. For some reason. Or is it that you don't want your brother to see me? For some reason? I see. And who are the Priors? I thought your brother was called Jack Braithwaite.'

'It's the name of the place, The Priors.'

'I thought it was Ellerby Farm.'

'It's Ellerby Priors. It was a monastery till the sixteenth century. There's farmland with it.'

Pammie's heart lifted. Andrew, it turned out, must be someone.

'It's mostly ruined now,' Andrew said. 'Jack built some of it up and added a lot of sheds and so on. They farm the land and run a God-slot.'

'God-slot?'

'Yes. He's very religious. They're God-botherers. Sort of community. Retreats and hacking mangel-wurzels. Not my style. Jack's by way of being a Rev. Maybe a saint. And he's old – much older than me. I was a menopausal surprise.'

'So you don't think I'm fit to be introduced to him? It's not very bright of you, Andrew, I must say. If we – and what about Mother Clare? She'd have been so thrilled if we'd known all about this in Guildford, we'd have been much happier about Faith. Well, really! I've done hassocks for Guildford Cathedral. Get in and come on and don't be so stupid.'

Still he hung in the road.

'Now that you've told me,' she said, 'let me tell you something. I am a religious woman too and all the way here I've been wanting to ask you if you couldn't stop for a moment before we get there to say some prayers.'

'About what?'

'Oh yes I have, so don't look so blank. About Faith, if you really want to know. You and I together, Andrew. But knowing doctors . . . Well, doctors get put off, I can see that. I should have followed my instinct. Andrew, pick up this baby and hand her over to me now. I want to see to the cot, and yes – I think I'll change her so that she's as she should be when she arrives. I'm very good at it. Oh – *pretty* girl. There. Angel-bird, lamb-child.'

When Faith was back in the cot, squirming a bit, making talking noises and snuffling, giving the occasional squawk and hoot, Pammie said, 'Get in, Andrew. I'm going to say a prayer now and be damned to you. And then let's get on to your brother's.'

'A prayer?' said Andrew. 'What for?'

'Well, for Faith. For her life.'

'Bit over the top, isn't it? I'm not into it, Pammie. And she'll be getting plenty of it soon. And for ever.'

He hurled himself into the car, started it up, roared away in it, peering all the time across the partridge figure of Pammie, smart in her red-brown wool suit, until there appeared at the side of the lonely road, rising black and high, a stone cross. A track led off from it down a steep hill and out of sight.

'What's this?' Pammie was bright with excitement and words were pouring into a rehearsed narration for Coombe Hill. 'An old *cross* – how fascinating! I'd no idea you were so erratic, Andrew. We all thought you were so very set and conventional. I'd no idea you were even from the far North, you know – I thought maybe somewhere like Leicester – until just before dear Holly . . . Do what you like, I shall pray by myself now as we go along. I feel I have Holly with me now, in the car beside me. I feel I can mention her name now in a Christian, *croyant* way, now that I know your brother's a parson. Oh my goodness, I do feel better.

'Dear Holly – so *good*. Didn't your brother adore her? I feel nothing can go wrong now for little Faith. I feel it. "Ellerby Priors". I knew it. What a good man, your brother. I must have met him at the . . . Did he take the service? No, of course he didn't, it

60

was the vicar, and not at his best if I may say so, but I don't remember another dog collar. Oh, he doesn't? Well, so few of them do now. Which one was he? I suppose he's unmarried. The really splendid holy ones seldom are, you know, even now. I hope he has some good women there, though, for Faith. Well, you *said* so. Will there be deaconesses? I hope he's not against WPs. Is it Catholic or Anglo? Andrew, you might have told us, you know. Is he ascetic? Or is it one of these love-and-kisses places? I can't care for that, I have to say. It takes me all my time to face The Peace in church, this newfangled stuff they have, and what's more I know that absolutely everyone feels the same as I do. You can see the whole congregation getting fidgety when it's announced, even the parsons. I mean, in *public*! You should see the poor old souls at St Saviour's. All their lives they've believed in keeping themselves to them-selves and now they have to turn round and grin at each other and nod their heads and shake hands. And they see each other nearly every day anyhow and half of them don't altogether get on. Sometimes, you know, there's kissing and *caressing*! No one can really take that, you know, unless it's black people. Is it going to be that sort of place, Andrew?' She tried to imagine – she saw – negroes in a monastic ambience, *in flagrante delicto*, rolling in the heather. She began to edit delightedly for Coombe.

'You should have told me, dear Andrew. All these hours on the road and we've been keeping to trivialities and worldly things, though I did like The George at Stamford. Anyway, too late now and I'm going to pray for the baby. How is she? Can you look in the—? Yes. Oh, angel darling! I'm going to pray now quietly to myself, so just shut up.'

'Too late,' he said. 'We're here. We have to undo this gate.'

'I'll undo it, my dear. My shoes don't matter.'

'No, you pray if you want to.'

'Did you?' he asked as he climbed in after shutting the gate behind them.

He drove down the last of the track, which turned through a medieval and broken-down gatehouse and became a large, paved, unweeded court. Surrounding the court were the remains of ecclesiastical buildings, some of them with agricultural machinery bundled into them. A line of prefabricated huts had been built in the courtyard and a small block of Portacabin water closets nearby. The huts had coloured mantras stuck to the windows and different-coloured front doors. Some of the Portacabins had holy-looking posters gummed to them, too. There was a line of heavy shoes outside one of them. Drab chickens ran about and there was rather a lot of rubbish – not serious rubbish but bits of nylon rope, cardboard, blown-about paper, and metal stands for some sort of leisure equipment, and several unlikely canoes.

'You can't pray properly in sixty seconds, Andrew,' she said, affectionately now. 'Just look at that lovely architecture. What a wonderful east window that must have been. All empty to the air now. But how lovely.'

From one of the huts four or five bulky Eskimo-ish people were emerging. They wandered off towards the Portacabins seeming to give promise by their incurious, in fact rather disgruntled, expressions that Ellerby Priors was not going to be a kissing-and-caressing sort of place.

'By the way,' said Andrew as a bell began to clank

62

somewhere and another sound joined it for a brief moment, a sound as if someone were revving up some mournful trumpet. 'By the way, Jack is married. He married not long after I did. And there's a child, a boy. And here is his wife.'

– 9 –

'Jocasta,' said Andrew, 'this is Pammie. And here is Faith.'

He lifted out the cot and Jocasta held out very small brown hands for it.

He said, 'No. Heavy. She's a whopping great baby. She was nineteen inches long at birth. I'll take her in,' and they all walked across the courtyard and through a decrepit studded door marked 'Office' in runny painted writing, Jocasta saying not a word and Pammie looking around for signs of lunch.

'We're a bit late,' said Andrew. 'I'm sorry. It's been a big day.'

Jocasta said that Jack would be here in a moment.

Nothing happened.

'Is he well?'

'Perfectly,' said Jocasta.

'Well, here's Faith.'

Jocasta looked quickly in the direction of the cot that had been put upon a table and was tipped up somewhat because of the clutter. She looked away. Faith regarded her with solemnity.

'She's been an angel,' said Pammie to keep things going. *Most peculiar*, she thought. *Utterly silent woman, rather oriental-looking and snooty. Not what you'd expect*. 'She's been an angel since the day she was born. I've had her all to myself for the past weeks, so I know. Not a sign of trouble. I've had no broken nights, not personally. I don't know why these young mothers complain about being tired. I've had no children of my own, but with decent daytime help – and I did have a night nurse and a first-rate health visitor and our own GP, who is private but I always think that's money well spent – she's been no trouble at all. And the social services are absolutely *marvellous*, of course – I hope you have them up here. There's just a trace of a sticky eye. Well, I've really *adored* doing it. I shall miss her frightfully.'

Jocasta looked at her. She said, vaguely, 'Yes.'

'You see, I knew Holly.' Pammie looked at Andrew and the look said: She *shall* be mentioned. It is the best way for you. 'I knew Holly. Holly was the light of many people's lives. I know it's perhaps too soon to mention all this in general conversation, Andrew, but you and I have got to know each other on this journey, haven't we? Soon I'll be gone. I'm really Thomasina's friend, Mrs Braithwaite, or I was. I'm afraid she's disappointed us. But . . .' she looked again at Andrew, ' . . . there's not one of us who wouldn't have done anything in the world for Holly.'

'He's here,' said Jocasta.

The baby suddenly went stiff all over, red of face, tremulous of lip, for some cataclysmic event seemed to be taking place in the passage outside, as if many heavy things had suddenly collapsed. It was a surprise that such a gentle man came in, and smiled shyly. He went straight to Faith and opened his eyes wide at her, and she grinned.

'My goodness. I believe she smiled,' said Pammie. 'That was an *amused* smile.'

Jack went over to Andrew and put his arms round him and rocked him, turned to Pammie and said, 'Forgive me.'

'Forgive you, Jack? Why?' said Andrew.

'Late, late, *late*, I suppose, Andrew. How do you do? Pammie?' He looked at her with intense and admiring interest. '*Pammie!*'

'She's famished, Jack. We had a croissant in Stamford.'

'It's full of history,' said Jack; 'very beautiful, a sort of miniature Oxford. It was spared by Cromwell.'

'*Food*, Jack. And offices of the house for Pammie. Me, too, in a moment.'

'I'll show you where,' said Jack to Pammie, still staring most lovingly. Jocasta made no move. 'And then we'll go to the refectory.'

He put his curly head back round the door after he'd left with Pammie to say, 'You'll follow, Andrew?'

The office died into silence. The baby had fallen suddenly asleep and through the slit of mullioned window in the stone wall a light fell across the mess surrounding her on the desk; papers, files, posters, telephones, some of them broken, word processors, dull screens, printers, tangled wires, and a pile of yellow T-shirts stamped EP. Metal chairs in a dusty corner sat in one another's laps, curving forwards in a toppling pile. In a niche stood a crucifix with cobwebs. On the walls were pegboards with curling old notices. They were to do with services, walks, activities, discussion groups, mealtimes and weekly terms preposterously cheap and out of date. Beneath the cross stood a vase of last year's dried-up heather.

From Faith's cot came snuffles as sunshine fell across her, too, and Andrew moved over to the narrow window and leaned down to look out through it, his back to the room, his head resting on an arm above the mullion, blocking the light.

Jocasta walked to the cot, looked briefly at the baby, and moved away to the door.

'I'll go now,' she said.

He leaned to the thick grubby glass and drew a line down it with his finger. Looking out over the courtyard, he said, 'I want you in my arms. I want you in my bed. I want my tongue in your mouth. I want—'

Jack came in again and said, 'I've persuaded The Missus to give us a bit of something as well as the soup. Bit of fish. No – leave her, she'll be fine. I'll send someone along. Jocasta has to do the school run but there's plenty of help. What a very nice woman, your Pammie. I must just round up the Tibetans for Evensong.'

When the two brothers had left the room Jocasta waited a moment and then she, too, left it, without looking towards the cot again.

– 10 –

Jack Braithwaite had lately been having trouble with
Ellerby Priors, an experimental community that was
his passion. He had founded it uncertainly years
ago, when ruins were cheap, with the intention of
gathering up a clientele from the slums of the
North-East, though 'slums' was a word not in
fashion then, like the word 'poor'. Both had been
swept away with Beveridge in the Fifties, returning
in the Eighties translated as 'deprived areas' and
'underprivileged', and they were what Jack cared
about. He especially wanted to help the orphaned
and children at risk or in care but in fact never
turned away anyone the social services sent him.
When the underprivileged were in short supply, for
the children seemed to come in waves and in
smaller waves came the government money to
support them, Jack struggled on with what was left
of his own funds and what he could earn off the
farm, which, because of the soil and the climate, was
not much. The menus shrank.

At first he had worked on a monthly basis, but
lately had taken to offering weekly terms and even
weekends for tired housewives, who often fell in
love with him and rolled up their sleeves to help. He

looked deeply at them in Christian love. He wasn't averse, either, to the terminally but not dangerously ill, though these had been dropping off lately, probably because of the menus. Many were ready to starve in the scruffiness of Ellerby Priors, to shiver in its dusty, freezing dormitories, to be near Jack, but the authorities and sometimes husbands felt otherwise.

Jack, with a great surge of the spirit not unknown to him, had lately decided to launch out among the homeless and the exiled. His last batch of the deprived had been very depressing. Classified Tyneside/Aggressives, they had proved a failure. Most unresponsive. The perfectly adequate medieval accommodation they had pronounced worse than home, the sparse but healthy meals, country air and counselling opportunities had not satisfied and there had been some embarrassing escapes, one whole batch walking out before Vespers, hitching a lift across the moor road after pushing over the Saxon cross and spending a gaudy night breaking up the Whitby promenade. The newspapers had reported this as a 'break-out of abused children held at an isolated moorland detention centre' and a correspondence had begun in the press about public safety. Jack had received questions from the Home Office.

It was a wonderful relief that in the midst of it all Jack, trying to dissuade the county council against the need for electric fences and guard dogs, received notification of a consignment of Tibetans for whom he had been angling for years. Great files of letters, and then faxes even, had passed between Ellerby Priors and Darjeeling, where a Tibetan Centre valiantly but rather glumly soldiered on. Jack and

Jocasta had visited it on their honeymoon.

Jack, scholar of Balliol without a string to pull in the world before he arrived there, had turned into the sort of man who had connections. His general air of abstraction and loving kindness caused him, without even trying, to be endlessly invited to high tables and the well-heeled abodes of antique men of letters. Presents came to him which he at once gave to the poor. Cheques went to the upkeep of Ellerby Priors. He fascinated women of all kinds and ages, and people worked for him for nothing – though they often fled at last in tears. Jack was incorruptible.

After the marriage to Jocasta much of Jack's social life had ceased, but Cambridge had invited him to meet the Dalai Lama on his exiled visit there, an occasion Jack remembered precisely though he often forgot his own telephone number. He and the Dalai Lama had discussed the Classics and the concept of divinity and the future of violence and the standard of the King's College breakfast. Jack prayed for the Dalai Lama every day and it seemed to him at once that these miserable prayers had been rewarded when a notifiction was delivered from the post van, roaring out heavy-metal down the moorland track, to announce that between seven and nine exiled Tibetans would be arriving the coming Wednesday. It was the Monday morning after the inflammatory Saturday of the Tyneside Aggressives, and this gave the resident staff of Jocasta, one woman and two lads (The Smikes) just time to clean up the beer cans, put together the broken furniture, and stick up the cracked windowpanes with cut-out mantras that Jocasta and her son Philip spent all day Sunday painting in

70

bright colours. Jack had been sent down to Whitby to the launderette with all the blankets.

Jack was exalted by the arrival of the Tibetans who came toppling out of a battered grey bus from Liverpool in the dawn, not many days before Andrew's Toyota. The Tibetans had quite put Faith in shadow. Family, as is stated in the Christian gospels, you don't have to get on with; in fact, it's unlikely that you will and often you even have to ditch them. Exiles and refugees and people who have been politically duffed up, on the other hand, must be cherished, put in your own conveyance, taken to some resting place and the bill paid in advance. Up to now the exiles Jack had taken in had been random and proud, outspoken about the Yorkshire weather and often surly about the one stipulation Jack made: that in return for a home at The Priors they must attend for an hour each day one short religious service in the chapel.

This he insisted upon even to the death of his venture, and he looked with his customary shining welcome but also a little anxiously as the Tibetans gathered up their belongings from the bus and walked across the cloister courtyard to their sheds.

– 11 –

'They'll be there now.'

'Who'll be where?'

'Well, Andrew and the baby. You know quite well what I mean, so don't pretend.'

'I'm not thinking about them.'

'Well, I am.'

'If they can't ring up or drop a line . . . It's not much to ask. Never consulted. We're vegetables now to him. Vegetables. That's what we are. I'm not happy, Dolly.'

'You never are happy, Toots. You never were.'

'I'm not happy about the baby, in with all the loonies. I feel like writing to the authorities – well, the authorities'll be round there. They'll see soon enough. I won't go near the place. The farming side, yes, but what's he want with the loonies? Jack gets no better with age. They'd all be a lot better off in their own homes. He's as daft as he was at school.'

'They don't have homes. The ones he has at present, they certainly don't have homes. They're from Tibet.'

'Tibet! They should have stayed there.'

'You know perfectly well what's happened in Tibet. I don't know, you never stop watching the news and yet you've got no idea of what's going on when it links up with here. You can't imagine being thrown out of your own home. I know I can. You never stirred even when you could have done, got a better job at a better school. You never left this parish. Tibetans are very well-thought-of people. It'd do you no harm to practise a bit of peace and quiet like they do. Meditation's what you want. I'd like to have the chance.'

'They sound a lazy lot to me. No fight in them. And I don't care – that Dalai Lama looks a funny fellow. We had a master at the school like that in 1932.'

'Be careful what you say, now. Don't be blasphemous. It's a serious religion.'

'Hairless blighter. Knew all the answers, yet he never spoke. Like that Greek chap – my memory's going – sits watching you on the sidelines and only drinking water. To think a granddaughter of ours . . .'

'She's not likely to turn into the Dalai Lama, Toots. Why don't you have a walk up to the seat? I'll listen for the phone.'

'Phone. They'll never phone. I'm not to be told what's happening. I'm not to be told if there's been a crash on the motorway. *I'll* be the last one to hear. I'd have thought that flesh and blood might have been given consideration.'

'I must say,' said Dolly, burrowing about in the wardrobe that had been inserted into the old dining room to take Toots's clothes, 'I hope Andrew knows how to look after her in a car. It's a tremendous way they're coming. They'll need nappies, and how do they manage the feeds? Heating up bottles in a car. She'll be four-hourly still – that's a feed and a half –

a tiny little thing like that. They'd have done better on a train, like we always did. Oh, I do want to see her.'

'Well, so do I want to see her. That's what I'm telling you. You can forget Andrew. Forget him. Hard as nails. Son or no son, we're nothing to him now. But her I do want to see, and it's our right. They could have brought her down here first: it's almost on his way. He never thought tuppence of Jack.'

Dolly, who had made a cake and looked out old cot-sized blankets, Andrew's old crib, several teddies, a monumental feeding bottle made of glass with a teat on each end, and a tin of baby milk bought secretly from the chemist and hidden somehow from Mrs Middleditch, said, 'Much better get her there and the journey over and done with. Ellerby's to be her home. She'd best get there and settle. They'll be cuddling her to bits. It's just tonight I'm worried about. Where's she to sleep in that cold place? I hope Jocasta's made everything ready.'

'That'll be the day.'

'Now don't start, Toots. Let's keep off that subject. Here's your scarf and I'll get your frame for you and we'll walk to the seat in the sun. I'll leave you there and come back for you in half an hour.' *Somehow*, she thought, *God give me strength. Why can't they phone? Why can't it just ring now? And when they do bring her he'll just give Andrew hell and pretend not to look at her.*

Batting about among the coats in the passage looking for his hat she addressed her God. 'Wherever's Holly gone? Why Holly? Who's to look to the child, us so old and useless and all of them so foolish? (Yes, I'm *coming*.) Why couldn't You have made Jack a good old-fashioned parson instead of all this hobnobbing with Buddhists and the EEC and everything? And Andrew marrying south. Who's to see to this child? I ask You – who's to see to her?'

She followed Toots down the garden path as he proceeded behind the walking frame, slowly, looking left and right with dignity, like a king making a public appearance before his subjects.

'Time that parsley was thrown out, it's rubbish. Great Scot, that onion bed! Get that lot up before anyone sees it. They're a disgrace.'

'If you think I'm starting on onion beds . . . That's Philip's job. Haven't I enough –?'

'Well, and then you talk about bringing up a baby.'

'We'll never see the baby,' she said, suddenly sighing, holding the front gate open for him to sidle through. 'I begin to think it's all talk, this baby.'

Her mind made one of the leaps it had been taking lately. The baby had not been born. Holly was not dead. This afternoon she would write to Holly and ask her what she wanted for Christmas. She might even ring Holly and ask her if the baby had reached Ellerby safely. She shivered and tried to get back to some idea of the present but at the same time wondered whatever Holly's phone number was now. She used to ring Holly sometimes from the upstairs extension when Toots was at his worst, just to hear her cheerful voice.

'No, we won't be seeing the baby,' she said to Toots.

'Now then,' he said, 'that's my line. Forget it. Don't upset yourself. There's a handkerchief in my pocket if you can reach. Leave me to do the moaning. We'll have a sherry later. Oh, strike a light – here's Ghent to Aix.'

Mrs Middleditch was waving and flapping down the street.

'They've arrived, they're fine. I came right round to tell you. Put you out of your suspense. Very good journey, not a hitch.'

'We've just stepped out of the house,' said Dolly. 'Well, isn't that – just the *minute* we step out of the house. They couldn't reach us, so they had to ring you. Oh, I do hope it wasn't a nuisance.'

'No, I rang *them*,' said Mrs Middleditch. 'Just thought you'd like to be out of your miseries.'

Toots turned from her and began to pace doggedly towards the seat.

'Go back in, Dolly,' said Mrs Middleditch. 'I'll sit with him a bit. I understand him. I don't mind if he creates. Then I'll bring you both a bit of liver.'

– 12 –

Jocasta had opened her eyes on Andrew for the first time six years ago in a hospital bed and seen a serious tall man in a very clean white coat frowning at a clipboard. A stethoscope hung round his neck correctly. He looked large, Olympian, remote. She thought, *A doctor,* and sank back into shadow.

Andrew had seen a tiny brown woman who opened the moist eyes of a chimpanzee. A sexy mouth. The round eyes stirred him and to forget such a surprise he removed the sheet from her and examined the long wound across her body, jagged across the base of her abdomen above the shaven mound of hair, the lovely thighs. He examined the clips and the bruises and said to someone, 'This might be cleaned up.' A pause. 'Oh yes,' he said, 'and the catheter . . . I think there's not enough going through. Keep her on it for the time being.' With almost disdain he took Jocasta's hand and said in the voice they use to pierce oblivion, 'Everything's fine. You're going to be fine.'

'Was that the surgeon,' she asked much later, 'that doctor?'

'It wouldn't be the surgeon. You'll not be seeing him, dear.'

'But it was somebody. Somebody who looked important.'

'Oh, that'd be Andrew. He's hardly qualified. He looks the part, dear, and he does very well.'

Jocasta floated away, returning later to Andrew's face. She noticed his clean nails. He was still gripping a clipboard and she saw that he was younger than she was.

When he saw her eyes open he said, 'Hello there, Jocasta. What a nice name. How are you now?'

'Did you take the lot?'

'No.'

'What have you left me?'

'An ovary.'

'No womb? Was it cancer?'

'No. We did take the womb but you have had a child, so that's not so bad, is it?'

'I've had *one* child!'

'But there are plenty of women with none. Perhaps I might have a word with your husband.'

'I have no husband.'

Late that night they came to rearrange the catheter and set it up again. Dr Braithwaite had telephoned to say to keep it going.

'Is he worried?'

'Dr Braithwaite is always worried, dear. We're not worried.'

'Where is he?'

'At his home for once. He's usually here night and day.'

'Night and day,' she said.

'Shall I tell you something? Last night while you

78

were asleep he came in and drew the screens round and stood looking at you. He does this sometimes. He stands thinking. But this time it was for half an hour. Don't say I said so. Dr Braithwaite is our favourite. We don't want to embarrass him.'

'What sort of a *doctor* is he?' she said. 'I don't care about your favourites.'

'He's very caring, dear.'

The next time he came to see her they drew the screens round and he sat beside the bed. He said, 'I see you're thirty. It's early for a hysterectomy. I'm so sorry.'

'I buggered myself up,' she said. 'Oh, don't look like that. I say these things to most people. I forget. What I mean is I've been living a messy sort of life.'

'I see.'

'Don't look so stunned. Haven't you met *anyone*? Just bodies, I suppose.'

'I meet people every day who say they have buggered themselves up but they don't look or seem like you.'

'I'm sorry.'

'Will you tell me what happened?'

'Nothing happened. I grew up and had a child. Then the framework packed in.'

'It doesn't happen like that. Were you promiscuous? On drugs? Undernourished? You look so very small. You look a *good* woman.'

'I buggered out off to India and played music. Beads and sandals and smoke. Had the child there. It was after RADA. I failed RADA.'

'A hippie?'

'A bit old for that. I'd got in a mess here. I couldn't get a job. I was trying to find myself.'

'You sound like a schoolgirl.'

'What was I like inside? Have I a disease?'

'You have some dis-ease,' he said. 'Physically you will be all right now, but watch out for depression. It hits people a week or so after this business.'

'I shall watch. And what shall I do when I see this depression coming into sight? Have you any medicine against the dark?'

He got off the bed and patted her hand. 'I'll look in tomorrow.'

Soon he knew that Jocasta had nowhere to go, that her child was being cared for by a friend in a bedsit, that she had long since broken all her ties with England and that she was still searching for the meaning of life. She told him all this in a restaurant a month later after he had taken her to a fleapit cinema to see *La Strada*: the mute waif and the tramp on the eternal road to nowhere, sleeping on heaped rags, the retarded girl shining with love and joy.

'I want to be her,' Jocasta said. 'No luggage.'

'No purpose,' he said. 'Where do you come from, so dead against purpose?'

'Child of the time,' she said.

'Don't be arrogant. You were born twenty years too late. The times now are full of purpose. Money and graft. What's your politics? What's your religion? You're not of the time, you're antique.'

'I'm an animist. I put bunches of flowers round the boles of trees and say prayers to Creation.'

'And skulk round Richmond Park looking for magic mushrooms and eat nothing but brown rice and wear trailing skirts and don't wash. Stop lying.'

'I did all that. I wash now.'

He thought she looked neat and composed. She

moved her fingers about fastidiously on the table-cloth. She wore one blue ring. Before she left to go back to her little boy he said, 'You ought to be seeing my brother not me. He's the unworldly one in the family. You're his sort.'

'What sort are your sort?'

'Women? I've never had time for them.'

'You must have had women,' she said. She had a cool clear voice that carried across the restaurant and he looked about him. The restaurant was round the corner from the hospital. Other men's girls said this sort of thing but Andrew was considered senatorial. He gave off an air that great standards were expected of him. Many of his colleagues found him a drag.

'I think,' she said leaning forward and taking both his white hands, 'I think you're really a bit of a joke, you know. You're pompous.'

He read the bill carefully and counted out the money to the nearest penny on the inside lid of an auntie purse. He wore a grey cardigan and collar and tie.

'But,' she said, getting hold of his wrists and sliding her hands up inside the cardigan sleeves, 'I could teach you so much. I adore you.'

A week later he took her to Ellerby, stopping off at Stamford for the night on the way. He had bought her some clothes and signed in for both of them as a married couple. He lay watching her unpack, run herself a bath, wrap herself in the big white towelling robe from the back of the bathroom door. She ordered drinks in the room and sat looking at hers in the window seat far away.

'Come back to bed.'

'Not yet. I'm thinking.'

'You seem very much at home, thinking in a luxury hotel.'

'I am. I'm thinking of Philip. I'll have to do something fast for Philip. Annabel's patience is on the wane.'

'He'll be fine at Ellerby. I promise. You can begin a life there.'

'Will *I* be fine?'

He nearly said, 'Have you any choice?' and thought, *I'm a shit.* 'We can but see,' he said.

She unravelled herself and curled beside him on the bed. 'Oh Andrew, Andrew, you are so good. How can I live so far away from you?'

'I can't marry you. No question of that at all. You know that. I earn twelve thousand a year and I'll be living in the hospital for a year and a half more at least. It's no life for a wife. We'd last six weeks.'

'But afterwards. There would be a life to follow.'

'It would be a long wait.'

'I've learned to wait.'

At breakfast next morning at one of the small tables in the hall she ate two croissants. She looked well. She said, 'And where is this depression that was going to strike?' He said, 'I love you,' and she said, 'I would wait, you know.'

A week later he saw her off with Philip for Ellerby Priors, this time on the train, and was struck again by her composure, her knack of fitting her surroundings. In the hotel she had been the experienced guest; at Ellerby, the Art and Drama teacher designate, born for the job; here on the train she was the woman always on a train, waving as it drew away, expert at saying goodbye, never losing

82

tickets, money, baggage, the professional departer, causing no trouble. Philip, five, glared and pulled maniacal faces from his window as she waved a cool hand and turned to find her seat.

Andrew ached when the train was gone. That evening, when he managed to phone Jack and heard that Jocasta was safe there and already sorting dormitory linen and tomorrow was going for Art supplies and to see to Philip's new school, he felt worse. 'Get her away from work tonight, you bloody man,' he shouted. 'She'll be exhausted. Tell her I want to talk to her. She's still not strong.'

'She won't come to the phone, Andrew.'

'I don't believe you. Where's the boy?'

'Off somewhere. They both seem perfectly happy.'

London was a desert. The few hours' sleep he had in the hospital were troubled by dreams of her. Her face kept appearing to him during the day. Not a patient with a scar across her body failed to raise the image of Jocasta's lithe slight frame, her brown-silk skin. He had grown to love the scar, caress it, kiss it, apologise to her for it as she lay looking at the ceiling. Her lovemaking shattered him. Her past she never mentioned. The father of her son seemed not to have existed. Once he asked her and she said, 'He was nothing. I can't remember.'

'Where was Philip born?'

'I can't remember.'

'You forget everything.'

'I don't forget you,' she said. 'Not for a single minute of the day or of the night. Not for a moment do I forget you.'

*

In the face of fury from the powers above he got leave to go to Ellerby less than a fortnight later, reaching it at night with snow blowing against the windscreen and heaping up against the snow posts along the ridge road. Near the Saxon Cross the car began to slide and he gave up, wrapped himself round with everything he possessed, staggered down to The Priors, once falling up to his shoulders in snow. He banged on the door. It was at last opened by Jack, who thought he beheld a vision.

Jocasta had been sitting in the solar beside an old oil-stove cutting out coloured paper-chains for Christmas. Her hair was done up in a braid and she wore a long brown dress and the expression of acceptance of a dreary Gwen John. She had achieved the poverty-stricken aspect of the sur-roundings and scarcely looked at him. He went off alone to find a drying room for his clothes and it was Jack who brought him soap and towels and sweaters and trousers.

When finally they were alone, he said, 'You know I love you,' and she replied with the maddening slowness he had once so adored, 'I love you, Andrew, you know,' but she continued to cut out the paper. When he came near to touch her she said, 'I must keep to my own bed here, Andrew. Unless you will marry me.'

It was not the ultimatum that had shocked him, not the bargaining; it was the way she had continued carefully cutting out the paper.

'I am cold,' she said and wrapped a bald coat of Jack's around her. It made her look ugly and old.

He thought of the nights they had had and couldn't believe in them. They seemed months ago, not days. He thought of a party he'd had to go to the week before, all pub glitter and dirty rugger songs and falling beer glasses and young girls with bright lipstick, nurses worn to shreds with work and still managing to dance. Holly Fox had been there. He'd heard of Holly Fox. She had been wearing prickly bunches of holly over each ear and expensive high heels and a silk shirt and she came over to him, laughing, to introduce herself. They had made jokes about medical horrors. She had poured out self-confidence and hope. 'She's after you,' someone said, 'and she gets what she wants, Holly Fox.'

In the wild snowy night at Ellerby Andrew found Jocasta's room and she was crying in her iron bed. She was cold, she was lonely. Philip was being troublesome and she couldn't take all the religion. She wanted to come home.

Making love to her, she came alive again and he knew there was none other.

But in the morning she had disappeared and he found her, wrapped up in old jerseys of Jack's, writing intensely in a notebook by an icy window niche. She covered the writing with her hand.

He found he could not ask her anything, could not tell her anything. He knew that her love for him would drown him, that he could not live with such a passion, with the sense of being always emotionally outclassed. 'I would destroy you, I suppose,' she said. He said, 'Don't worry, I'm leaving. I'm going back right away. I see it's over,' and knew that she knew he was pretending she had been the one to tire.

Jack and some of the others – little Philip was there – walked up the track with him and pushed and shoved to get the car started, towed it along behind a tractor, gave him a shovel to put in the back in case he got stuck further on. He was back on the motorway in an hour, in London as night fell.

An hour later he was on duty. Happy Holly Fox came clattering down the ward on chic black legs. Her unassailable assumption of conquest. He smiled at her.

– 13 –

In the car now, going to fetch her son Philip from school, Jocasta sat silent beside Andrew with her eyes closed. He drove very fast along the moor roads until she said, 'We're not late, you know. Can't you slow down?'

'I'll stop if you like,' he said.

'No, just slow down.'

'I'd forgotten. You're afraid of driving. Even now?'

'I do plenty of it now. I get Philip back and forth every day. But I still hate going fast.'

'I'm sorry. I should have given you this car to go for him by yourself but it's only insured for me. Or I could have come by myself and saved you the journey altogether.'

'It wouldn't have done. I don't let him get into cars with strange men, or men he hasn't seen for six years – which amounts to the same thing if you're eleven.'

'I should have been the one to take Pammie to her train,' he said. 'I hadn't reckoned on Jack wanting to take her. I'm sorry. I've muddled it.'

'Jack seems smitten,' she said. 'Surprise, surprise. He puts us all on pedestals. He loves women.'

They drove along the ridge, where steep clefts either side ran down from the rim of heather to brilliant steep green fields. On the horizon stood the three huge golf balls of the early warning system.

'They still frighten me,' he said, 'even though they're obsolete now, aren't they? Do people still do sit-ins around them? When I was at school there were "observers" coming from all over the place. Americans. Russians. Now they sit there like kids' balloons.'

She had shrunk down in her seat in the Toyota, her ankles demurely crossed like an old woman's. Dressed in black pants and sweater and her hair pulled back in a knob, she looked like a resting ballet dancer. Her hands were clasped so tight there were white marks on the knuckles. Staring at the three domes, her black eyes welled up with tears. She said, 'Oh how could you? How could you have married?'

He gave the cough he reserved for bedsides before imparting bad news. 'It – well, it was taken out of my hands, Jocasta, that's all I can say. She was – very forceful. You met her.'

'I met a hockey-playing extrovert who never stopped laughing. A gymnastic outdoor Betjeman girl. A woman of no subtlety, a bossy, tiny-minded bourgeois. I'm sorry. I know she's dead. I shouldn't say it. You must be suffering, I suppose. In your way. But I can't help being honest.'

'Nor could Holly. She was as honest as you. I think that's why—'

'Oh, don't give me that crap.'

'No, I mean I think that's why I thought I'd be able to manage.'

'*Manage*!'

'Without you.'

88

'But *why* manage without me? I was there. I was yours. Why?'

'You soon found Jack. Every woman wants Jack and you're the only one—'

'Yes,' she said, looking for a handkerchief, 'I soon found Jack.'

'It looked like pure malice. The timing of it.'

'No,' she said, 'not malice. It was a way of still being near you.'

'And now look what's happened. If you were free now . . . Jocasta, I'm trying to tell you that I'm a man who's made very few mistakes in his life but not marrying you was one of them.'

'And do you honestly believe,' she said, 'truly in your heart, that I would ever consider marrying you now even if I were free as the wind? Do you have any idea how much you've hurt me? And how much better the man I've married? And how much happier I am than I could ever have been with you? And how much *loved* I am now?'

They sat and the wind blew all around the car as if it might knock it over and roll it away. Long minutes passed. One car went by and dwindled away down the ridge and over the moor until it was a speck, and then was gone.

'You kept your secrets,' he said. 'What about Philip? You turned up in London with a five-year-old son and never a word about him.'

'Why ever should I?'

'You know everything about me. I told you everything. I told you long before we were lovers.'

'You never asked.'

'You were so beautiful, Jocasta. Like nobody else. You were like a brown nut. You were skintight like a Red Indian. You were still as a stone. You look no older now. You look untouched by Jack, or anyone.'

'Yes, I'm untouched by everyone. You look older. That great bald head. And your mouth is smaller. And mingier. And it sneers.'

She looked at him to see if she had gone in deep. She had. Bloody good. His transparent London pallor was flushed and his head tilted back in apparent disdain. He turned on the engine and said, 'We'd better get on.'

She put a brown claw on his arm then. Still looking ahead of him, he switched the engine off again. 'Let's get out,' she said.

They walked, a few feet apart, until they came to a long narrow dip in the heather, a swath of green turf scattered with dry black sheep droppings. When they lay down here the heather rose up around them, encircling them, so that they could not be seen by anything but a bird. They had melted into the moor. At the edge of this grass there were bilberries and the sharp arousing mineral smell of them mixed with the sweet smell of warmed grass. She undid each button of his shirt tidily and slowly, one by one. He pulled her sweater over her head and they held each other, she remembering every knob of his spine, he tracing the pattern of ears and jaw and neck, remembering how to undo the pile of black hair to let it fall round her shoulders like a shawl. He put both arms round her, his face in her neck, amazed that she could be so small. 'I think you've shrunk,' he said, and she said, 'No. You have forgotten.' They lay still, folded in to each other, heart upon heart, breath mixed with breath, until they grew warm in the October day, glowing, melded together. 'Now or later?' he said, but she did not answer.

Finding her mouth, he said, 'Now or later?' and she said, 'Now.'

'Right. Finish. Bell. You can all go, and good riddance. Philip Braithwaite, stay behind.'

Philip looked up in mild surprise. He had been drawing passionate lines against his ruler across a piece of graph paper. It was a French lesson. He ambled up in friendly fashion to the master's desk as the others scattered for buses home.

'Hi,' he said. 'Something up?'

'Shut up and wait. Straighten yourself up. Stop being insolent.'

'I only said . . .' Philip helplessly spread his hands. 'I never said . . .'

'You're to go to the Head.'

'What, *now*? I can't.'

'You're to see the Head now. He's waiting for you.'

'I'm sorry. It's not possible. I have to meet my sister. I'm not exactly mad about going to the Head anyway.'

The French master closed his eyes. He clenched his jaw. 'Philip, you haven't a sister. Will you kindly, most graciously, most accommodatingly, get the hell out of this room and go to the Head.'

'OK. Don't hit the ceiling. I'll go, but I've only a minute. They're bringing my sister when they come to collect me. She's only a baby. She can't be kept hanging about.'

He went and burst into the headmaster's office, forgetting to knock. The headmaster, who was standing looking out of the window, told him to go out again and come in properly.

'Sorry, wasn't thinking,' said Philip and retired.

91

There was silence. The Head opened the door and saw Philip wandering off down the corridor and about to turn the corner. 'What the hell d'you think you're doing, Braithwaite? Come back at once.'

Philip turned, smiled and gave a sketchy wave. 'Oh lord – sorry. Wasn't thinking.'

'I should like to beat you,' said the Head. 'I should like to flay you. I should like to hang you from the light cord. I should like to fling you from this window on to the cement of the school yard and see you founder.'

Philip looked interested and then very sad. 'I'm glad my stepfather can't hear you . . .'

'*Philip Braithwaite*, I have asked you here in order to find out if something is wrong. Something more than ordinarily wrong. We know you have your troubles. We know you live in a lunatic asylum on the moors. We know you are but a simple child in an adult world. We know that your family is beset with God and that God hides His Face, probably exhausted by you all. But we also know that you are a very intelligent, perfectly sane boy with potential to do anything on this earth you set yourself to do. Why, then, will you tell me, do you refuse to attempt to do any work, freak out at every games period, get lost at dinner time and cause general havoc wherever you go? I know I've asked you all this before, several times a week, but today is the end of the road. The end of the *road*, boy.'

Philip looked innocently bewildered. 'It's been all right today. Quite a pleasant day,' he said. 'Sir,' he added, as the Head's face darkened. 'I just had to go down into Whitby to buy a present for my sister.'

'You know perfectly well you're not any of you allowed into Whitby in school hours.'

'There seemed no one to ask.'

'But it is not *allowed*.'

Philip looked pained. 'I told you. I had to get a present . . .'

The Head sat down at the desk and pointed at a chair on the other side of it. Philip sat. The Head covered his eyes with his fingers and then uncovered them to grab Philip's wrists as he stretched forward to pick up an ornament on the desk. 'You bloody little twerp, put that down.'

'It's ormolu. *Sir*. Very nice. Lovely. We've got some Tibetans—'

'Philip, I've had enough. The school has had enough. You lie like an Arab. Look, we're going to have to expel you.'

Philip brightened.

'I should be a happy man, a fulfilled man, if I could only expel you and see the back of you for the last time marching out of that door. Unfortunately, I can't. I tried. I can't.'

'You mean when you got the assessors in? When you wanted me to go to the Dyslexic Centre?'

'I do. And when you spelled "Here" H I Y, I thought we'd got rid of you. But you overdid it. Overacted. As you do.'

'Well, I got interested in the Maths.'

'Unfortunately.'

'And they made a mistake.'

'So you told them.'

'They did. I wasn't exactly mad about telling them but—'

'That will *do*, Philip. The point today is where has all the Art paper gone? That's all I ask. You were working alone in the Art Room last week and all the paper is now missing. Four large rolls of it.'

93

'Why should it have been me?'

'Was it you?'

'Well, yes. You see—'

'*Philip!*'

'I wanted it for the Tibetans' mantras. We'd run out. Jocasta had something or other on her mind. I brought some back. I'll replace it, honestly. My mother's been awfully busy getting ready for the baby.'

'Baby?'

'My sister. She's just been born.'

'But I saw Jocasta last week . . . You mean there's a *baby*?'

'Just come. I'll be seeing her for the first time this afternoon. They're probably waiting outside for me now.'

The Head looked nervously over his shoulder out of the window and saw a Toyota he did not know approaching the school. Jocasta, light as a leaf, got out of it, her hair floating down her back.

'I'm afraid I shall have to speak to Jocasta and your stepfather again,' he said wearily. 'Philip, Philip, what are we to do with you? Not today, though. I'll make an appointment. Can you give me some satisfaction about the Art paper?'

'Oh yes. I'll get it back,' he said as he stood up. 'I'm sorry,' he added at the door, a smile of delirious enchantment breaking across his face. 'I'd better go. You've been very understanding, sir. Actually, "lie like an Arab" – isn't it a bit racist?'

The Head roared.

A moment later he watched the boy trot across the school yard towards the Toyota. Jocasta, on seeing her son, got back in her seat and sat looking at herself in a little glass and applying lipstick. A man not Philip's stepfather was at the wheel and as far as the Head could see there was not a trace of a baby.

– 14 –

'I believe that car was Andrew's. It looked like Andrew's. My son-in-law.'

The nice old Jaguar swooped down the high ridge road into a village with soft grass growing down its middle on either side of a stream. There were sheep wandering about and ducks sailing and waddling. A village shop.

'Oh this is so charming,' said Thomasina. 'So lovely to be here after horrible Scotland.'

'Horrible Egypt,' said the general, who had been enjoying Scotland until yesterday and was bemused that Thomasina had elected to leave it. He had been bemused by many things about Thomasina, to whom he was not married but on behalf of whom he had been signing his name in hotel registers for severals weeks. The events of the recent past, the months since Holly Fox's death, were proving startling to the general, whose life had gone steadily along since he left the army nearly twenty years before and even more steadily when two years ago he entered a calmly accepted widowhood in Berkshire, near his old garrison. He had been enormously enjoying his disciplined life and finding it very entertaining until his visit to Challoners

Health Farm for his joints, and the first sight of Thomasina.

It was not at all that he had fallen for her lustfully, as old men so sadly do. The general's love for Thomasina involved not a jot of desperation. It was seeing her there and recognising a dying breed, his breed, the breed of woman he had always been easy with, a woman untouched by the shabby, messy world that now surrounded him, belaboured him on the television, on public transport, from advertisement hoardings, even in the theatre, the world where everything hangs out. The last time he had been to the opera he had seen somebody in the audience in a vest.

Abroad was not so bad, or at least the abroad he had known so well. India was still recognisable, the beggars more prolific and even more demanding, but there were still hotels there where, on a good package, you could find people wearing the right clothes and speaking in the right voices. Shepheard's Hotel in Cairo was virtually gone – the Shepheard's Hotel that had twisted his heartstrings once – but there were still gentle and spacious havens. There were still, for example, punkahs against the heat in Singapore, though nowadays the fans were worked by electricity and not the toe of a boy. You could still meet an old friend in the Cricket Club and the Straits Chinese were very efficient people. You had to respect them. They had the Club on a good financial footing.

But on the whole he stayed at home. He rarely looked at travel brochures now. The attempted afterglow of the empire there he found embarrassing, as he did the Royal Family, whom he had abhorred since they had gone public and made love in front of the camera. There were one or two of the Royal Family who were all right. The Queen, of course, and Princess Alexandra. About Princess Alexandra he even had very faint (and very secret) fantasies on the edge of sleep. He rode with her in Abyssinia and Tanganyika in the old days – narrow beautiful jodhpurs – or he fished with her in Scottish burns.

The first view of Thomasina across the salon at Challoners behind her silver teapot had given him an excited lurch, for she had Princess Alexandra's legs and narrow skirt, and when she turned, as he called across to ask her if she were famous, Princess Alexandra's crooked smile.

After Thomasina's tragic departure he had worked vigorously to find her again. He had not been able to extract her address from the place but they had promised to forward a letter. There had been silence. He had at last discovered the reason through a mutual acquaintance run to earth at a party given by a Surrey GP. 'Used to be married to old Herbert Fox. Quite something. Nice woman. Didn't remarry. Very wrapped up in her daughter, who's just died, I understand. Yes – only about a month ago.'

The general tracked down Thomasina and found not Princess Alexandra but the creature now anathema to all her friends. Thomasina encased in glass, untouchable. He also saw her bravery. He saw it in her clothes and careful make-up and flawless social manner, and he still felt, beneath it all, her charm. In the intensity of those first days it is just possible that the general caught a glimpse of Thomasina herself.

He felt a great warmth for her, a wish to be near

her, to touch her elbow, enwrap her, take her to leisurely expensive places in his immaculate old car. He wanted to take her to meet the remnants of his own old background, where he knew she would appear deeply, effortlessly at home. She looked so unselfconsciously well-heeled, too. *I could comfort her*, he thought. *If I were younger I'd say I was in love*.

This thought gave him delicious amusement as he went swooping about in the Jaguar. *Seventy-two*, he thought with pride as, approaching Kensington High Street, he cut in on a little Renault driven by a man like Tony Blair and pressed the button that let down the Jaguar's roof. He took to keeping the roof down in all weathers: to wearing a tweed cap. He began to notice girls' legs in the autumn sunshine. He found in Hyde Park one day that he was thoroughly, positively happy.

Not that he'd ever been an unhappy man. Very lucky. Keeping going. Usually possible to find something pleasant to think about. Good health the secret. No bees in the bonnet. No love troubles.

Love troubles, he thought. *Ridiculous. Couldn't do it now*.

He began, though – as he made his toast and porridge for breakfast in the shiny kitchen in his house on the edge of the garrison, calendar on the wall marked off with perhaps a dwindling number of things to look forward to, telephone these days ringing rather less frequently and the dear old dog dead – he began to remember love.

They were hazy creatures, like somebody else's, girls from a pre-war book, girls whose names . . . There came a warm zephyr of a memory, something to do with Egypt, a weekend with a girl at Karnak in the Summer Palace during the war. He had been –

what? Under thirty. He remembered a summer frock and a string of little pearls and sunset over the Valley of the Kings. Madeleine. She had been very shy. He'd met his wife Hilda soon afterwards at a noisy tennis party in Hong Kong and loved the way she smashed the ball about and looked so big and sensible and believed in the Empire. *Madeleine*, he thought. *What became of her?* And saw, amazingly, the line of her dress on the terrace of the Summer Palace half a century ago, her fingers tangling in the pearls. He saw that he had suppressed all this – good God, where was it all coming from? Blonde, blonde hair. He saw her longing eyes.

I missed something, he thought. *Bloody fool*.

Continuing the essential ritual of his day, after dinner on the kitchen work-top he poured himself a double Scotch and switched on the ten o'clock news. He switched off when it was over and found that he had not registered one word, but that the Egyptian sunset was still about. He picked up the telephone and fancied that Thomasina's voice was as Madeleine's would be now.

When he took Thomasina to dinner the next evening at his London club he cleared his throat, examined the moulding on the ceiling and suggested that what would do her good would be a package tour to Egypt. 'For me, too,' he said. 'I should like to see Egypt again. Buck us both up. What do you say?'

But Egypt with Thomasina was not to be the gentle time with Madeleine. They began in Cairo with a non-luxury hotel. There had been no tour available so they had simply bought a couple of airline tickets and made reservations for themselves in something that sounded quiet and where there would be no Americans. The hotel had turned out to be far from the Nile, down a maze of dirty streets and looking over an empty sports stadium, and the general spent the first morning trying to change the reservations, with no success. They had a bad lunch in a restaurant smelling of hamburgers and then trailed about the Museum of Antiquities. Tutankhamun's head was out on loan and round every grubby sarcophagus a dirty fellow with a beckoning finger tried to lure them off to see secret horrors in dark corners denied, they were assured, to the general public. 'Dead babies covered with hair,' one demon promised them.

The general led her away towards the Bazaar but something had happened to the sky. It had turned the colour of uncleaned copper and sand was uneasily snaking the streets. They took a reluctant taxi, in which the driver had been curled up on the floor, to visit friends of the general's dead wife. Valerie had married romantically on leaving Cambridge an Egyptian economist. The apartment was in Stygian darkness owing to a power cut and the darkening sky. 'But we always need the lights on in here, anyway,' said Valerie. Dusty sand lay deep on shelves and tables, in folds of the curtains, along the top of the sunny but fading photograph of Girton girls in caps and gowns, in 1938. The husband sat slumped in a broken chair, his long yellow hands hanging towards the floor. There were little cakes that tasted of sand. The apartment was on a lower floor of an old six-storey block and at intervals loads of rubbish were chucked from above and fell past the window to land with a thud in the street below. The hostess moved with dazed dignity, carrying milk jugs, paper napkins. Sand-wiches garnished with parsley the husband turned from with disgust. Suddenly he asked about this year's Boat Race and they all tried to remember it. Valerie mentioned the general's dead wife, Hilda, and then burst into tears.

That night the sandstorm closed the airport and for two days Thomasina and the general stayed in the hideous hotel watching the cars in the streets below being coated with sand as thick as a deep snowfall. The snow was solid and dark and did not melt. The city was silenced. Somehow they forced a cab to take them to the airport to see if they could get to Karnak on the second evening, and found themselves marooned there, alone except for a party of giant Texans in T-shirts, stetsons and boots. No Egyptians were to be seen except for those bundles of rags blurred into mummified shapes all over the lounges, the duty-free, perhaps even the runways, sleeping till the sand had settled and drifted away, God knew when.

Utter silence covered Cairo. They joined up with the Texans, who were drinking Glenfiddich – which improved things no end – and at last accompanied them to their suite in the Mena House Hotel beside the Pyramid, a fee like the national lottery jackpot being demanded by and paid to a doleful cab driver who implied this would be his last drive on earth. In the Texans' suite Thomasina and the general drank more whisky, ate smoked salmon, talked about racing, entered a violent argument about American politics, were found somehow a single room in the hotel, into which the two of them crammed, became lovers and awoke the next morning to a curiously muffled but sunshiny world.

Thomasina glittered as they caught the plane to Karnak next morning, the general held his head high and the security man in the airport pinched Thomasina's bottom as she stepped through the gate. The general smiled so lovingly at a stewardess that she blushed and brought them a half bottle of champagne.

At the Winter Palace, where crowds of tourists sat on suitcases weeping at the total failure of all bookings, their air of Olympian confidence, the general's marvellous trousers and Thomasina's tall relaxed figure unfussed among the life-size palms on the grubby marble somehow produced a key a foot long and a room with doors so high they would have admitted giraffes. The bed in this room, which was Farouk Dynasty, was covered in old brown satin. A basin and ewer stood at a tilt on a stalk of twisted metal and from a shadowy dressing room an old gentleman was evicted wearing a long pale-pink robe. He said that he had been expecting to spend the night with them in order to clean their shoes.

Laughing like school children, they ordered dreadful sandwiches and even more dreadful wine and slept together for the second time. In the morning they opened shutters upon the Valley of the Kings, gold and rosy in the dawn, and watched matchstick people with boot-black faces and pastel-coloured robes prancing and jolly on either bank of the Nile. And the Nile ran fast and green, busy with feluccas sharp-winged as ancient birds on a frieze.

Thomasina and the general did not refer to the events of the night, though they both knew they were more precisely and deliciously remembered than even those of the night before, wreathed in sandstorm and whisky; but on the terrace at breakfast they often caught each other's glance and smiled, and the general tenderly asked her if she'd like more coffee. When they crossed by felucca to the tombs, he said, 'I hope you're as happy as I am, Thomasina,' and she smiled and took his arm.

There was a change, though. As they stood in one of the patterned walled tombs of a young queen, there was a little bundle in a corner, the dust of a child. No one knew, said the guide, if it were a miscarried child or a child dead just after birth, but it must have been a child greatly loved or desired to have been buried with such honour. Thomasina said nothing, but afterwards the general remembered the moment. Thomasina's coolness, which had left her at the Mena House for an almost languid glow, returned, and at the dinner table that night she began to work out the expenses of the trip, insisting she pay half. When he protested, she said that times had moved on since his day and she was nobody's mistress.

In bed later he lay in silence and she moved towards him and caressed and cajoled but didn't apologise.

It was a different sort of lovemaking, Thomasina almost ferocious, and the at first reluctant general very surprised.

On the plane home she read a book about the royal houses of the Ptolemaean dynasty and the general thought that he had never seen her more beautiful. He was now as much in love with her as a dizzy boy. He dropped his money about, mislaid his passport, longed for the night. He would even have agreed to staying in Cairo again, even at the hotel overlooking the stadium as they had planned first, but when she said No, home, he agreed. He would have agreed to anything. He wondered when she would tell him that she would marry him. Pale England in the autumn light, the smooth broad road from Heathrow, the luxurious taxicab, the traditional talkative driver, made him feel as if life were just beginning again – real English life as it had once been. He was exalted.

It was only after they were in the taxi and the general leaning forward to tell the driver where in London they should go that it became clear to them both that neither knew where that was.

Thomasina was leaning back, looking reflective.

'My club?' he said.

'Very well.'

'Covent Garden,' he said. 'We can have dinner there.' *But not sleep there*, he thought: *I can't take her to bed there.*

It was a huge distance. On his own the general would have taken the tube or a couple of buses to Berkshire. And the general, Thomasina thought, had not seen her mock-Tudor house near Edgecombe. They sat silently considering these facts.

Thomasina said as the taxi with thirty pounds on the clock reached central London, 'I think we'll make it Waterloo, if you don't mind, Giles. I think I'd like to go home.'

'Right,' he said. 'I shall come with you.'

'Absolutely no.'

'You are being ridiculous,' he said, wondering how he had displeased her.

But she was first out of the taxi and had paid the fare before he had even begun to negotiate the suitcases. She seemed not to notice his annoyance.

He strode off and bought first-class tickets for the train and was ahead of her at Guildford station, finding another taxi fast, helping her aboard; but again lost face because he didn't know the address. He looked stonily at the large house, the overgrown garden. Apples had splattered down among the trees on the front lawn; rambler roses over the trellises needed cutting back. It was a garden he'd like to get his hands on. They waded through the papers and letters behind the door and stood on the parquet and Persian rugs in the hall as she read some of the postcards.

'Shall I open a window or two?'

She frowned, looked at him, read a postcard over again.

'Do you really live all alone here? Is it safe? Great garden all around and right off the road. Bit of a temptation to people, isn't it?'

To his amazement (it was three o'clock in the afternoon, for God's sake), he found himself longing to take her to bed again. *And seventy-two!*

'I'll get some coffee,' and he turned to where he thought there might be a kitchen.

'No,' she said. 'Don't. Stay here.' She went over to him and stroked his cheek. 'I'm sorry. So sorry, Giles. Could you just stay in the hall? I'm going upstairs to change and wash and . . .'

'Very well.'

When she came back he was sitting on an antique oak stool much too small for him, fist on either knee, and her heart melted for a moment. She said, 'It's just it's this house. Spindleberries. Where we lived. I can't come back just yet. I thought I could. I find I can't.'

106

'I understand.'

Not once had she mentioned Holly's name since they had met. He waited.

'I think I'd like to go to Scotland now,' she said.

'Now? Scotland?'

'Yes, I think I'd like to go to Scotland. We might get sleepers.'

'Out of the question.'

She seemed to brighten up. 'I'll make some tea,' she said, 'Sit down somewhere. You're overdone.'

Later he found on the phone that there were no sleepers for weeks and at her disappointed face said that they might perhaps drive there tomorrow or the next day. Do the old car good, he said. But not straight off. Bit of rest first. Plenty of friends there – places to stay, and good bed-and-breakfasts. Cousin in Caithness. Lovely in the Highlands just now.

She looked bewildered and then relieved, kissed his forehead as she passed his chair, watched him pick up the suitcases and led him upstairs. In her bedroom she said, 'If you went to get the car now and picked me up here in the morning . . .' but he said, 'No, I'm not going to do that. I'm staying here tonight.'

'You can't sleep with me. Not here.' She was looking over his shoulder.

'I'll sleep in another room. I'm going into London for the car now, and I'll be back here about ten.'

'Can you get dinner somewhere?'

'Of course.' He looked stern. 'You have something in the fridge, I dare say?'

She looked at him scornfully and let him out of the front door, from where he had to walk a mile to the station.

All evening she paced about the house, agonising that he wouldn't come back.

At ten there was no sign of him, nor at half past. She had made up a bed for him and turned up the central heating, picked a few flowers, put together a tray of drinks and taken bread out of the freezer for morning. The house felt frighteningly still and she was wide awake. *Jet lag*, she thought. *I'd better not drink. Yet I never get jet lag and all I've had is horrible aeroplane champagne.*

She couldn't remember if she'd eaten anything since and went to the kitchen, where she found a crumby plate from her supper and some pants and stockings drying on the Aga rail. Upstairs her dresses had been hung up, her sponge bag emptied. She must have been quite busy. She rang Pammie for the third time but there was still no answer. At last she went into Holly's old room. Baby clothes lay in soft neat clumps. Teddies and old dolls were in a box. There was a crib and baby blankets. She sat on the bed.

This is a big step. I am here. Tomorrow I'll start thinking. He will not come back and I shall write to him and finish it off. Good clean break. He was a nice man. It was mad, really. I'm amazed I could remember how to do it.

The lights of the Jaguar swung across the garden, then across the bedroom, and in a moment he was at the door with another suitcase for Scotland and wearing a tweed suit. He smelled of very good soap and walked in as if she were his wife of years. But he made no more enquiries about sleeping quarters and no comment when she said, 'No – not there,' as he made for Holly's room. She opened another door.

'D'you want the landing light left on?' he asked. 'I'll leave my door open.'

She heard him moving about his room, the click as he put down his watch on the bedside table, the little rattle as his cuff links were dropped on the dressing table. She heard him brushing his teeth, drawing back curtains, opening the window a little. The creak as he lowered himself into bed.

Good God, men, she thought. *They're bloody awful. Where have I brought myself? What do I want? Why can't I let myself go? Or get rid of him?*

'It was Andrew's car,' she said, 'and Andrew in it. My son-in-law.'

The general swivelled a tired eye. Thomasina was looking lovelier than ever, he thought, her skin clear from fresh Scottish air, a couple of days' fishing and some splendid rain. He could not look at her without delight. And yet . . .

'Your *son-in-law*? There was nothing up there at all, Thomasina, just the moor.'

'No. There was a car by the roadside. It was Andrew's Toyota. Holly used to drive it.'

He thought, *I must be very careful now, and very kind.*

Before she could have time to wait for his reaction to Holly's name being mentioned at last, he said, 'Oh, I'm sure there are plenty of Toyotas around here, you know.'

'He was with a woman. A very small dark woman. They were sitting talking. Miles from anywhere.'

'No, Thomasina. It would be an extraordinary

109

coincidence, wouldn't it? Wasn't your – wasn't Holly married to a London doctor?'

'There was no sign of the baby in the car, I think,' said Thomasina.

He said carefully, 'Ah. A baby. I think I heard there was a baby.'

'Faith,' she said. 'Ghastly name, isn't it? Better than Hope or Charity, I suppose. Well, it wasn't anything to do with me.'

'I'm afraid I had no children. We didn't have this problem.'

'Perhaps you were lucky.'

Then she saw his face.

'Come,' he said. 'We can get tea here,' and in the teashop, looking at the stream and the white wooden bridges outside over the stream, he said, 'If you would like to talk about . . .'

'Oh,' she said, 'not a bit. Terrible shock, you know, and I keep thinking, "Holly darling, how dare you? Just going off like that and leaving poor old Andrew." But you know, she wasn't one who would want us to *mope*. She was very sensible and positive. Awful bore it happened, but it does happen, doesn't it? Nothing to be done.' Her light voice was the voice he had first heard across the health farm drawing room. He thought, *And it's the voice of the lost*.

'And the – baby? Faith?' he asked.

'Oh. Well, I think she's not really my department. There are the other grandparents, you know, and a brother. They live up here. Just about here. Big Northern family all rallying round. Marvellous people, of course, Yorkshire people.'

'Will you mind her being a North Country grand-daughter?'

110

'Oh, you mean her accent? Well, of course not. That would be too bourgeois. And it can be very homely and nice. I'd have preferred a Scot, of course, but there. Andrew hasn't a trace of Yorkshire in him even though he's from a local school, I believe. Stuffy old stick-in-the-mud, but I have to say you could take him anywhere.'

'He must be very cut up.'

'Yes,' she said. 'Oh, do look at that sheep. Yes, it was strange seeing him just now with that woman. D'you know, it was the first time,' she said with an open and completely empty smile, 'that I realised old Holls had gone. Let's get on and find the hotel. Priors Meadow. It can't be far. Actually, it's quite near some of Andrew's family, I think. Next village.'

The general said carefully, 'So it could have been Andrew?'

'Oh yes,' she said. 'It was.'

Pammie at the same moment was settling herself in a first-class carriage as the King's Cross train drew out of York station and laying out for herself on the little shelf beside her the equipment for mixing up a knockout gin and tonic – brittle plastic beaker, three miniature bottles and a plastic swizzle stick. She was alone in the carriage. She kicked off her shoes, took a quick shuftie at the Minster in its cream-and-gold glory behind the scaffolding, wondered about a cigarette, lit a cigarette, lay back, closed her eyes and translated herself to Surrey.

You won't believe this. I'm not sure that I believe it. It was a riot. *Tibetans*, dear. Holy men. Yes, I am talking about Faith Fox and Andrew. She is to live in *ruins* on the North Yorkshire moors. The very strangest people you ever saw in your life and

111

Andrew, let me tell you, quite a different person. D'you know, he got out of the car in this great wilderness, every bit as wild as Dartmoor and not even the cafés and coaches, and he went striding off into the heather leaving me all alone? Well, cold feet, I suppose. His brother, well, you would never, never, dream they were related. Much older. He looks a different generation from Andrew, but masses of curly hair and not grey. He's a sort of evangelist, I suppose, and his wife's tiny and black. No, I don't mean *black* black, I mean sort of dark. All over. Sort of heart of darkness. Gaunt and tiny and intense. Not my sort at all, I'm afraid. You can see she'll be very attractive to men. Great eyes in a little head. No trace of the North about her. I don't know where he can have found her. Rather plummy voice, actually. Overdone Oxford sort of voice, quite old-fashioned. But young, she's young, and she's not a Sloane. Arty. There was a child about somewhere, quite an old one, I think, but I didn't see it. You couldn't think anyone so tiny could have produced a child. She just stands about, looking at you.

Most frightful lunch they gave me. Some sort of salt fish. I expect it must have been got in for the Tibetans, though it would have been a mistake, Tibet being so far from the sea. They probably never touch it. No common sense about. Yes, I saw some Tibetans. They were lumping about in some sheds. They looked fairly doubtful to me.

Cells, my dear, to sleep in. Workshops full of looms. They must have cost a bomb, yet there was no central heating and not a carpet or a curtain. Jack – the brother – showed me around. And, d'you know, Andrew never said goodbye. He went off

112

somewhere with Heart-of-Darkness and it was brother who took me to the train. Thought we'd never get here, he's a frightful driver, and we were in some sort of smelly pick-up full of beer cans. They'd had a batch of hooligans staying from Teesside. They take in the unloved. Our darling Faith! He kept wanting to stop and show me churches and bits of ruins and I had to be quite firm. As it was, I missed the train I'd booked a seat on and I had to jump for the next. I just managed to run into the buffet and grab a drink and leap into the train as the doors banged, dragging my luggage in off the platform. I hadn't *taken* luggage but this Jack had made me bring home a plastic bag full of potatoes. There was no sign of him but, just as we pulled away, here he is, wandering down the platform with his arms full of newspapers for me. The kindest man – but, you know, impossible. He dropped all the papers trying to wave goodbye. Very lovable man. He's asked me to go back, by the way, for a retreat. I retreated all right, straight back south.

She took a swig of gin and looked out eastward over the plain to low hills of hanging woods. A plump and amateurish white horse was picked out in the chalk and above it ran the line of the moor. She felt a surprising pleasure. Finishing the gin, she thought of Thomasina and could not see her anywhere near such a place. *I don't think he'd have asked* her *back*, she thought. *I think I rather hit it off with the evangelist. But by God, I couldn't have taken much more.*

What a day! she thought. *I'm getting too old for this. There and back to North Yorkshire by bedtime. That drive!* She had a frightening moment of being quite unable

113

to remember why she had come and this was followed by something even more unpleasant. It was like pain. It was guilty sorrow. She couldn't place it.

She fell heavily asleep, waking just north of London with enough time to do her face and look at her hair and wriggle herself tidy inside her silk-and-wool suit with the black binding (Harvey Nicks). She patted a black silk scarf, thinking, *Black. Oh dear, Holly's funeral. Oh, poor Holly Fox*.

Back home old Hugo wandered across to her with whisky. 'Child safe?' he asked. 'Settled in?' and Pammie stared, placing the anguish.

She had forgotten to look at Faith before she left or to say goodbye.

The two Smikes were waiting for the go-ahead to set off on their night out when the Toyota arrived in the courtyard on its journey from Philip's school. Philip got out and came over to them. 'Yer goin' down Middlesber?' he enquired in a voice that would have been unrecognisable in his classroom.

'Come back,' Jocasta called. 'Philip, come back and say thank you to Andrew for getting you from school.'

'Thanks, Andrew,' said Philip in Jocasta-speak, then, 'I said, yer goin' down Middlesber? Can ah coom wid yer?'

The Smikes continued to drink out of Coke cans. Jack's pick-up could be heard approaching the gatehouse from its trip to York and Jack climbed down from it and went over to Philip, smiling.

'Now then, Philip, what's this?'

' 'E wantster coom Middlesber,' said Smike One (Ernie). 'We's goin' down Retcer ont bikes.'

'That's a matter for Jocasta,' said Jack and looked across to the Toyota. His brother now seemed to be there alone.

'She's gone to look at Faith, I think,' said Andrew. 'Pammie get off OK?'

'Perfectly. Now, what about Evensong? I thought there should be a little welcoming ceremony for Faith. I thought maybe somebody might carry her up to the altar and I could bless her.'

Andrew looked uneasy.

'Perhaps Philip?' said Jack.

Philip aimed a sudden kick at Smike Two (Nick), who had just lit up a joint and aimed the match in Philip's direction. Then he went into The Priors, looking for food. Andrew thought, *Nasty little prick*.

The journey from school had not been agreeable. Philip had come, almost bustling, to the car in the school yard, climbed in the back and said, 'Hi, Andrew' (after six years). 'Where is she?'

Andrew, dazed from the journey out, warmed and sleepy by the delight of Jocasta's silky thigh beside the handbrake, the smell of her hair and skin, said, 'Where's who?'

Philip didn't answer. As they started for home Philip realised there must have been some mistake. He'd thought – he had *known* – that they were bringing his sister. He knew it was true. He'd heard them all talking and stuff being brought in and so on. Baby. Faith. He'd liked Holly. 'Holly's Faith' they'd all been saying. He wasn't mad about the idea of Holly being dead.

Faith. Coming to live up here. His sister. Like most dyslexics he had a hazy grasp of relationships. Nephews and nieces, cousins and aunts, they were more complicated for him than the construction of computer programmes that would have puzzled Aristotle and came to him like breathing. At eleven, grandparents he could just about understand, maybe because Dolly and Toots were woven into his life. They were Jack's parents and Andrew's parents. He knew this. Jack he had been told was his stepfather only, but he'd never enquired into that. He remembered a time in somewhere vile when there had been no Jack. Some house fully of dirty rooms in screaming streets. Bright red buses. Police sirens. Vaguely once a place called Earls Court where there had been acrobats. Jocasta had been there with some people – but no Jack, nobody he knew now.

'Well, but you are my grandparents, though?' he'd asked Dolly and Toots, and Dolly had said, 'Well . . .' and stopped. Toots had said, 'That's right, boy. Twice over.'

The first and only thing Philip had ever made with Jocasta in one of her craft classes had been a wooden box that stood askew and was narrow at the bottom so that dirt got in the corners and everyone had laughed at it, but when he gave it to Dolly and Toots at Christmas they had been in raptures. 'Put that right there by my bed,' Toots had said. 'Now, that's not to be moved. That's for my papers,' and Dolly had shown it to everyone, especially Mrs Middleditch, who had said that her Bingham couldn't have made it at eleven and he was now a mechanical engineer. These were grandparently events, he sensed. Philip was rather mad about his grandparents.

'You got heather on your back, Jocasta,' he said, 'and bits in your hair.' She said nothing. 'Where's the baby?' he tried again. 'I thought you had brought the baby.'

'She'd had enough driving,' said Andrew. 'She's being looked after at The Priors. You'll see her when we get there.'

'Oh, I don't care about seeing her,' said Philip. 'I just wondered if you could have forgotten her.'

'Don't be a fool, Philip,' said his mother.

'I thought that Philip might carry up Faith this evening,' said Jack at tea, 'bring her up from the body of the chapel to the altar and then I could carry her down again and show her about to the congregation – the visitors and all the staff and everyone. The two youngest ones together.'

'You might do better to get one of the visitors. One of the oldest,' said Alice Banks, The Missus, the housekeeper. 'The one that looks as old as Shangri-La.'

'She's looking after Faith at the moment,' said Jack. 'Well, I think so. I hope so. Have you been to see her, Jocasta? You took her over there, Alice, didn't you, after you'd seen to Andrew's bedroom?'

The Missus said yes, but it had hardly been a question of handing over, the Tibetan lady had carried Faith off in her bosom.

Everyone laughed except Philip.

'Can I go with The Smikes?' he asked.

'Not again,' said The Missus. 'Not again. You can't.'

'Who are The Smikes?' asked Andrew.

'Our saviours,' said Jack. His smile was a light unto his feet. 'Can't do without them. They hold us all together.'

The Missus looked darkly at her plate.

'They're ex-remand boys,' said Jack. 'We've had them a while now. They decided to stay on after they'd done their community service. They were burglars. It's a great tribute to us. But no, Philip, you're not to go with them again.'

'Why not?'

'Because,' said The Missus, 'they're older than you are. They get you in trouble. The trouble they make is their own affair, so I'm told, since they're over eighteen. Now it's all girls and drink, and it's way too soon for you.'

'It's quite right for The Smikes,' said Jack. 'We lead them now, we don't command. We only can suggest right values.'

'Couldn't one of them carry up the baby?' said Philip. 'I'd just drop her or something.' He awaited contradiction.

'Well, if you think you would,' said Jack, and Jocasta said, 'He would. He's not to do it. Her father shall carry her, if anyone.'

'Actually, I don't see why anyone should,' said Andrew. 'She'll be having a christening some time, won't she? She's been jumped round enough for one day. Surrey ladies and Tibetans.'

'So, could I go with The Smikes? I could stay the night, if you like, with Dolly and Toots.'

'No, I don't like the way Nick drives,' said The Missus.

'Oh, come on,' said Jocasta, changing sides.

'They're wonderful drivers,' said Jack. 'People go on about young drivers today but they're better than we are. Wonderful reflexes. I wish mine were anything like them.'

'Oh, I dare say Philip will be safer with them than you,' said his brother.

Looking Philip over, Andrew felt a pang of remorse. He'd not addressed a word to the child in

118

the car, his thoughts being far from step-nephews, his hands trembling, his whole dishevelled being reliving the glory of the journey out. *What a day!* he thought. *Pammie and The George and all that prattle and getting lost and theology and losing courage and nearly going home to Mum and then arriving – and there she was. Oh God. And within two hours, naked in the heather. And now evensong.*

Andrew disliked boys. He disliked children altogether, really. He found them selfish, wrapped up in themselves, expecting attention and interest to be taken. He still couldn't quite believe in Faith. He hadn't been able to take her in at all. But there was something rather arresting about Philip now. Very honest. Yet complex. Well, he was Jocasta's, wasn't he? God knows who the father had been. Good old Jack, taking him on. The boy must have a queer sort of life.

'I'll be going down tomorrow to see Dolly and Toots,' he said. 'I could bring you back, Philip, if these Smikes drop you off there tonight.'

'Only if The Smikes promise to drop you off on their way *in*. We don't want you joining up with them in whatever their goings-on are,' said The Missus. Jocasta moved her fork about. Jack smiled. *Whose the hell's am I?* thought Philip.

'And you must be strapped in that bike this time,' said The Missus, 'and ring up the minute you get there.'

'I must write my few words for the service now,' said Jack. 'What do you say about Philip going, then, Jocasta?'

'Fine,' she said. 'Friday night. No school tomorrow.'

'Then we'll all go to evensong in ten minutes,'

said Jack. 'The visitors will be in the chapel already. Shall we gather up Faith and begin?'

'What about this carrying-up thing I have to do?' asked Philip.

'We'll leave it. We'll say some prayers for her, but perhaps we'll leave the presentation until some time like the christening when Dolly and Toots . . . And we might invite that good woman to come back. Jocasta – darling, what's the matter?'

'Tired,' she said. 'I'm going to lie down. I'll miss this.'

During the service the old Tibetan woman, who must have heard some rumour of a ceremony, took matters and Faith into her own hands. In the middle of a hymn in which the Tibetans did not join she suddenly arose with the cot and dumped it on the altar and went back to her place.

'Cheek,' said The Missus.

From the front pew, Philip observed Faith. Strapped on the slanting tray of the cot, she was looking down the tin church this way and that, alertly at the candles on either side of her, wonderingly at the sunlight dying through the metal windows. She began to drum her feet against the tray and opened wide her arms. Squirming rather angrily, she made a sound that might have been either laughter or tears.

– 15 –

'Are yer goin' ont sans?' yelled Philip over the racket of the motorbike. He was in a sidecar hitched to the bike's side with ramshackle hooks and twine. It bobbed up and down like a cockleshell boat. The Smikes, one behind the other, kept their faces forward. 'Don't drop me off at me gran's, Nick. Gi's a break, Nick.' The machine was slowing down at the end of Dolly and Toots's road. Usually Philip was tipped out near old Toots's seat beside the church and walked the rest of the way, but the slowing-down process was being a tricky one tonight and Nick, swearing, decided to pack it in for the time being and drive on. They went over the top of a low sandy roundabout with the sound of a cohort of cavalry, plunged on over a short dead-end of unmade road that led into the sand dunes, and bike and sidecar then performed a ballet in the gloaming across golf bunkers and low grassy hills and swooped down upon the seashore beyond.

It was dark. The sands were hard and wide and appeared to be empty. 'Let yer frottle art,' shouted Ernie to Nick. 'Let 'er go.'

'Yes, let yer frottle art, yer booger,' shouted Philip alongside, bouncing.

Nick obliged and the machine with a noise like a steelworks when they open up furnaces took off along the shore, weaving among half-submerged rocks and piles of seaweed and springing like a thoroughbred over a massive rusty sewer pipe. The waves drew back as they passed by.

The bike roared in a crescendo and then faded and stopped at last in a profound silence. Some faint cries reached them from the promenade. Ernie, the quieter Smike, let out a long halloo like a fox yapping and Nick began a paean of demon laughter. Bouncing slowly like an airliner after landing, the hooks of the sidecar suddenly broke and it went careering, with Philip inside it, out into the ocean.

When they'd dragged him out again and failed to re-harness sidecar to bike, they pushed them, with some difficulty – especially for Philip, who was in sole charge of the sidecar – up the deep grubby sand. When Philip reached the promenade both Smikes were leaning against a fishing boat, in conversation with friends. Trying to haul his charger up the steps, Philip called, 'Yer gotter 'elp me, Nick. It's 'eavy.'

'Poor little booger. Poor little soft booger, 'elp yerselluf.'

It was Ernie who came over in the end and got behind Philip to drag and heave the thing, though he looked the less strong of the two. Emaciated, tattooed and earringed, he seemed as he rose up the steps from the strand like someone rescued after weeks in an open boat. This was deeply misleading. Ernie's gentle appearance had stood him in good stead for years, particularly with women of the maternal variety, and had been to his great advantage as a burglar.

The bike and sidecar were brought together among the boats with the intermittent help of new Smike cronies, who had detached themselves from the open doors of the amusement arcade opposite and from the yards and wynds that joined the straggling, clapped-out ex-fishing town to the shore. There followed a big struggle to get the bike and sidecar re-attached and padlocked to the railings of a statue of a bewhiskered Victorian benefactor of the town staring out to sea above their heads.

The amusement palaces behind him wailed and blinked their lights. 'See yer, Philip,' said Nick making for the pub. 'Git off to yer gran's or we'll cop it.'

'Can I coom wid yer? 'Alf an 'ower?'

'Yer not old enough. Yer eleven.'

'I look more,' said Philip. 'Can I coom wid yer to t'video games, then, Ernie?'

Ernie, who had joined another gang, one of whom had an arm round Ernie's waist, said, 'Garn, Philip, git lost.'

'Oh, garn, Ernie.'

''Ow mooch money yer got?'

'Four pound.'

'OK then. Cost yer three.'

Philip handed over three pound coins and accompanied Ernie and his consorts into the arcade. Nick had already disappeared.

At first he let himself drown in the glory of the place, the glitter, the pulse and blood glare of the lights, the filthy floor, the robotic seducers bleeping and flashing, the tremendous satisfaction of the tin music, the shouts and laughs of the clientele. He drifted about, wondering which machine he should honour with his pound. Out of sight, he heard

Ernie's gang manning the video games and went to find them. Ernie was in thrall to a naked woman with bared teeth who was surging towards him down a mountain side, whirling a whip. He seemed enchanted, and when the screen went blank said, ''ere, Phil, gi's yer pound.'

'I can't,' said Philip. 'I need it.'

'Yer'll just wairst un. Gi's 'ere.'

'Nope,' said Philip, 'I'm not mad 'bout video games,' and he slid off down an aisle to the fruit machines where some of Ernie's mates were trading in Es. A small white pill changed hands for fifteen pounds.

'D'yer want one?'

'What's it do?'

'Yer'll never 'ave lived, mate.'

'If you've any magic mushrooms, I'd like a go at them.'

'I can't 'elp yer but I know a man as can. Seven pound. Mind, they make t'sky bleed.'

'Yuck.'

''S great, a great bleedin' sky.'

'I'm putting me last pound int fruit machine, so belt up.'

'Silly fool,' said Ernie coming up. 'That un's a dood. I'd 'ave tellt thee.'

'No, it certainly is not,' said Philip, in excitement turning back to his native tongue. Concentrating, he willed the machine to be his slave. *I'll bloody well, bloody well . . .* he thought. *I'll will the best thing there is on this earth. I'll spend all the cash on it.* In his trouser pocket – which was still his school trouser pocket, as Jocasta had gone to bed with a headache and forgotten to make him change – he felt the present he'd bought for Faith in Whitby in the lunch hour. It was a photograph frame. He'd thought she could put a picture of Holly in it for later on when all the people who'd known Holly were dead. It would be important. He'd have liked a picture of his own father, but Jocasta you couldn't ask. He must be dead. A lot of people seemed to die before Philip had had the chance of . . . He wasn't mad on people dying.

Fastening the fingers of one hand round the edge of the frame, he thought intensely of the child on the altar with its arms spread out and swung down the lever on the machine with force.

Ernie was still saying, 'Well, there goes a fuckin' pound if ever,' when, with a gaping metallic vomiting, money began to shower from the machine all over the floor.

The Ernie brigade were there like pups round a dish of meat and Philip in the middle of them, kicking and punching. A fight began, at first rather merrily, then with just a suggestion in the satanic dark of an intermittent flash of something in someone's hand that clicked open. It came closer, but then Philip felt himself taken by the shoulder. He was pulled away and outside, on to the promenade.

It was a kindly-looking man in a tweed jacket and rather unusual shiny black trousers and trainers. Having hauled Philip away, he at once let go of him, most politely. 'Bad types in there, lad,' he said. 'You don't want anything in those places. Where's your parents?'

'They're somewhere about.'

'You weren't alone in there, then?'

Philip thought of dastardly Ernie. He and his lot had got most of the money and were still fighting.

'That wasn't your brother, was it? With the gold earring and no hair?'

'They're all gold earring and no hair,' said Philip in standard English to match the man's. 'That's Ernie's gang. Nick's. lot, not so often, but he's in the pub somewhere.'

'You have two very poor sorts of brother,' said the man.

'They're not my brothers,' said Philip. 'They are *not* my brothers. I have no brothers. I have one sister. Ern and Nick work for my stepfather. They're just looking after me until I go to my gran. I'd better get on there now, by myself. I don't need them at all.'

'Fish and chips?' said the man. 'There's a good chippie down Nelson Street.'

'OK. I can pay,' said Philip. 'I got quite a bit of that off the floor.'

'Wouldn't dream of it,' said the man. 'My invitation. Come on now, and then I'll walk you to the grandparents.'

It was a caff, not just a take-away, and the tables were a cheerful red. The sauce bottles were warm brown with gunge round the tops and the salt cellars were made to look like tomatoes. There were ceramic vases with imitation pink chrysanthemums in them and good loud music. The crackle and swish of the hot fat rose and fell excitingly as the chef, who was unclothed from the waist up and had a towel round his neck like a boxer, swirled about in the vats with a long ladle. A huge plate of golden fish and chips was slapped down in front of Philip.

'Aren't you having some?'

'I have already dined,' said the man.

Philip thought that 'dined' was the sort of thing Jack might say. Or dear old Holly. Must be OK.

126

'Eat up,' said the man, leaning easily back. 'Then I can take you home or they'll be worrying. Where do the grandparents live?'

Philip was airing fish on the end of his fork. 'It's too hot. I can't eat it any faster.'

The man stared intently.

'They live – oh, quite near.' He couldn't for the life of him remember.

'How near?' The man was leaning forward now. 'Take your time,' he said, watching Philip. 'Your glasses are getting steamed up. You ought to take them off. I'll look after them for you if you like.' He seemed to be trying to find a pocket. Philip removed his glasses but put them in his own pocket, where they rattled against the photograph frame. It seemed to have got broken, he thought, either in the amusement palace or in the sea. As he took his hand away from the shambles within, still airing fish on his fork with the other one, he felt it taken in a vice-like grip under the table and directed towards the shiny stuff of the man's trousers. There it was pressed against something hard and slippery and hot.

Philip dropped his fork, picked up the plate of fish and chips one-handed and slapped it unerringly and equally hard in the man's face. The man's scream was still going on as Philip reached the street outside.

He fled down the back street beside the fish shop and on to the high street where there were plenty of people about. He tore through the pedestrian precinct full of well-lit shops all selling refrigerators. As he approached a police station he thought he'd maybe better slow down; then, as the street became shabbier and darker, he began to run again. He felt wet on his leg and thought he would be sick, but coming to a halt under a street light he found that it was only blood. The clinking in his pocket must be broken glass, either the frame or the specs. He tried to drag some of the tangle out and found a smashed frame and a severed leg of the specs and a cracked lens. He thought, *Now I've done it, I can't see. I haven't a clue where I'm at, as they say*, and fancied he heard the man's padding feet behind him.

He began to race on, turning about here and there, on and on over the cobbles of the old side streets, and at the end of one of them saw a stretch of the doleful dark promenade again. He turned and turned again, and ran on. When he found himself this time on the top of a slope leading to the sea he felt very tired.

If I could bloody well read, he thought. *If I could see the street signs. You'd think I'd remember the address. I'd remember if I heard it or could read it. I'd better go in a pub or something and ask. Braithwaite's not all that common a name.* He found, however, that he was frightened of this idea. 'I'm not exactly mad about asking,' he said, aloud.

Two people came stepping in a dignified way out of a building on a corner of the seafront beside him. They had such a look of respectability that Philip, remembering the man, melted in shadow, but one of them, the woman, called out sharply, 'Hello? Hello there?'

He kept quiet, but, miraculously, she then said, 'Philip? I know who that is – it's Philip. Philip Braithwaite, whatever are you doing out by yourself at this time of night? It's nearly nine o'clock. Does Granny know?'

'Not actually,' said Philip.

128

'I knew you the minute I saw you,' she said. 'I said to Mr Middleditch, "It's Dolly's Philip." I knew you even without your glasses, you don't fool me. Where are your glasses? Good gracious, you're bleeding. And you're wet. Wet through.'

The Middleditches marched him between them through the streets.

'Just leaving the Chamber of Commerce Ladies Night,' shouted Mrs Middleditch through Dolly's letter box. *Mercifully*. Now open the door, Dolly. We've found Philip and he's pouring with blood.'

– 16 –

Dolly was answering the telephone in the passage as Mrs Middleditch began her assault through the letter box. From the room near the front door where Toots lay, there rose his howls and roars. 'That bloody woman again. Middle of the night. Bring out your dead! Christ, can't she leave us in peace.'

'Just a minute, Jack,' said Dolly on the phone, 'there's someone at the door. Who is it?'

'Could you let us in, Dolly? Now?'

'Yes, I'll just find the key. I'm on the telephone. Yes. Hello, Jack? Yes, Philip's here.'

'I forgot to ring earlier. Just checking.'

'Yes, they've brought him. When shall we be seeing you?'

'Tomorrow. I'll be down in the morning to fetch Philip back.'

'And you'll bring—?'

'Tell you tomorrow. Something about a gummy eye.'

Dolly unlocked the front door, saying, 'Just Jack to see you'd arrived safely, dear. He'd never said you were coming. Oh dear, oh dear.'

'We'll say nothing tonight,' said Mrs Middleditch. 'It's too late tonight. No need for the police, though

130

who knows? If it hadn't been the Chamber of Commerce and I had not been coming out at that particular— Oh, good heavens!'

Toots had put up the volume of his bedside radio so that the News boomed out as it might have been across Las Vegas.

Philip slid past his grandmother and out of sight.

'I'll have to go. Mrs Middleditch. Is Mr Middleditch . . . ? I'd like to give you both a cup of tea but Toots isn't too well. Thank you so very much.'

'I'll be back first thing in the morning. There are some questions. See to the bleeding.'

They departed.

'Bleeding? Oh Lord – whatever –?' Dolly went into Toots's room and tried to make herself heard above the latest stockmarket prices, which were reverberating off the walls. Toots lay as in rigor mortis and Philip stood by the fireplace picking bits of glass out of his pocket.

'Philip, dear, oh dear. How *late*! They shouldn't do it. Those awful boys dropping you off this time of night. Whatever's Jack thinking of? No idea . . .'

'And nor has your mother,' said Toots from his catafalque. 'Nor the whole damn lot of them. Down on that bike in the dark. Had you a helmet? No. Eleven years old. Have you done your homework? No. What's the matter with this country? Tell me. What?'

'No discipline,' said Philip.

'No discipline. And skate-boarding.'

'Skate-boarding's over years ago, Toots.'

'Whatever it is now, then. Drugs. Filth. They're selling the stuff open now to anyone, all ages, twenty pounds a time.'

131

'Fifteen,' said Philip.

'*What*?'

'Don't be so silly, Toots. Philip doesn't know anything about drugs. He's at a private school and he knows we all love him.'

'What's that blood?' asked Toots, eyes still apparently shut, nose raised to the ceiling.

'It's a photo frame. It broke in my pocket. I've sort of twisted my glasses, too. I guess I can't see till they're mended. Just as well I can't read or I'd be getting held back.'

Dolly came to him with TCP and hot water in a pudding basin and some bandages from a Red Cross box they'd kept since the war.

'Funny thing to keep in a pocket,' said Toots, 'a picture frame.'

'It's just a present.'

'Lot of shoplifting going on at the moment,' said Toots.

'Toots! Will you be quiet! Don't listen to him, Philip. He's a silly old man. He wasn't like this once, you know. He was different when I first married him.'

'I didn't nick it, Toots. I bought it for Faith to put Holly in. Have you got one of Holly?'

'Beg your pardon,' said Toots. 'Apologies. But you smell of fish and chips. That could be something of a private matter.'

'Whatever has fish and chips to do with shoplifting? I tell you, Philip, your grandad's not quite right in the head.'

'It could have a bearing,' said Toots. 'Telling the truth. There's no fish-and-chip shop between here and Ellerby Priors. And no picture-frame shops, either.'

'I bought the frame in Whitby at dinner time. And I got a blasting for it at school. There was going to be some sort of welcome ceremony for her – for my sister – they said. Something in church. I thought there'd be presents. Jack was giving her a pound, he'd found.'

'A welcome? Well, bless me, they never said one word to us. You'd think we'd be invited. D'you know, we've never seen her, Philip. Not even a photograph.'

'Oh well, it all fell through in the end. First yes, then no. I just got this idea there might be. They'd said something about me carrying her up and then Jack would take her and show her round the church, but it didn't come off.'

'No bloody discipline. Where did you get the money?'

'For the frame? Oh, I had some. I've been making a bit lately.'

'Now, Philip.' She had bathed the leg, taken away the water, returned with tea and chocolate cake and a hot-water bottle and sat him in an armchair. 'Now, do just be careful what you say. You don't have to pretend with us.'

'No, it's true. I have made a bit. On an investment. Just simple stuff. I invested a pound. Made about fifty. I'm lucky. I lost a bit of it again, well, most of it, but I've a good scheme. It's concentration. Toots, I could tell you how: you just will something very hard, *really* try.'

'Like you do with your reading.' Toots opened an eye and Philip looked into it. They both laughed. Only Toots could refer to the peculiar nature of Philip's dyslexia. Only Toots could say that not one boy in his day, in all his teaching years, had ever had it except for the obvious loonies. 'Maybe I'm a loonie,' Philip usually said. 'You make a good case for yourself,' usually said Toots; 'd'you want to play chess?'

'D'you want to play chess?' he said now.

'No, not tonight,' said Dolly. 'At this time of night Toots is meant to be asleep. You're not playing chess. Philip's had a big day.'

'I wouldn't say that,' said Philip. 'This and that happened. Faith coming and that.'

'Now then,' said Dolly, knees apart. She picked up a sock of Toots's she had been darning. 'Now then, tell us all about her.'

'Truth, mind,' said Toots. Philip glowered at him.

'She's pretty beautiful,' he said, finishing a third piece of cake. 'Very beautiful. She has thick black curls and dark-green eyes. Lovely ears. And she smiles all the time. Her hands cling on to you. When she yawns she's got a pink tongue. Her nose is very pretty, like a lion cub's, soft and flat, and she smells of roses.'

'Roses,' said Dolly. 'I wish they'd called her Rose. Is Andrew very fond of her? However can he bear to leave her?'

'Yes, he seems very keen on her. He's mad about her, I suppose. I expect he's settled a lot of money on her.'

'And is she going to be happy up there, d'you think?'

'Well, she's awfully fond of me.'

'She is?'

'Yes. Actually, I took her out. She was brought to meet me from school. Jocasta and Andrew brought her.'

'Yes,' said Dolly. 'I thought they would bring her. That was nice.'

'And on the way home she cried and Jocasta couldn't cope and Andrew just said, "Pick her up, Philip," so I did and she stopped crying at once. She just looked me straight in the face and smiled at me. She's got lovely teeth.'

'Teeth?' said Dolly. 'But she's not three months yet.'

'She's advanced,' said Philip. 'They say she'll be walking any day. She looks as if she could talk if she set her mind to it. Actually, Andrew said when we got back and I carried her in for tea, he said, "You can see that baby idolises Philip. She has both arms round his neck." '

'Philip . . . ' Dolly was grave. But Toots said, 'That'll do, Dolly. Let him be.'

Soon Philip said he might as well go to bed and wandered off to the room they now called his. Dolly went off in her slippers to get him another hot-water bottle and creaked up the steep stairs with it. He lay in his clothes, fast asleep on top of the covers, and Dolly took off his shoes and lifted his legs up and covered them and tucked the hot-water bottle wrapped in an old petticoat of her own well down near his feet. She managed to drag off his zip jacket without waking him, wondering a little about the coins that kept dropping out of it. She noticed that his face was filthy and longed to get a flannel. 'I'm getting hopeless,' she said. 'I see nothing these days.'

'Tomorrow will do,' she said, and sat on the bed beside him for a time, looking at the sharp little face, the red mark of his specs on the bridge of his nose. Still not much more than the face of a baby himself. What a queer idea he had had about the face of a baby! His clothes seemed very damp and there was a breath of salt water about him. And Toots was right. There was a very definite smell of fish and chips.

– 17 –

Pammie woke next morning in her bedroom of chintz and bits of dressing-table silver to the familiar sight of dear old Hugo standing at the window in his schoolboy dressing gown. She was sitting bolt upright in bed staring at him and wondered why. It must have happened before she noticed him and so could not be simple surprise. There flooded in then the dream of – how long? – a second ago, the terrible dream. A dream of the baby, Faith Fox.

'Good Lord, Hugo, you frightened me. What's wrong?'

'Nothing. Beautiful morning. Glad you're awake. It's seven o'clock.'

'*Seven*? Well, I don't know— Is she crying? The nurse is there. Oh!'

'Grass needs a last cut. I'll tell Sears. Sopping wet. Heavy dew. The baby's gone, Pammie. Back to her own folk. You're not awake.'

'No,' she said. 'Hugo – awful dream. About the baby. I can't remember it.'

'You're done in,' he said. 'I'll get some tea.'

She waited in the sunny room, listening to the comforting sound of cars going down Coombe Hill towards London, Hugo letting Thomasina's dog out

137

on the lawn, the postman's voice admiring the pompon dahlias. It was warm and still. *Home*, she thought. *I am home too. Yesterday. What a day! That baby.*

'Will you be able to make it?' Hugo put the tray of tea down on a table, trembled some into a rosy china cup and tottered across to the bed with it.

'Make what? Lovely tea, Hugo. Make what?'

'The wedding.'

'*Wedding?*'

'The Seton-Fairley wedding. Farnham.'

'My God, no! Not *today*. It can't be. How can I? I've nothing ready, have I? Oh yes, it's back from the cleaners. Oh, *not* today. I *can't*. It's halfway back to where I was.'

'Hardly say that, dear. Under an hour. Car's coming for us at eleven; then we can have a bite somewhere.'

'Oh, I can't go. Out of the question. We'll write later and say it was a bug. I've sent the present – that's all that matters. We hardly planned this.'

'I've had my tails cleaned,' said Hugo, making a noise drinking his tea. 'I like old Seton-Fairley. Must be ninety. Shan't see him again.'

'That's morbid. Oh, great heaven, *Farnham*. Is the water hot?'

In the bath she thought again of Faith Fox, tried to see her face, her strong, stout little body. She had hardly held her. On the journey, giving her the bottle of milk as the nurse had shown her, she had been delighted with herself, delighted with the waving arm that sought and patted her face. The child so good, so quiet. The nurse had said, 'A paragon.' Well, one almost wondered . . . But no.

One could see from her eyes there was nothing funny about her. Nothing retarded or queer there. Dear little soul. Just through and through good.

Let's leave it at that, she thought, finding new tights, getting down to her nails among the silver scent bottles. 'Dear little soul. You know I had her for nearly two months just after she was born? *No* trouble.' She was attending Faith Fox's wedding now, Faith Fox the image of Holly but quieter, more perceptive, gentler. Here came Pammie, twenty years on, chatting and edging along towards the reception line-up, towards the white, white lilies of little Faith's bridal bouquet, bridegroom tall, impeccable, his face a haze, but Faith a star, bending down to Pammie. *'Pammie,'* she cries. 'Oh, darling Pammie. She saved my life, you know, when I was born. Just about brought me up.' There stands Thomasina with her smile. Nobody near her.

Old. We'll all be so old by then. Thomasina's boyfriend will be dead and gone and so will Hugo. Wonder what the rest of us will look like. Much the same, I suppose. We've all beaten the flab now. We've all kept our dogs to walk, and our golf. We do our exercises. I don't see myself changing or getting ill. I'll wear the blue thing today. Not my favourite, but I've overdone the yellow lately. I'd have liked yellow somehow for October but the only decent hat is—

The phone rang during breakfast and she thought. *Thomasina. Very thick with the Seton-Fairleys – oh!*

For where was Thomasina? She'd have to be there, old S-F and Herbert being such buddies long ago. Somebody or other godmother to Holly and all that.

So, she thought, *I'll be seeing Thomasina today, will I? Very interesting. I'll stare her out. Stare her down. I can't talk to her. Yes, someone said she was back from Egypt.*

'Any word of Thomasina, Hugo?' she asked as he came from the phone.

'No, it was some nutty fellow talking about potatoes. Had you got the potatoes and he hopes they weren't a trouble.'

'Oh. Oh yes. That's Jack. Andrew's brother.'

'What, ringing from up there?'

'Yes.'

'Bit extravagant this time in the morning, isn't it? Are you all right? I said you were getting ready to go to a wedding, so he rang off. I thought I heard the child crying somewhere, but he didn't seem to be noticing.'

Pammie said, 'I shall have to ring. Not him. Andrew. To see if the baby's all right.'

'Dammit,' said Hugo. 'Damn and blast it, Pammie, it's for Andrew to ring you, all you've done for him. Glad it's all over and this place back to what it was.'

'Yes,' she said.

'Not that I didn't like it,' he said. 'I rather liked the smell.'

'Smell of the baby?'

'Yes. Don't they say it's like new bread, a baby in a house? Pretty woman, the nurse.'

'A lot of clutter,' said Pammie. 'I'm glad it's over.'

'Not picking up Thomasina, are we?' he asked in the car. 'Easy to do.'

'Hugo – I've just asked you if you know where she is. Nobody's seen her since she went off to Egypt with that man.'

'Oh, jolly good,' said Hugo. 'I remember now there was a card from her yesterday, from the North

140

somewhere. Northumberland. "Coming home by stages", or something.'

'It's probably a week old. She'll be home by now and we'll see her today. I hope you'll ignore her, Hugo. Don't let me down by behaving as if nothing's happened. We've all had Thomasina up to here and if she's been in the North and "coming down by stages" you'd think she'd have looked in on her one and only grandchild on the way. I saw a woman just like Thomasina yesterday – as a matter of fact, now I think of it, in a Jaguar – when I was being taken back to the train and I thought for one moment, "It's Thomasina – come to herself again and off to see the baby," but of course it couldn't have been.'

'Why not?' Hugo liked Thomasina. He hadn't been able to keep up with tales of her rampages of bad behaviour and didn't much care about them. He was one of the few people who had found Holly the lesser woman, both manipulative and rather thick.

'Rather thick girl, Holly,' he said now.

'Pull yourself together, Hugo. Holly's dead. You know she is, so don't pretend you're senile.'

'That little Faith,' he said, 'looked like a better bet. Smiling away.'

'Hardly, at two months,' said Pammie, who had been reading a child-development book or two since the summer. 'They don't smile for a long time. It's parental fantasy.'

'Yes, she did,' said Hugo. 'Got hold of your finger like a vice. Tried to eat it. Put it right in her mouth and chewed. Grinned.'

'Hope it wasn't all nicotine, then. When was all this going on? I'm sure I hadn't time to be tootling at the baby. What I'd like is a real rest now. Abroad. About three weeks in Cyprus.'

141

'We might go to the North for a weekend maybe,' he said, 'when you're not on the Bench. See the set-up there and how the child goes on. I'd rather like it.'

Pammie found then that she only wanted to go north again by herself. She couldn't see Jack and Hugo getting on. There was absolutely nothing religious about Hugo and he'd be hostile to the Tibetans. *Why ever do I want to go back, anyway?* 'I want to be shot of the lot of them and concentrate on the Ladies' Cup,' said Pammie. 'Anyway, if that was Thomasina I saw, she won't be there today. She couldn't possibly get to Farnham by two o'clock.'

– 18 –

A substantial part of Surrey had been put on hold for the Seton-Fairley wedding, to which seven hundred people had been invited. The police had been augmented by special constables, cones had been seconded from several motorways and parking-meter attendants moved in little coveys about the main street, directing cars to the excellently organised car-parking facilities behind the church in the grounds of some organisation that the Seton-Fairleys nationally organised. Strings of penguined middle-class males threaded their way about the churchyard or stood in knots or hurtled wildly through the tombs looking busy and blasé at the same time. Most were pretty mellow after a luncheon laid on at the local, where some of the girls were still running about and squeaking in the queue for the Ladies. Dozens more were making their way to the church in the extraordinary overdressed condition that the occasion demanded – vast hats, tiny miniskirts, long floating velvets, leather, art-deco jewellery, odd waddly shoes with sequins or teetering Sunset Boulevard heels. Others, making quite another statement, had gone for sloppy silk sweaters and skirts and shoulder bags and greasy hair and were ex-girlfriends of the bridegroom. Their purpose in acceptance of the feast was to show him, and the bride, what the hell.

The bride's family was still a quarter of a mile away, in a gleaming house and weedless garden, fortifying themselves with dry sherry and egg sandwiches. The marquee on the lawn for last night's party was empty now, greenish light within, smelling of grass with only yesterday's embattled flower arrangements standing on the last of the trestle tables and folded cloths. The bride was pretending to be bored, the bridesmaids being frisky or cool as the mood took them, the father feeling confident and not half bad-looking, pulling down the points of his silver-grey waistcoat before the mirror. The mother was being anonymous and unruffled. The grandfather in a wheelchair had closed his eyes and a step-grandmother, Madeleine, was walking in the garden.

Cars arrived and took people away. The bride's car waited, beribboned. A little rain fell and everyone groaned. The sun came out and was greeted like the Holy Ghost. Everyone looked gorgeous. *Gorgeous*. From the front door you could hear the bells of the church coming in fits and starts on the breeze across the meadows.

On the bridegroom's side hunting was the big motif, the pages being dressed in hunting pink and awful gobbling hallooing noises issuing from his guests arriving at the church, stepping out of cars, acknowledging one another among the gravestones. Talk was of cubbing. The bridegroom and best man, well known in hunting circles, which now of course included the saboteurs, were nearly struck by eggs as they walked up the church path and there was an exciting rumour that a demo had been planned for the middle of the service. The bride's grandmother, seeing some saboteurs standing rather apart at the church gates, went across to them to make herself pleasant, thinking they were servants or village people. Some of them pressed pamphlets into her hand, which she clutched along with her service sheet.

As tall Fiona in taut cream satin, her colossal backside hidden by her great-grandmother's veil, walked up the aisle, Madeleine found herself, during the first hymn, examining photographs of the bleeding gobbets of dead foxes in the mouths of hounds. She waited anxiously for her stepson to return to the pew after the handing over of the bride so that she could ask him to explain.

But her son was in his own world, smiling in the obligatory way at his wife as he stepped in beside her to the pew, the wife keeping her eyes forward, steady as the Queen. When his stepmother began to flap the fox photographs at him, he ignored her.

She turned then to the row behind and saw through the mass of hats and heads Thomasina and a tall man being hustled in late to a pew with some cousins, the last two seats in the church. 'My dear, *do* look,' she called, flapping the pamphlet. 'Whatever can they be?' A grandson on her right said, 'It's OK, Gran. Forget it,' and tried to turn her round. 'Oh dear, I hope I can,' said Madeleine, quite loudly for such a gentle woman. She looked again at the photographs. 'Quite awful. I hope you'll come and have tea with me soon, my dear.'

People were either ignoring Madeleine or smiling kindly at her. One or two were saying, out of the corner of the mouth, 'The grandmother. A bit gone.'

Thomasina managed but a glacial smile. Thomasina's escort, who looked flushed and stern and not at all at his ease, gave Madeleine a piercing blue stare.

'Good afternoon, Giles,' said Madeleine. 'How lovely, darling. Do you remember Egypt?'

The great concourse rose at this moment like a surging sea to sing *O Worship the King*, and close family were ushered from the front pews towards the vestry to sign the book, Madeleine now sitting beatifically still until someone came to fetch her and lead her off too. She stopped a couple of times on the way to shake hands with the choir and seemed uncertain what to do when she reached the altar, stopping again to smell some flowers.

'Who is that beautiful woman? How does she know my name?' asked the general.

'Some sort of grandmother,' said Thomasina. 'Madeleine. Early Alzheimer's. Or so they say. She's been like it for years. They think she puts it on. Men still go mad for her.'

'I only know the groom's lot.'

'But what did she mean about Egypt?'

'I've no idea.' He cleared his throat and stood yet straighter. Madeleine. The arthritis was no joke today.

'Are you all right?' she whispered in a wife-like voice which enraged him so that he could not reply but turned towards the happy couple, who were now swimming up the aisle with their train of relations behind them. He was relieved to see Goofo, the father of the groom, who gave him a quick and military nod as he passed.

Of the grandmother there was now no sign and he thought that she must have been kept back in the vestry, by some minder perhaps, or taken out by a back door. He did not know whether to be thankful or not.

But looking down he found Madeleine at his side in the pew, carrying a rose she had removed from the arrangement on the font and sliding a grey silk glove under his elbow.

'I'll come out with you, darling,' she said. 'You don't mind, do you, Thomasina? Where are Herbert and beloved Holly? Oh – and isn't there a dear babe?'

The sternness of the face of the general had established itself long before his arrival at the church. On reaching the porch and hearing the first hymn, he had said they should not go in but wait outside and mingle unobtrusively with the rest of the congregation afterwards during the photographs. Thomasina had paid no attention, but swept in. It was two-twenty. She had said they would be late and they were late and she was satisfied. He, who was never late, could not believe that it was he, Giles, who was tiptoeing so prominently down the aisle behind her. Nor could he believe that he had driven three hundred and seventy miles since breakfast after making love to this woman last night.

They had retired to their bedroom at The Priors Meadow Hotel after their long drive from Northumberland and the momentous conversation at the village teashop about Holly and her child. Thomasina, lovely in her country clothes, her hair wound on top of her head in a coil, hair left to begin to grow nonchalantly grey, which only a few women can get away with as an added attraction ('Why should I care? I'm beautiful. I don't need to attract men, for goodness' sake'), was being the perfect companion. Giles knew they were being noticed at The Priors Meadow Hotel that evening as people who were probably somebody, and certainly from the South. He made himself especially courteous to the waitresses though they were not allowing themselves to be generous with their charms. Most of the other guests had already eaten fast and silently and gone off to their bedrooms to remove their shoes and watch their television set. It was a moorland hotel well known for its away-breaks for the middle-aged: dinner at seven, five enormous courses, and all over by ten to eight. The general and Thomasina, eating slowly, found the lights being put out in other parts of the dining-room until their own table held the one remaining lamp. A sturdy waitress, grim of aspect, stood by them with the cheese as they finished their pudding.

'Are we slow?' asked Thomasina. 'I'm so sorry.'

'You're all right.' She insinuated the cheese between them on the cloth. 'But we like to get cleared up. We've a way to go, all of us, to get home. It's five miles over the top.'

'We'll hurry.'

'Tek yer time. Put the cheese you don't eat under the glass bell. It can stay till morning.' She left them, turning off switches around the bar outside. 'I'll leave you the one to see your way,' she shouted through.

'It is ten minutes past eight,' said Giles. 'By God, I know what they mean about another country. I couldn't put up with this. Do you know, when I was stationed at Catterick I went to a village hop and asked a girl to dance and she said, "Take my friend, I'm sweating." '

'There are bad manners everywhere,' said Thomasina. 'Andrew's are perfect. They're quite nice people up here, really, when you get to know them.'

'We are, are we?' said the waitress stamping by again in a gigantic turquoise padded coat. 'Now, don't forget your room key or you'll be in trouble. There's no one on at night but there's a doctor's phone number by the bed that you have to have by law and most folks coming here are old. I'm not bringing you any coffee; it'll only keep you awake.'

'My God,' said Giles, beginning to undress in the anonymous flower-sprigged bedroom. 'I'm beginning to feel like London again. I wish we could get off right after breakfast.'

'I should be going to London tomorrow,' she said. 'Well, Farnham. It's the Seton-Whatsits' wedding. I accepted three months ago.'

He had slid beside her into the bed, had caught her hand, had hauled up his bony old frame on top of her and let it fall bonily down. His other hand was beginning to do daring things, and Thomasina, after the Scottish and Northumbrian nights when she had been inattentive or sleepy and very different from the way she'd been in the Valley of the Kings, was giving promise of renewed interest.

Tired, he thought. *Well, she's no chicken either. It's a long time since she had any of this – utterly good woman that way, I'd think. Golf and so on. Until we met. Made for each other. Beautiful woman, still –* 'Oh God, Thomasina, you smell wonderful.'

'Couldn't get my hair done in time, anyway.'

'What?' he said, falling back exhausted a while later, extremely happy. 'Hair? Hair's perfect.'

'For the wedding. In Farnham. Seton-Fairley.'

149

On the edge of sleep, his head on her neat breasts, his chin on her rib-cage, his moustache making the rough patch on her skin of which he was becoming rather proud, he sat up.

'Seton-Fairley?'

'School friend's daughter. Herbert's school friend's daughter. Mad on hunting. Farnham. Must get up and wash.'

When she came back to the bedroom – she had put on the trousers of her silk pyjamas and seemed to have tidied her hair – 'Good God,' he said, '*I'm* going!'

'Where?'

'To the Seton-Doings's wedding. I think. She's marrying my ADC's boy.'

'I can't remember who she's . . . But it's Farnham Castle, two o'clock.'

'I'm invited. I accepted. We'll have to go.'

'Darling – *Farnham*. We're on the Yorkshire moors. Have you sent a present?'

'Yes, of course. Tea knives.'

'Well, that's all right. They'll never notice. I have too.'

'What, tea knives?'

'No. A wok.'

'That's not the point. I'm afraid, Thomasina, we'll have to go. Perfectly possible. Five or six hours and we can leave here by eight o'clock.'

'What about clothes?'

'Ah, clothes. Have you something?'

'Well, I haven't a hat.'

'Tell you what, we'll leave at seven and go round by the garrison and I can get my gear and we'll find you a hat of Hilda's.'

'Hilda?'

'My Hilda. My wife.'

Thomasina looked extremely thoughtful. 'You mean,' she said, 'your wife's clothes . . . ?'

He looked ashamed and said, 'Difficult business, disposing. Never know what to do. Would welcome a bit of help on that, actually.'

He got out of bed and put on dressing gown and slippers.

'Giles?'

'Going down to see about the bill.'

'There's no one there. You know there isn't. The lights were all put out.'

He took off the dressing gown and sat on the edge of the bed and thought. 'I'll get it first thing in the morning. Ask for it at seven. We can't leave without breakfast. Now, don't worry. We'll make it. I can't miss it. I was at Alamein with Goofo.'

'Goofo,' she said, and was silent for a long time.

Then as he was beginning to breathe in what sounded like sweet sleep she said, 'Yes, of course we must go. It decides everything. You can't just ignore a wedding you've accepted for. I know people do. The young, mostly. It's a fashion. But we're not . . . And I'll be able to see Faith some other time. Any time. I could get the Teesside shuttle any day of the week; it's a half hour flight.'

He woke at six and padded to the loo, pleased with himself that he could go through nowadays, though he was only just in time this morning. He stretched himself before the bedroom window on his way back. Glorious morning. Heather magnificent. Miles of it. Wonderful dawn. Mist in the valleys.

A smell of heaven floated in, gold October light, sharp clean air. As heady as spring, really. The baby could hardly suffer, being brought up here instead of Surrey. What was it she'd said?

'Thomasina?'

She was asleep.

'Did you . . . last night . . . were you saying something or did I dream it? Are you wanting to see the baby?'

'What?'

'If you are, my dear . . . My dear, if you are – you are wanting to see the baby – no question, we'll see the baby and Holly's husband's people, of course we will. The wedding's nothing.'

'Why ever should I want to . . . ?' She turned from him, eyes shut.

'You said so. Last night. As you were falling asleep.'

'No. I said it settled it. I needn't go. Great excuse, darling, really. It'll be a nice wedding.'

He saw that her face had lost its quiet mask of sleep and now wore another: one of amused weariness.

'I'm afraid we are not going,' he said; 'we are going to see this child.' Then he asked what he had not dared before. 'Thomasina, *why* not? Why are you such a coward?'

Twenty minutes later, swooping out of the bathroom, she called out, 'Giles, I think you'd better hurry up and get the bill if we're to get off before eight. We're never going to do it by two if we have to go round by your house.'

'We don't. We're not going, not to the garrison nor to the wedding. You want to go to Faith. I know you do. Why can't you just *go*? Thomasina, I know what I'm doing. If you don't face what's happened to Holly, if you don't face the fact that Faith is part of Holly—'

'You have no idea what you're talking about,' she said. Her face looked old, her mouth a trap. 'You and your childless wife.'

*

152

'A last chance,' he said in the car. 'North or south? This place where Faith has gone is ten minutes away. I've looked it up.'

'I must go to the wedding.'

On the grind south neither of them said much more. Cars and lorries roared and spun along, nose to tail, three columns. Past road works, accidents, and police cars sitting in side roads waiting to pounce, they drove, jerking and manoeuvring through the costive approaches to London, round London, out of London.

The general's red-brick box of a house seemed to hold no interest for Thomasina. As he dressed for the wedding upstairs she sat downstairs doing her fingernails on the edge of a businesslike oak desk, not looking out of the window where there were playing fields and skin-head soldiers running. The general, immaculate, came down the stairs, holding several hats made of felt and feathers and a plaited and limp pink turban with a gilden brooch. 'I'm afraid Hilda wasn't great on hats,' he said.

Thomasina had walked away to the hall mirror then, taking a silk scarf from round her neck. She wound it round her head and pinned it with her own brooch, whereupon it became a delicate if slightly precarious hat. 'We must go,' she said.

The house was bleak about them. She saw lists pinned up, memos, framed mementoes of a directed life, many photographs of the regiment and a decoration mounted behind glass in a frame in the hall. The Queen's signature. The place she felt suddenly as a trap, an airlock. Who was he – the man she had clung to naked for three weeks of loving nights, three weeks of days when she had delighted in looking so perfect with him, perfect for him? So safe, so adored. But whoever was he?

'Do you love me?' she asked.

It could not have been a worse moment. The general in his morning coat was checking his watch. 'We'll just about make it. Come along. Sorry about poor Hilda's hats.'

She thought, *And how can he possibly know me if he can offer me her hats?*

Better end it, she thought as they tiptoed agonisingly late into the church, she first, smiling her lovely apologetic smile at faces here and there ('Thomasina's here,' whispered old Hugo to Pammie. 'Man she's with looks a bad-tempered cuss.' 'Don't look,' said Pammie) and Giles behind her, chin out like the rock of ages.

Giles stood to attention through the remainder of the service, trying to breathe steadily and become unnoticeable inside the kaleidoscope of colour, the stained glass of the windows, the pink of the bridesmaids and pages, the creamy, foamy mass of the large, smiling bride, the emerald and silver of the vestments, the flowers everywhere – late roses, phloxes, michaelmas daisies, country things – the young men out in force in their gladrags, the urgent, painted girls, clever and silly, self-interested and yet yearning. Long, long lives ahead. He thought of love and youth. Could he really love Thomasina? He hardly knew the woman. *Better end it*.

The old woman in front of them turned round to him – beautiful woman, old as time, quite bats, obviously rather fun though – she turned to him and said, 'Hello, Giles darling. Do you remember Egypt?'

As Thomasina and the general were sitting down at
their moorland hotel for their gigantic breakfast at
seven o'clock before their long journey of discord to
Surrey, ten miles away across the heather Jack was
walking in the wet mist of his fields, conversing
with God.

At The Priors the view shone and glittered. The
heather was rosy, swimming in miles of light like a
coating of pink bluebells. Wet sheep stood in its
wooden stalks, silvery on the dark deserted moor
roads. Larks were plucked up from it like fish on a
line, fluttering and spluttering with enthusiasm for
the sunlight. Below them the clefts in the moorland
were filled up with mist so that the heather seemed
broken with white water. These lakes were just
beginning to smoke, drawn up like the larks
towards the sun.

As the mists drifted upwards, sometimes masking
the road and the sheep and the heather on the
ridges for several minutes and leaving things wetter
than ever so that the sheep steamed too and the
hard patches of road shimmered with mirage, as it
all drifted upwards, the valleys emerged brilliantly
green. Little round knolls with trees on top cast

miles of shadow over farmland and fields. The ragged ruin of The Priory arch stood over Jack's sheds like an elephant above chickens. It held itself nobly, the sun streaming through the stonework to settle on the prefab jumble of shanties Jack had somehow been allowed to build in the cloister. A number of tombstones had been moved to stand near the gatehouse in a cluster, tipping a bit, their shadows behind them.

Jack went in to his tin-can church now and lay face down, arms outstretched, prostrate in the sunlight, thanking God for the wonder of His grace.

Then he went out and unlatched the door of the chicken houses, determinedly not looking towards the Tibetans' quarters. It saddened him to think that Himalayan people could like to stay in bed in the morning. He had hoped his folded moors might have enlivened them. They were after all mountain folk who would probably never see their own land again. He was having difficulty, more each day, in getting the Tibetans to work in the fields and hoe the late vegetables, which tasks had been part of the deal of their coming. The weather was so warm compared with Lhasa's, the air so easy, and the conditions of life he considered so close to God they ought to bring healing. Jack was the last person to make anyone work any harder. Jocasta in the handicraft and artistic department of The Priors had much more success with the women at the looms. Slowly cloth was beginning to be dyed as they had seen it in Darjeeling on their honeymoon visit to the Tibetan Centre there. Jack tried not to be jealous of Jocasta and was pleased that the newest tenants at The Priors seemed contented enough. He loved to hear the drone of meditation and music coming from the sheds and found that it more than made up for the amount the Tibetans ate and their passion for confectionery. Seven pounds of Cadbury's chocolate fingers and three of chocolate wheatmeal had been consumed in a month. But the perpetual political discussion and rowdy quarrels among the younger ones, all conducted in Liverpool accents, rather disappointed him and the late leek crop went unplanted. He was glad when the two Tibetan men suddenly packed off.

But about the Tibetans' attendance once a day for worship in The Priory he was adamant. He did not care if they conducted their own meditations but he insisted that an hour of worship in the interpretation of God's name must be undertaken. He had assumed that this would come easily to Buddhists and left them to it and they did turn up more or less every day. But in the matter of weeding they needed instruction and they did not present themselves for that. The Smikes, who had been undergoing intermittent instruction for three years, were still not distinguished hoers and the rest of the staff at The Priors were all overworked already with cooking and laundry and teaching and keeping the shabby place going.

Oh, thought Jack, *if Andrew could only stay here a while, it would not only help The Priors but calm him, the poor guy.* He would have liked to work beside Andrew in the fields, two brothers hoeing together in a biblical sort of way. He hardly knew Andrew now, but it was Andrew who had brought him Jocasta, his dark jewel, his strange princess. And, of course, Philip. Thinking of Philip, Jack paused in the shed where he was trying to find a sickle in an unholy clutter of tools. He was unable to get anywhere near Philip, and Jocasta wouldn't speak of him.

I ought to be able to imagine, he thought. *I ought to be able to feel close to Philip. I ought not to expect him at eleven years old to be helpful in the fields, with his school work to do. They say he's very clever, though I must say his handwriting doesn't suggest it. We don't know what sort of life he's had. Jocasta will never say. Pretty rough, I dare say. No spiritual guidance. Jocasta keeps her counsel about Belief. It was God directed Andrew here. Andrew is a good man – fine doctor. To try to help Jocasta he brought her here to me. She was only one patient among many. A routine operation, he said. I never heard exactly what.*

And now Jocasta was his. His own, his one love, his great love before God. It was wonderful of her that she never let him say so.

And her celibacy. So magnificent. He began to hoe, edging cruelly and expertly round the carrots, destroying weeds, worms, creatures of all kinds – and that must be the reason for the Buddhists refusing to work, now he came to think of it. The celibacy was hard on him, he had to say. He felt deprived, though he prayed nightly for patience. He would love to have a child. God had not yet answered him.

At eight o'clock he left the fields and returned to The Priors, where nobody much was about except hens. He found that the eggs had not yet been gathered, filled his pockets with them and cradled the rest in his hands. In the kitchen The Missus was standing over a pan of porridge. He filled a kettle (she was in one of her remote moods) and made coffee for himself. He said, 'Maybe Philip would like an egg.'

'Philip,' she said, 'as I'd have expected you to

remember, is not here. He's down Teesside with his grandparents, so-called. Oh yes, and The Smikes didn't come home.'

'I'd forgotten,' said Jack, smiling at something through the window. 'And where is the baby?'

'The Tibetans came for her early. They're good with her. She seems to love them.'

'I'll walk across,' he said. 'Andrew's taking her down to see Toots and my mother today. Exciting moment. I wish I had time to be there with them.'

The Missus said, 'She's not looking her best. Her eye's inflamed. Her granny won't think a lot of that.'

But Jack was not listening. He had seen Jocasta walking across the scruffy cloister wrapped in a purple shawl, and forgot all else. He went out to her and brought her in.

– 20 –

'Dolly,' bellowed Toots. 'Dolly? Where are you? Can't you hear me, Dolly?'

Bumps from the bedroom above. Complaints and sighs. 'I'm coming. Whatever is it?'

'Door bell.'

'Door bell? Whatever—? Half past six in the morning? You're dreaming.'

'Door *bell*.' (It rang piercingly.)

'You'll wake Philip. For heaven's sake, be quiet. On and on.'

She was downstairs and peering from his bedsit window without her teeth in, her hair long and grey, the ghastly old coat again in play. 'I shan't answer it. This time in the morning you never know. It might be burglars. Oh, good gracious me, it's The Smikes. Now what in the world . . .?'

Ernie and Nick trailed in and were summoned by Toots to stand before him, side by side at the bottom of his bed. 'Great Scot,' said Toots. 'Strike a light. The riffraff of England.'

'I'll make some tea,' said Dolly. 'You both look worn out.'

'Not with any work they've been doing. Give me back twenty years and a good leg, I'd have the pair

160

of you up on that farm knocking weeds down a penny-piece a row *and* cleaning up that filthy yard. Days off all the time. Eating your heads off like you were still in prison. It's the hard world now, boys. They ought to bring back hanging.'

All four began to drink from teacups, Dolly giving no countenance to mugs. For a while she was coming and going with half slices of buttered toast.

'I'm sorry there's no marmalade. At least there is, but it's only Silver Shred. Mrs Middleditch got it for us but it'll have to go back. If either of you two is going past the supermarket you might change it for me. I'll wrap it up. I like a dark marmalade but not that awful stuff with whisky in it.'

'Dolly, will you shut up about marmalade. Just sit down and look at this filth. Come on. Let's hear why you're here.'

The Smikes stood pale and dirty in slept-in clothes.

'Come on. Where did you spend the night? Truth, now.'

'In a boat ont prom. Under t'covers.'

'Why aren't you at Jack's? There's acres of experimental courgettes—'

'Night off,' said Ernie.

'Bike wouldn't start back,' said Nick. 'Full of sea water.'

'Sea water? Great Scot. My godfathers!'

'Sidecar coom off. Philip was bashin' it. It ran into t' sea.'

'Philip never said a thing about it.'

They looked more alert. 'Hast seen 'im?'

'Well, he's in bed upstairs, dead to the world. Arrived here about nine o'clock.'

'Nine twenty-one,' said Toots. 'So he was with

161

you, then? I thought as much. Stinking of grease and chips.'

Nick and Ernie appeared to relax. Ernie sat down on the bed and Nick switched on the electric fire and began to rub the bit of his back between the shoulder blades against the mantelpiece.

'OK, then, was 'e?'

'We don't know what he is until he's awake. Mrs Middleditch found him wandering and brought him here and he's asleep. He was off soon as look at you, in all his clothes. I couldn't get him into night clothes. Why ever didn't you drop him off, Nick, on your way down? If Jack finds out . . .'

This thought seemed to hold no terror for The Smikes. Ernie asked Toots for a fag. Toots said no, pointed to two upright chairs beside a clothes airer Dolly was setting up, and glared. 'Sit,' he commanded. 'The pair of you. You're no better than dogs.'

'I taught you,' he said. 'In my time. In my C stream. My boys. Gallows fodder. It's looking at the likes of you breaks my heart, lying here. Whatever good did I do? Forty years a teacher. Gold earrings, long hair, skinheads. What's going to win the 2.30 at Doncaster, then?'

'Gold Flake,' said Ernie.

'Heart o' Day,' said Nick.

'Get away with the pair of you,' said Toots. 'Nicholas Nickleby. Dead cert. Put me a fiver on it.'

'Toots?' said Dolly.

'Gi's the fiver, Toots,' said Nick, who was undoing his jeans to reveal a wallet stuffed with notes.

'You'll get no cut on this,' said Toots. 'You didn't look after Philip. We know he's no joke to look after

162

but it's no excuse. You've been lads on your own yourselves. Philip's a lad alone. I've no use for you.'

'Get on,' said Nick. 'Philip's got 'undreds round 'im.'

'And would you have been suited brought up up there, then? Sermons and Tibetans?'

'It's good for a laugh,' said Ernie.

'Oh, 'e'll be OK,' said Nick. 'We stick it out, don't we?'

'We've given Jack every loyalty,' said Ernie suddenly lapsing into radio-speak, quite emotionally. 'We support Jack all the way. Jack 'as nowt to complain of in us. 'E's a nutter but 'e's OK. 'E'll do. I reckon 'e needs us to keep in touch with everyday life. I'm a Nationalist meself and I don't see what we need with foreign 'omeless. We're pretty near 'omeless, us two, ant we? Nick and me? It's us 'e ought to be putting first. But we're all like 'is children, Jack. 'E's OK.'

'He has a child now,' said Dolly. 'The baby. Is she nice? I've done you both a bit of bacon. Tell me about little Faith. We haven't seen her yet.'

'She's OK,' said Nick.

'Now, Nick, I asked what is she like.'

The Smikes pondered and looked into their hearts. Nick saw the buggy tray, a bundle strapped across it. Ernie saw a hump in the folds of the Tibetan woman's anorak, the Tibetan woman glaring as she marched away with the hump towards her own domain. 'She's great,' said Ernie. 'Comfortable.'

'Comfortable is not what you call a baby you've never seen before. Who's she like? Not like Toots, I hope.'

'She's more like thee, Dolly,' said Nick, surpris-

163

ingly. He wiped off his plate with bread and tossed the plate empty on Toots's bed. 'She's bonny.'

'Blue eyes, I suppose?'

'Oh aye, blue eyes. One of them's all gummed up, they were saying. They were saying they'd have to take her to 'ospital.'

'No! Oh dear. Well, it does happen. Mind, it never happened to either of mine. It's all in the washing powder and the cotton wool you use. And clean hands.'

'The Tibetans is looking after 'er.'

'Smear themselves in rancid butter?' asked Toots.

'Be careful, Toots; that's racial,' said Dolly. 'I've just seen Mrs Middleditch coming.'

'We'll be off, then.' Ernie and Nick rose as one man.

'Don't you want to see Philip?'

'Naah,' said The Smikes together. 'Tell 'im: see yer,' said Nick.

They melted from the room, down the passage, out at the back door and across the cement yard. They knew their way around this house as they knew their way round a number of houses in various parts of the Tees estuary, and perfectly well in the dark. From Toots and Dolly's house, though, they had never lifted a thing, and nor would they, ever.

– 21 –

Suppose yourself a gargoyle or perhaps a bird, or a very small photographer hanging in the basket of a very small balloon up in the vaulted shadows of the roof of the great hall of Farnham Castle on the occasion of the reception for the Seton-Fairley wedding. You will find yourself looking down on a carpet of constantly blowing flowers planted tight from wall to wall. Floating up to you there will be echoing, yapping waves of celebration growing louder and shriller as time goes by. More flowers are constantly cramming themselves through the great doorway of the hall, weaving into the throng like a stream merging into the sea, disappearing at last into the general movement of the tide. There is a serpentine pattern among the flower-heads of coloured chiffon and straw and velvet. They press forward towards a border of alternate black and coloured flowers standing in a row on an underplanting of red carpet. The stream of purples and pinks and greens and yellows and black-and-whites and heliotropes sways up to this little line of the knot garden. Each flower-head bends towards another along the line and then withdraws as in a dance. The little shrieks and exclamations that arise from the line are more perilous and fragile than elsewhere. The glitter of glass, the popping noises like pistols in the corn here and there about the hall, make the flower heads nod and toss a little faster. The feeling now grows gayer. The flowers grow dense as cloth, a tapestry of tight stitches. The music begins.

Stay up there in the rafters for comfort, for Farnham Castle is not one of the great castles of the world and seven hundred flower-heads is its capacity. More than its capacity. Or, if you must – swoop down. Down you go, down and down, and you are standing close, so close up against the backs and fronts and heads and hats, angling your own head so that the domed fronts of men and the brims and chins of women don't get in your eye or sweep your drink from your hand.

And watch out for your feet or they will be trodden to bits by the unseen army of shoes below. Close your eyes against the cigarette lit up beside your left eyeball, tilt your head back against the teeth of mouths laughing. To survive, light a fag yourself, swig down some champagne (it isn't sparkling wine) and start making little screams and signals of your own to anyone, anywhere. 'Aren't you ——?' 'I'm ——' (whoever you are). 'But I'm *sure* you are.' 'Wherever was it we –?' '*Years* ago.' 'How lovely!' 'And how is Deirdre, Angela, Sydonia, Humphrey, dear old Miles?' 'Dead – oh, I'm so sorry.' 'So sorry, darling.' And so on.

There were two considerations at the Seton-Fairley wedding that were of prime importance to both families: one, that the reception should be held in the Castle to show that each side could feel they had rank and, two, that there should be the utter maximum number of guests, three hundred and fifty a side, and all of them closely interwoven to prove level pegging in the social register.

With seven hundred, it is possible that you will not get anywhere near a soul you know. In the depths of the seething flowery streams it occurred even to Pammie (who knows most of the world) that she and Hugo might attend and leave the reception never having seen a familiar face except for the bridal line-up, assuming they should ever reach the bridal line-up. Hugo hoped at most to get a word up there with old Puffy, though even that depended on whether old Puffy could still stand up. He'd been a bit shaky at his retirement and that was twenty years ago.

And Hugo himself wasn't looking too good, thought Pammie. How was she to get him somewhere to sit down? A drink? A canapé? (No food to speak of at this do; who but Christ could feed seven hundred cheek to cheek?)

'Hugo, my love,' said Pammie, 'keep round the edges. There's a thin place here. Stand in it. Don't move until I get someone to find you a chair,' and she stood him beside some silent and unintroduced people all wondering what to say to one another, waiting for alcohol, smiling tightly. She turned away and battled out of sight, the crowd closing behind her.

But Hugo had his stick and leaned on it, and smiled and waited and soon found himself taken up in some undertow and drawn with the silent companions towards the happy couple standing on the red carpet. As he was moved nearer the line he found he couldn't remember who the hell any of them were at this awful bloody wedding, and to get over the fright of this he concentrated on someone in the line who was delivering a top-speed rundown into the ear of the woman on his right, describing all who approached.

'Very old friend of family, second cousin or so over from Singapore, Daisy's aunt, old family retainer, Rosie very nice, not sure of the one on the stick, Thomasina Fox coming next but three, old Herbert's widow, lost her daughter, bit of a mystery about a baby, didn't expect her . . .'

Hugo nodded and mumbled his way along the line, nobody knowing who he was, which rather pleased him, until he came to Puffy in a wheelchair at the end.

Puffy was looking broad and remote with bloodshot blue eyes and white moustache. He was leaning back, abstracted, like a Viking plotting murder and pillage.

'Great day, Puffy,' said Hugo.

'Got a drink, Hugo?'

'All in good time.'

'Ha!'

Hugo passed along, content, and then stood about waiting for Thomasina. As she fell away from the line he put out both his arms, stick or no, in an attempt to embrace her. But she seemed distracted. For a moment she didn't even seem to recognise him. *She looks haunted*, he thought. *Bags under the eyes. And whatever has she got on her head? Looks like a rag, and it's coming undone.*

'My Thomas*ina*!'

She looked at him, the famous smile forgotten, and he thought, *By God, she's in a mess*, and he took her lean arm and tried to lead her away. She said nothing when they had to stop in the crush, only glared at him. Hugo remembered something of Pammie's about not speaking to her. He hadn't the faintest idea what to do next and the glare began to put him off balance. He prodded his stick into the ancient slabs of the floor, grabbed two drinks from a passing tray, passed one to Thomasina and looked desperately round. There was an old silk shoulder nearby so he grabbed it and turned it towards him. 'Hello. Hello – Hugo Jefford. You remember me? I wonder if you know my friend Thomasina Fox? Er?' and Madeleine, turning round, smiled at Thomasina and held out her hand.

Standing like a quiet queen, Madeleine said, 'My dear, I think we might escape from here, don't you? I was thinking of baked beans. I had no lunch but egg sandwiches. We could find a café somewhere?'

Old Hugo, roaring with bewildered laughter, backed away and disappeared with relief into the mêlée and Thomasina tried to do the same.

'No, no, but I mean it,' said Madeleine. 'It is so important. I've been trying to keep you in view since the church. To tell you about *Giles*. So important.'

She smiled once to left and once to right, touched an arm or two, and took Thomasina's hand. She then led her graciously away, a passage opening up for them. Somebody bossy, some sort of grandchild, tried to suggest otherwise, but Madeleine ruffled its hair with her free hand and passed on.

Thomasina, following, looked back to see if Giles's head was in sight. It usually stood above other heads like a king palm tree, but it was not there. She thought, *He's gone, then. He's left me. I thought so.*

Madeleine was disappearing into a Rolls-Royce and Thomasina followed. The car swooped off in the direction of the town centre.

'A side street,' said Madeleine to the chauffeur, 'we want a side street, and a snack bar will do nicely. Though we're really after baked beans. We're famished.'

The chauffeur looked in his mirror and then away and the car slid down various alleys and stopped outside something called The Sulawesi Johnnie. 'How delightful,' said Madeleine. 'Sauce bottles on all the tables. Now away you go back and thank you so much. I hope you haven't long to wait for whoever's chauffeur you are, but I expect you will have. I suppose you wouldn't care to join us? No – well, I'm not surprised at that either, two old bats like us. Come along, Thomasina.'

– 22 –

Jack was out again with the hoe, his shadow still behind him, the ground still white with dew that looked like snow, and it was all of half an hour after dawn. With every shove of the blade he said, *Jocasta*. He had stopped praying. *Jocasta, Jocasta*, said his mind's voice. For she had come across the cloister and into the kitchen and her purple shawl had fallen round her feet and she had put her arms around him. She reached nowhere near his shoulder and her head was sideways against his heart. She had said nothing but had held him and held him, and he had said, 'Jocasta, Jocasta.'

The Missus at the porridge pot had pursed up her mouth and said, after a wonderfully long moment, 'Well, it's ready. If you're coming for it, that is.' She hadn't liked looking at them standing together as he had buried his face in Jocasta's hair and said, 'Jocasta, Jocasta.' The Missus hadn't known where to look. 'Shameless. And they don't sleep together. You know that, don't you? No, they don't. Him soon as not kipping down anywhere, in the church all night sometimes. Off his rocker, poor old Jack. So funny, Andrew every inch the proper doctor. Never think they were brothers.' The Missus had been a

171

mill girl in Lancashire. Her life now was Jack. She had accompanied him on the last disastrous venture, of which nobody spoke. She was old, vain, plain, and knew it, but The Priors revolved around her because of her unique talent for creating a feeling of guilt in anybody who crossed her path. 'I am old and weak and my life is done but I have run a spotless course. See thou doest likewise,' said every pore and nerve-ending of The Missus. To see Jack and Jocasta standing as one being a few feet from her, Jack breathing deep into Jocasta's hair – it was unknown. It was indecent. Jocasta was doing it to disgust. Jack was of course oblivious.

Jocasta released her husband and went away and Jack sat and ate The Missus's porridge, his face alight with contentment. He smiled at The Missus when she said there'd be no bacon for anyone else if the Tibetans were to have any. The kitchen, the courtyard, the chickens scratching in the tombstones, the throb of music and some shouting from the Tibetan quarters in the early winter sunshine – it was like the first morning of the world. Jack was sure now, unequivocally, that The Priors was the guiding light that God had instructed him to build in a heathen and poisonous world.

Andrew came in and sat down to wait for his bacon and eggs and Jack saw in him a man of sorrows. No wife would come over to him and wordlessly take him in her arms, trustingly, not caring who saw, not needing even to speak any endearment because they were one, one person. Oh poor Andrew, poor bright Holly. How could he bear being without her? Much less than half the purpose of his life must remain to him. Holly so strong and vivid and indestructible. And not a sign of self-pity in Andrew. Not a flicker.

'Andrew,' he said, 'I think we should say a prayer.'

'What *now*?'

'Now. A prayer for Holly.'

'I'm off to see if there's more bacon,' said The Missus and Andrew said, 'Sorry, Jack, I'm off to Toots and Dolly.'

'But it's not eight o'clock in the morning. They'll hardly be up.'

'I have to drop in at the hospital in Middlesbrough with Faith. Someone ought to see to her eye.' But he put a hand on Jack's shoulder as he passed him to pour himself tea.

'I said that about her eye two days ago,' said The Missus, slapping down burnt bacon on the table before Jack, who looked at it vaguely. 'Nobody deigns to listen to me.'

'I did. I am,' said Andrew.

'I was one of a large family,' said The Missus.

'And I'm a doctor. There's a test they can do on the eye. Sometimes it's just a blocked tear duct but sometimes not. She would be kept in overnight and back by Monday.'

'Not round here, she wouldn't,' said The Missus. 'There won't be a bed for six months and by then the eye will have cleared itself.'

'I'll get her in,' said Andrew.

'You won't. That doesn't do up here. You're not in your own place south now. Say you're a doctor and you're back of the queue. Not that that's so dreadful. I never found doctors so wonderful. I helped with me mam. Could do the lot – break the waters, untie the cord round the neck. Minute it gets tricky it's "Shall I leave it to the nurse?" That was

173

doctors. Not that I'd speak against the profession publicly. I know my place. Oh yes. But I could massage that eye right with my thumb in ten minutes.'

'And damage the nerve and give her a squint for life. No thanks. I'm taking her down there and then I'll go on and pick up Philip from Toots and Dolly. I'll take Jocasta with me, OK, Jack? Might take her along the beach a bit. Leave the baby for Toots and Dolly to google over for a bit.'

'She's somewhere near,' said Jack, 'she's just left. Take her by all means. Jocasta gets little enough time away. She needs a change.'

Eating toast fast, not looking at Jack, Andrew said, 'Great. We'll be back by lunchtime, then.'

So Jack went back into the field, moving slowly, step by step, down the courgettes. He stopped once or twice to reflect. Once, he picked the pale-primrose trumpet of a flower. He ate it slowly to the last stamen and looked up at the sky. His life was together at last. New year, perhaps a child?

– 23 –

When The Smikes had left and Mrs Middleditch had also departed, carrying an armful of Toots's washing up the street and leaving an atmosphere behind her, Dolly began preparations for the visit of her widowed son and grandchild by draping Toots's best clothes over various pieces of furniture and switching on a second bar of the electric fire to make sure all would be properly aired. Long woollen leggings which he called his knickers and a long-sleeved woollen shirt that would go over the long-sleeved woollen vest he wore in bed and changed on Saturdays were spread across the armchair. Clean socks were put side by side on his bed table and his suit and braces laid across the sideboard with a clothes brush beside them. A new red tie hung round the clock on the mantelpiece. Dolly then came hobbling from the kitchen with beautifully polished black shoes, one of them with a built-up heel. She moved the bed table away from the bed, turned back the bedclothes and brought the walking frame up beside him.

She watched him heave himself over and out and his pyjama trousers fell down round his ankles as they did every morning. She walked behind him down the passage, holding them up. He said, as he did every morning as he led this procession of two, 'Give over. Let them drop. I'll step out of them,' and she said, 'There are some standards you don't let go,' and why couldn't he take the time to fasten the cord? And he said, 'Not worth it just for down the passage.' It was their morning refrain, their matins.

In the invalid bathroom built out on the draughty extension to the kitchen where there had once been a maid and a charwoman under Dolly's eye, she opened the door of the plastic bath as he stepped from the trousers. She helped him out of the pyjama jacket and vest and steadied his shrivelled body on its thin shanks through the little door. She held him as he lowered his thin old bottom on to the bath seat. She ran the water carefully, the cold with the hot, squeezed it warmly over him and soaped all down his back, remembering it when it was young, its muscles like ropes. He'd had hardness and glow to him then. He sat hunched forward now, munching on nothing, staring at nothing, hating the feel of her hands on him. 'It's work for a nurse, this,' he said, the daily introit, and she said, 'Don't be so silly. You'd do it for me.'

He knew he wouldn't. He could never wash an old woman. He knew too that she knew he didn't dislike every aspect of this bathing and soaping. The once irascible, fierce, invincible Toots had discovered that he liked to accept care, as babies accept.

'Well,' he said, 'they'll be on their way.'

She rinsed him with an old sponge they'd long ago brought from Greece. 'Give me that flannel,' he said. 'You're not doing down there.'

'They may well be,' she said. 'There's a lot to do,

176

so get out. You've to shave yet.' She dried him, helped him into his dressing gown with protecting arms and sat him on a cork stool before a mirror that came out like a fake boxing glove on a metal spring, but he couldn't see to shave himself.

'Put your glasses on,' said Dolly.

'I can't get the enthusiasm,' he said, 'when I see the problem. Looks a lot better blurred.'

'Blurred, it looks like an old tramp,' she said. 'Like this designer stubble. Like that Nick.'

'Give us the razor here, then. That's a good point you made.'

There was the ritual drying of the face, the combing of long-gone hair, the procession back to the bedroom, the slow sacrament of dressing. He heaved himself into the Windsor chair with a table in front of him as she toiled about making the bed, hauling at a heavy cover that was meant to make it look like a divan. She came and went with the night bottle and then hid it in a drawer. She knelt before him to ease on the shining shoes. She tied their laces. 'I could do with my coffee,' he said, and she said, 'Well, you can wait till I've dusted and hoovered round.'

'The brasses could do with a rub.'

'They were done yesterday.'

'There's no fruit in that bowl.'

'I'm opening a window before I'm fussing with fruit. The smell in here's disgusting. That's what comes of sleeping where you live all day. We should be out of this house and in care.'

'Living up at Jack's, you mean?' said Toots. They gave each other a glance of understanding and agreement. 'That Jocasta having us sit making cut-outs,' said Toots. 'Like a snake she sits.'

'I don't see what snakes have to do with it.'

'Where you going to set down this baby when they get themselves here?' he asked her. 'Clear a space now somewhere.'

'We'll put her on the end of the bed.'

'Well, mind you sit yourself in the upright chair for him to pass her over to you. That other one's far too low and you'll drop her.'

'He's a doctor, Toots: he knows.'

'I'm not going to hold her, mind. I'm not strong enough. I'm not well up in babies anyway. I'll be standing back today.'

'You know you'll hold her, given the chance. You know you've always loved babies.'

'Can't stand them,' he said. 'Is that the gate?'

'They can't be here yet,' said Dolly. 'I'll get your coffee and your pills. I might just put the dinner on. He may stay.'

'By God, I should hope he does stay. Not seen him in a year and him widowed and a father and you say will he be staying for his dinner. By God, I'd not be suited if he didn't stay on till after his tea. There's no question about it. I'd take it very badly if he didn't stay.'

'Well, she may not settle, Toots. She may cry. She's unlikely to be settled up here yet and there's this gummy eye. He may want to get her home.'

'What, to yon rural slum? She'd be better off here for cleanliness. Have you looked at Philip?'

Dolly pulled herself once more up the narrow staircase with the scarlet and blue turkey carpet and the polished brass stair rods and examined all she could see of Philip, which was a tuft of hair and a bundle of clothes. She had something for gummy eyes somewhere and began to rustle about in cupboards. She gathered up some glass baby bottles she had put out already and came step by step downstairs again with them. She submerged the bottles and ancient teats in boiling water for a good long sterilisation, then creaked upstairs again for the baby clothes she'd been gathering up from church bazaars for a year, ever since she'd heard that Holly was pregnant. They were in layers of tissue paper on top of her own lavender-smelling underwear. Very pretty. She came awkwardly down the stairs again clutching them with some old toys of Andrew's; a plaster angel to hang over a bed, a mug painted with 1950s sprites, a bone teething ring with a bell on it and a stringy bit of blue ribbon old as the child's father.

'What's that ket?' asked Toots. 'Hello, there's the front door. They're here.'

'Never. I didn't hear the gate. It can't be.'

Nor was it. Only Jocasta came sliding into the room. They hadn't even heard her enter the house. She said, 'Hello, Toots – Dolly,' and sat sweetly down on the bed with her hands folded, her feet not touching the floor. 'You both look very smart. You must have got up early.'

'Well!' said Dolly. '*Now* then. How lovely!' She always sounded pleased to see people, even if she disliked them. When she saw them in her house she forgot whether or not she disliked them. It was unconscious caution. The gods of hospitality were always on the watch. They could avenge, and Dolly was frightened by her old age. Judgement loomed. Across the room Toots sat on his throne looking ahead into the electric fire, moving his bad ankle up and down against the bar of his walking frame so that it squeaked rhythmically. He waited for Jocasta to wince.

'Can't I go and help him in with her?' said Dolly. 'With the carry-cot? I'll go down to the gate.'

'He couldn't come,' said Jocasta. 'I'm on my own. He's halfway. I left him at the hospital. She has this gummy eye. He sent me on to say he's so sorry but she ought to be looked at straight away. I dropped them both there and I'll pick him up on the way home.'

'She'd to go to *hospital*? With a gummy *eye*?' Dolly's eyes were round.

'They may not take her in. She's had so much excitement, though, the last two days, Andrew thinks she shouldn't be shown around yet.'

After twenty minutes, she left them as quietly as she had arrived and without going up to see Philip. 'I'll leave him for you, Dolly, may I? He loves it here.'

'Well,' said Toots, 'that's something anyway,' and he took off the red silk tie and undid the collar stud.

– 24 –

They sat for some time waiting for the baked beans
and a pot of tea, Madeleine touching the forks on
the plastic table top, smiling at the salts and
peppers. She looked around her once and bowed to
someone with severe acne and dressed from head to
foot in leathers at the next table. He had a huge
hairless head. The open leather jacket showed a
gold ring through one of his nipples. He pretended
not to see her.

'So sad,' said Madeleine. 'Chemotherapy. It's not
necessary to lose your hair now, you know, so long
as you see to it that you have the right surgeon.'
Turning back to Thomasina she leaned over to her
and tucked in a corner of her scarf-hat. 'There,' she
said. 'Just the tiniest bit astray.'

Thomasina's hands flew to her head. She said,
'Oh God, I know. It's all I had. Giles and I were on
holiday in Yorkshire this morning and we'd quite
forgotten the wedding. I'd a dress that would do but
no hat.'

'It's charming,' said Madeleine. 'But what about
him? Had he the gear?'

The lad in leathers gave her a look and she said,

'*Gear*, dear, yes. I'm not an antique.' He rose and left the café.

'We went to get it. To his house. In Berkshire. It's been a long day. Actually . . .'

'Yes?' Madeleine leaned forward with love.

'Actually, when we got there he offered me a hat of his dead wife.'

'Hilda's! Oh my dear, I'm so sorry!'

'It had a pheasant's feather in it.'

'Yes, it would. Oh my darling girl! So it's over, then?'

Thomasina unwound the scarf and shook her hair. She said, 'I'm sorry. I really can't – I can't remember you. I *am* sorry. Maybe we should have had some champagne and then I . . .'

'I wonder if it's licensed here.' Madeleine looked luminously at the girl behind the counter, who said, 'You what?'

'I don't suppose you're licensed? My friend needs a little brandy.' The girl stared. 'No – I'm afraid, quite hopeless,' said Madeleine. 'My dear, you are Thomasina Fox. I don't know you *really* but I know *of* you. Through Pammie Jefford. Now, I have a hopeless memory these days but I'm sure she never told me you'd married dear old Giles.'

'I haven't.'

'Dear child – well, I'm old enough to call you child – *dear* child, I'm so glad. I can talk more freely.'

But she stopped and looked gently round the restaurant, as forlorn a little place on a Saturday afternoon as you could find; the hard bread rolls, the gluey slabs of chrome-yellow flan behind glass, the bag-woman in the corner rustling through newspapers, the two girls all paintwork and thighs leaning their heads towards each other, talking in whispers, the sad young man with a book by the window. 'I always think that Sarajevo must have been like this.'

The baked beans arrived. They looked quite good. The teapot followed. It had strings hanging out of it round the lid, each with a label saying there was a teabag on the other end. Madeleine asked for some real milk instead of the liquid in the plastic pots but the girl didn't hear. Then Madeleine said, 'But you were *holidaying* with Giles. Would you mind if I asked – is there anything now in the way of lovemaking?'

When Thomasina attacked the baked beans without a word Madeleine continued to sit serene. In a few moments she poured more tea for them both, dribbling it a bit into the thick saucers. She began to spear the orange beans singly and daintily with her fork.

At last Thomasina said, 'I'm sorry. I don't talk about my private life.'

'Oh, that's such a mistake,' said Madeleine. 'Oh, I so wish that I had had someone to tell me what a mistake that is. You have to have *someone*. But there – I expect you have Giles.'

'I hardly know Giles.'

'Yet you make love with him. You didn't say no. I wonder what he's like. I yearned to know once. I'd guess now he'd be pretty brisk, but that would be better than he was when he was young. He was absolutely terrified then of the whole idea. Not only of sex, but of love. And of course I was terrified too, and so well brought-up. I went to Karnak with him, you know, if you know where that is. It was wartime and I was a Fany (yes, isn't it lewd?) and he asked me to go to the Winter Palace for the weekend. I was in such a *fit*, dear, about contraceptives. I had no idea what to expect. All I knew was from school. One of the big girls had told me that the Ancient Greeks used to use butter and of course you couldn't get butter in the war and it would have seemed a frightful waste. So I just went and hoped for the best. But dear Giles, there was nothing like that at all. He kissed my hand on the Saturday night and we both went to our separate rooms. You wouldn't believe it, would you, all the books you read, but that was quite usual then. Oh I *burned*, dear, in my bed. I left my room unlocked and a huge Egyptian man came in during the night in a long pink thing and asked to clean my shoes and there was no telephone and I said that I should have to scream and then the man went away. I think I was probably very lucky, although the Egyptians are very pleasant, polite people and it may have been no more than affection. I told Giles in the morning and he created a frightful fuss. Well, you know, I expect they all thought my room would be empty, though it would have been more flattering if they had thought *Giles's* room would be empty and he'd be in with me. He was tremendously apologetic. I think he knew that he'd behaved badly. Very tamely. But, you see, neither of us knew the rules. They were in a state of flux in the Forties. Well, they probably always are. But oh my dear, so shy. That's why he needed Hilda.'

'What was Hilda like?'

'She was like a gun, dear. She went boom. Boom, bang, smash. Tennis nets fainted at the sight of her.' Madeleine leaned sideways in her chair. 'Boom and smash,' she repeated to the two whispering girls, nodding her head. 'Boom, smash.' The girls looked insulted and then hostile. Soon they, too, left the café.

'Oh, Thomasina, Thomasina, do be careful. He's probably more positive now but at heart he hasn't changed at all. Even in appearance. I knew him. Recognised him after fifty years. That's rare – even rarer in a woman, of course. But he has that wooden army face, you know, like the Duke of Wellington. The narrow army face not the plump one. Giles never drank. Just the same jaw as the Iron D – and, of course, I knew each plane of Giles's face, each nostril, darling – thank God youth passes – and each finger and nail on his nice hands. His hands have changed, by the way – has he arthritis? Poor Giles. But it is such a good face, you know. Such a beautiful face that I'm afraid it may have made a barrier between you. We all of us, you know, want a man sometimes whom we don't have to know too well and if he's handsome it's used as a substitute.'

'My husband was like that,' said Thomasina. 'He was a surgeon.'

'Oh yes, of course he was, poor man. But I expect you were a great help to him.'

'I've nothing to do with Medicine.'

'No – I mean in calming him down. From all the excitement. A surgeon's job must be so overheating. It makes them feverish – or sometimes ice-cold.'

'I'm afraid,' said Thomasina, 'I don't think I thought of that. I lived in a bit of a world of my own. It seemed to be what he wanted.'

'He probably admired you no end,' said Madeleine. 'What work did you do?'

'Oh – nothing. I was a very keen gardener.'

'Ah, that's what they say in *Who's Who* if they don't do anything at all.'

Thomasina blazed scarlet. 'I am a very good and

serious gardener.' She closed her teeth over a forkful of beans, dragged the fork out empty and slammed it on her plate.

'Darling – I'm so sorry. Children?'

'What the hell d'you mean?'

'You had some children, didn't you? It's more than I did. I've only steps. Barren as the fig.'

'So was Giles,' said Thomasina.

'The poor fellow.' Madeleine sat with an expression of true and profound grief. 'I expect that was Mildred. They don't have many, tennis players. I suppose the wires get twisted. Giles needed children.'

'So what about you?' asked angry Thomasina.

Madeleine only leaned across and touched her hand. 'What about your daughter?' she asked very clearly. 'What about your daughter, Holly?' She let her hand become a handcuff round Thomasina's wrist. 'Your daughter died the other day, I hear, and there is a baby. And I understand you will not see the baby. Why not?'

'This is utterly none of your business.'

'Yes it is. I see a shuttered woman turning to a clammed-up man to save her from the rest of her life and I know that she is laying up for herself nothing but another coat of varnish, like those unhappy quiches on the counter. Oh yes, my dear girl. You'll both look your parts convincingly until you die. You'll take each other down the last years like two beautiful illustrations out of the old England we all love and mourn. And you'll go nowhere. *Nowhere.* Even the lovemaking will be dignified till it peters out altogether, which will be about three weeks after the wedding. It's a bit dignified now, isn't it? You haven't said a thing about it. Is it not the sort of thing you could do to a comfortable de Souza

186

march? Tum-te-tum? Tell me I'm wrong – that it's between two who love each other and long to know each other and love each other more. You can't. You know it is a barrier, the sex between you. Isn't it?'

'It is not,' cried Thomasina, red in the face, almost weeping. 'It's pretty good. Very nice. Sleeping with Giles is the most exciting thing I've done in years. I don't say so. Neither does he. D'you think we're French or something? But we *will* do. We're good at it. The first time was in a sandstorm.'

The café had fallen still. Even the bag-woman had stopped rustling. The young man by the window had laid down his book and taken off his reading glasses and the girl behind the counter had let the microwave ping unheeded.

'And the granddaughter?' Madeleine was in with a thrust as Thomasina began to cry. 'This granddaughter?'

'I've had enough,' wept Thomasina. 'I've had enough of motherhood. What the hell can *you* tell me about its pain! Do you not know, woman' – she stood up – '*my daughter is dead.*'

The general and a boy and a girl, all in wedding clothes, stood in the doorway and the general was at Thomasina's side as she turned to fling herself in his arms. Then she flung herself out of them again, making for the open door, and he went after her and held her from behind by the shoulders, looking round the assembled company with a mixture of terror at being found in such a place in such a way and valour in his determination that nothing would make him retreat from it.

The boy and girl slid down on either side of their seated step-grandmother and the girl looked over at Thomasina and said, 'You mustn't mind, Mrs Fox.

Honestly, she's dreadful but it's not her fault. She's, you know, Alzheimer's or something. It's terribly sad. She says terrible things. But then she forgets them.'

The great car that Thomasina and Madeleine had arrived in stood at the café door again with the chauffeur picking his teeth inside it. He'd done a lot of weddings. They'd been saying a thousand bottles of champagne had gone into this one.

'I'll walk,' wailed Thomasina. 'Giles, let's get away.'

'Of course,' he said. 'We'll go straight home.'

'We'll take her back to Puffy,' said the girl. 'Not that he's much better. Come on, Gran darling.'

Madeleine looked around her, bowing separately to each customer, favouring the young man with the book with a caress on the cheek. 'An intellectual,' she said, and in the street, 'Darlings, I've just been telling Mrs Fox that this little place reminds me of Sarajevo. I don't mean the awful Bosnian business, I mean the outbreak of war – The Great War, before even my time. The breaking of nations. The old world disappearing overnight throughout Europe when the silly driver of the emperor's carriage got stuck in a back alley and there was the gunman who'd missed the first shot in the main street having a cup of coffee. Bang! Everything changed. The flower of all our countries gone.' She paused. 'But then, you know,' she said, 'not quite, for here are you, and here am I and there is the general and that nice woman Thomasina Woolf. She wrote *The Waves*, you know. And there have been other turning points. There are. All the time. *All the time*. Thank God.'

'You got her?' asked the grandson.

'Yep,' said his sister.

'Come on, Gran darling. Home we go.'

– Part Two –

– 25 –

At the beginning of December Jocasta sat in the workshops with the Tibetan women cutting paper and half-listening to them talk. The Tibetan men had disappeared. No one spoke of them. Under the coarse, hairy coat of the oldest woman, Pema, Faith lay sleeping. She seemed seldom to be in her cot. A little hammock had been rigged up for her in the visitors' quarters and there she slept now at night. She was with them in the daytime, too, except when a health visitor announced a routine visit and then somehow she was always to be found in the main buildings with The Missus or Jocasta about. But she often became fretful there and was returned to Pema quickly. With Pema she never seemed to cry, passing her days in a sling under Pema's bristly coat, almost hidden, like a chicken under the wings of a hen.

The art class was busy this morning with a huge collage planned for a Nativity tableau on Christmas Eve. The Tibetans were not excited by it. One of them, a girl with good A levels at Liverpool, was wild to get into the Slade. The Priors was only her temporary billet while she waited for interviews. She was building a portfolio in a rather absent-minded way when she wasn't spending time on the telephone sharing long silences with a busking boyfriend in London.

The girl was dismissive of mysterious Jocasta, who had been out of touch with what was going on in Art colleges for over twenty years. The girl sulked and lolled, looking Jocasta up and down, disagreeing with all her theory and practice and scratching her hands through her raspberry-red hair. Only her eyes were Tibetan; her clothes and accent aggressively scouse. *Silly bitch*, this girl thought as Jocasta's fingers cut and pasted, *with her posh voice*. Jocasta was talking today about negative space. 'Negative space, for Chrissake,' said the Tibetan girl to herself.

Negative space, thought Jocasta, snipping at shredded silk, daubing it orange for sunrise, *is where I live*.

Oh what to me the little room
That was brimmed up with prayer and rest . . .

She had stopped sleeping with Jack long ago, long before Andrew had returned with the baby. Jack had understood. He had understood perfectly, he said, the urge for celibacy in a woman no longer young and particularly in Jocasta, who had been on an unearthly spiritual plane in India. They had met so late, he said, looking at her with love. Everyone, The Missus, The Smikes, the hangers-on around The Priors, thought Jack was a fool to love Jocasta, who was a cold fish. Jack never complained, seemed to have no conception of infidelity or treachery in anyone. His trust was ridiculous, childlike. He looked, he loved.

But he does want me in his bed, she thought, *and otherwise brimmed up with prayer and rest. And Andrew did let me go. He ditched me. He made a political marriage. And look where it got him.*

But yet there's something good in Andrew. Something

fearless, unchanging. Look what happened. Within an hour. He could have held me for ever. He still could hold me for ever. He shall hold me for ever.

He bade me out into the gloom, she thought,
And my breast lies upon his breast.

'D'you never think of going home?' she asked the sulky girl, the Tibetan bohemian. 'Isn't it a bit easier now? Couldn't you get back somehow, at least to Nepal? It's your continent, your culture.'

'I'm not goin' back to that sort o' painting, thanks very much. It's only boys do it anyway and it's all copying old Buddhist stuff. Might as well work for Disney. Coom on, Jocasta, let's get to it. Let's hear this negative space.'

'It's what we're doing here,' she said, and smiled over at unsmiling Pema. 'Move over a bit, could you, Pema, while I open the screen up. Shouldn't you put her down in her cot for a while?'

Pema didn't speak. Knitting without dropping the hump across her chest that was Faith, she waddled to another part of the workshop and sat with her back to everybody. Laying down her needles, she adjusted the baby and began to heat up milk.

'So,' said Jocasta, 'we do this. We block in roughly and then in detail, first sketching, then drawing, then the layers of colours and textures. Cloth – oh, all the substances we want. Grit, glitter, granite chips, bits of heather, coal-dust, beads, baubles, ribbons, glass, net, everything. These are to surround the subject only. The suburbs of the city. The city, we leave bare. We almost reject it. We ignore it. We have no feeling for it, no plans. We do not allow ourselves the concept of a subject. We let it materialise. It emerges by our creation of the material around. Its clothing, if you like. The material is in part its creator: the material is the cause. If we do this faithfully we find in the end that the subject of the work shines out the clearer, apparently of its own accord. Life of its own. It's a way of arriving there by standing back, letting the Creator create so we sometimes get a big surprise. Well, here of course we know what the centre of the thing is going to be because it's for the Christmas do in the chapel. It has to be the Nativity in the centre, obviously. But the idea is that perhaps the central object will be revealed more dramatically, more clearly, if we don't overwork it. Don't work at it exclusively or even at all. Sometimes the subject can only be found if it's crept up on like this. The central point of this picture can turn out to be more than we can bear to reveal directly. Sort of wearing dark glasses. Perpetual light is, after all, unbearable. Well, for mortals.'

'Is it religious, then?' the second Tibetan woman asked. 'Christian. Obey the doctrine and the faith looks after itself?'

'Or Buddhist?' said a third.

'God, let's hope it's not Buddhist,' said the A-level Liverpudlian.

'It's Methodist,' said someone. ' "The trivial round, the common task, would furnish all we ought to ask." Be good like that, keep your eyes down, and you'll get God as a prize at the end. Right at the heart of it all.'

'If you like,' said Jocasta, who kept off God, 'or it is peace, truth, karma, a goal.'

'Keeping your eyes down,' said the other older woman of the group. She held up the thing she was stitching. It was like a little rectangular kit of framework sticks crossed at the corners, the fabric bound round and filled with a pattern of wools in

194

three colours: a black circular pupil, bronze iris against the oval white, a dense, small tapestry about four inches by four. The third eye, held aloft, its last strands not yet all woven in, overlooked the little group. Jocasta shuddered.

'It's not a very adventurous idea,' said the Slade-girl-to-be.

'I think it is, quite,' said Jocasta; 'it is quite brave. And it's a patient way of working with sometimes a great result. I've been surprised almost every time by what comes out at the end. If you push all your ordinary tricks and gimmicks and – persiflages – out of the way. Stop thinking of faith.'

Oh what to me my mother's care, she thought,
The house where I was safe and warm,
The shadowy blossom of my hair
Will hide us from the bitter storm.

Oh Andrew, Andrew, Andrew . . . but how can I leave him? Jack is my mother and my father and he keeps me safe and warm. Or he would if I would let him. But Andrew, oh come in under the blossom of my hair, oh damnation, oh sex. Oh my love.

Pema came across to them again, walking calmly, and sat. She began to feed Faith Fox her bottle of milk and the child's round pink hand like a starfish stretched up and traced a pattern in the air, then patted and stroked the old woman's cheek.

Outside the wind blew. The time was most certainly winter now and becoming cold. Most of Ellerby Priors had been closed down until the spring came. No more groups would be coming, no public events or days of meditation or farm visits. The curling lists on the notice boards could all be taken down now if somebody remembered. When the Tibetans left in the spring the guest sheds would be closed. The refectory had already been cleared and shuttered, the main priory dormitory stripped, and such heating as there was drained down. The skeleton staff of The Missus, The Smikes, Jack, Jocasta and Philip drew in each night round the stove of the old kitchen. Snow could sometimes begin in December and the steep road off the ridge was regularly blocked during January. The deep-freezes had been filled by The Missus with bread and chunks of long-dead Whitby cod and the barn was full of Jack's potatoes and swedes. There was discussion about the economics of buying half a frozen cow; about how maybe this year it would make sense for Philip to be a full boarder at the school rather than Jocasta having to walk to the cross and coax the car alive and brave the moor road four times a day.

Oh when, oh when, shall I see Andrew? thought Jocasta. *And when he does come back, whatever shall I do? How shall I behave? Surely he'll come at Christmas. He'll want to look at the child. I want him to take me back with him. Yes, I do. And I should. It is right and normal that I should. It's healthy. And I want to do something for Philip. There's nothing here for him. He's not like a child. He's not like any of them up here anyway. They're North, that's all there is about it. They're as intelligent as us. Doctors' and solicitors' children. A private school I said I'd never countenance. They learn French in a fashion. But they're different. It's not the voices, it's the glowering looks they have, and they're so rude and they're North. My God, I hate it here.*

And he spends all his free time with The Smikes and the old funnies at the seaside, so-called grandparents. Oh, but I have no money. I've left all my own life behind me. I'm going nowhere. Teaching Negative Space to Tibetans. I'm lost. Oh, how I want him. Andrew.

– 26 –

Hugo Jefford had been prophetic when he said that the Seton-Fairley wedding would be the last chance for him to see his old friend Puffy, husband of drifting Madeleine. It was Puffy, however, who survived the winter and Hugo who that warm autumn left the world. He left it suddenly, without any goodbyes.

And on such a lovely morning. The dew was on the Coombe Hill lawn and the marks of his bedroom slippers on their last journey suggested some passing giant or summer snowman marching from the house towards the three great garages. He had brought Pammie early tea that morning, a habit that had somehow established itself since her uncharacteristic oversleeping the day after her return from the North with the bag of potatoes. Hugo appeared to enjoy this new duty. He had stood drinking his own tea at the window, looking over his garden, as Pammie sat up straight against her pillows, sipping and glaring ahead of her.

They said little and pretty well the same things each morning. 'Busy today?' and 'Remarkable weather. Extraordinary autumn, this,' and 'They say it's cold in the North.' 'Yes. Odd. It's like spring here.'

Hugo had stood hunched with his broad old back to her, his ears sticking out. The rising sun shone through them and turned them rosy. 'You ought to get your hair cut,' Pammie had said. Looking hard at his back she felt impatient. She felt young. She felt undervalued.

'Hardly there to cut,' he said; 'not like this wretched lawn. He'll have to go over it again.'

'So you keep saying.'

'So he keeps having to. Makes a fearful hash of it. I'd like to have a go myself.'

'Well, do, if you want a stroke.'

'Stroke, my foot.'

'I don't want to stroke your foot. And I don't want to be landed with someone like poor old Puffy. It's probably Puffy who sent poor Madeleine off her marbles. I mean right off her marbles.'

'Or vice versa,' said Hugo. 'We're very lucky, Pammie, you and I. We're so fit.'

'Well, I'm hardly Madeleine's age, if you don't mind my saying so. You used to be always telling people I could almost be your daughter. Almost.'

'Almost,' he said. 'I told the nurse you could, you know. Just to stop her getting ideas. Then she said, "Well, I could be your granddaughter." ' ('And I don't care,' she had also said but Hugo didn't say so now.)

'You liked her, didn't you?' Pammie all of a sudden found that she too liked Hugo and as much as ever. 'Bring me some more tea. You're an old reprobate.' She pulled his head towards her by one of the rosy ears and kissed him.

'That feller's in the garden now,' he said; 'I can hear him. I'll just nip down and catch him. Tell him to get the big mower out, not the Flymo. When it's dried up a bit he could get a cut today.'

'You'll catch cold.'

'No. Lovely morning. Fresh. Like spring.'

Pammie never saw the dark footsteps in the unruly grass because, by the time she discovered Hugo dead beside the Bentley, round which he had been manoeuvring the mower, they had disappeared. Hugo had been mistaken about the gardener. It had been the postman he had heard. He had taken the letters from him and then walked to the garage. He bade the postman a courteous goodbye, took the garage key from its compartment behind a loose brick, wheeled out the mower and leaned to the self-starter.

His death flattened Pammie as nothing in her life had done. It put into proportion deaths of the children of friends and all attendant emotional shocks and sorrows. The weeping for Holly Fox over tumblers of whisky, Holly's angry funeral, everyone seething at the behaviour of others, the distaste of the whole bazaar for the superficiality of Thomasina, the righteous disgust for her love affair, even the comfortable pride Pammie had begun to develop for the baby: all were revealed as things of a slight order. Most of them she now identified as boredom or self-indulgence, self-importance with almost a whiff of prurience. And most of all Pammie was revolted by her hearty behaviour at The Priors, that madhouse full of cranks. Whatever had she been doing there? Not one's own sort at all. Religious fanatics. She had behaved like a schoolgirl rushing up there with the baby. She had been wanting to show up Thomasina. Now she was ashamed of herself. Seedy eccentricity was not the world of Coombe and it was only a seedy eccentric with a very nice face who had been gushing all over her up there, not someone you could know. You couldn't possibly ask him to dinner. Nor, if it came to that, the laconic brother either. Secretive Andrew, running off in the heather. Not her generation and certainly not her friend. He was no more than the son-in-law of an ex-friend, and she should not have pushed into other people's lives. Riffraff lives. Not worthy behaviour for the wife of Hugo. Hugo the good.

Childless and alone in the huge house except for Hugo's sorrowful old dog, Pammie surprised all her friends by her heaviness and inanition. Hugo had after all for years been no more than a benign shadow seated with glass and newspaper under a standard lamp, Pammie a stocky seraph flying past him at intervals, eyes fixed on her own ploys.

But Pammie the great organiser of Surrey rituals now could not even give orders for the funeral or the wake. Pammie the paradigm of common sense and courage in the face of disaster, so decisive and practical, now allowed letters of condolence to pile up unanswered, gave up her magistrate's duties and her golf and her singing. Bridge she just about managed, 'for her mind's sake,' she said, 'and as long as nobody says anything', but she was withdrawn and looked disagreeable and her partner grew fidgety and then sniffy. There was a vulgar, old-persons' sort of row and that was that. Pammie stayed home.

But the worst of the loss of Hugo was how it attacked like a killing virus the very gut of Pammie, her sure, religious life. Froze it. Set it in aspic. God melted under its strobe light. And this hard cold light seemed to Pammie to be some sort of poisoned present Hugo had sent her posthumously from wherever it was he had gone when he fell, face forward, across the mower as the late autumn roses sparkled at him through the open garage doors. Hugo's going pierced that layer of Pammie that she had confidently labelled Christian and out of it spilled only a ragbag of old rubbish.

She examined this ragbag as soon as the stately funeral was over. It had been a rustling, whispering, concerned but not very upsetting funeral. There had been much good fellowship, several rows of stout old gentlemen in long dark overcoats ('Was old Hugo *Jewish*?'), massive wreaths, and several unknown pale new partners from his old city firm. The nurse they'd had for Faith had been there with a white handkerchief to her face, and two or three rather nice-looking women Pammie could not place. There had been white moustachios in cricketing ties. Old Puffy had been there, leaning back in his wheelchair examining the vaulting of the church roof as if in search of angels. He had been attended by a young man in pinstripes with a bowler hat beside him on the pew. Someone said it was a butler. He had wheeled Puffy past Pammie at the church door and bowed. Puffy had said only, 'Bad news, old girl, bad news.'

Madeleine had been absent but Thomasina had been there (without the general) and so had Andrew Braithwaite, with a little dark woman Pammie felt she knew. She wondered if it was a girlfriend and thought, *Oh how splendid*, before all the petty Holly Fox business slid out of her head again. She could not even remember, as they all roared out the last hymn, *Fight the Good Fight*, she could not remember the name of Holly Fox's little baby, who had lived with her and with Hugo under their rose-tiled roof. She could not conceive what she had ever had to do with the child.

But then she saw before her Hugo's face again, the face she had so terrifyingly been unable to recall since the day he died, and his voice saying, 'Gets your finger in a vice. Smiles at you,' and there at last, before the final verse, she began to cry.

It was Thomasina who looked after her. After the funeral she saw to the guests back at the house, ran round after the caterers had gone, tidied up, gathered the service sheets, the tickets from the wreaths, put them on Pammie's desk, said she would deal with them. She had brought whisky and little sandwiches for the evening, for both of them, as if there had been no rift, no death of Holly, no general, no Egypt, no Faith. A little warmth began to ease its way into Pammie again.

Thomasina was now the image of her old self in her gold jewellery and smart shoes and she guided along a conversation almost macabrely ordinary. She suggested that Pammie should come back and stay with her at Spindleberries at least for the next week or so. Later they could talk about holiday plans. Hadn't Pammie been thinking of Cyprus? They discussed Apex fares, then the appeal of going soft and travelling at least Club Class. They discussed dates, fitting them in around various summer appointments: the Chelsea Flower Show, the Cheltenham Festival, and so on. They might go at Easter . . . Or what about Christmas? The cadences of the sentences suggested the old way of things again, that after a stone sinks the water does eventually stop rippling. Their two voices worked for the future, towards a long-term forecast and, damn it all, a pleasant one.

However, the old way of things for Pammie had included her habitual and lengthy conversations with God, which had filled up much of the time when she was not attending to her almost perpetual interior monologues addressed to friends and acquaintances. These monologues now had ceased. Pammie had discovered that they were no longer important, that the unconscious recipients of the monologues were no longer important. She had, she found out, only addressed them anyway to the unimportant. To the Jinnies and Vinnies and Daffies and Janes. Hugo had never been addressed as he had never intruded on any of her dreams, sleeping or waking.

And now that he was gone all that she wanted to do in the world was to talk to him, and not in her heart or her interior monologue but in her everyday easy voice. And likewise with prayer. Prayer was an intrusion. It was not God she wanted, it was Hugo.

And, when it came right down to it, what had all this 'communion with God' really meant? Why 'God'? Why should there be 'a God'? She had never of course believed in a physical sort of God with arms and legs and private parts and so on, she was a bit better educated than that. She had read her A. N. Wilson. But she had believed in the God of the Apocalypse, in the great formalised throngs of the heavenly host, in precious stones and the horsemen prancing, the halo round the Light of Lights, the great eye that beholds.

She had believed that inside the eye of light there dwelt the essence of love, of love for her, Pammie (and Hugo), whatever she did or said so long as she attended to her worship and said the General Confession in church every Sunday and behaved through the week with a weather eye on doing what is right. But then Holly Fox had died.

A random nonsense.

And now Hugo had died. Wordlessly. One minute drinking tea at the window, the next a sad lump over the mower. Gone. And where? To the hosts of the Apocalypse? To eternal rest? He'd had eternal rest ever since he retired and quite a supply of it before that. What had he ever known about himself? What had she ever really known about him? Why had he wanted to marry her? If she had ever thought to ask him, would he have been able to remember? What had he seen in her as the years went by? A woman tearing about. Church on Sunday, leaving the house in her car at seven forty-five sharp. She had always prayed for him but had of course never said so. Back to breakfast she had zoomed, boiled eggs, *The Sunday Telegraph*, drinks before lunch, snooze, Bridge or the garden, a few friends round, easy telly, supper on knees, bed. What on earth had it all been about? The day God gaveth. 'A good Christian life,' the vicar had said, but what on earth was Christian about it? Christ had said sell up, go out and preach. He had said He brought not peace but a sword. She thought of Hugo happily eating crumpets every day at four o'clock in the centrally heated lounge.

Pammie considered Christ. She walked all round Him. She began to talk to Him, questioning Him keenly as if He were one of her old clients at the Citizens' Advice Bureau. What evidence had He for his doctrine of love? Why should God love her? Ridiculous, when you thought about it.

And what about the texts? 'In the beginning was the Word' – and yet Christ left behind words that now appear to be phoney or mistranslated or mischievous. It appears that we can't understand a word of the Gospels now unless we know both Greek and Hebrew. Mary is no Virgin, just a 'young woman' loosely related to the goddess Diana. As for the Resurrection . . . Pammie had never had the least difficulty with the Resurrection until the bishops got on to it. And some of them were homosexuals. And some people say that Christ was one. And that Judas was only misguided and Pilate a tragic hero. 'Do we all have to go out, then, and get ourselves a theological degree?' she enquired of Jesus. 'And where will that leave our good works, the fruits by which we are supposed to be known?'

'I'm afraid I'm having to cut down on my voluntary work,' Pammie wrote round. 'Since the death of my husband I am having a great deal to do with his financial affairs.' This was not true. Hugo had left things magnificently trim. She wrote a great number of these letters. To the vicar she made a telephone call, not wanting to make her resignation from the flower rota too formal and wondering if he might suggest when he heard her voice that he come and talk to her. But the vicar took the news bravely and rang off.

'What cock!' was the next stage, 'what absolute cock it all is!' and, as she said so, something like a heavy old mackintosh she had never much liked fell away from her shoulders. 'I don't really believe a bloody thing,' she said aloud and listened to herself. She prickled with excitement. She eyed the face of Jesus. (Because there's no doubt that He had a face. She didn't doubt the historical figure. She wasn't saying some consortium of magic had made Him up. Oh no.) She eyed Jesus, the middle-class carpenter of Galilee, and said, 'I can't begin to see why we're all so conditioned by You, a Middle-East cult figure with a three-year work span, dead two thousand years. Look where it's got us. Inquisitions, Northern Ireland, Bosnia, the Crusades. Look at this country. Packed once with saints. Holy Ireland. My eye! Rivers of blood, rioting, louts, thugs, football hooligans, mugging, all the churches dropping down. North-South divide. The whole world is a north-south divide. Fighting over religion every-where. From the beginning. Absolutely all the time. All of us supposed to be united by the Cross. There's only the Catholics now that bother with the Cross and even the nuns didn't send more than a note after all my years of Wednesdays.'

And all this Muslim business.

At this point the face of the Christ began to get hazy, much like the face in the coloured aquatint in Pammie's Confirmation Bible where the hair hung down the shoulders in ripples and The Saviour of the World sat in a white nightgown beside a well, with flowers growing in and out of His toes in the grass.

Well, you could see why Hugo had never bothered with any of it. Just sat rattling the newspaper. Oh, how she wished she had known how stupid she was being. He must have thought it. But he had known – how clearly she saw it now – he had known that her religion then, her church life, was all emptiness. He had never said so, never teased her, but he had known it was all show. Entertainment. Play. Oh, Hugo had been so wise. So clever. All the money he had made and without seeming to try. Tears came as she thought of Hugo sitting wisely, and saying nothing. The only man who had simply listened to her. Had loved her – well, had adored her. Look at all the things he had heaped upon her. She could go shopping and buy anything she wanted, anything in the world, and she still could, for the rest of her life. All she had to do was walk along to the bank. The bank was a limitless pot full of money. Or she assumed it was; she'd never been a spender. No time. *Oh, beloved sweet Hugo, when you think of some men. When you think of the deep certain order of my life with him here, and then of those shipwrecked people in the North, that mad place.* She meditated on the face of Hugo until it was surrounded by a great crater of light, Hugo swirling about somewhere in the depths or heights of it, and the trumpets sounding all about. *Well*, she thought, *I suppose it'll take time to get rid of the imagery. To reach full atheistical purity of thought. But I am on course now for a clean break.*

And when she next went to see friends for drinks it was Advent Sunday and someone was going on about Advent calendars for children. 'Will Thomasina send one to the baby, I wonder?' asked Jilly. Everyone else had rather laid things to do with Thomasina aside by now but Jilly took things slowly and rather hung on to them, and not too many of them since the gin had taken a stronger hold. 'Don't be silly,' said Nicky, 'it's only a baby. Poor brat, I feel like sending her a Christmas thing myself.'

'Maybe *you* will, Pammie?' said Didi.

Pammie examined her nails and said, 'Oh, I've given up all that rubbish. Christmas and so forth. I've forgotten all that Thomasina business. We can suffer far too much for other people.'

207

An anti-Christmas, anti-Christian gesture she felt must now be made. It must cut right into the heart of her life to show the change in her. Good sense. An appropriate good time. The heart of her life, the place that reflected all she now stood for, all that dear Hugo had stood for, was her house with its silk chairs and matching footstools, its fat curtains, gold wallpaper. She would transform it now into the sort of place she was convinced that Hugo had always wanted. Something to proclaim his wider-than-suburban success.

She would transform the house, beginning with this room. She would fling out the mahogany, sell the upholstered suite, give away the Victorian watercolours on the walls, replaster to remove all traces of the individual picture lights above each canvas, and she would throw away the huge portrait of herself that Hugo had never really liked, had said looked as if she was dying to consult her watch. Yes. And she'd scrap the fitted carpets and have instead a room that Hugo's young successors in the firm might envy, a young room that she should have made for him long ago. The floor would be black tweed; the walls, one coral and the rest white. Enormous floor cushions to sit on and in one corner an arrangement of Japanese lanterns, all hanging at different lengths, some almost touching the floor. She'd have oriental scrolls on pins and a tray of sand sculpture and a few big rocks on a glass table. She would get down to measuring it all out at once.

Pammie walked over to the garage where Hugo had kept tools and plumb lines and measuring rods. It was the first time she had stepped inside since his death.

The mower, of course, had been put away and all was tidy, but looking around for metal rods and measures she saw on a high shelf, almost out of sight behind the oil cans, the mail that Hugo had received the morning of his death.

It was mostly nothing. A few charity things. Some junk mail. The telephone bill she was pleased to see because she had thought it lost. There was also a rather grubby-looking letter stuck over with a Save the Trees label. The address was written in copperplate handwriting and the postmark was Whitby, North Yorkshire.

– 27 –

The Missus had gone. One morning, a Monday, she was not at the stove of the Ellerby Priors kitchen crashing with pans. As everyone appeared for breakfast, one by one, a bitch of a wet day, rain trailing across the courtyard in curtains, swirling down off the moor and quite cold at last, there was no fire lit, no table laid. Philip and (surprisingly) The Smikes arrived first. Philip had to be got to school. They stood about and after some time in came Jocasta, who sent Philip up to The Missus's room to see if she were ill. He came back to say that the room was empty and all her things gone, her car not under the gatehouse and how was he getting to school and it was maths.

Jack came in from the chapel.

This was unthinkable. The Missus had been about for many years, ever since she'd heard Jack preach in Rochdale the year he was ordained.

The Missus, Alice Banks, a sharp little woman, fierce and silent. Her family had been in the mills. She was registered as a Card, was The Missus. She hated joy. Joy got to her. Her *bête noire* was Gracie Fields, the world-famous Lancashire lass of her youth whose nightingale voice had drawn the crowds around her like shawls in their mutual birthplace. A golden creature, all laughter. 'I wouldn't cross t' street for 'er,' had said Alice Banks, The Missus. 'Loud clart. She were comin' back round t' mills that day and they give a holiday to stand int streets for 'er, yellin' and carryin' on. "Are yer not comin', then, Alice?" they said and I said, "I'd not cross t' road till 'er." I went ower t' church instead.'

She didn't say that Jack had been preaching that Friday, a young man like an angel, for she never discussed emotion or devotion. She had stayed behind after the service – the screams for Gracie loud in the street – and taken tea and buns with Jack and the slender congregation. Jack had asked her job and she'd said, 'I don't have un. They've closed t' prints,' and glared at him. 'I can cook,' she'd said, she never knew why. 'That I *can* do,' glaring harder, fit to kill. He had left with the impression that he had met a little bit of rough black jet that could cut you to bits but would never crumble.

He remembered Alice Banks when he went to his first parish and a vicarage the size of a college, a kitchen floor glazed with damp, silverfish flitting between the loose wet tiles, and he had set about finding her. She was there within the week, mouth like a cut, unsmiling eyes, hair of a witch. She looked round the ghastly place and got out her apron and a bucket. And never left him.

She never took a holiday ('Where would I go?') and seldom spoke directly to Jack, although she had made up her mind that he was now her life. She muttered as she worked, was unpopular in every parish, treated all-comers as honoured peasants lucky to be allowed audience, sent them all

211

(including, once, a bishop) round to the back door, and returned meat to the butcher with covering notes saying, 'This won't do for his reverence.' She had been seen in the henhouse haranguing the hens, urging them to point-of-lay. 'Git yersens movin', 'e 'as two eggs to 'is supper.'

The Missus had few possessions and, it appeared, no family. At Christmas there arrived only a very few shabby-looking cards, to which she paid scant attention and often didn't open. She was almost always silent, though if you did want any life to flow from her you had only to mention Gracie Fields.

She loved Jack. Of course she did. She was not in love with him, although she thought about him most of the time, for she saw him as beyond desire; but she was obsessed, nevertheless; by his gentleness, his innocence and his loving looks. They had been the first she had known. The day when, some weeks after her arrival at the first grisly vicarage, she took it upon herself to attend to his laundry was as much a stage in her spiritual life as a novitiate's first vows. Thereafter she rubbed away each week at his socks and underpants and shirts as at a sacrament, always washing by hand, hanging everything out ritually in neat even loops along the clothesline. She ironed and light-starched the oldest of his frayed handkerchiefs with the care of a wardrobe mistress for a star.

She began to knot for him, polish his shoes, restore his chaotic shirts, change his sheets and pillowcases, buy his shaving soap, toilet paper, toothbrushes, which he never acknowledged or noticed and seldom paid for.

Her cooking was dreadful, but Jack didn't seem to notice this either. She spent hours at it, boiling potatoes and cabbages to pulp, turning chops to cinders. She stood over him watching it all go down, stamping in with the second course, puddings like stone, custards covered with mackintosh which she slopped all over the plate from a height. Her expression was at these moments at its least terrifying, its nearest to fulfilment; the Creator surveying Her handiwork and finding it good.

Jack throve. Had it not been for The Missus everyone agreed that he would long ago have left the world, for he never ate unless food was set before him, and his appearance if left entirely to him would have been John the Baptist between locusts and unlikely to impress either the diocese or the Arts Council.

He paid her whatever she asked, which was very little, and had no idea of her needs. She was never ill, never elsewhere. In none of his ministries or ventures had he ever entered the room where she slept. At one place it had been a mattress on the floor of a cellar, but she did not tell him. As evangelical adventure after adventure came to grief under Jack's shining innocence and carelessness, she moved along with him to the next. She even went with him to Oxford, where he was housed for a time in a college, and found herself a job as a bedmaker and sat it out silently. Her conversation, when it came, when it was sometimes forced from her over cups of tea, harked back always to the same subject: Jack, the difficulty of working for him yet his obvious superiority to everyone else in the world. She had feared Oxford. She imagined that plans might be afoot there to trap him and tame him: Oxford, where Jack might forget the open air and where collars were not clean. When he went off with the gift of a disciple's money to set up a centre for Christian farmers in the Yorkshire Dales, where agricultural suicides in the winter months are not uncommon, and when the centre turned out to be a roofless stone shed on the open moor, she set about finding The Priors. Some said helped him buy it. Some said bought it for him outright.

She was growing old now, the cooking worse than ever, the cleaning long in abeyance, for her eyes were fading; but she was still there, still Jack's angry-looking champion, and whatever curiosities appeared in his professional behaviour, whatever hours he kept, when he lay prone on the moor or said the Offices of his faith all night long in the chapel alone, she accepted it with respectful silence. This was the form. This was Jack. He was hers. The marriage had not shaken her. She had detested Jocasta on sight but saw in her a woman without an inkling of how to put herself out for anyone, and therefore, she reasoned, Jack would need his housekeeper all the more.

Far and near, the marriage had been an amazement. It had enthralled all those who had ever known Jack. Celibate, saintly Jack – and pushing fifty! However had it come about? What sort of proposal had there been? How had it ever been accepted by this smouldering, resentful-looking intellectual gypsy, a woman who never aimed to please, sat apart, never seemed to do more than tolerate even her own son? Jocasta, it was said, would mark the end of Jack's greatest asset in life, The Missus.

But Alice Banks had no concept of physical jealousy. The lusts of the flesh had never come her way. Vaguely she knew that marriage is brought on by passion as pneumonia is preceded by fever. Passion she called daftness. Children resulted from it, but the process by which children were attained sounded to her as unpleasant as hospital treatment, ridiculous as morris dancing or Gracie Fields. She could not see how it could be practised for delight.

Poor, poor Alice Banks, how she hated happiness. Nothing so clamped her jaw as people appearing before her and expressing exuberant pleasure. When Holly Fox had paid a visit, prancing over the kitchen flagstones exclaiming and shrieking and lifting the lids off saucepans in a girlish, mischievous way, it had been a grim moment for The Missus. Holly's sunny smile had got her nowhere. When she had reeled back with a startled but kind smile from a pan full of pink mince, saying faintly, 'How delicious,' The Missus had very nearly slapped her hand with a spoon. 'Delicious, we'll see. It's what his reverence has Mondays, that's all. There's a table to be laid, young lady. It's twelve o'clock.'

When Toots and Dolly had asked The Missus how she had liked Andrew's wife she had said only that she was the music-hall type.

That first shrivelling winter when Jocasta had arrived, inert and beautiful in the corner of the kitchen, she had ignored The Missus. The Missus in turn had ignored her. *Sour little rabbit. Even that pale scrag of a little lad she's got has more life in him.* The Missus hated children but Philip she noticed, and at length found herself disarmed. His eccentricity and honesty and good looks were what had drawn her to Jack; and so with Philip, but, unlike Jack, Philip had attached himself to The Missus like a rather delightful flea. She began by snapping at him, then giving him orders, screaming at him to clean himself up, he wasn't in India now. She seized his shoes in exasperation and polished them, seized his hair and cut it with the kitchen scissors; in time she started playing cards with him. He called her Alice, as only Jack did, and she began to call him Phil, as only Jocasta did. The Smikes, who had known The Missus for years, would watch the quick-witted card games between the boy and the fierce old woman with wonder.

The Missus saw to Philip's school uniform as the years went by, had food ready for him when he got home, helped with his writing with an intense and astonishing patience, sometimes placing her claw of a hand over his and guiding it round the loops. Sometimes she thought, *I dunno. He might be Jack's own. 'E's not slow, 'e's original, that's what 'e is. 'E's 'imself.* 'Jocasta,' she'd shout. 'It's four o'clock. Get off for that boy, you'll be late.'

The fact that Jack and Jocasta did not sleep together did not interest The Missus at all. But once, this winter, after six years, Jocasta had come floating through the kitchen and put her arms round Jack in her presence, and they had stood close – close, close, close – for so long that she had been disgusted. And a little afraid. *What a show! Trying to tell me something. Nasty.*

She had stuck it out. She had gone on stirring at the porridge and her kitchen had survived undefiled. It had been Jocasta who had disentangled herself from Jack's long arms and left the room. And The Missus had reigned on.

Yet, three weeks later, The Missus, Alice Banks, was gone. After more than twenty years, gone. No note. No word. And why? And where?

'There'll be an explanation,' Jack said, looking desperately round. He was frightened that perhaps he had been told and forgotten. Some visit. Some break.

But The Missus never left the place, or just into Whitby or down into Teesside to see Dolly.

'She'll have gone to her family in Rochdale. There must be some trouble. We'll get a letter. I must have been told. I must think what she said.'

'She'd have said goodbye. *Has* she a family?'

'She doesn't say goodbye,' said Jack. 'I don't think so. I expect there's some family about somewhere. She'll be back.'

But then, her belongings? Her clothes? All were gone from the room over the gatehouse below the guest room in the hospitium. Alice Banks had been no jackdaw but Philip – who had often visited her room to tell her stories as she knitted and listened to Radio Two turned up full blast and said, 'Very well, then, stop romancing. Let's have a spot of truth' – Philip said there had been quite a lot of boxes and newspapers and shoes in rows. All gone now.

Then Jimmie, the postman, stopped off and said that she'd passed him in her car down the ridge, going towards Teesside estuary, the Middlesbrough road. 'She weren't lookin' herself,' he said, 'in a felt hat.'

Andrew said that he and Jocasta would follow The Missus – go down to Toots and Dolly and find out if anything had been seen of her. It was afternoon by now. Philip, who had been taken to school by Andrew, would have to be brought back either by one of The Smikes, who said it was their day off again, or, heaven preserve the child, by Jack. Jack drove sketchily and often turned up at the wrong place, thinking it was a different day and a different mission. Jocasta said no. Not Jack. '*Right*?' She had blazed up like a fire. Everyone stared. 'Jack's not to go for Philip. I'll go. He's not safe.'

'But we have to talk,' said Andrew, following her out to the car. 'You must come with me to Dolly's. It's the only chance we'll get.'

'I can't risk Philip. Jack's driving's lethal. I've risked everything else. I've risked everything for you, Andrew, from the minute I met you. Right up to last night. That's it.'

'Last night can be explained. If we can find her, we can tell her.'

'Nobody explains to that woman. She knows everything, judges everything, forgives nothing. Always Jack, Jack – she's obsessed by him. Oh you fool, fool, fool, Andrew! You knew her long before I did. Jack's her reason for being. She'd die for him. To keep him from hurt is what she thinks she's born for. You and I are nowhere. She'd cut our throats.'

'Then how could she leave him?'

'I don't know. Shock. I think I'll go for Philip.'

'OK, then. I'll go down to Toots. I'll take the baby. They still haven't seen her.'

'Do what you like. I've had enough,' she said.

'So why did you come to me last night?'

She drove off, Andrew watching as the car passed under the gatehouse arch and out of sight. Then he turned and went into the kitchen, where his brother was standing about wondering whether to make tea.

'I suppose we might tell the police,' Jack said, looking childish, with hanging hands, his face quite old. 'Do you suppose . . . ' there was a great pause ' . . . that I have neglected Alice? I've never sat down with her to talk, you know, not for years. It's possible that it has suddenly come to her that' – he looked up like a penitent – 'I am a very selfish man.'

Andrew took the drooping teapot from his brother's paw and made tea. He did not look at Jack.

They sat and faced each other across the great oak table. A sense of The Missus, black with contempt, hung about the room.

Andrew thought, *I shall tell him now. There will never be a right time. We are alone, for once. It must be done.*

Yet he ought to ask Jocasta first. Jack ought to be told by them both together. He could not bear Jack to hear it from somewhere else and there would probably be a letter from the bloody Missus woman tomorrow, telling all. No, he must tell Jack now.

If of course The Missus could bear to hurt Jack, by letter or in any way. Her flight surely meant that she could not. Her flight was the most abstruse hint that she could give. She would never be able to keep the great hurt that was being done to Jack to herself, to live with it, to watch it happen again and again whenever Andrew came up from London, to watch the unspeakable foulness of it grow familiar. To see Andrew grow easy, smug, sated; to see Jocasta's lazy joy.

The surprise was that The Missus, the night before, hadn't charged him with the enormity of it there and then, head-on in the doorway of his bedroom as she stood there with her pathetic torch. A pointing finger, a loud Lancashire voice shouting, rage and disgust. But she had vanished. At one moment holding the door open wide, her black hair in ridges of metal clips, her midget body swathed in an old brown coat of Jack's trailing on the floor over her nightie, wellingtons on her feet, torch shining on the bed – and he had turned in the bed and seen it all, over his bare shoulder. He had been covering Jocasta, yet she might – must – have seen Jocasta's face, sideways on the pillow, her hair loose, her eyes dreaming. Then the doorway empty and The Missus gone.

And Jocasta had said, 'Don't worry. Stay with me.'

Andrew had climbed out of bed and dressed. 'Stay with me,' she had kept saying. His horror had not been because of being found out or because of what he had done, but because Jocasta had said, 'Stay with me.'

Then fear had come flooding in. He had felt Alice Banks's terrible unblinking eyes.

'Stay with me, Andrew.'

And he had said no and run for it.

Left her alone, not even shutting his door behind him. He had gone across the courtyard to Jocasta's room and sat in it for the rest of the night, taking pleasure in growing colder and colder until dawn came sluggishly and he heard sounds about the place. Over in the dormitories the visitors were stirring and he thought he heard his daughter crying.

The thought – more than the thought: the bright imprinted image – of Holly was suddenly there with him. She seemed to be waving from somewhere or other in a blue dress.

They were in California, picnicking on a jaunt through the gold-rush towns on the way to the Big

220

Trees. Rolls of airy cottonwood floated and scratched about the road ahead of them. Lean men with walnut-creased faces sold walnuts from roadside sacks. A hot fog had come down over the plain, then lifted and left blue air. They sat beside the road together with a thermos flask and sandwiches in the sun – Holly had never taken to American food though she never let on. She would ask scrawny, health-mad LA women to tea and give them little egg-and-cress sandwiches and butterfly cakes, little boat-shaped bridge rolls spread with the Gentleman's Relish sent out by Thomasina from Piccadilly.

'Darling – look!' Far away to the east a snowy fluted blue-white feather lay across the sky.

'What is it?'

'D'you know,' he said, 'it's the High Chaparral – we are actually looking at the High Chaparral.'

She licked Gentleman's Relish off a roll in the sharp autumn air and they laughed like kids. They behaved as though they'd been granted a vision. *'High Chaparral,'* they shouted.

'Oh, I'm halfway to heaven, Andrew. All I want's a baby to make one out of the two of us. We'll call it High Chaparral.'

'Or Klondyke Kate,' he said, 'or Cottonwood, or Redwood, or Gentleman's Relish. You are the Gentleman's Relish.'

The air so clean and gold, the road so white. It stretched so straight and empty over the plain.

Why ever did we come back? he thought. *This bloody, shabby, threadbare, worn-out country. Grubby and poor as a Balkan republic. Medicine in chaos, hospitals closing, no bloody money, tiny, racist, divided North and South, living on its past.*

As he shivered in the crumbling medieval ruin that in the South or in Scotland, even in Ireland, might have had a spot of limewash to brighten it – on the Continent it would have been restored with plaster or pulled down – Andrew saw The Priors in its soggy hollow of the moors as a trashy place, a sentimental notion, cranky, quaint, nostalgic, a half-baked idea of a revival of early Christian asceticism.

'Taking in the poor' – and who are they? Liverpool Tibetans, whatever that means. How could Tibetans get here? Phoneys. Frauds. The whole set-up run by a lunatic, and the lunatic my brother at that.

As it grew light Andrew went looking for a bath but found someone ahead of him in the vaulted bathroom, the geyser roaring angrily. Instead he pulled on some clothes and went out into the first frost of the year, over the courtyard to the sheds. He thought he'd take a look at Faith and found her being dressed, lying on a mat in the steamy dormitory.

Behind her on a shelf there were little lamps flickering. The air was scented with sweet oils. One of the women was praying over the lamps one by one. There were only four Tibetans now, and there were five lamps. Pema, who was bending over his child, looked up at Andrew and then away. Faith lay naked, arms and legs kicking in ecstatic jerks, eyes watching the flickering line of the lamps. She arched her back and complained about being fastened into the nappy, then flopped down again and raised her legs in the air. Far above were her pink feet. She examined her toes. She conversed with them. Her eyes reflected the lamplight. She looked as far back as she could over her head at the ceiling.

'May I take her?'

'No. She has her bottle now.'

'Later?'

'Oh yes. If you like. Come, come; come, pretty,' said Pema.

'She's mine, you know.'

'She's her own girl, right?' said the A-level girl.

'She has good eyes,' he said. 'That right one's cleared up well. Hospital didn't do much good. Just needed time.'

'She sees fine,' said Pema, who had used a salve out of an old cough-sweet tin she kept about her. She'd smeared it over the eyelids every day for a fortnight. 'She sees far away over the mountains.'

And she's mine, thought Andrew, walking fast up towards the ridge. *I must remember*.

His total lack of feeling for the baby, Holly's baby, frightened and shocked him. He tramped off piste into the frosted heather half hoping he could get lost in it.

Oh my God, my God, the child is mine. No one can take her without my permission. I must get her away from here. Learn to like her. Have to, now. All over here now. Shall go today. End the thing with Jocasta. End this vile mess. Oh God, how terrible. But he could not say 'End this sin'. It was a great sin. To lie with a brother's wife. He could not say it, only feel it deep, deep, far out of words.

He saw The Smikes shambling about below him as he turned and set off bleakly back again. Philip, shoelaces trailing, school tie in a noose, crossed the yard. Then, not wanting to, trying not to, Andrew watched Jocasta and Jack walking side by side to

223

breakfast together, Jocasta composed and neat, Jack tall above her, smiling down. Jocasta was walking calmly towards the kitchen, where reigned The Missus, who had confronted her in the night.

I'll leave now, Andrew thought. *Just go. Send for the child later. Pammie Jefford might come for her. I could even . . .* and, though he knew no reason for it, his eyes all at once brimmed with tears . . . *I could even go to Thomasina. I could beg her.*

With a surge of longing, for some sort of absolution, for the chance of letting in a corner of light on the chasm left by the death of Holly not filled but deepened by the obsession for Jocasta, Andrew thought, *I might tell Thomasina everything.*

He had seen her at the funeral of Pammie Jefford's husband, which he'd gone to out of gratitude and respect for Pammie and hoping ridiculously that Jocasta might be there. And Jocasta had been there. And without Jack, who was tied by the farm, as ever. Afterwards he had spent the night with Jocasta in a hotel room and he had thought there had never been such abandon and happiness and anguish. As he had put her on the train back to The Priors, they had both been dazed, drained, drenched by the night.

Now, the terror of The Missus with her gorgon head of steel, her terrifying passion for Jack, the voice of Jocasta saying, 'Stay with me,' and the sight of her walking unconcernedly beside Jack towards the kitchen for breakfast prepared and presided over by The Missus. And the memory of the child he could not love who stretched up confident arms to things he did not understand, had her eyes fixed on invisible things – all this, and physical exhaustion, too, gathered inside him a well of shame, a glut of shame, a need for cleansing.

It was Thomasina's face at the funeral of Pammie's old man, the face he had known as cynical and witty over the betrothal champagne, bright and competent at her daughter's wedding, unbearable to contemplate in the antiseptic gleam of the health farm, absent at Holly's funeral, blank and lost as she passed him in the Jaguar on the ridge with the ancient boyfriend; the face that he had seen last at Jefford's funeral was a face grown old. Thomasina an old woman. Yet alive now in some sense and perhaps ready now freely to receive, freely to give.

I'll go to Thomasina, now, he thought. *She will take Faith now, I know she will. She will take me. We could live together near London, out of all this, the three of us.*

So right, so beautiful, so inevitable did this solution seem that the night hours, the knowledge of sin and chaos, went into the shadows, thinned, evaporated. He started walking down towards The Priors again as one shriven, even as one blessed.

And he found a cold room, no fire in the stove, no table laid, no food to be seen, everyone gathered helpless and unbelieving.

'Gone?' he said. 'She can't have gone.'

Jocasta turned away and began to cut bread, which she passed round. Philip found some butter and jam and began to eat. Ernie Smike filled a kettle with cold water and slapped it on the cold stove, which had gone out. Nick Smike said there was an electric kettle somewhere, maybe over with the Tibetan lot, but did nothing to find out. Philip opened a can of Coke and swigged it from a hole in the top and said, 'So, who's getting me to school?'

When Jocasta's car had disappeared with Philip,

Andrew had stood in the courtyard watching it away, thinking that he had seen Jocasta for the last time. For the last time.

But he could not just go. This morning. Just leave the place and the baby – now. It would look suspiciously wild. He must speak to Thomasina first. Or to Pammie at any rate. He must see Jocasta again and discuss what to tell Jack. He must tell Jocasta, tell her that now that he and the baby and Thomasina would be living together in the south he would not be coming back up here again. Ever. Over. Except of course now and then to see his parents. They were getting old. He'd neglected them for a long time. But he could visit them without coming up to The Priors. No one need ever know of any rift between the brothers.

And, come to that, was there, realistically, any need to tell Jack? Tell him everything? Or – well, anything at all? Jack's shining soul, God help him, would never for an instant suspect. Never suspect his brother's sin. There. He'd said it. Christ! Sin. Not much talk of sin these days. We don't live in classical times. Oedipus. Phaedra. Jocasta. Vengeance of the gods – all unknown now.

We're all trivial now, thought Andrew, *hardly Titans falling from heaven, lost gods lying blinded along a darkened plain. No one believes in heaven. Religion's an affected joke, patchwork, ridiculous, easy to forget. 'Love' is talked about all the time, 'adoration' even, but not in relation to God. No eagles now. All sparrows.*

He thought of silly Holly, sexy and laughing and obvious, of her child in the lamplight, of Jack's narrow sweet face. A wonderful face. His fortune. Women loved it. Always had. Even old Pammie in her pearl studs and her million-pound house.

226

And Jocasta?

There had been a sensual, submissive quiet about Jocasta walking this morning beside Jack after the tempestuous night. Jack's hand had touched the back of Jocasta's neck for a moment as they had passed through the door to the kitchen and she had not shrunk away. Jack had looked down at her with love.

A great wave of longing for Jocasta filled Andrew now. Jocasta, my Jocasta, his heart called.

Her voice calling after him, 'Stay with me.' Was it, maybe, after all, not unforgivable?

– 28 –

When Pammie saw the letter on the high shelf in the garage above the spot where poor Hugo had laid down his head for the last time, she stood for a moment looking at it. She took it in her hands. The junk mail and the phone bill she put in her pocket. She examined the old-fashioned handwriting on the Yorkshire envelope.

She wondered why she felt so still. Then she realised that she wasn't talking to anyone. The relentless, exhausting inner voice that accompanied her everywhere, even in dreams, was quiet. She had no desire to share this curious event. And at the same time she had the mad notion that the letter must be from Hugo. That he had got it to her from wherever he had gone. And then she thought, *I'm going mad. It must be a letter of condolence*, and walked into the house.

Standing once more in the rosy drawing room about to be demolished in favour of Japan, she thought, *But it couldn't be. He wasn't dead then*.

She considered a letter of condolence for one's own death being put into one's hands ahead of time by the postman. The Black Spot. Enough to give you a heart attack.

But it hadn't been opened. Maybe – stretching up to the shelf and then stooping down to the mower – it had been Hugo's Black Spot. She saw it happen. Yet, even so, the voice of the full-time whispering raconteur, the entertainer of unsuspecting Jinny and Laura and Didi and Wendy and Thomasina, kept silence. For more important than the telling of this macabre little happening, Pammie found, was the happening itself.

And after all, here it was: it was a letter of condolence before death – a letter written two days before Hugo's departure to greener lawns.

'My dear Mrs Jefford,' it said, 'I was so sorry . . .'

It must be from some seer.

But it went on. 'I was so sorry not to have been able to see you properly on to the London train the other day and now I wish so much that I had not burdened you with the potatoes. I very much blame myself after your incredibly tiring day for insisting that we stop to see the church of St Ethelswitha and St Eadburga (who was, of course, King Alfred's mother) and the lovely market town of Stokesley. I very seldom drive these days on account of absent-mindedness and I misjudged the time it would take to get to York. The full glory of the day was upon me, the mixture of sorrow and joy. Our Holly's death and the arrival of Faith at The Priors have rather disoriented me. I don't believe any of us has ever thanked you for the valiant rescue of my niece, but I promise you it will never be forgotten by her family. You and your husband are welcome here not only to see the child but whenever you wish to come for a holiday, to stay as long as possible. We have, as you saw, plenty of room! I should like to say that your bracing presence and common sense –

and, if I may say so, your lovely face – steadied us all on a very emotional day and you are remembered in our prayers.

'There is much I want to show you. Our Tibetans. Jocasta, whom you did not really meet. Faith's grandparents, who are very keen to meet and thank you. God bless you. Until your next visit,

'Jack Braithwaite.'

One would have expected this from Andrew, she thought, sitting on a velvet humpty, gazing at the doomed mock-Adam fireplace with its twirl of heather in the grate like *Country Life*. She had found the heather pushed into the top of the bag of potatoes.

The whirlwind day in Yorkshire returned to her. She had forgotten most of it. It seemed distant. Mixed with guilt. The guilt of having left Hugo alone when he had had such a short time to go. That in turn had led to the guilt of having neglected him during the time when they had housed the baby.

Not that she had ever hung over the baby. Like all childless women, Pammie did not believe in hanging over babies. 'Babies need letting alone and if they cry they cry,' thought and declared Pammie, who had never been kept awake by anything in her life. Her dogs as puppies had been banished to an outhouse with a nice rug and a ticking clock for company. They had been very well-behaved dogs; you hardly knew they were there. That is how, she had told the night nurse, she should treat Faith.

Hugo had done more hanging about over Faith than she. The baby had never gripped her finger and smiled. Pammie had a secret notion that it hadn't gripped Hugo's finger either. He'd been so dotty. It was probably the nurse's finger he'd caught hold of.

No. That wouldn't do. Hugo had been faithful. Always. Proud of her and her busy life. Found it commendable. Funny. Liked the way she biffed about. Made jokes about it. She'd liked the jokes and overdid the biffing to have more of them, pinning up lists of future events and phone numbers all over the kitchen, getting Christmas finished before anyone else. All the presents bought and wrapped by December the first. Dear old Hugo.

'*Your lovely face.*'

Well.

She reread the letter, wondering why exactly she liked it so much. *There wouldn't be much bought and wrapped at The Priors by December the first. Or the twenty-first. The state of that office place. And that boy's hair. Looked cut with the kitchen scissors. And the old witch stirring over the stove. And the grease in that refectory!*

She began to consider what she knew of Christmases in religious institutions. Her Christmas cards had often pictured such scenes. *Rollicking tonsures. One couldn't imagine a Christmas card depicting The Priors, not unless it was an appeal for the Third World. But such lovely country. It must be looking beautiful now, probably under snow. Thomasina suggested Cyprus for Christmas but they hadn't done anything about it yet. Not one word from the dreaded Andrew. Good of him to come to the funeral, of course. The little dark woman with him must have been the terrifying Jocasta. How good of Jack to send her to stand in for him, especially as she was obviously his wife only in a very bohemian sort of way. She didn't look the type you ordered around. Maybe she was one of those romantics – those Arthurian romantics, playing at courtly love, that you hear about still. Though not likely. She must have wanted*

231

to come. I wonder who had the baby overnight. Not a word in this letter about how the baby is doing. Probably hasn't noticed. Unworldly. Not exactly the family man. A bit crazy.

'Lovely face', he says, 'if I may say so.'

And thinking of Hugo's old noddle wagging up and down over the baby's cot Pammie remembered it was Hugo, the morning he died, who had suggested they go north to visit The Priors, together for a nice weekend, and she rose from the humpty, crossed the room and dialled the number.

As the phone rang far away in the cold old ruin she hung on and on, looking out at her garden through the magnificent potted azaleas on the windowsill to the odd rogue rose still dancing and springing about untidily, brilliantly, eight feet high above the box parterre, the odd gold leaf, the odd still-juicy branch of singed and shrivelled buddleia. A desultory blue pyre rose from the last hedge-clippings over on the bonfire place behind and in front of the mirrored trellis and drifting leaves lay all over the grass. *Whatever would Hugo say?*

The phone rang on and on in the office of The Priors, for so long that the Tibetan girl came over at last from the sheds, Faith hanging fore and aft under her arm. But by the time she reached it Pammie had rung off.

'Yes? Hello?' Jocasta, getting out of the car from the school run, saw the girl coming from the office into the courtyard. 'D'you want something? What's under your arm?'

The girl put the roll of padded matting up on her shoulder. A face looked out, like an owl in a hollow tree.

'Oh, Faith. Well, she's warm enough anyway. What do you want?'

'The phone was ringing.'

Jack came from the direction of the chapel, carrying a bucket. '*Yes*? The Missus? Where is she?'

'I missed it. Rang off as I picked it up. Been ringing on and on. Driving you crazy. I went over to try to stop it.'

'Why was no one there?' asked Jocasta.

'I had chickens to feed.' Jack lowered his eyes before her.

'Where's Andrew, then?'

'He's gone down to Toots. In case Alice is there. Or in case they've heard something from her.'

'I thought he wasn't going down there again unless the baby was with him. They're very upset they haven't seen her.'

'I know. He felt he couldn't. She wasn't ready.'

'Pema says 'er eye's gone wrong agen,' said the girl. 'And there's a message from Pema. She says there's more food needed in the sheds. We're out of everythin'.'

'The Missus isn't here today, I'm afraid.' Jack looked helplessly at Jocasta. 'Somebody else will have to take over.'

'I don't cook,' said Jocasta.

'Well, you can eat with us lot if yer like,' said the girl. 'Just get us in some stuff, like. Or I can go down Whitby. I could get some takeaways.'

'Well, I've a class now,' said Jocasta, 'if you're all ready?'

She walked with the baby and the girl to the studio shed while Jack went alone to the office and wondered what to do. Sitting in all the dust, he moved his hands over the mess of papers. The hands were dirtied by the chicken mash and he remembered there'd been no soap in the bathroom this morning. There was a button off his shirt cuff and he pressed the edges together hopefully, wishing they would stick. He thought of Jocasta's neat clothes. *They don't do things for men any more*, he thought, and drooped. He had a facility for this, almost sensuous, a wilting of the frame, head bowed in humility. God watching.

He thought of his mother waddling up and down that passage in the house on the estuary over fifty years. Ten and thirty times a day with offerings for Toots. Paddle, paddle. Carrying Toots's beautifully polished shoes with the pressed laces.

The telephone rang.

'Hello? Hello? Missus? Alice?'

'I'm sorry, no. Is that Jack Braithwaite? This is Pammie Jefford.'

He couldn't imagine who that was.

'I've just seen your letter.'

'My letter?'

'Written just before my husband died.'

'Oh. Yes. I do hope that it was helpful.' Then he remembered her. 'Oh, I'm so sorry. I didn't write about that. I purposely sent Jocasta instead to the funeral. The farm . . . I felt that prayers for you would be more valuable. I do hope so. Letters of condolence only have to be answered. I didn't forget you, my dear.'

'Thank you.' *He sounds ninety.* 'No, this was a letter you wrote me earlier. About the day I spent with you. When I brought Faith. I've just found it. It had been – mislaid.'

There was a pause, growing long. Pammie in Coombe felt herself grow shy. When she realised that Jack had forgotten about the letter and the affection in it, she found to her great surprise that she was crying.

'I brought you the baby.'

The pause continued. She had been cut off?

Then Jack said slowly, 'I don't suppose you could possibly . . .'

The wallpapery room swam, the pot plants trembled. Pammie found her handkerchief. She said – and it came out aggressively – 'What?'

' . . . come here again? We're in a bit of trouble. My old housekeeper has, well, actually disappeared. I don't like to ask. I hear you're very high-powered. Justice of the Peace. On committees and so on. Can't pretend it's comfortable here.'

'I'll let you know,' she said and rang off as the room came back into focus.

She tossed the letter into the flower-painted wastepaper basket, chucked the measuring rod for the home improvements on to a chair, went into the kitchen and made coffee. She poured the coffee into an ornate green and gold cup, placed a silver teaspoon in the saucer, carried the coffee to Hugo's old study and sat in his polished swivel chair. She sat. *Bloody cheek*, she thought. Then she swivelled round in it, full circle. Once. She dialled Thomasina.

'My dear! Now, whatever do you think about this? What do you think I should do? Yes – *now*! So I gather. Gret crisis. *Oh*, yes. Some sort of walkout by staff. Yes, I gather that too: storms in teacups – they're never without them up there. Not enough to do. They're all a bit mad. Hysterical. Life full of nothing but incidents you and I could fix in five minutes. It's the North. These people talk about them afterwards for years. Oh no – my dear, I am *not* smitten. Yes, I know he's charismatic or whatever they call it. He's years younger than me and he's married. In a sort of way.

'Imposition? Well, I don't know. *Is* it, Thomasina? You? No, you shouldn't be the one to go. Don't let me mess you about, suggesting that. You know how we all felt about Egypt, but that's your affair. You don't have to grovel. Yes – OK, then. I'll leave it. I won't say another word. You've been very good to me since then. Nobody could have been kinder.

'Andrew? Haven't you heard from him? He's *dropped* you! How could he, you're Holly's mother. It just isn't done and even if he's from the back of beyond he's a gent. Yes, I know he's worked off his feet. He looked awful in Yorkshire. His brother's twenty years older, different generation, but he looked the better horse, I must say. Quite young, really. Jack Braithwaite's the sort that doesn't age. It's all that curly hair and the Thomas Hardy look – though, mind you, Thomas Hardy wouldn't have lasted up there ten minutes. No golden harvests and lands of the great dairies up there, Thomasina dear. No cider apples and greenwood trees. A frightful barren place. How he does it with only two village idiots – well, you've been there. I'll give you some of his potatoes.

'Thomasina? Thomasina – are you there? Yes, I'm better, of course I'm better, I started to feel better this morning. Hugo wouldn't have wanted . . . I had a letter from him this morning. No, of course not. From Jack. Written just before dear Hugo set sail. Very nice. Lovely letter. It's what I rang for.

'Yes, it would mean no Cyprus for Christmas . . . I did just wonder, well, it's occurring to me now, actually, I suppose you wouldn't feel like spending Christmas at – well, northwards?'

'I'll ring back,' said Thomasina.

A crash from the kitchen had signalled a crisis from the general, who was making wine on the end of the kitchen table.

'Trouble with the bungs,' he said.

'Pammie,' she said carefully, as she swept up the green splinters into a long-handled dustpan with a long-handled nylon broom – her fingernails so pretty, not a crack in the lacquer – 'Pammie on the phone. She's thinking of going up to see the baby again.'

'It's far too far to go up and back in one day.'

'She *indicated*,' Thomasina handed him the dustpan of debris to carry across the kitchen to the litter bin with its white plastic lining, 'that she might be going to live there.'

'My God!'

'And also she wondered if I'd like to go too. Join her there for Christmas.'

'Alone?' he asked, not looking at her, showering out the broken bits of glass.

'She didn't say. She hasn't actually agreed to go herself yet. She's had some sort of loving letter from Jack. She doesn't know it yet but it's the letter he writes to everyone.'

'But isn't he married?'

'He married a hanger-on of Andrew. To comfort her.'

'Who told you that?'

'Well – Holly, actually.'

'And Holly?' He went over and put his arms round her. '*Holly*? Go on then, Thoms.'

'Well, Holly was rather naughty really. It wasn't a bit like her. She just said once that Andrew had told Jack to have pity on one of his troublesome ex-patients and take her off his hands.'

'Jack was *obliging* Andrew? How very odd.'

She started laughing and the general joined in with a few snorts.

'I mean,' he said, 'dear Jack doesn't sound exactly Heathcliff.'

'I don't know,' she said. 'Some women go mad for skin and bones. I do rather.'

'And you can't call Pammie Catherine Earnshaw,' said the general.

'I didn't know you were an intellectual, darling.'

'No fear. I saw it on a telly ad. I say – it's rather good to be laughing, Thomasina.'

She was frying (in butter) tiny pieces of liver with sage, dropping them deftly into the pan.

After lunch they were going to Bentalls of Kingston to see after a new eiderdown for Thomasina's bed, getting rid of the vulgar duvet. Then home in time to walk the new dog in the lanes.

At six, over sherry, the general said, 'Happy, Thoms? Not hankering after the blasted heath?'

She said, 'Shall we watch *Blind Date*? It's so awful. I adore it.' She eased off her shoes.

'What thinking?' he asked at bedtime before he set off for home, kissing her cheek.

'Nothing.'

'Tell me.'

Both knew that it had nothing to do with the fact that he was going home.

She closed her eyes and he took her by the shoulders.

'Say it, woman!'

'Wondering,' she said, 'what to buy the wretched baby for Christmas.'

'Why not say "Faith"?'

– 29 –

Toots gave a bellow from his bed at teatime and Dolly came running, to find him pointing a furious finger at the dark winter window. 'She's out there.'

'Who? What are you on about?'

'Her. Middleditch. Standing out on the grass, looking in.'

'Don't be so soft. When did she ever not walk straight in through the door? It's what you can't stand, the way she comes in. It's years since there was by your leave.'

'I tell you, she's out on that grass, looking puzzled.'

'It's too dark to see anyone looking puzzled. It's too dark to see if you're rambling,' said Dolly, 'but just in case you're not . . . ' She tapped on the glass and called, 'Mrs Middleditch? Hello? Don't stand in the cold.'

No reply came from the frosty garden but some scuffling sounds were going on in the direction of the front door, a kind of stamping.

'It'll be the boot scraper,' said Dolly. 'She's been in the flower bed. She's gone off her head. What we have to put up with, being old, the sort of people we have to know, and all in the name of charity. It's the worst thing she's ever done, walking in from the flower bed.'

'She'll have buggered up the bulbs. I've a mind to tell the police.'

'Maybe it isn't her at all. It might be muggers.'

But in burst Mrs Middleditch in her broderie anglaise and good cardigan and zip jacket and mackintosh and muffler. She erupted before them.

Curiously she seemed to have nothing to say.

'A cup of tea, Mrs Middleditch?' asked Dolly.

'Oh, no, thank you. I have to be getting back. Actually, I've been thinking . . .'

'Oh yes?'

'I wondered if you'd both like to come round to me for a cuppa?'

'Dolly can go,' said Toots at once. 'It's after dark. I don't stir after dark.' His zimmer frame was by the bed, his calliper alongside on the blankets like a sword on a tomb. A thriller lay across his chest and bottle of whisky which could be reached at top speed was in the cupboard. 'Do her good. Never goes out.'

'Is it a birthday?' Dolly warily asked.

'No, no. Not at all. But . . .'

They had never seen her hesitant. Nonplussed.

Toots thought, *He's left her. About time.*

'*But*,' said Mrs Middleditch, 'we have a visitor and we don't know what to do with her. I think one of you should come to her since she won't stir. It's that Alice Banks.'

'At your house?' The Missus?'

'Yes. She's landed.'

'Now you must have asked her, Beryl,' said Dolly, using the given name on account of the seriousness of the moment.

'Asked her? Never. I hardly know the woman.'

240

'She must be confused. She's confusing you with us. She's never been very normal.'

'No. I don't think so. She calls me by my name. Arnold would be more *au fait* with what to do about her. Tonight he has to be out, of course, with his work for the Boys' Brigade. She's settled in and her car's locked up in the road. For the night, it looks. Packed with stuff.'

'She's not been in that car – I don't know when I remember her off in that car,' said Dolly. 'What if it snows? She'll never get back.'

'Packed full,' said Beryl Middleditch, flushing, 'to the gunnels. Packed up with shoes and boxes and heaps of rags. There's an electric kettle and a whole pack of grapefruits. I'd think she's left Jack.'

'Dolly, get your hat on,' said Toots. 'And wrap up: it's a cold night. Go after her and bring her round here. I'll settle this.'

'Oh, I'm sure there's no need for that.' Mrs Middleditch was bewildered by another's taking command. She hadn't known Toots at the height of his authoritarian powers. This was part of the trouble. She treated him as an old chap. 'It's just that I find her rather confused,' she said.

'Talking about Gracie Fields, I dare say?'

'Well, as a matter of fact she is.'

'Yes, she does.'

Dolly departed with Middleditch. Toots shot out of bed and, ignoring the hardware around him, made for the cupboard on flat but confident feet. Sitting on the bed end, he took a good swig and filled up the bottle to its previous level from a bottle of ginger ale kept for the purpose. The whisky tasted filthy because of this process having been followed many times before, more ale now than grog. But still, there was something left to cheer the heart. The telephone rang and, being made amiable by the noggin, Toots eased himself down the passage to the hall chair and picked up the phone.

'*Toots*!' said Thomasina? '*Dear* Toots! You have a phone by your bed.'

'Who? Thomasina? Well, my godfathers! Thomasina. I don't believe it. How are you? By Gad, we think of you. Dolly's out. There's a mad woman sitting in somebody's house. How's our granddaughter?'

'Thank you, dear Toots, for your lovely letter,' she said. 'I'm sorry. I couldn't answer. I went to Egypt.'

'Very nice.' He thought, *I mustn't forget to ask after Holly*, and then remembered. He was doing that sort of thing nowadays. 'By Gad,' he said instead, several times, 'Thomasina!'

'I was thinking of coming up.'

'Then you'll stay here,' he said at once. 'We've three spare rooms now that I'm downstairs. And bring that sexy green dress.'

She laughed and said he was a disgraceful old man and who was the mad woman down the street? He listened carefully, on his better ear, to her southern voice. Her face came back to him.

'It's very nice of you to ring here,' he said. 'We can't be very interesting to you.'

'You were always riveting, Toots. The things that went on.'

'I remember you coming visiting here once,' he said. 'I remember you sitting on the piano stool. The first time they came back from California, the three of you together. You've lovely legs.'

'Yes. I remember.'

'I said "You have lovely legs".'

'Now then, Toots. Toots –' she said ' – I was just ringing. Wanted to hear you.'

'You're a brave woman, Thomasina.'

'Oh no. I ran to Egypt.'

'Well, who wouldn't run? If we'd lost Jack or Andrew, I don't know how far we'd run. If we had the money. That was our advantage. By, but we pitied you, Thomasina, how we pitied you. We wept for you, and for all of us.'

'Don't, Toots.'

'Baby lovely, I hear.'

'Yes. Well, I expect you know more about that. You'll have seen her often.'

'Well, now then, as a matter of fact – they're very busy up there, you know. And there's the weather. There's always something going on. We'll be going up there for Christmas, unless it snows.'

'That's what I was going to say. Christmas. If I could come up for Christmas – no, we'd stay in a hotel, I wouldn't land the two of us on you. I have a friend. There's a hotel up on the moors near The Priors. But we would see you both, Toots, wouldn't we?'

'We'll be there,' he said. 'Unless it snows. They're putting on a Christmas show up there – three kings and so on, and Faith's to be christened. Nativity thing.'

'And we would see *you*?'

'You would. I'll make sure of it. There's sixes and sevens up there at present with this mad woman. Barmy about Jack for twenty years and she's made off with a car full of shoes. Left him. Housekeeper.'

'Not The Missus! Well! If she wants another job, tell her there's one down here for her. A dotty old lady and a man called Puffy. We – my friends and I –

243

are desperate for them.'

'Oh, everyone's desperate about old folk,' said Toots, 'I can't think why. Everyone's desperate about us two. "Where will it end?" – they hang about the gate saying it to each other – "Where will it end for the pair of them?" That sort of thing. You know, life's very comfortable. It's laughable if you don't read the papers. There's some terrible fools about. But it makes entertainment.'

Ringing off, she thought, *I like those people so.*

Ringing off, he thought, *Well, how about that, then? Thomasina! Lovely woman. Beautiful voice. Like Holly's.*

Dolly, having tottered home and into the over-heated house, found him prone upon the bed with his braces loose, and smiling.

'It's The Missus all right,' she said. 'Just sitting there. She doesn't say what she's up to but she can't stop talking and I've had to say she can come here if she wants. I don't think she does. She's laid back on that peach settee with her shoes off. And – Toots – she does smell of fry.'

'What's the matter?' She looked sharply at silent Toots. 'What's this grin about? Have you been in the cupboard?'

'I've been having a conversation,' he informed the light fitting, 'with Apple Green.'

'You rang her? You're drunk.'

'She rang here. Just for a chat. What about that, then? Nice as pie. Voice like the Queen.'

'Thomasina Fox rang *us*?'

'Aye. She's coming to stay,' he said, 'Christmas time. Never a dull minute. She's coming and The Missus is coming. By the way, I've fixed The Missus up with another job.'

– 30 –

Jack scarcely ever visited his parents, though probably he had not realised it. When The Missus flew to them, however, or virtually to them, for the alighting on Mrs Middleditch was only a preliminary settling, it was obvious even to him that he must be the one to fetch her home again.

Jack was not one to seek explanations. Others came to him with their troubles, at which he never seemed surprised. Other people's troubles were his workload. They poured them at his feet like offerings and were comforted by his loving face, or at any rate a face that had set into practised loving lines. His face was a strange face. It sometimes looked quite wooden. It always looked innocent, with candid eyes you never surprised or found assessing.

What lay behind the eyes was a mysterious area for Toots.

But then, Jack had always been a puzzle to Toots. If he'd been anyone else's son he'd have said he was plain dippy, a cartoon loony, but, since he was his own and Toots had his pride, he kept quiet. 'Wonderful boy,' they'd all said when Jack was at school, the school where Toots taught. Toots had watched him effortlessly collecting honours. At the university Jack had won a cricketing blue and a First in Physics before becoming entangled with God. Then followed certain spells in the wilderness, ordination, and more spells in the wilderness. For some years Jack had been cut off from his parents and the North, descending upon them only once or twice from nowhere, sitting smiling in their kitchen, thin as a skeleton, looking at the food Dolly put before him with historical interest, faint reminder of old pleasures. Cricket talk with Toots had been the only thing to raise a flicker of interest.

Toots had grown silent, too, with disappointment. He and Dolly did not discuss Jack together then. Only after the arrival of The Missus and the subsequent more or less straight course of Jack the parish priest did they begin to drop his name into general conversation again. They began to wonder sometimes if after all Jack might reach the high office everyone knew – of course – he deserved. Such ludicrous bishops about, not half as clever as Jack. Dolly always believed he was in with a chance, until he fetched up one day almost on his own home pad, The Missus in attendance like a snappish Sancho Panza, and began his crazy venture on the Yorkshire moors.

By Gad, he's been a funny fellow, the now bedridden Toots thought. *Whatever was it we did wrong?*

He had never once discussed Jack's career with him, never once said that he had been saddened by the fading of the golden years. Now he just brooded on the whole thing from the bed and, when the various Middleditches of the town enquired not quite innocently about Jack, Toots was taciturn but never judgemental. There were private explosions sometimes, though, and as he grew old some weeping sometimes in the night that Dolly knew about. The recent arrival of the Tibetans was the worst thing yet, in Toots's mind, after the bizarre marriage to Jocasta. 'The Snake', Toots called her. Jocasta had represented the depths of Toots's mystification and sadness about his son.

For Dolly, Jack had never done wrong. He could never disappoint. He was unique, her first-born, her star. Andrew, born so long after, walked his steady road uphill towards the London hospital, got clear of his old home, and his parents' friends informed them of how proud they must be, overdoing it rather to try to blot out the embarrassment of Jack. Dolly would have none of it, cutting in on Andrew's praises with anecdotes about her first-born. 'It was Jack had the brains,' she would say. '*Oh*, yes. Andrew was just run-of-the-mill. He was the one who had to work. It all just came to Jack.'

The small bedroom that had once been Jack's Andrew had moved into when his brother went to university, as it was a few feet bigger than his own, but when Andrew left home it became 'Jack's room' again. Dolly carried all Jack's things back into it and moved Andrew's out. She kept it clean and tidy, the old school books dusted on the shelves. She secretly wished she could reconstruct Jack's chaos again, the rubbish she had not been allowed to touch, the greasy plates shoved under the bed and forgotten, the dangling icons, the furniture eased into the middle of the room and surrounded by newspaper screens.

'But *why ever*, Jack?' (His wonderful young face.)

'It's too big. I don't need all this space.'

'Why do you sleep on the floor?'

Jack had grinned and looked away and Toots had said, 'You're a fool, boy. You do no work, just lying there. You'll fail.'

But inside the paper screens something must have been going on, for Jack always passed out top.

'Well, I'm sure – I don't know,' Dolly had said proudly.

Sometimes even now she sat alone in the narrow room. She said to friends that it was a way of getting a break from Toots, the stairs now being far too steep for him. She sat in the three-cornered art-nouveau chair beside the iron bedstead and looked out at the church spire across the allotments, the steelworks behind blossoming scarlet and gold. A solemn church bell. She thought of little Jack hearing the dreary thing all those years (she forgot Andrew) and wondered if that was what had been wrong. *If we'd put him looking over the street or towards the sandbanks*, she thought, *there might have been less religion. But he was a lovely boy*. She sat dreaming of his gaiety. Now when Jack came down very occasionally to see them she had to adjust to the fact that this gaunt, hesitant man had been the quicksilver larky boy who had never once given any hint that what he wanted to do was try to live like Christ.

'Very funny boy, your Jack,' Mrs Middleditch had said after Toots had been insulting her more than usual. 'I remember him, just. He used to like sleeping under his bed. I never thought it was quite nice.'

Yet even Mrs Middleditch was balked by the Jack of today. He met her torrents of instruction to the world with a sweetness – and silence – that threw her off course. She would have liked to tell him a thing or two like you ought to be able to tell a parson, but then she'd known him as a boy and that was always difficult. She'd like to have told him about Toots's drinking and betting with Nick Smike, and the trouble Dolly had bathing him, and his poisonous rudeness to people – quite respectable people – and Dolly's breathlessness going upstairs. But the disturbingly loving face of Jack had her beaten.

She pursed her lips as one who might say much, but 'please yourself, if you don't want to ask'. She scratched the backs of her hands, shuffled on her bottom hoity-toity, wondering how she could get across to Toots and Dolly that Jack was not the Lord God. Now and then she hinted he might do more for them and described the wonderful sense of duty in her own son, Bingham, who lived at home at forty-three and saw to all their shopping.

When Jack at last arrived in quest of The Missus it was with Philip.

It was a cold and nasty day well into December – he hadn't hurried. He was wet, with no coat over his cassock, and Philip not much better in an anorak that had a broken zip and was much too small for him. Jack sat down in the Windsor chair and stared gently at the electric fire. In and out of his mind floated the conviction that God must be with him since Mrs Middleditch hadn't spotted his car at the door and was not yet present. Toots lay staring at the ceiling. Dolly looked down at Jack's wet shoes. One of them had a string for a lace. Philip had disappeared upstairs to wash his hands. 'Is he still washing them?' she said. 'He was at that last time. Every half-hour. I wonder if his bladder's wrong.'

'Is that possible at eleven?' Jack still examined the electric element. 'We'd better get Andrew to look at him.'

'Is Andrew still up there?'

'No, no. I mean next time.' He felt Dolly's eyes shift to his soil-begrimed hands and put them out of sight.

Toots said, 'So you and Philip are down here on your own, then?'

'I'm sorry,' said Jack. 'You'll think I'm making excuses, but they wouldn't let me bring her. I was driving. No one would hear of it.'

'They're ready to risk Philip, then?'

'Well, he's quite a help. He warns me of the traffic lights.'

There was silence between the three of them, all apart yet all aware of what the others thought.

Jack said, 'You're both coming, then, on Christmas Eve? To the christening? And Jocasta's putting on a tableau. That's all fixed if Mrs Middleditch can only bring you and take you back. Faith will be just three months old, I'm to tell you. I'm told it is a lovely age. The eyes have cleared up – they come and go rather. Pema has been going on to Jocasta, saying that a baby looks its brightest and best at three months and all the crumpled red look gone.'

'Pema,' said Dolly. 'I hope we shall be meeting Pema. Whoever she is.'

'Oh, she's been magnificent with Faith,' he said. 'Or, at least, so we all thought.'

'It's funny,' said Dolly. 'Nobody ever tells you about a new baby without saying it hasn't got that crumpled red look. What is it? I've never seen it. Mine were lovely babies from the start. You looked like a curly little gold cherub, Jack.'

Jack's bony Savonarola face lengthened the more.

He had had terrible days since the flight of The Missus. Andrew had announced that he had to be on duty, the first Jack had heard of it, and Jocasta had said she must be on call for meeting Pammie Jefford, to which Jack had agreed. He had been overcome with shyness at the thought of meeting Pammie himself. The Smikes were useless, forever alleging it was their day off or they were too busy in the fields. Then, an hour or so ago, just as he and Philip were setting off, the A-level girl had come wandering by to say that all the Tibetans would be leaving The Priors at Christmas.

'Ah,' he had said, looking away from her.

'Sorry, Jack.'

'But the looms? It was all done for you. It's a charitable trust. Registered. Charity money. You were to stay into next year.'

'There'll be plenty want them. We could get them sold for you if you like. There's someone in Liverpool.'

'Ah. Liverpool.'

'Yeah. We're ever so sorry, Jack, but we don't like it here.'

'You mean with Alice gone? The food?'

'God, no, we like our own. No, it's just it doesn't work here, see. Someone has to tell you. It's different worlds. It's all daft stuff after Liverpool. It's not the teaching we expected.'

'Jocasta? You'll not find anyone better qualified. And all totally free, if you don't mind my saying so.'

The girl gave him a look.

'Well, don't you agree?'

'I guess,' she said. 'But she's old, Jocasta, see. We're sick of this negative-space stuff. It's as long gone as Picasso. Out of date, like. We want to get into New Art and that.'

'I'll let her know,' he said, standing like a pinnacle, staring towards the moor lane. 'We've spent, the charity has spent, a great deal of money.'

'I guess. But you'll get someone else. You might get intellectuals or writers' groups. They're cheaper.'

'Not through the winter. Oh, I might just say that there is a new housekeeper coming. Mrs Jefford, who brought us Faith. Would that make a difference? I think she will be a very dependable woman.'

'I saw her. Christ, Jack, you haven't a hope. Lipstick and lady-dresses. She'll never last here. Oh, and we've told Jocasta already. We told her last week. And the lads.'

'The Smikes know? Jocasta knows?'

'Yeah. Actually, Jack, Nick's comin' wid us.'

'Nick? To Liverpool?'

'Don't go for me! I'm not bothered. "Suit yourself," I said. "Come if you want." But I tellt 'im it wouldn't do 'im no permanent good wid me.'

'You and Nick?'

'He thinks so. I don't. Not permanent. I'm getting to art school next year, the Slade if I can, and I will.'

'Nick is leaving Ernie?'

'I guess.'

What Jack was looking at then in his parents' house was not the red bar of the fire but these revelations, particularly the bombshell about The Smikes, who had been in the Braithwaite family for years. They were not brothers. The name was a literary joke they both understood but pretended not to. They denied any education. They were not lovers either, Nick sturdy, short-legged, scowling, watchful-eyed, level-headed, Ernie away in a world of his own. They were mates, that was all they had told Jack when he took them on. Neither paid attention to the other's partners and behaved as if they didn't exist. Ernie expected Nick's girlfriends to be slags and never addressed them. Nick, 'on principle', whatever that meant, did not speak of the gay community of the esplanade fun palaces and considered them boring. He worried, though, about Ernie and Aids and occasionally lectured him on the subject, buying him packets of coloured condoms as if they were sugar candy. He urged him to go for his check-ups. They were like unidentical twins. Some bond forged before their times in prison held them, probably Toots, who alone in their schooldays had reached the small but deep areas of their unpreposessing souls. After prison, it had been useful to get some work out of Toots's dotty son and it had been Toots's fierce eyes not Jack's holiness that had made them behave on the whole very well as hirelings at the crazy Priors.

Nick and Ernie had moved about the landscape of Cleveland since then as a pair, always together. You couldn't conceive of one Smike without the other.

'Might I ask' – Jack looked hard at the girl – 'what is to happen to Ernie?'

'Well, 'e'll 'ave ter fettle, won't 'e?'

So that Jack had been more than usually distracted on the journey down, what with the flux of The Missus, Nick and the Tibetans, the imminent arrival of the scarce-known southern matron Pammie – she might already be on the train, unstoppable now even if Alice Banks decided to come back after all.

The withdrawal of the Tibetans would mean the withdrawal of funds. The Arts Council allowance that was all that saved the place from total collapse. *And the baby?* he eventually thought. *The baby without the Tibetans?* Would Pammie take her on again? As well as the housekeeping? Obviously not. Jocasta, then? But he knew that Jocasta would not.

'Who's going to look after Faith, then?' Philip had asked in the car.

They were groaning along in low gear through sleet that fell on the miles of simmering chemical works. A caravan park lay in their foothills along the main road, old flaking grey vans sunk down in frozen mud. Some were boarded up, but on the step of another a child in nothing but a T-shirt stood braying at a door to get in. Piles of rubbish lay around in long shallow puddles of rain. It was inconceivable that whole lives were being passed in these tin cans, but from one the white old face of a woman looked out, chewing and ruminating like a beast.

'A terrible place,' said Jack and prayed for all who dwelt in it, closing his eyes to do so and narrowly missing a bus.

Philip yelled.

'You'd better get yourself round there now, lad,' said Toots (the boy looked tired), 'before that woman brings her round here and sits listening in to it all with us.'

'She'll sit listening in round there,' said Dolly.

'No,' said Jack. 'I'll speak to Alice alone.'

'She'll be ear to the door. Can you not take Philip with you to stave her off? He's Alice's friend, aren't you, Philip?'

254

Jack rang the Middleditch bell pull, Philip beside him on the step, and they found The Missus seated on a shell-pink armchair like a sack of coal against a sunrise.

Jack sat down on the apricot settee and Philip stayed outside in the passage examining the brass medallions on the walls and triumphal certificates of the Boys' Brigade. Mrs Middleditch looked him over unenthusiastically before moving into her lounge to preside. She had dressed seriously for the interview in bottle green, with court shoes and earrings. She moved to the piano stool and cleared her throat.

Jack said, 'I wonder if you'd be very good and get poor Toots a hot drink?'

'We ought to get this settled first.'

'It will be. I'm sure. Could I ask if Philip might go with you?'

'I'm fine here,' said Philip from where he was easing out the metal floor of the hall-stand with scientific interest.

'Stop that at once,' said The Missus and Mrs Middleditch together, and somehow Philip and Mrs Middleditch were side by side in the street and heading along the terrace for the other establishment, Mrs Middleditch coatless and insulated only by her wrath.

Silence fell between Jack and The Missus, Jack basking for a moment, thankful that his professional pastoral manner had not quite left him and that he'd got rid of the opposition. Then the silence grew, and the deeper it struck, the shyer he and The Missus became.

'Have you been comfortable?' he asked in the
end.

'It's been satisfactory.'

'It is very good of Mrs Middleditch.'

'No. It's what she lives to do. Get in on other
people's messes. And I'd no option. I'll send her a
present.'

'Send? So you are coming home, Alice?'

She looked over his head at the plastic head of an
Airedale that was attached to the wall with its
tongue out.

'This is a right tasteless place,' she said. 'Keeps
showing me all over it and it's scarcely two up, two
down. She's had her downstairs WC done up
low-level glaze. Avocado. Joined tank, and a lavvy
brush got up like an owl. Taps gold-plate, dead
common.'

'But, Alice, she's not even a friend of yours. You
landed on her. Don't you see how good—?'

'Bed that soft you can't get out of it of a morning
and running about with cups of Ovaltine half the
night. You can hear them on and on talking about
Toots and Dolly – and you. And how Philip's being
neglected and fourpence in the shilling and that
Bingham! Stinks of scent. You have to open the
bathroom window so's to let in the filth from the
works – it's disgusting, but it's better. That
Bingham's far too fat. He eats rubbish. They all do.
Over the telly. She puts a sheet down. And he's
forty-two.'

'Alice—'

'Little pasties all half-cooked. Never a decent
meal. She's got a negligée. This Arnold's supposed
to be the great man for running the church but it's
all desk work. Never speaks. Not person-to-person.'

'There is absolutely no reason, Alice, why he should.'

'And she took me clothes and put them through her washer. Said you can't be too careful, coming from farms. I ask you! Left me a great dressing gown to get into, all appliqué reveres. Far too long. Sitting in that box of a kitchen you couldn't get past me, watching all me clothes going round as if it was typhoid. The thing began to scream. That was the drier, if you please, all in one, like the WC. They come out bone hard, past ironing – not that she does any, just smoothes them over them Aga domes. Ridiculous in this hen coop, Aga's just showing off, half the size of the house, boils the place out. Not a decent bite for breakfast, mush, skim-milk and hard apples. I'll get 'er some bacon before I go.'

'So – you will be leaving?'

'Oh aye, Jack. I'll have to go. I can't stay 'ere with satin reveres, I'm not Gracie Fields.'

Again there was silence.

'Alice, could you perhaps tell me . . . ? After all you've been to me, all you've done for me – I know I'm not aware of things sometimes, but what have I done in particular to make you leave me?'

'Nothing.'

'Nothing? Then—?'

'It's the rest of them. It's not right.'

'Has someone insulted you?'

'Not me. Nobody insults me. Not even this Middleditch. I'm going to give her me auntie's gold brooch while she's still deriding me round half Cleveland. That'll shame 'er. No. It's not me. It's you they humiliate, Jack. And I won't have it.'

She sat glaring.

'Well,' he said, 'but, Alice, it doesn't happen, you

know. I don't notice, and so it doesn't happen.'

'You can be humiliated unawares,' she said darkly.

'I can take it.' He moved across to her to take her hand. It looked unnaturally clean, softer, older, very small. He kissed it.

'You can leave off that rubbish, I'm no film star. I know me limitations and I'm old as your mother just about. But I won't sit by to see you humiliated, Jack, and so I've got to go.'

Looking into Jack's candid eyes the enormity of what had happened at The Priors swept over Alice Banks again, the horror of the scene in the gatehouse, the shattering of the whole structure of the Christian presence which she had thought Jack had created, the shock of watching the anonymity of sexual desire. Andrew's vacant face turned to her. His sweaty back, Jocasta lying there, her legs wide, her skin shiny.

'Where shall you go?'

'There's a job south. Someone of Holly's.'

'Alice! A job south?'

'I've not even been to London,' she said proudly. 'I've never been drawn. I've met plenty of them, God knows, and I'm not impressed. I keep myself apart and I shall do. But I'll go south now if I have to. I'll go anywhere. Don't ask me no more, Jack.'

'Very well,' he said. 'It's a mystery.'

'Oh, please stop,' for tears were coursing. Her warrior's small head seemed to be vibrating as if it were balanced on a shuddering volcano. Her hands gripped the great black handbag on her knee. 'If you could see to my stuff I could go tomorrow. Toots knows all about where. It's convenient. I'll go.'

'I'll see to things.' He knew he couldn't but maybe

Jocasta might. Or Pammie?

'Pammie Jefford is coming.'

'So. I'm replaced. It didn't tek long. Very good. Very good.'

But the tears still flowed.

'I'm going to take you out to lunch now. Just you and I and Philip.'

'I couldn't eat.'

'There's a very good fish-and-chip shop.'

The tears lessened.

In the chip shop she and Jack sat together to heaped plates; Philip had refused to budge from the car. The Missus after a time began to pick about, then to apply herself. She asked for more vinegar and said the plastic tomato cruets needed a scrub. She spoke of the insanitary aspect of the chip-maker's naked torso above his swimming bath of boiling fat. ' 'Is very sweat'll drop in it,' she said, 'and look at them disgusting tatoos.'

– 31 –

Madeleine and Puffy were not native to Farnham. They did not live at the house of the bride in whose garden Madeleine had been drifting on the morning of the Seton-Fairley wedding. That had been her husband's family territory.

Puffy travelled only to important weddings and funerals nowadays and even these were having to be rationed. He lived with Madeleine in East Kent, on the coast, but with no view of the sea. This did not worry Madeleine as she forgot the sea until she saw it again, but it troubled Puffy. He thought of the sea a great deal, tipped back in his orthopaedic chair.

The tiny room he sat in was furnished in Madeleine's aristocratic lack of taste – frills and rosy covers and dozens of photographs in tarnished silver frames of people with dressed hair, a swirl even of a royal signature (Edward VIII), everyone a little sepia. Limoges and Dresden were dotted about and a small television set was hidden in the Adam-style fireplace behind gold-and-white cupboard doors. Madeleine found herself these days spending more and more time away from this low-ceilinged sitting room where Puffy floated like a giant balloon. She had plenty of help, which she took for granted. She had always been an employer of staff. There was a skinny cleaner and a young man called Henry Jones who would do anything, even feed Puffy little bits of food into his mouth like a mother blackbird. Henry Jones cooked a midday meal and always looked in at night to see that the old pair were all right. Henry was what Madeleine called a pansy and Puffy might have called a woofter if he had been able to address the subject. Henry was very fond of old ladies and of Madeleine's swimmy green eyes.

'But I've simply no one for the *nights*,' complained Madeleine. 'Our only difficulty is the nights. Well, that was always the way with marriage, wasn't it? If the nights are all right, then ... How very outspoken I am! Poor old Puffy.'

Agonised by her beached-whale straining to hear the sound of the sea that was becoming only a memory on the horizon to him, Madeleine had lately taken to calling for a taxi to get her to the London train, and then, wondering at about Ashford whether she had told Puffy she was going, getting off, ringing him up, missing the next train, getting into conversation with people on the platform, sometimes joining their train and finding herself home again.

Or not home again, which was worse. Once she had taken off with an Indian student who said he was a horticulturalist and ended up with him in the Chelsea Physic Garden and writing him a cheque for fifty pounds. She took him out to tea and found she hadn't a penny in her purse to pay for it. When she rang Puffy to ask him where she had been going in the first place, he panicked and struck the alarm

261

signal on his breast, but that did no good at all because when the police arrived he had forgotten the reason for summoning them. Henry Jones wrung his hands over the Chelsea Physic Garden and said that the student might have been a serial killer. Something was obviously going to have to be done.

But Madeleine would not hear of moving to a Home – or even two Homes – and had become convinced that all would be resolved if she could only get a little break on her own. Just a tiny one. No, not with Puffy. 'Beloved Puffy,' she said, 'but I can't get near him in that chair or near anything else. He's swelling like a watermelon. He's a bull in a china shop. He's tethered but he's still a bull. I must get away with darling Giles and that woman. Henrietta. Very nice woman, but nervy. I could probably help her. So hard on Giles. Let's see . . . three months. He'll just be beginning to think of extricating himself. I don't believe in health farms. You form attachments that would be unthinkable if you were in your clothes. Massage makes you careless.'

A little of this she hinted to Giles, whose telephone number she had procured and was making use of several times a day, leaving many messages when he was out.

'I'm afraid Thomasina and I are going to Yorkshire for Christmas,' he told her. 'We're not sure how long we shall stay. I'm sure you wouldn't want to leave Puffy over Christmas.'

'He never knows when it's Christmas,' she said. 'I shall just tell them not to put up any decorations and hide the cards.'

'That seems harsh.'

'Don't be sentimental, Giles. We can pretend it's Christmas when I get back. Then I shall have two.'

'Won't he hear about it on television?'

'No. He hates television. Well, he used to like it but he hardly sees anything now. He can't read the newspaper either. It's the angle of his head.'

'I'm sure the social services—'

'Oh, no need at all. He has all sorts of people coming in to see him. They read to him and bath him and dress him. I'll just tell them to keep off the newspapers and not to let him switch on the wireless.'

'You are a ruthless woman, Madeleine.'

'No, Giles, I am a pragmatic woman, unashamed. I've lived far too close to Puffy for years. In foreign parts, you know – so much more space.'

'I never thought there was a lot of space in Hong Kong.'

'There are different kinds of space. Space for little separations. We were so wonderfully looked-after. *Such* fun.'

'Madeleine, if you're going to talk maids-before-the-war like a ghastly old dowager, goodbye. It's suburban of you. You are a woman who has had everything she ever wanted.'

'Ah,' she said, 'but not for the nights.'

She won of course. A conversation with Thomasina, whom she had also run to earth, led to Thomasina's conversation with Toots in the draughty passage of the house on Teesside, and then to the journey of The Missus south to pass her Christmas in a foreign land.

'But you can't mean that you've arranged for Madeleine to come *with* us?' Giles had such a look of

263

horror that it was almost a smile. 'My good girl, it'll snow and she'll wander out and get pneumonia and die. Wherever could she stay?'

'Wherever shall *we* stay, come to that?' Thomasina looked very thin today. Rather lost. 'I'm sorry, I've decided I can't take that place on the moors with the whiplash waitress and I'm not staying at The Priors.'

'It would be insulting not to, wouldn't it?'

'No. It's not fit for anybody. I've done it. With Holly and Andrew. It is vile.'

'But – Faith – lives there. Your grandchild. Isn't that the reason we're going?'

'Oh, Giles,' she said, 'stop being a fool. Actually, Pammie Jefford will be there.'

'Pammie *Jefford*?'

'Yes. She's going as housekeeper. I told you she's rather keen on Jack. She's religious. Andrew will be there, too, I imagine. And there's Jocasta, Jack's wife, and her little boy and some serf people who work there. Oh yes, and some Tibetan refugees.'

'It does sound rather full. Yes.'

'Doesn't Madeleine know anybody up there? Someone with a decent house where we could all go?'

'It's rather short notice for Christmas, isn't it? Less than a fortnight now.' However, he rang Madeleine.

As usual, all his exasperation faded at the charm of her voice. The face he saw in the air was at once graced with the young shining hair of a girl; the body was slight and wore a silk dress. It sat on the terrace at Karnak. Its green eyes watched the Nile.

'Hello, Maddie. We were just wondering if you'd thought of anywhere to stay up there. We're not really fixed up yet. Not too comfortable, I hear, Thomasina's grandchild's place. Had you planned something?'

'I'll see to it,' she said. 'But, do you know, your wonderful Thomasina has actually *found* me someone. A housekeeper. She's coming down on the coach and I was just going to ring and see if you'd meet her at Victoria and take her across to Waterloo to catch the Dover train. Henry and I will meet her there of course.'

'Well . . .'

'I'll ask Pammie Jefford,' hissed Thomasina.

'We'll ask Pammie Jefford,' said Giles. 'She's a—'

'Oh, I know who Pammie *Jefford* is.' Madeleine had acquired Pammie's number, too, and the number of The Priors. 'She's up there already, I think, or soon will be. She's the new housekeeper and they're sending the old one down to me. That's to say, to Puffy. *Such* nice people. Rather a strange man answered the phone. Beautiful voice but not worldly, I'd think. Seven-thirty?'

'Seven-thirty?'

'At the coach station tomorrow? Seven thirty *a.m.* of course. She's travelling down overnight.'

'She must be mad.'

'Oh, nonsense, Giles. It's only nine hours. I thought we might all travel up that way, as a matter of fact. It costs twenty pounds instead of hundreds and they have a video and hot drinks and a WC and Big Macs. It's not Dickens now, you know. Not post-horns and outside seats. It's a bit tight round the knees – wouldn't do for Puffy – but we're all slender. Goodbye, darling, I must get Henry to see to the new person's room.'

*

'We are to meet this woman,' said Giles, 'at the Victoria Coach Station at seven-thirty a.m. We are then to cart her across London and put her on the train to East Kent. Why? Why us? Why at all? Is she infirm? Who fixed this ridiculous transportation of labour? It is inane.'

'We?' said Thomasina. 'Not you, Giles, I'll go. It's my affair. I did it. On the phone in a silly moment. Why should you?'

'Because I can stay overnight at my London club and you can't. Leave it all to me. I'm responsible for Madeleine. We should never have gone to that wedding.'

'You are very good. This is really my affair.'

'It takes two to make an affair,' he said.

'About such things,' she said, 'Giles . . .'

'Not just now.'

'You are looking shifty.'

He was hurt. 'I have never been shifty. That I have not been. I'm going now. What do you want from London? I can walk over from Waterloo to Soho and get some pasta.'

'Oh, lovely.' (She thought, *Better! How easy we are together again. How married we seem.*) She said, 'Thanks. See you for supper, then, tomorrow?'

'Oh, long before that. Tea. At the latest.'

That evening she turned out the rest of Holly's school things from her bedroom drawers and packed them up for Oxfam, even her school reports and her bears. *In the morning I'll nip in and get some figs for supper. Nice after pasta. Figs and cream. Or with fresh oranges. Funny old thing. Getting to be part of the fabric. And maybe a cake for tea.*

*

266

All through the night the coach thundered south bearing Alice Banks away from all she stood for, the rectitude of the unswerving North.

Jack had brought her to the coach. They had been driven by Mrs Middleditch with Philip sitting in the back. Mrs Middleditch had not left the car. The Missus had said goodbye and thank you to her then, but had not been able to say a word to Philip, who sat glumly not looking at her, unravelling a thread in the upholstery. Jack and she together carried her three cardboard suitcases and watched them being stowed in the coach's hold. As she climbed aboard, laden with plastic bags and packages, Jack panicked. The sight of her back going away from him, her head not turning, was unknown.

'*Alice!*'

She did turn then. There were people behind her wanting to get on and Jack was in everyone's way. In his old cassock and scarf and ragged duffle coat and a weird yellow semi-balaclava The Missus had once knitted for him he looked an unlikely divine, too intensely concerned with his passenger. Love and distress were in the air.

'Alice, there's no need for you to go. It's not too late.'

'It is too late.'

'But what have we done to you?'

'Move along, git on,' said the driver, trying to get to his perch. Everyone was aboard now. 'Git off, missus, if you're not comin'.'

She glowered down at Jack.

'All these years, Alice.'

'It's more than I can tell you. You'll find out and you'll understand me then. But it isn't my place to say.'

'Could you write? Write about it? When you get there?'

'I'll see.'

Her intense love for him she disguised with a thrust of her pointed chin, a turning away, a dropping of parcels, and she disappeared down the centre aisle of the coach as he stepped back and trotted down the side of it to see where she settled. But alas, the windows were dark with tinted glass.

'It's to make it go faster,' someone said. 'There's no waving off any more. Same on the trains. You don't get much seeing-off at all now, it's all self-help.'

Jack stood feebly waving at the bus's shadowed flank and then its vanishing backside, before taking the midnight road back to his parents' house. He was not being trusted with the moor road home at night.

And Alice sat in the bus regarding the back of the seat in front of her hardly twelve inches from her nose. Beside her reclined a blond gorilla, who began to snore at Boroughbridge, kept snoring through Wetherby, over the Leeds roundabout, along the Doncaster bypass, through Sherwood Forest, Stamford, Peterborough and the A1 interchange. At first to her left were the Cleveland Hills, invisible. To her right, beyond the gorilla, was the darkened plain that lifted itself far away into the Pennines and the Lake District and subsided again south towards her own Lancashire. Through the night the coach vibrated with the snorts and farts and coughs and moans of people's dreams. Lads swilled lagers in the back and at one time there was some shouting and a clattering of cans and tuneless singing.

Shadows blundered up and down the aisle to the WC. The drinks bar alongside it clonked and fizzed. The atmosphere grew fetid and foul. By Worksop quite a few people were smoking. In Northamptonshire, somewhere beyond the Oundle turn-off, Cambridge to the east, The Missus realised that she had not moved a muscle since she stepped aboard.

She reflected objectively on this, presupposed the pains in her joints and decided they could be postponed if she didn't disturb them. She risked uncrossing her feet and recrossing them the other way, winced, and shut her eyes. She did not turn to the packet of sandwiches on her knee. She forgot the thermos of tea Dolly and Toots had insisted upon, Toots even ringing Mrs Middleditch about it and Mrs Middleditch saying what sort of woman did they think she was, she knew her duty.

In the dawn The Missus saw London for the first time, grey and windy and strung with millions of lights like lighted barbed wire in grey air. Hendon came and went and it could have been anywhere. Stockton-on-Tees, say. Swiss Cottage was nothing of the sort. St John's Wood just blocks of flats. Lord's Cricket Ground was a stretch of wall. As they reached Baker Street, Oxford Street, Marble Arch, where she might have seen the big shops, at last she slept, leaning sideways on the gorilla's elbow like a small dead tree. Buckingham Palace with its tumbril spikes was left behind unnoticed, and in the bleached dawn the coach surged into Victoria Station.

Alice found that she could scarcely move. She was longing to pee but never, never, would she use the upright coffin provided at the back of the bus and

269

certainly not now when the coach was stationary. Maybe there would be somewhere else? As she stood waiting for her luggage she was nearly knocked over several times.

'OK, missus?' asked the driver and the familiar title made her small green face soften.

'D'you have toilets down here?'

'Over there, missus.'

'What happens to me luggage?'

'Is someone here for you? OK then, I'll watch it.'

But she was not sure of this and began to gather the luggage and her packages together in a heap against the coach-station wall, making trips back and forth. She hid the smaller bundles behind the bigger ones. But still she disliked the idea of leaving them all, and there were notices saying you mustn't. *That would be bombs*, she thought. She looked about her and saw that David Niven stood nearby, observing her from lamp-post height. 'Miss Banks?' If he was a mugger or a kidnapper or a rapist it was odd that he knew her name. He was springing about now like a grasshopper, calling up a taxi. All of seventy. Whoever was he?

'Hop in. I'll take you somewhere for breakfast.'

'I need the WC.'

'Oh yes, of course. I shouldn't think they're very nice here.'

'I can see the sign. I'll not be long.'

Looking back doubtfully at the luggage and the man presiding over it, she thought, *Or maybe the Anthony Eden type.*

She made off and once inside the ladies room didn't want to leave it. She felt a little weak and sick and was not at all sure she wasn't dreaming. *All them buses*, she thought, threading her way back among them. They were multiplying as she watched, nosing in like great salmon returning to their birthplace. There was Edinburgh, and over there Exeter, and lined up ready for off, just spawned, was Liverpool. And Glasgow. The board beside Liverpool had Preston written underneath in smaller letters. It'd be stopping there. Not far from Oldham and Wigan and Bury and Bolton and Rochdale. Home.

She was almost swept away by the desire for the Rochdale bus. What would they all say, eh, when she walked in the door, her mam at the fireside with her knees apart making toast on the brass fork with the Medusa head on it, and her dad supping his tea? 'Saucering it', he called it, and no shame. *And that cat. It'll be that pleased to see me. They all died in the war, though.*

'Miss Banks? Hello there. Are you all right?'

The general armed her to the taxi and they drove up Victoria Street and over the river, which glimmered in the winter morning but Earth had many things to show more fair than the buildings that looked down upon it.

'We'll have some breakfast on the platform,' he was saying. 'There's a good snack bar. There's rather a long time to wait, I'm afraid.' (*Over an hour. I suppose I must stay with her. Good God, what to talk about?*) 'Never here before? Good gracious me. That was the River Thames – so sorry it's dark. And there's the Shell Building. In the distance you can see the National Theatre. Concrete but dressed with a pattern of planks.'

Alice remained unmoved. They left the taxi and on Waterloo's great staircase she spoke at last.

'What's this, then? Backstreet India? Why don't they move them all on? 'Umans in cardboard boxes is a disgrace.'

At the ticket office she insisted on paying her own fare, insisted so ferociously that people turned to look. She returned the stares. 'I've seen this ticket queue on the telly,' she said. 'It was on the news. Someone got murdered in it once for not being quick enough.

'I'm from the North,' she told the man behind the glass. 'I can't think what I'm doing down 'ere.'

'Nobody can,' he said.

The general wondered, too. He wondered very much. There was no porter, no trolley to get the luggage up the escalator, which Alice wouldn't use anyway though she'd been on the ones in Middlesbrough Binns. They had to make several journeys up and down the stairs alongside. Then they trundled it all by slow degrees along passageways and down a stairway to the platform for the Dover train, and then halfway along this to the snack bar, which was shut up and in darkness.

Rain was falling silver and cold on the lines, spitting and hissing against the roof. Now and then a blustering wind flung drops in handfuls across their legs and feet. The overhead signal boards that predicted coming trains creaked. They were all blank.

'Ha,' said the general. 'Well.'

'No trains,' said Alice Banks. 'It's no better here than anywhere else.'

'My dear, none whatever,' said a sweet voice. Seated on a bench, wrapped round with rugs, a fur hat on her head and the *Financial Times* on her knee, sat Madeleine.

– 32 –

Philip, after refusing to go into the chip shop with Jack and Alice, had decided that he couldn't even accept the glossy newspaper parcel of cod and chips Jack had come out waving at him through the car window. Jack had gone back inside and stood looking helpless, whereupon The Missus had said, 'Give us 'ere,' and risen to her feet.

'Just you eat it,' she'd shouted through the glass to Philip. 'Open that window. What's wrong with you?'

'I want to wash my hands. I don't like this chippie.'

'You've just washed your 'ands at your granny's and you can go and wash them there again in 'alf an hour if you want.' She had rattled at the car until he opened his window for her to drop the package in.

Jack's face had brightened when he saw her coming back into the chippie without it. The Missus had not quite disintegrated after all.

After he'd left her at Mrs Middleditch's and arranged about the journey south for the following night, he and Philip had set off back to The Priors, and at the caravan park Jack stopped the car without warning and gazed at the site. It was the

273

bleakest of days, worse than this morning. It was four-thirty and workers were going home. The narrow old trunk road had now for an hour or so become a teeming motorway. A car behind missed bashing into them by two inches and faces from following traffic blazed at them sideways as they passed.

Jack had stopped in the fast lane.

'You'll have us dead, Jack.'

Jack stared tenderly at the mobile homes.

'What's up, Jack?'

'I was thinking. Philip – when the Tibetans go at Christmas, there are people here we might approach.'

'These aren't homeless. They're *in* their homes. They may like them. They'd think you were after rehousing them.'

'I feel I should make contact. I don't think this is accidental. I think we may have been directed here today. I think I should call.'

'Oh please, Jack, no. I want to get back. I've got my homework and I'm going over to the sheds to see my sister.'

'Five minutes.' Jack manoeuvred the car on to the hard shoulder and went walking about the caravans, but nobody seemed to be answering his knock. 'Oh, stuff it,' said Philip. 'Stuffation and grot.' A man had come to the door of the fourth caravan and Jack leaned down to him ceremoniously. Then disappeared inside with him. Not long afterwards he reappeared with the man and walked with him towards the car. Philip, his face squashed against the glass, was looking down and saw dirty trainers in the mud and above them shining black trousers. It was hardly a glance upwards, but eyes met.

The man in his elbow-patched jacket turned and made off back to the caravan.

'Well, most interesting,' said Jack, 'most interesting fellow. I've left our address. He seemed quite enthusiastic. I don't know why he made off like that. Very well-spoken, educated man. An intellectual. This car is a brute to start.'

'For God's sake, get on with it. Quick, get on with it.'

'Not like you to be rude, Philip.'

'I want to see my sister. Get me home. He was horrible.'

Jack brooded. 'Little Faith,' he said, 'dear little Faith.' He imagined a stout and homely soul following on from Pema. Perhaps a fine old gypsy woman. Or a Traveller. The woman gazing from the caravan window, eating a pie? He saw the blotchy face soften, grow gentle, self-respecting, as the child was rocked and serenaded. Maybe the wife of the intellectual man?

And if not her arms, whose? he wondered. *Jocasta's? Oh let it happen. Slowly, slowly. Let her take to Faith. One day a child of our own.*

'I believe you really do think of Faith as your sister, Philip. I wish Jocasta felt more for her.'

'Yes, it's funny. She always wanted a girl.'

After an age – they were climbing now up Sutton Bank, spluttering and groaning, leaving the sprawl of the works below – Jack had said, 'Ah.'

Then later, 'I didn't know that, Philip. I hope it doesn't upset you? Make you feel unwanted in any way? I'm surprised she told you.'

'Oh, Jocasta tells me everything. She told me when she was beginning to think of marrying you.

She actually asked my advice. I was quite young, too.'

'Ah.'

'I said – d'you want to know what I said, Jack?'

'Well, I suppose I do really want to know.'

'I said, "Jack's OK, but I don't think we'll like living up there for ever. It's going to be lonely." '

Jack said nothing until, at length, 'And you, Philip? I expect you must be rather lonely. As you expected?'

'No, I'm not now. I like it OK. I wasn't exactly mad about it till Faith came, but now I'm not an only child any more it's fine.'

'You'd like real brothers and sisters, I expect?'

'Faith's real.'

'You are extremely fond of her, aren't you?'

'Well, she's the only one I'll ever have.'

'You never know. You never know, Philip.' He looked beatific again. Light perpetual. Hope perpetual.

'Yes I do. Jocasta's had all the parts you need for childbirth taken out. Didn't you know? I'd have thought you'd know. She's got this great scar across her tum. You must have seen it, Jack, don't be daft. Andrew did it. He helped the surgeon when he was young. What's wrong with this car now? We nearly went over the edge. Shall I drive? I could. I drive the tractor for Nick.'

'I believe,' said Jack twenty minutes later as they reached the cross, 'you may be a bit wrong there, Philip. Wasn't that just something like an appendix or a peritonitis business?'

'D'you mean you've never even *asked* her? Jack, you're crazy. I mean, *I* asked her and I was little. She

276

said that I'd have had to know anyway because it was only fair to me.'

'Only fair,' said Jack. 'I see that.'

The only person he had told of his longing for a child was The Missus. He had not told Jocasta. He had assumed she must know. Any wife would. Naturally. Now he thought that somehow The Missus must have discovered about Jocasta's barrenness and that she had never told him of it. Maybe Andrew or Philip had somehow let it out – Philip playing cards with The Missus in the gatehouse. The Missus couldn't cope with treachery. She smelled it a mile off. Her ferocious face belied her capacity to be deeply shocked and when shocked she fell silent. She collapsed and ran. Out of pity for him The Missus would have sunk deep into herself, glaring, crashing the saucepans, become remote, ready to kill Jocasta for embracing him in the kitchen with her open eyes full of love. Alice was a woman awkward when it came to imparting bad news. Or any news. A difficult, heavy little woman. *I don't know why I kept her so long*, Jack thought, and shocked himself.

But truly The Missus had reacted ridiculously. The trouble was that she deeply hated Jocasta and had done from the beginning. She had simply been waiting for the final coffin nail. He should not have allowed such hatred to fester at The Priors. He must put things right. The first thing he would do when he reached home was tell Jocasta that he loved her and put things right.

He went straight to her room, knocked politely, waited for permission to go in, and found her with her hair loose and an open book face down on the

277

bedcover, staring at the door. She looked as if she had been lying like this for ever, staring ahead.

'Jocasta.' He sat down at the end of the bed. 'In bed early?'

'I was cold.'

'Tell me, do you – did you hate poor Alice Banks?'

She said at once, 'So you know.'

He was surprised that she leaned forward then and picked up one of his hands. She stroked it and laid it against her cheek, 'You know.'

'You're crying.'

'No,' she said.

'Your eyes are enormous. You're so beautiful, Jocasta.'

'I love your eyes, too,' she said. 'I love it when you look like that. All raggety-baggety. You're a loving old Don Quixote. I want to have you in my arms.'

'Then why – why ever? Why won't you ever . . . ?'

'Well, it's not like that.'

'Like what?'

'Sex. I've told you so often. I can't. I just can't. Darling, how could I?'

'You shouldn't have married me without telling me. You must have known then that there was no chance. How could you not have told me? I'm Andrew's brother, for God's sake.'

'But then I couldn't have married you, could I? I wanted to. And you would not have married me. Well, you *shouldn't* have been able to marry me. I should hope not, anyway. I'm the sinner.'

'Of course I would have married you,' he said.

'What? Even knowing . . . ? No, Jack. No!'

'It was Andrew brought you to me. It wasn't his fault you were his patient. You talk as if he'd violated you. He had no choice but to bring you here

278

to me. Yes, he should have told me and you should have told me, that's all I mind about. I could have coped. It's all so sad. But it wouldn't have changed my mind. You know – I am so hopeless I'm beginning to wonder now if you did tell me and I somehow simply forgot.'

'*Forgot!*'

'Well, maybe Andrew thought I knew. In some way. That he'd told me sometime at the very beginning. We've never been close, you know. We never had conversations – he's a different generation. And of course he has no time for religion.'

'Well, heavens. It's hardly a thing he would have dropped into a conversation. It's nothing to do with religion.'

'I truly promise you . . . Of course I'm not, well, happy. Of course it changes the future – our future together. It can't be the same now. But "blame you"? No. I can't. I couldn't. After all, how could you help it, my poor love?'

She stared in disbelief. She dropped his hand. The eyes that had been full of affection and loving tears had changed. He saw a younger, harder Jocasta, the one Philip's unknown young father must have met. The Jocasta who had lived by her wits in India after school, the pot-smoking, seriously trendy, guru-seeking, guru-rejecting Jocasta, a King's Road and Carnaby Street Jocasta, a brown-rice, barefoot, Streatham Common Jocasta. The eyes said, What sort of dope is he? You can carry forgiveness too far. He makes me sick.

'You've no anger in you, have you?' she said. 'No passions? You're not even going to throw him out. You'll have him back for Christmas. You won't even hit him.'

279

'*Hit* him? Hit *Andrew*? Of course not. Why ever should I hit him? He liked you, grew to know you. It wasn't unethical. You'd ceased to be his patient. He was sorry for you and brought you up here to me for a home. I fell in love with you and we were married. He has done nothing *wrong*, then, before or since.'

'Jack,' she leaned forward and took both his hands, 'Andrew and I have both done wrong and doubly wrong not telling you. I am very, very, very sorry. I have never felt this before. I suppose it was The Missus told you. That's why she went off. She couldn't bear it. She has a strain of purest vitriol inside her. She'd kill for you. She discovered it and went. It's a wonder she didn't stay for breakfast and poison Andrew and me together.'

'Oh my dear – come on.'

'Oh, my love, I'm sorry.'

'It's not that serious,' he said. 'I don't think she'd have stayed, as a matter of fact, if we'd *had* a baby. She likes Philip but that's because he's not childish. She's never paid the least attention to Faith.'

Very slowly she said then, 'Do you mean that it's just because you won't be begetting any children by me that it matters? That that's what it's all about? Yourself?'

'Well, partly. Naturally. The other part is your not telling me it was a hysterectomy.'

'And otherwise you don't care?'

'Not at all. Not in the very least.'

'But, Jack, Andrew and I have betrayed you. Philip and I will have to leave you. Andrew and I knew that when we saw The Missus standing staring at us in the doorway.'

'My dear. My dear sweet girl, you are being theatrical. You and I are *married*. We love each other.

Whatever does the gynaecological stuff matter? I mean, it's not as if you and Andrew had been having an *affair*, is it? Poor Andrew – just look at his face. He'll mourn poor Holly, I'm afraid, for the rest of his life.'

– 33 –

Every few minutes trains were running into Waterloo East station to tip out their contents. Hundreds of people surged forward, wave upon wave, at a stiff jog-trot towards their daily bread. The trio waiting on the down-line platform was jostled about several times and Alice Banks's suitcases were at continuous risk. No sooner had one train left than in came another. The crowds were being sucked towards London for their execution.

Alice watched and could not see one contented face. *Poor stock*, she thought, *most of them half-breeds. Black and curly, greenish-grey, blotchy brown, some white – well, pink. All of them glazed over like they've got New Forest disease and need their ointment. No shepherds. No dogs to guide them.* They all seemed to know the way, though. Off they went up the slope in a huddle, butting away at each other, left wheel and out of sight. Not one of them turning to run for it. Nobody coming back. *Like death really*, thought The Missus. *So much for London*.

She thought that she'd like to tell Jack of it. It might be a thing for a sermon. Then she thought not, for there was nobody anywhere near Ellerby

Priors the least bit interested in the London rush hour. *Fancy*, she thought, *Philip must have seen this. It was his home once.* She thought of him, a sharp-faced baby in a pushchair.

And that Jocasta. There's plenty places she knows about, and us with no idea. You wonder how Philip's grown up natural at all. He's had a break away from all this anyway. He'll be stuck back in it soon, though, mark my words. They'll all be tipped back down here, that Andrew, that Jocasta, Philip. They'll never get heard of more. You'll see.

And me down here, she thought, *whatever am I down here for with this fond pair? Not one of us knows why. The balance of my mind must be disturbed, like in the papers. I've always got the balance of it back talking to Philip in the past, but here's something you can't talk about with Philip, nor yet with Toots and Dolly. You can't tell the best people things like this. That Smike pair, they'd take it. A fancy-boy and a common criminal. I'd not tell that Middleditch one breath. Give her a whisper and next morning it's in the* North-Eastern Gazette. 'What's that?'

'We were just saying, Miss Banks, that perhaps we shouldn't wait on this cold station for an hour. We think we'll take you for some breakfast at Lady Madeleine's club.'

Alice could think of very little to say to this.

'You must be so tired. We must find you somewhere nice to sit down.'

'I've been sat down all night.'

'But – a good cup of coffee?'

'I 'ave me sandwiches.'

'We feel it's not very pleasant here.'

'What I don't fathom,' said Alice to Madeleine, woman to woman, 'is what you're doing 'ere your

283

age at all before eight o'clock in the morning. You was to meet me t'other end. You must have got up bright and early to get 'ere in time to take me back down again. Are you taking me back? I'd say you ought to be careful of yourself.'

'Ah,' said Madeleine, looking up at the blank train-times indicator.

At once a message flickered up on it announcing Alice's destination. 'Arriving one minute,' it said. 'Front four coaches only.'

It arrived.

The general seized the luggage. The Missus clutched her parcels, and they ran. 'Don't *change*, cried the general, sounding like a romantic film, and The Missus found herself in an almost empty compartment, bound for East Kent. 'You're to cross the footbridge when you get there and there'll be someone meeting you,' he cried.

'Who?' she shrieked back through the window – but Madeleine could not be asked. She could only just be seen far away up the platform under the indicator, her fut hat, her opened newspaper.

'Don't worry,' called the general guiltily, 'please don't worry.'

And The Missus's baleful face disappeared into the dark morning.

Jack awoke the morning after his conversation with Jocasta to find that he no longer loved her.

The knowledge astonished him. The experience of falling out of love was not new, he had done it often, seldom with women, of whom he had little experience, but he had lost other passions. Mathematics had left him early. Physics had deserted him at the university just before his final examinations and he had walked out of them. The passion for Oxford, where he had gone next, to learn some Architecture, had been intense and he had for a time walked in the Celestial City. Then one blustery dead day in the vacation it had withered and died.

The ensuing passion had been for God and that had led him to ordination and to his affair with Holy Church and its rituals, its ancient words, its magnificent music, but all this had weakened when he came upon the Muslims in Bangladesh, the Buddhists in India. God Himself he had never abandoned, quite sure by now of his need for the everlasting arms to comfort and hold him at the end of his every adventure.

There had been women, crowds of them, but only

for gazing at and loving in a perfectly pastoral way. He had seen splinters of God in each and had enjoyed adoring all of them, but he could scarcely remember a name now, hardly a face. Some radiant moments only.

Jack's passions consumed him but vanished always, and it was this aspect of himself that saddened him and gave him his rueful, gentle face, the face that was his fortune and disarmed the world. But he wondered why God had deprived him of the talent for fidelity he would have so much enjoyed. In the end he had decided that his incapacity to concentrate on being faithful must be treated as his Pauline thorn in the flesh, the cross he had to bear.

And at last he had been rewarded. Jocasta had walked in and at once swept away the years of his fickleness. Lost, ill, looking for love, here was God's requested gift. She was the only one he had ever asked to marry him and he was in terror lest, should she accept him, he would at once go off her.

She had given him no answer for weeks, but kept out of his way, spent most of her time in her own room or the Art rooms, wandered the countryside by herself, gone sitting about in cafés in Whitby, begun to take an intense interest, at last, in her little boy. Jack had kept his distance and his regretful face, allowing himself to look increasingly unparsonic, rougher, to remind her of her hippie years. He had stopped washing for a while, and eating, worn threadbare clothes. He was a man who suited a hollow face and as it grew more so he thought this might attract Jocasta, remind her of hungry seductive India. In the fields those first months at The Priors she saw him standing with his cassock hooked up like a medieval French saint. At night over the stove he sat in contemplation, his face turned from her, trying to despise himself for such affectation.

She would sit apart drawing or sewing, sulky, almost ugly, he thought. Not entertaining. A bore. And he waited for these conclusions to bring the blessed release from his obsession. And then she would look up and smile wearily and he was wild for her again. 'Marry me, marry me,' he begged in a silence she could feel. She would gather up her stuff and leave the room.

At length she had said she would. It was directly after Andrew had visited with Holly Fox, after they had become engaged, and Holly Fox had looked at Jocasta and said – in front of her – 'Golly. Aren't you *wonderful!*' Holly Fox had said, laughing, to Jack, 'I've told Andrew I'm jealous. His patient, if you please! Shocking!' Holly Fox had tried to be friendly to Jocasta, who had seemed tongue-tied, quite overwhelmed, had tried to keep out of sight. Holly Fox had grown noisier and slightly embarrassing.

Jocasta had kept her thrilling distance from Jack until their wedding and straight after that she had caught some virus and they had still not slept together. Two nights later they had joined up with the ecumenical expedition to Nepal, where they had slept in sleeping sacks in community huts and he had scarcely been alone with her. He had been happy enough, though, seeing her so excited and grateful for being in the mountains.

On that expedition everyone as usual fell for Jack, which he as usual accepted. He did not notice, because he was so taken up with her himself, that nobody talked easily to Jocasta or seemed to want her company. He would of course have expected them to keep their distance. She was his wife. 'My wife,' he kept saying, watching for reactions. There seemed to be none. Neither Jack nor Jocasta mentioned to anyone that they were on their honeymoon.

Then home again. Sometimes Jack thought that his unprecedented continuing passion for her was only because she still would not sleep with him, and he half feared the moment she would change her mind. Thus the idea of possession was spiced with danger and he had to discipline himself not to think of it. It became in the end a superstition. He must not, must not, think of it or the worst would happen. All would be lost.

During the latter part of the honeymoon trip she had seemed to be growing nearer to him and would smile up at him from the seat beside him on the truck. Leaning from a parapet over a road one day high above two tremendous ice-green rivers that converged at a place called Marriage she suddenly took his bony hand, and he kissed her small brown one, the hand with his ring on it. That day he risked buying her – he was no great one for presents – a necklace made of chunks of red amber, which she stroked and put against her face and let him hang round her neck, though she didn't say thank you.

When they got back to England she put the necklace away. She seemed cold and dismal and not quite well. Philip, who had spent the honeymoon with The Missus eating chips and learning Bridge, seemed unmoved by their return.

In time they slept together, but it wasn't a success. She was passive and apart and he was unnerved.

She made him feel inexperienced and feeble. There was always the suggestion in her that she was living somewhere else, listening for another voice, waiting for a different caress. This made him unable to think her frigid, which was troubling, too, but more troubling was his fear, very secret, that, should she change and grant him the passion he knew she possessed, he might as usual back off; run for God again.

And this he deplored. He loathed himself for it. Inactive. Timorous. Maybe masochistic. Perhaps he was that nastiest of monsters, the apologetic rapist?

And so the balance was kept, and on he suffered, and soon Jocasta had told him of her wish to be celibate, at least for the present, and would he understand?

But he was never unaware of her, wherever she was in The Priors or the studios or the fields. He prayed for her and for himself endlessly. Then was grateful. He was proud of having her, of the impact she made when people saw her first. 'That astonishingly beautiful woman.' He was always amazed that she was even supposedly his.

And for six years they had lived like this, his obsession holding fast until for some reason – it was about the time of Holly Fox's death – a cold wind began to blow from somewhere upon Jack. When he had heard of Holly's death he had put down the phone, turned to Jocasta and told her before going off up the moor. And he'd seen something shocking in Jocasta's eyes. He couldn't place it. 'Holly Fox is dead.' What had he seen? Delight and fury, both together. It was very bewildering. Very terrible.

Knowledge goes ahead of the expression of it as the blow strikes ahead of the pain and the axe drops ahead of the sound of the chop. When Jack had gone up to Jocasta's room last night, at once after Philip had told him she was barren, he still imagined himself in love with her. Tired and cold and hungry after the ghastly day – even Philip turning and screaming at him down in the caravan park – as he sat on her bed he was still adoring the long hair loose on the pillow, the neat fingers folded over the back of the unread book.

That night he had fallen into deep sleep and woken with the thought that some enormous trouble had come to an end, a huge stone tablet lifted off his chest just before it crushed him for ever. He felt dizzy. Not himself at all. He got up and walked over to the chapel but could not pray. He decided to prostrate himself full length before the altar as he had done at his ordination, offer himself utterly to God.

Yet there he stood, unmoving, not even thinking. Standing. In the church there was no sense of any presence, not even his own. No love here. No godliness. He might have been an empty body, a creature long dead and forgotten, like a ghost of the monks who had lived here in the past.

The air was icy. The wooden cross on the shabby altar very small. Meaningless. The dawn had not begun and though he stood for ages watching the east window, it scarcely lightened. He thought of summer mornings here after nights that scarcely happened, when the sky never really grew dark, one of the most beautiful things about the life of this place.

I shall never leave it, he thought. *I shall always need to be here. And the dark in the winter always shifts at last.*

He knelt to say the Office but it was evasive. He tried to say the Magnificat but it faded out. At length, instead, he said, 'I do not love her. I have stopped. It is simple.'

The window began to lighten above him and soon some sort of brightness struck through and fell across the stone floor. 'It was an inordinate love,' he said. 'It was wrong. "Nought shall separate us from the love of God." But she has separated me from it. She filled my being and my being should be filled only with God.'

She was in the kitchen ahead of him, wearing a hefty grey sweater and old trousers, her hair on top of her head untidy, in a rubber band. Without The Missus, the stove was still sulky and cold. The electric kettle had disappeared and Jocasta was filling the heavy iron one to take to the fire in the refectory. Her cold fingers poked through the ends of her mittens.

She said, 'Not much bread. I'll have to get some,' and he thought, *This is the woman. The woman who has tried to destroy me. I have been screaming for her and about her to God and now I'm screaming against her. But how ordinary she looks.*

'Sugar, Jack?'

She is so quiet. So ordinary. It is only Jocasta. My Jocasta. I've manufactured a demon out of her.

But as she made tea and came back and walked about the room, went over to the door and called across the courtyard to Philip to make him hurry, like any boy's mother, Jack knew that something had happened. It had happened last night as they talked and she had said that she and Andrew had betrayed him. And her eyes had hated him for saying it didn't matter. For being simple. 'You can carry forgiveness too far,' her look had said.

So. She had reached the same conclusion as he. Long ago maybe. And it had taken him six years to be out of danger. Out of love.

'Oh, Jocasta,' he said now, 'I'm out of danger.'

And she looked over at him with her usual lack of curiosity. She yawned. 'What?'

' "Not as if you and Andrew had been having an affair",' he said, and stood watching her. She brought him the mug of tea and he drank it. He said, looking out of the window, 'I'm in the clear, Jocasta. You're free of me. I don't love you any more,' and when she looked at him he saw her eyes become unclouded, wide and alive.

When she said, 'Oh Jack, whatever are you on about now?' he was silent. In the silence he saw her at length grow frightened and knew that he had come through to the unconcern that had so reliably ended his every passion every time.

He swam again towards God, allowing himself one fleeting moment of avenged delight.

And yet the day went on as usual. Not another word. 'I'll pick up the rest of the Christmas stuff after I've dropped Philip off,' she said. 'I can't do anything about lunch. Can you find yourself a tin of something? Or could you go over to the Tibs? They always have something even if it's marshmallows. Or get them to come over here. I'll bring something frozen for supper. I've some paint to get near the supermarket for the backdrop for Christmas Eve so I won't be early back.'

'Backdrop?'

'I've told you. I tell you every day. Nativity

tableau. Abstract thing. It's going to look all right.'

'Don't be too late. It will snow today.'

'I'll stay in Whitby till it's time to fetch Philip home again.'

'Don't worry about here,' he said. 'It may well be today that Pammie Jeffreys arrives. Jefford? Jefferson? If she broke the journey last night she might even be here by lunchtime. She'll take over. I suppose there's a room ready?'

'Will she start in straight away, then? Are you paying her anything, Jack?'

'Paying her?'

'Well, why should she do it otherwise?'

'D'you know, I never thought about it. She's very well-off. I don't think she'd accept money.'

'But why should she come?'

'I didn't beg her. I scarcely asked. She jumped at it.'

He remembered the reassuring voice over the phone. He remembered her capable kindness. *Such a steady, sensible woman.* He saw her open face. *No hang-ups there at all. Pretty. Getting on a bit, but a delightful woman. Rather innocent. Deep Christian too, someone said. Surprising from that neck of the woods.*

(*And she was taken with me.*)

'I'm off,' said Jocasta.

On the top road sleet was falling. The three giant golf balls were dirty white shadows above the clean snow.

'Horrible drive,' said Philip to his mother. 'Jocasta, could I board next term?'

'Yes,' she said at once, 'you certainly *could*. I thought you hated the place.'

'Oh, it's OK. They do go on a bit, but I know them now. The Head's OK.'

'You'd miss going down to D & T's. Are you doing better?'

'No. But they're not bad.'

'Are you sick of The Priors?'

'Yep.'

'I see.'

She dropped him at the school gates and he went without glancing back or saying goodbye. *Boys do that*, she thought; *girls don't. Right up to being men they go without a backward glance. Until they're old and then you have to prise away their fingers. Philip has never kissed me or put his arms round me or given me one present. In London he just dreamed about. Sometimes looked me over. Hardly knew who I was. That's Communities for you. I thought they'd make us all stronger. His father the same. Beardless boy, saffron robe. Beads, pot, parents Maida Vale with chequebook to call him home. Mind-blown lazy lout now, I dare say. Maybe banker. Never heard of Philip. Never shall. Oh, I truly believed in all that, I truly did.*

Philip's not like him, she thought. *Not like me either. Nor anybody. My lamb. Could Jack afford boarding fees?*

Then the new knowledge flooded in. Jack would not be finding any more money for Philip now, or for anything else to do with her. The minute Pammie whatshername arrived, she and Philip would have to go.

Last night's conversation and this morning's revelations had swept away the last six years. There had been a weight about Jack she had not felt before. She had seen him angry sometimes, but not sickened, almost poisoned with surprise. *Could Andrew run to school fees? Would he if he could? Could Jack just order us to leave?*

Jocasta realised all at once and quite certainly as

294

she eased the car down off the moor towards the treacherous hill into the town, peering forward through the clotted windscreen, which the wipers were trying frenziedly to clear, that Andrew didn't want her either and that she had known it for some time. She had known it even when he packed her off up here six years ago, before he'd even met Holly Fox. He had found her a burden even then. A sexual delight, but a burden. He had enjoyed her as a serious temptation, the only thing in his life that had made him skid off course, the only unwise thing he'd ever done since he was born. He had needed it, his liberating rebellious act twenty years late, marking the moment when at last he stopped trying to please his Jack-crazed mother.

But the returned desire for her, Jocasta, after Holly's death had been self-pity. It was the reaction of any young man widowed, to take a woman as different as possible from the wife so that in bed there would be no comparisons and out of bed there need never be a loving thought.

It was because he couldn't bear to think of Holly he came back to me. So much for his scratching on the window the day he brought Faith. 'I want you in my bed'. In time, when her memory fades, he'll find another Holly and in the end he'll muddle which was which.

Everything alters,
And one by one we drop away.

I don't want either brother, thought Jocasta, *and of the two I need Andrew even less.* 'Right,' she said as the car slithered into the supermarket car park beyond the quay. *He took away my womb but I don't have to be grateful. Anyone could have done it. I wish it had been a woman surgeon – why are there no women surgeons? – a woman would not think of it as tissue and blood but my female gender, the source of life. Has Andrew ever considered the source of life? Poor Jack, of course, thinks of nothing else, and look where it's got him. Holy poverty on the Yorkshire moors and sycophantic ladies from Surrey.*

Well, 'We're all mad here, said the mad hatter'. The whole bloody wash-bag is mad. My trouble, I suppose, is I'm not mad enough. I brood and suffer but I've no mad passions. I never had. I was never born.

At the supermarket checkout, paying for the turkey, she saw Ernie Smike standing by the doors, presumably waiting for the weather. He looked forlorn in black. He was alone. She said, 'I thought you were working with sheep today,' and he said, 'Do us a favour,' and nodded at the storm. 'Anyway, it's me day off.'

'D'you want a lift home?'

'I got me bike.'

'You can't bike in this. I'll take you. Come and have some coffee.'

They sat in the coffee shop, a strange pair, Jocasta almost invisible, but precise inside a huge duffle coat she had picked off the back of the kitchen door, Ernie towering above her, beringed in ears and nose, his hair short to nakedness, his weighty leather jacket somehow suggesting more nakedness beneath. His head jerked to the music playing inside the black discs over his ears. Tinny reverberations enclosed him.

'Give it a rest, Ernie.'

'Sorry.' He switched himself off.

'What's the matter with you? You look more miserable every time I see you.'

'D'yer wonder at it?'

'You mean Nick going?'

'Oh, let 'im. 'E'll be back. That bitch won't keep 'im.'

'Something wrong somewhere with you, then?'

'You could say.'

'Love trouble?'

'Nar. Is Philip goin' down 'is gran's this week? I can tek 'im.'

'I don't want him to. I don't think he wants to, as a matter of fact. Something happened down there the last time ha had a lift with you. He's not himself. He's forever washing his hands.'

'Yeah – well.'

'What happened? He went out with you and Nick, didn't he?'

"E just hung about. 'E got to 'is gran's.'

'Was he out with your lot first?'

' 'E went off to Dolly an' Toots.'

'There are things in your part of the forest, Ernie, I don't want Philip to know about. I'm not having Philip going the way you went. I mean it. I'm not enlightened about gays. See?'

'Thanks a bunch. So what about you, then?'

'You are being insolent.'

'You're to be the model for 'im, are you? You and Andrew?'

'You're being insufferable.'

' "In-siff-er-able". You was an unmarried mother, wan't yer? I'se no time for slags. Wan-parint families. An' what yer do fer yer keep now?'

'A great deal more than you do. And I teach.'

'Teach wogs 'ow to colour pitchers.'

'Ernie,' she said, 'don't. Don't say these awful things. It's not like you. I'm sorry for what I said about gays, but – I'm all Philip's got. It's not like you to be foul to me. What have I done? It's Nick going, isn't it?'

'It is not. Nick's life's 'is own. If you want to

297

know, it's Jack. An' Toots an' Dolly.'

'Jack?'

'The way 'e's bein' used. Innocent, that's Jack. I 'ates seein' 'im made moonkey of and Dolly an' Toots too, widout a clue. We're not daft, you know. Nick an' I 'ates yer – you and that Andrew. That's why The Missus went.'

She said, looking away, 'I shall soon be going too. I shall be taking Philip. Andrew won't be coming back. He'll probably take Faith away.'

'Get on. Don' flatter thesen. What good does it do Jack everyone packin' off – and Nick goin' and wogs an' all – who's to look to Jack? That's what you don't give a fuck for.'

'Somebody's coming from Surrey.'

'From down there? That bossy posh dyke? Gi's a break, Jocasta, it'll last five minutes.'

'I'm going for Philip. Do you want a lift?'

'I tellt thee, no. I'd not take no lift from thee.'

She sat meekly as he lumbered off.

She saw nothing but sorrow and mess, a pool of unhappiness. She tried to find some spark of meaning in their lives, in any of their lives, one by one, and she couldn't. And yet she knew there was some central matter there if she could only catch hold of it. Sometimes, now and then, she had caught a breath of it. A sunlit day. A sigh of breeze. She nearly caught it now, here in the warm coffee place, people about, laughing and yattering on about Christmas. Happiness. Fading. Lost. She let it go.

I'll go for the paint, she thought, *finish the backcloth. That's all right anyway. It'll be good. I'll finish it whatever, before I go. I'll leave it for them, even if they throw it away afterwards. It will be my present to Jack. Forever. God knows if he'll have a clue what it means. But it is the best thing I've ever done in my life.*

She passed Ernie near the early warning system globes, head down over the bike, helmeted like Camelot. He raised a great black arm in greeting as she went by and she tooted back, surprised and pleased by the salute.

So pleased that she found tears in her eyes.

He's only a kid, she thought; *poor little soul, what is there for him? Nick gone, he'll be in trouble in five minutes. All Jack will do is pray for him and stand around helpless. Poor lad, he's never made a good decision in his life. It'll be drugs and Aids by the time he's thirty. Poor little rat.*

'Where's Philip?' asked Jack when she reached The Priors.

She said, 'Oh God – I forgot him.'

'And so, my dear Madeleine, who's to meet her at the other end, if I may ask? I thought you were?'

'Goodness, no. I only got up to London last night. I have my Christmas shopping to do; one can't do it in *Deal*. Dear Henry's meeting her.'

'How can he know which train? And who's Henry?'

'I don't think anyone knows which train these days. I'll telephone him in a minute. They amalgamate them all, you know. If they don't get enough in one train they let it lie about and fill up with the ones aiming for the next one. I wonder what they do with the extra drivers. Oh, it's all so different, Robert—'

'Giles.'

'Giles. I often wonder if there *are* any drivers, as a matter of fact. You never see them. Each end looks exactly the same, like caterpillars. I expect it's all computers. Darling Giles, how we all take our lives in our hands. It was so much safer in the war.'

'We must telephone Henry whoever-he-is at once,' said Giles. 'I don't think that woman's been about much.'

'She seemed very much in control to me. Very *au*

fait. Not at all overawed by anything. She's like these people you see in television plays or on the radio. You rarely meet any in real life. I don't think these creative people, writers and so on, go about very much outside their own sort. Much less than Alice Banks. Of course, you don't *have* to. Look at Balsac: far too busy to do any research. But then, he knew something to start with.'

'I hope she gets something to eat on the train,' said kind Giles. 'She must be eighty.'

Madeleine looked vain – and indifferent. 'They put a trolley on at Ashford. Henry's my *man*, Giles.'

'Your man?'

'Those trolleys are marvellous when they remember to put them on. Curry sandwiches. Beer. I do rather enjoy beer. Shall we go to the Academic Ladies?'

'Whoever are they?'

'My club, beloved Giles. Where I stayed, of course, last night.'

'Why "of course"? I thought you couldn't leave Puffy overnight. I thought that was why we had to find you Miss Banks?'

'And you did find me Miss Banks, you and dear Thomasina, and I can't tell you how grateful . . . and I did get up and come to the station this morning at a very early hour to look her over, didn't I? Whatever would we have found to talk about if we'd gone down together to the coast? No. I've seen her. She will be marvellous. So now, you and I shall set off for the Club. I'll give you breakfast and you shall give me lunch. Don't be silly, you've *plenty* of time. Then we'll do a little Christmas shopping and go to the cinema. We'll go to the Chelsea Classic in the King's Road.'

'It's been gone these twenty years, Madeleine.'

'Ah,' she said, 'they disappear before you can say you loved them. "What's become of Waring . . ." '

Giles paid off the taxi and they went into the Academic Ladies' Club, where various academic ladies were quietly eating toast.

'Breakfast's over,' said the severe academic lady on the desk.

Madeleine smiled at another one chomping bacon in a corner.

'We are only *obliging* Dr Crass.'

'Then do oblige us. We are ravenous after a journey.'

'You had breakfast at seven o'clock, Lady Madeleine, at some disturbance to the kitchen.'

But breakfast was brought. When the coffee had been returned and replaced for some that was hotter, Madeleine smiled around the shabby pastel dining room, lightening the colourless December day.

'Coffee's good.' Giles was warming up, too, beginning to accept the bizarre morning (and still scarcely after nine). 'What a surprise, you and I here together, Madeleine.'

'Not exactly. Such a chance. To meet alone. After so *very* long.'

The sunlight on her skin lit the pale freckles on her hands. A fawn blotch like the map of Northern Ireland shaded her left cheek. He felt love and sadness.

They lunched at the Royal Academy and proceeded on foot to the Sainsbury wing of the National Gallery ('Such a strange hobby for a grocer') and then on to the Courtauld exhibition in the Strand.

'We might have tea in a McDonald's. There's one

by the Law Courts somewhere.'

'Can you sit down in them?'

'You're not *tired*, Miles?'

'Giles. No. Wonky leg.'

'Oh, men and their legs. Tea, my dear child. China, please.'

'I think you order from the counter, Madeleine.'

'Then you shall order for me. Child, excuse me. May we have a *smoking* table, please. A silly thing to have to say; it sounds as if we're on the slopes of Mount Etna. What? *None* of them? Oh how strong-minded you all are these days. What a curious menu – all kinds of fried things and sauces, and three o'clock in the afternoon. I shall have the chicken nuggets – no, the fish.'

'Fish?' Giles was having a cup of tea.

'Yes, it'll save us bothering with any dinner. I shall dine at the Club.'

'Madeleine,' he reached for her hand, 'you'll do nothing of the sort and you know it and you are lying. You'll ring up some old flame and get taken to Claridge's.'

'You're my only old flame, Richard.'

'Rubbish. Giles.'

'Giles – you are my one volcano. My con-flagration.'

'Well, I'd never have guessed.' (*Why the hell couldn't she have been like this at twenty?*)

'Giles, how strange, they've put this fish in a paper bag. Inside a bread roll. And where are the knives and forks?'

'I don't think they have them. Shall we order two milk shakes?'

'How lovely. I feel American – fish and milk shakes at tea time. Ralph, d'you see how they're looking at my fur hat? Am I overdressed? Ralph, it's years since I had such fun.'

'Giles. Yes. I suppose life's not very jolly for you with Puffy, poor old boy.'

But she said at once, 'Life is no fun at all *for* Puffy, that's what one has to remember. England has died for him. He probably suffers more than any of us. He looks the stupidest of us, but he is in fact the most intelligent. I'll never leave Puffy, Giles. Never. He is heroic and wonderful. Yes, please, delicious tartare sauce, and what a pretty little plastic thing it's in, just like an aeroplane. We can take it home, where there will be scissors, and spread it on something. No, Puffy is a wonderful man. That's why I have employed this excellent though expensive woman. Dear Thomasina – so clever to find her. Thomasina, Giles, will be in time a woman who can accomplish anything. Anything. She will become the strongest of us. At present she's only the most astringent. The most inarticulate and very much the loneliest. But she will become the strongest.'

He saw her into a taxi, *en route* for some Scarlatti and her granddaughter, whom she'd got him to telephone from the McDonald's wall phone. 'She's the fat one who got married the other day. A frightful wedding. They kept blowing hunting horns and all the people round the church gate were wanting to chop up foxes. I'll tell you all about it one day.'

'Anthony,' she said from the taxi, 'think whether you can cope with somebody so *serious* as Thomasina. She might kill you. Goodbye, my love.'

Crossing the bridge back to Waterloo for the train to Surrey, he remembered he was supposed to have been buying pasta for supper and reaching Thomasina well in time for tea.

– 36 –

The grey-faced Missus slept through most of Kent, missing the hop-poles and the oasts and the regiments of poplars protecting the bagatelle boards of the orchards. A refreshment trolley did appear at Ashford but it had run out of tea. She asked for a cup of water but was told that the urn was dry. There was Coke at a pound, orange fizz or alcohol, and she gave the fat teenager with the sad face a look.

'Can't you get another job?' she asked.

No, she was told, and: 'They've even stopped us using the lifts to get an urn fill-up at the depot. It's to save electricity.'

'I'd run up and down the stairs if I was you,' said The Missus, and the trolley wended its depressing way.

A station or so later, so did the only other passenger in the compartment. The train clattered on through the desolation round the entrance to the French tunnel. At Dover the sea arrived and then the white cliffs with long yellow-ochre stains running down them from the rain. *Like lavatory pans*, thought The Missus.

A castle stood on a green hill, looking like a toy.

The Missus thought it not a patch on Whitby Abbey and probably a fake. The train groaned into a small tunnel of its own and stopped. In the dark silence The Missus listened to the whisper of the sea. The train ground out of the tunnel and for a time the sea seemed to be lapping its rails, slapping its flanks. Stony beaches lay below, like glittering whirlpools in the wet. The sea had a thick streak of blue-black horizon with bumps on it. France.

South, thought The Missus. *You won't get me over there. South does for you. I don't travel. Gracie Fields.*

The train stopped at her station and she flung out her suitcases one by one, and then the bundles, climbing down after them. There was a nicely painted footbridge over the line to a ticket office, where hanging flower baskets were waiting for summer. Posh. A couple of damp-looking youths were horsing about the platform shelter but when they saw The Missus they ran off. The Missus couldn't understand what they said. Maybe they were over from France.

She gathered her belongings about her in the shelter and sat on the cold bench. 'I'm not shifting till I'm fetched. That's the head and tail of it,' she said. Rain clattered on the roof and the wind blew. 'The long and the short of it,' said The Missus. She began to eat her sandwiches, which were damp and limp as wet handkerchiefs but very welcome. After half an hour she said, 'That's the top and bottom of it. Here I stay.'

A figure was crossing the bridge towards her. Dressed in a pillbox hat and a short cloak that swung as he walked. He stood before her in the shelter and looked her over.

'Miss Banks?'

'I am.' She crumpled her sandwich paper and stood up and held out her hand. It was ignored.

'I am Henry Jones. I am the Seton-Fairley manservant.'

'Oh, you are.'

'I am in charge of staff.'

'I see.'

'I'm very sorry to be late but I have only just received the time of your arrival.'

'It doesn't surprise me. I thought they'd forget. Where's the car?'

'I'm afraid the Seton-Fairleys are both too old to own a car.'

'Well, the taxi.'

'Taxis have to be ordered in advance and it is no great distance. You seem to have a lot of luggage.'

'Well, I'm supposed to be here for permanent. Get me a taxi.'

'I'm sure we shall manage.'

Again the cases were heaved up, the bundles clutched, and they set off, Henry Jones swinging his cloak ahead of her along the edge of the little town, up a steep wooden staircase to the ramparts, down into a cobbled street of medieval houses.

'They've got this in York,' said The Missus, 'but bigger.'

'This is one of only three perfect medieval towns in the country, built on the old grid system. It attracts a particular class of person. We live to a great age here, what with the golf and the good medical attention. Like Frinton. We have standards here.'

'Didn't think there was anything perfect in this country any more.'

'Times have certainly changed,' said Henry Jones,

inclining his head. (*Thinks he's a butler. He's seen that film. Can't be thirty. Nice boy, though.*) 'For example, staff is very short these days. Living-in-staff, that's to say. I'm worked off my feet about the town. I look after half a dozen. Dying off now, of course, a great many of them, the India and Kenya expats. You used to be able to get eight different kinds of chutney in The Stores. I should prefer one place only but it's out of the question. I get calls from all and sundry. Often at night.'

I can imagine the sundry, she thought. 'Is everybody old here, then? Sort of sheltered accommodation place?'

'It is elderly.'

Godalmighty, thought The Missus.

'Here we are,' said he.

She was surprised to see that the Seton-Fairley establishment was far from large. It was also far from medieval, being a sensible bungalow on a 1950s estate protected from its neighbours by a wattle fence that waved a little in the rainy wind. A heavy roof was clamped down over low compressed-brick walls. The metal windows had rusty trickles of damp from the corners and were shrouded in thick net curtains. Inside, in the stingy sitting room, was a gleaming orthopaedic chair of giant proportions, a hoist with handle and bar hanging above it like a gallows. On the chair, reclining at a steep angle, lay colossal Puffy gazing upwards at a small chandelier.

'This is Miss Banks,' said Henry Jones. 'Colonel Seton-Fairley.'

Again The Missus held out her hand and again it was ignored. She regarded him.

'I shall make tea,' said Henry Jones. 'The colonel and I have had our lunch.'

When he had left the room The Missus with difficulty walked round the chair. Puffy blew air out of his lips and turned his head away. The Missus saw great legs, the fat paws of a bear, the head of a dying lion.

'Thank you, Mr Jones,' she said when he came in with the tea, 'I'll manage now. I'll cook myself something. I've come a long way. Off you go.'

He was halted by this. He had removed his pillbox hat and his pigtail lay over his shoulder.

'You remind me of our Ernie,' she said. 'A very nice boy, though you'd not think it to look at him. Quite my favourite except for Philip. I'll tell you about Philip later on. Now Ernie stays aloof. Feckless but good-hearted. Not like his friend Nick, oh dear me no. Nick's not your nancy-boy type, he's been a burglar. There's a lot of crime where I come from. Very rough place now.'

Henry Jones made to speak.

'A lot of good things, too, mind you. I'll enjoy telling you. From the telly, you see, you get the wrong picture. Different habits. Shaking hands for one. It's thought to be polite with us, shared with France, though I'd not go near the place myself. Well, it'd be us taught them, the Normans. We'd likely been shaking hands before the Normans, having natural good manners when you understand us. Maybe from the Romans. We still have history up there, you see. Not that Nick type, though. Mind you, if Romans is Italians I'd doubt it – they're all for kissing. No, where I come from we're formal. Surnames and titles. So you'll be Mr Jones to me and I'm Miss Banks. Now, if you've poured that tea for

309

the colonel you can go.'

'I'm afraid that I am in charge here, Miss Banks—'

'Not now, you're not, Mr Jones.'

'I think your manners are not French at all. They are uncouth.'

'Now then, stop that. I'm old enough to be your granny and you don't talk to me like that. Leave your phone number in case there's disaster in the night. I'm not sure of this hoist. Well, I'm not sure of nursing at all and it wasn't mentioned, but we'll see how we get on.'

'I think that you and I should have a discussion . . .'

'Yes. Well. When her ladyship gets herself back's time enough. Just take me things to me bedroom, will you, and then get yourself away.'

He went.

He turned with a petulant flourish at the door but she waved him on. She looked her bedroom over and thought little of it after the hospitium, returned to the sitting room and again walked round the chair.

'Did you get any decent dinner?' she enquired.

A blue eye rolled in her direction and a surprisingly soft voice, high and courteous, said, 'Thank you, yes.'

'You've drunk that tea?'

'Just now.'

'No cakes or biscuits?'

'Alas – not allowed.'

She went to the kitchen and saw that salads had been put out for supper. She began to cook a pound of pork sausages she had brought with her in one of her bundles and when they were thoroughly blackened and shining she added onions and a lot of butter. In the speckled fat she made fried bread and carried it all on two plates along with a fresh pot of strong tea into the sitting room.

'How do you eat?'

'I fear,' he said, 'that you feed me.'

'It's sausages.'

'I'm not allowed sausages.'

'Oh, bugger that,' said The Missus.

She experimented with the chair and at length managed to manoeuvre it into a more upright position. She pumped at a lever to lower it and stuck a bit of sausage into the rather dizzy Puffy's mouth. He munched.

He finished two sausages in this manner, then some bread and butter as well as the fried bread. She held the teacup to his mouth. 'I can do that bit,' he said, and took the cup into his paws.

She left him to it and took her own plate on her knee.

'We'll have to see to a civilised table tomorrow,' she said.

'D'you play cards?' asked a gentle voice.

'I do.'

'There's cards in the sewing table.'

'Well – a sewing table. We had one in Rochdale in 1940. Is it for Mr Jones? He looks a sewing sort of man.'

'Now then!' said Puffy. 'He's just a bit of a romantic.'

'He has to be kept in his place. I'll deal.'

They played for an hour, and she brought him cocoa.

'He'll be back to put you to bed, will he, or do I do that?'

'No, no. That is for the nurse.'

311

'Whoever else have you got?'

'There is a gardener and an odd-job man and there's the woman. And someone called The Silver Lady for the forks. And Henry Jones. And the Social Services call, and once a month someone comes to take our blood pressure. And the barber. And the doctor once a fortnight. Madeleine often misses the blood-pressure nurse; she's away a great deal. They think I'm past doing anything.'

'You're not past taking two pounds off me in an hour's bezique.'

'I could take more off them. You're a very good player, Miss Banks. But where's the use? Where do I spend it?'

'On all these servants, sounds like to me. I'm a good player because I play a lot with a little lad where I live. Mind, we don't play for money there, it's religious. By, you do look better than when I walked in: you've a sparkle in the eye. We'll play again tomorrow.'

'Miss Banks,' he said as she got up to answer the door to the nurse, 'you'd better hide my sausage plate. It will put them in a frenzy. They tell me I haven't many more tomorrows.'

'Well, they may as well be good ones, then,' said The Missus.

– 37 –

The fearful weather and wind off the sea continued for a week after the departure of The Missus. Dolly and Toots thought of little but how she was getting on, and how the rest of them could possibly be managing up at The Priors.

The Priors filled their lives. They telephoned endlessly, sometimes getting a reply, more often not. For three days now they had not, and discussion raged about whether the lines were down or whether everyone was away with sheep or whether – this was Toots's view, strongly supported by Mrs Middleditch when she sat in on the matter – Jocasta somehow knew the tone of their telephone calls and did not lift up the receiver.

'And that baby,' said Mrs Middleditch – often – 'how is she getting along? You've not seen her yet, have you? What a shame. You'll be missing all her early little habits. They go so quickly. And the first smile. I must say if the weather was anything like, we'd take you up there ourselves. We'd drop everything. Very happy to. Bingham would be only too glad. He's very fond of old people, you know. It really hurts him to see them neglected. He often says to me, "Mother, you need never worry we'd put you in a Home. I'd never allow it." But then, Bingham's not just anyone. I'm very fortunate.'

'I'd put that Bingham in a Home,' said Toots when she'd gone. 'I'd out the whole bloody lot of them to a Home.'

'She means it kindly, though, Toots. You know, when the weather improves, if it does before Christmas, I'd like to take her up on it. I mean it. I'd like to go. I don't care about being beholden. I could make her a gingerbread. You never know with Christmas. What if it snows? We ought to take any chance we can, if it fairs up before.'

'We'll go our two selves alone,' he said.

'You're being ridiculous.'

'In a taxi. Just hang on. Hang on.'

Dolly woke, after several more days of sleet in the wind and the rattle of torn rose thorns against the glass, to darkness – no sign yet of dawn – and a strange silence. It was profound and she at once decided that it was the silence of death and went flopping downstairs without her slippers and not even stopping for the coat. Toots was lying with all the curtains drawn back on the dark. The church clock boomed out five.

'That's the clock,' he said.

'I know it's the clock.'

'The wind's dropped. That's why we hear it so loud. It's to be a grand day. You'll see. What's the matter with you?'

'I thought you were so quiet. The quiet brought me stark awake.'

Dolly never caressed Toots. For years she had not held his hand. But his days and nights were long and they both knew it. At some point they would be

314

over for one of them. They both knew that that day would finish the one that was left.

Out of the window a low moon bowled along just above the trees, lighting the frost-crisp garden. 'Still as doom,' said Toots. 'We might get up there today.'

'Wherever?'

'Up yonder. Priors. We ought to get there. Right away. Get yourself ready.'

'It's five o'clock in the morning.'

'It'll take time to get straight. Taxi place opens eight o'clock. We order it right off. On the dot. Get ourselves dressed, breakfast done with, all left shipshape. We could start now.'

'We'll have to tell people we're going, else we'd cause a hue and cry. We can't just take off.'

'We're telling no one. We're off. We'll take the presents, then they'll be off our minds. You're all set with them? All done up? And that cake you've made. And there'll be keys to find and doors and drawers to lock and money for the man – did you get our pensions? And I'll need my suit.'

'You'll need your breakfast. If you don't calm down you'll have a seizure. I never heard . . .' She went off and started breaking eggs.

'No call for eggs,' he shouted. 'Hot tea's all we want. And hot-water bottles.'

But he ate the eggs and wrote out some lists to be left lying on various stretches of the mantelpiece. While Dolly was upstairs dressing, he hauled himself along the passage to the bathroom and got himself into the warm combinations waiting over the radiator. Leaning on the zimmer he waited for her to bring him his clean shirt.

'You should by rights have had a bath,' she said. 'I don't like you going all that way without a bath.'

315

'There's none of them there spends time on baths from the look of them. That Jocasta's a dirty-looking—'

'Now then, stop that. She's got a dark pigmentation, that's all. Come here while I comb your hair, such as there is. Then I'll get the luggage together.' Up and down the stairs she tramped with Christmas presents. 'We could get the taxi man to carry down the chair.'

'What chair's this? What are you giving away now?'

'I'm giving her the chair that was her father's. Faith. The nursing chair. It's not big and it's a good chance. Mrs Middleditch'll just make a song and dance if we ask her. There's no room in that Bingham's car, it's all for show.'

'Don't start trying to get it down yourself, then. We've to get hold of the taxi yet. They're not the sort at that place I'd want going round the bedrooms. We'll see the whites of his eyes before we ask him.'

Toots was fast losing confidence. He fumbled for the taxi number. He wrote it down clearly on a page in an old exercise book and added: 'Taxi Ordered 8.10 a.m.' He closed the book and put it away.

'Get on, then, Toots, order it. Here's your frame. You can get down that passage again if you try. I want to put my hat on, it's nearly quarter past. They'll be open.'

'I'll give it five minutes. I'm a bit lame this morning. Can you not do it? I've the number here. I'll listen.' As she went off to dial he wrote in his financial diary the name and address of the taxi firm and then 'Maximum £5'.

'Thirty pounds, he says,' said Dolly. 'I've cancelled it. Out of hand. It's a try-on.'

316

'We'll see about that.' Toots sprang off the bed and humped off down the passage at speed. He seized the phone.

'See here, what's all this? My godfathers! Toots Braithwaite, lad, d'you know who you're talking to? We're off on a Christmas visit. Thirty pounds, you're highwaymen! I remember you. Red-haired. Five A. You were rubbish. Aye, well, I dare say it is a long way but it's a clear road this time in the morning and there's no snow falling. We'd have heard if it was blocked. Aye, we're ready. Been ready an hour. You can come when you like. Twenty pounds, then? Ridiculous. All right, since it's Christmas. I'd have thought you'd have done it for nothing, old people like ourselves, going to see their only grandchild. Have you a good taxi now? Last one stank of cigarettes and drink. And you've got to get a chair down.'

'We're going,' he said. He looked very nervous now. 'Don't forget your heart pills. We ought to take the hot-water bottles. I'm not joking. But we're not taking that plastic bed bottle, mind.'

Dolly had dropped into sad silence.

'What is it?'

'We might get stuck up there, Toots. We'd be a nuisance to them. We're old people. It's selfish putting the mountain rescue on alert. It's what we've always said ourselves: people are plain selfish going off this weather in ordinary shoes and no proper clothes.'

'We've good clothes and shoes and we're not leaving that taxi. So don't be so silly. "Climbing". It's not Everest and crampons. It's Sutton Bank in a station taxi.'

But as they waited he wrote several more notes.

One he propped by the mantelpiece clock for those who would perhaps need information. 'TAXI 8.30,' he wrote. 'THE PRIORS. Return journey commences 2.30 latest. Estimated arrival home, five o'clock latest. Aim for 4.30 sharp. Tel. No. see hall table, lines possibly down. Documents bottom wardrobe.' He repeated the information in his notebook, adding, but not showing Dolly, the name of the funeral director he favoured and the telephone number of Andrew's London hospital. 'Milk,' he said, 'cancel', and began to write a note to be attached to the front door knob.

'That's just inviting burglars, you're going off your head. Here,' said Dolly, 'I've done up the thermos and I'll fill the hot bottles when I hear the taxi.'

'Eight thirty-five. Not here. The bugger's late. It's all off.'

'I'll ring again.'

'No. It's all off. Forget it. We're not right. We're wandering, Dolly. It's dotage. I don't know what we were thinking of, setting off this daft game. I'm not feeling very well. We'll have to call Middleditch.'

'It's here,' she said, from the front door. 'Here's your coat.'

At The Priors the low moon lit the ruined arches and the moors but left the dell where the new buildings stood in darkness. There were sheep clumped up together in the dipping place beside the chapel, keeping each other warm. Sometimes there was a cough or a rattling short bleat from them, but they stood as they had done all night, tense but quiet. Here and there the moon lit their eyes, green staring lanterns. They were to be Ernie's job today. These

318

were the sick sheep brought away from the others. He was to anoint their green eyes with penicillin. Jack would hold them, Ernie squeeze the ointment over both top and bottom lid and let each sheep spring away. Ernie was good with sheep, better than Jack, whose hands were too slight to hold them steady. Nick was strongest of them all, but awkward. The two wide-shouldered Tibetan men had helped once but hadn't caught the knack. It had made Jocasta wonder if they were Tibetans at all. Jack had said perhaps they worked only with goats. The Missus had said for her money they weren't from any mountains, all they liked was rice and you don't grow rice in the Himalayas. Jocasta had said Yes, you do. The matter rested. The Tibetans went back to their sheds and ate chocolate.

'What happens if you just leave their eyes?' the A-level girl asked Ernie, and he had said, 'They go blind. They stoomble about.'

'Does it matter?'

'It does to them. And they break their legs and walk over edges. It's nasty. It's very infectious, this disease.'

'Maybe it's what Faith had.'

'You never know.'

Jack, listening, considered whether the maggots of sheep might serve for a sermon on seeing, but did not see Faith in the picture.

Jocasta was best of all of them with sheep, small as she was. She had hard hands. Ernie wanted her help today rather than Jack's and had suggested it and it had been agreed. The backcloth was nearly finished and Philip was now boarding at school. They were going to get on with the job at first light, for it would take most of the day.

319

It was now five days since The Missus had left, four since Jack had killed Jocasta: that's to say, killed the dark fairy who had haunted him since the minute he met her. The woman who moved about The Priors, now, he saw for the first time. She was deft, thoughtful, abstracted by her own thoughts, but efficiently getting on with each day, managing well the curiosities of Alice Banks's ménage, preparing rather nice food, helping all round. Maybe she had always been so. Neither of them spoke much. Neither mentioned either the Missus or Andrew.

And, to Jocasta, Jack now seemed sterner, more self-reliant, without a trace of homage for her. He gave sensible orders to the lads, did the accounts at the kitchen table at night undistracted by her presence or by anything. He made phone calls about orders of feed, subsidies, veterinary bills. He never consulted her. Maybe he never had. She watched his lean body out over the fields in all weathers, never tired, never considering the life hard. She liked this.

They were at once aloof from each other like people dazed after an earthquake and yet aware that they shared something cataclysmic known to no one else. It was not so much that each was sloughing the other off as that they were both becoming aware of what had been there all along, unshared under the skin.

So that the day when Jocasts had sat so quiet and lost in the Whitby supermarket and had forgotten Philip had been the day when she was not so much beginning to change as beginning to emerge under her own colours. When Jack had almost hit her when she came home without Philip she had been terrified and not tried to hide it. She had shielded her face and gasped. Jack had been horrified, both by himself and by the fact that the cowering had looked so experienced. Jocasta had been hit before.

He'd said, 'Oh Jocasta – oh, God! I'm sorry. You didn't really think I would . . . ?'

She'd said, in the controlled, old-world, educated voice that her hippie years hadn't touched, 'No, no. Of course not. I'll go for Philip. It's no distance. I'll go now. I'll ring him. He's mine.' She was shivering.

'I think Nick might go. Or Ernie. Wherever they are.'

'I'm afraid for Philip, in the sidecar.'

'Yes. Of course. Come and sit down.'

In a while he said, 'I'm going to phone the school and ask them to keep him for the night. No, don't argue. The Head's wife is a nice woman; she's suggested before.'

'Has she? Yes, Phil likes her. I expect they think we're not their sort.'

When he brought her a mug of tea he said rather distantly, 'All fixed. Quite all right. I'm so sorry, you've had a lot to bear lately, Jocasta.' And she thought, *He sounds like some counsellor.*

When she had drunk the tea she said, 'So have you, Jack.'

They both thought of Andrew. There had been no word. And no word of The Missus. Nor of Pammie, whose date of arrival was still vague though Jack had telephoned her affectionately several times, Jocasta in the same room.

'I've done all the big shopping now,' she said, 'all the stuff for the Tibs. And our turkey. It'll have to go in the freezer. It's a shame, but it's just too long a time to leave it out. It was too early, really, to do the

Christmas stuff today, but if the weather goes really wrong . . .'

'Could you – do you know how to cook a turkey? That's if you stay, of course.'

'I could cook a turkey, I suppose. If I stay.'

They sat on, looking into their tea mugs.

'I hope it's big enough. I can't make out how many are coming.'

'A host of motley,' he said. 'There's Toots and Dolly, they're the essentials. They still haven't . . .'

She was looking at him and he held her stare. There was guilt in the air. She said, 'I know. They haven't seen her yet. It's dreadful. Andrew and I did try. We nearly made it, you know, when they decided to keep her in the hospital, but the weather . . .'

He said, 'And we have been otherwise engaged.'

He was disappointed when she got up then and began to unpack all the shopping. 'Must you do that?'

'A lot of it's for the freezer, it can't hang about. The Tibs need theirs right away, they're almost out. They're doing all their own cooking now.'

'Yes. Jocasta. It's Nick and Ernie's night off. We are on our own tonight. Is that going to be all right?'

'Yes. All right. I bought some smoked salmon. I had a cheque sent for Christmas.'

He thought, *Andrew. I won't eat Andrew's smoked salmon. Or maybe it's another man. The father of Philip, whoever he is. She's a dark woman.*

'It was from Thomasina. To buy you a present in case something stops her coming.'

'She'll make every excuse not to come, I'm afraid. She always does. Ever since poor Holly . . . I don't know why.'

'She's still very frightened of seeing Faith,' said Jocasta.

'Is she? I'd no idea.'

'I knew you hadn't,' said Jocasta. Had it not been the raw, exposed, adulterous Jocasta, he'd have said she was looking at him with simple kindness. Almost affection. 'She's afraid of hating her, Jack.'

They sat at supper together at each end of the table, both of them in sweaters and boots. Jocasta saw that Jack's fingers were purple with cold. 'We should wear mitts to eat,' she said. The wind howled outside through the broken stones. 'Poor sheep tonight,' she said. 'I hope Toots and Dolly are all right.' She looked at Jack. 'It's time I saw them again. I was taken up with . . . all that other business the last time.'

It occurred to them both that if they were to take Faith together to her grandparents it might seal this evening they were passing together so extra-ordinarily. So quietly.

'I don't get on with Toots,' she said. 'Your mother's all right.'

These were things she had never said.

'Nobody gets on with Toots, I'm afraid.'

'He has a right to see Faith,' she said, surprising herself. 'I'll drive you down there if you like.' She waited. There was a very great pause and she felt afraid.

'Oh, there's no need. Pammie Jefford will want to go down and they're keen to meet her. She's a jewel of a woman.'

'Very well.'

'Unless of course you particularly want to go?'

*

She thought of her last visit to the old creatures with Andrew, though Andrew hadn't reached the end of the journey. She thought of the delirious hour with him on the way home, the wonder of being alone with him as her lover again. The clinging together, the warmth of him, his skin, the certainty of him. She waited for the familiar surge of love and longing for Andrew to warm her to the heart. She concentrated on the first time she had seen him after Holly's death, here, in this room, at the window, the child on the table ignored. His head leaning on the glass, 'I want you in my bed. My tongue in your mouth.' She waited for the lurch of lust.

It took its time coming. It subsided feebly. She saw herself, this now older creature, shabby in every way, morose, looking down at empty hands in a cold kitchen with the man who was her uncaring husband.

Quickly she said, 'Jack, we must take Faith to them. Right away. Anything could happen. They're old. If they were ill, or if it snowed so they couldn't get here, they'd not see her even for Christmas and it would be scandalous. I don't mean it would be *thought* scandalous, though it would; it would *be* scandalous. Oh, you childless people – oh Lord! I'm so sorry.'

'It's all right,' he said, quite kindly. 'Yes, we'll go. If we can prise the child from Pema.'

'Let Pema come too. She'd get on with your mother and give Toots plenty to talk about for months.'

'I'm not sure that Toots—'

'Oh, never mind him. If you won't go down with her I'll take her myself. Or I'll go with Philip.'

He stared. 'Of course I'll go,' he said.

'With me? Are you sure? Alone?'

'I will. We'll go together, there is nothing against it. We won't tell them, just turn up. They're never out.'

'I have a chicken. I could cook it tonight. Oh yes, and I bought a chocolate-log thing.'

He thought, *This is Jocasta. We sound married. We never did sound married. This sounds like an accustomed marriage.*

Unable to go on with this, he jumped up and said he was going across to the chapel.

Steam rose from the huddle of sheep and also from the sheds of the Tibetan women as he crossed the cloister. The smell of spice from the sheds was so pungent he thought, *It'll make the sheep's eyes water*, and then: *Rather a good joke, that. I must tell Jocasta.* After his prayers he came back across the courtyard and thought that the wind had dropped a little and that it seemed warmer.

'It is warmer,' she said in the morning. She was dressed for out-of-doors, standing by the hot stove they'd all now mastered. 'It's definitely warmer. There's still frost and it'll be snowy on the top but we could drive there perfectly well if we're careful. I'll go over and ask Pema and they can get Faith's foods together and her stuff. They'll want to dress her up.'

'Oughtn't we to be doing all that?'

'Some hope. Pema won't let anyone near Faith. Jack . . . ?'

'Yes, I know.'

'Pema's going to be bereft. Do they really mean it, that they're going?'

'Don't ask me. I understand nothing,' he said, suddenly sounding like his father.

The low moon lit the sheep as Jocasta crossed to

the sheds to tell of the visit. The A-level girl was there. Pema, she said, was not well. Yes, the others could get Faith ready but better not tell Pema she was being taken fifteen miles away. Let her think she was just going to spend the day over in the kitchens.

'If you're all going away for ever, Pema will have to get used to being without her.'

'I'll say,' said the girl, 'that's what we tell her, don't fret. You can't reason with her. She's very old. And look what she's been through. Ten years ago she walked out of China. Six hundred miles. You lot knows nowt.'

There was no sign in the sheds of Faith, who was in her hammock slung in the roof struts, subsumed into the place, into the smells of spices and cigarette smoke, dark cloths and the flickering row of lamps that the third woman – there seemed to be only three Tibetans to be seen now – was lighting. The lamps were arranged along a shelf. They had grown fewer, too, the last weeks.

The girl had told her there was a lamp for every human soul living at The Priors. Jocasta wondered for a moment about Faith wrapped tightly in the nest of these cocksure foreigners. She realised that she was putting her mind into the mind of the baby and felt obscure unease.

In the house she found Jack holding up an old flannelette blanket. The carrycot Faith had arrived in was standing on the table.

'I think it may be too small for her now,' he said, to her and his own surprise.

She said, 'My goodness. Yes. I suppose it is. Obviously. I don't notice these things. Phil always travelled on my back. I'd better have her on my lap in the car.'

'Won't Pema want to hold her?'

'Pema's ill,' she said. 'We're going alone. You'll have to drive. You can't hold her. You'll forget she's there.'

'I'm not exactly the best driver . . .'

'You are,' she said. 'You can. Oh, Jack . . .'

They packed up the old car with Christmas presents, in case Dolly and Toots didn't make it on Christmas Eve, and the carrycot full of Faith's belongings. They carried Faith out to the car. As usual she was passive and sleepy. Ernie appeared.

'These sheep's left to me, then?'

'Get Nick to help you.'

'He's useless.'

'Get the Tibs.'

'Where'd yer be widout me?'

'Lost,' said Jocasta, and smiled.

Ernie stood looking after the car, wondering if he'd seen aright. The two of them together with the baby.

When Nick came frowsting out of his room with the A-level girl, his arm round her neck, Ernie said, 'Yer to 'elp me, the pair on yer. They're away down to Toots an' Dolly. Jocasta's pleasant.'

The moon had set and the sun was reluctantly rising as the car made the ridge road. The white moors stretched pure. The sheep were all down in the pastures and there were no birds, the road silken, lavender-pink, as the low sun shone between miles of empty frozen heather.

'What time do we get there? Ten o'clock?'

'Maybe a bit later but it will be just about right,' he said. 'They'll be up and dressed. It takes them ages.'

327

'Take care, Jack. We slithered. You'll destroy the Saxon cross.'

But Jack was taken up with the glory of God arranging itself down the valleys, the sky turning to ice-blue above the early warning system of the golf balls.

– 38 –

Toots sat in noble silence for the first five miles. Dolly was keeping up a loving monologue addressed to the taxi driver, saying how good of him this was. So early. Such a wintry day. So hard on him to have to turn out at such an hour and then to be having to hang about through lunch, waiting to bring them home. She was absolutely sure there would be some lunch for him and anyway she had brought mince pies. Yes, it was a remote place but he'd find it very interesting and there was only one field gate to open now. When she and Mr Braithwaite had been younger and driven their own *very* nice little car, such a good little car, she'd been able to jump out at every gate for him to drive through. There had been seven gates. It was still a lovely drive of course.

After another few miles she asked him if he knew the way. Well, what a shame. But it didn't surprise her, there were very few Teesside people bothered with the moors, it was all Spain and Tenerife. Five miles more and she informed him that her son, who lived on the moors, was an unusual person. It was a priory they were going to. A ruined priory. Her son was a clergyman.

The driver lit up a fag.

Toots said, 'Put that out, boy. Mrs Braithwaite has a chest.'

The driver put it out. But spat.

'Oh dear,' said Dolly, 'it does seem a shame to ask you. People used to smoke all the time before the Tory government. It must be hard on you now, when nobody does.'

'Plenty do in this taxi,' said Toots. 'It stinks. Here, watch out. Where are you going? Left here – left over the bridge. By gad, the river's full. Look at that snow up the top there. Rotten rattle-trap taxi, this. Filthy, too. Is it going to get there?'

'It's the recession,' said Dolly. 'Everything used to be so different. Leather seats and little tassels and concertina stools. Lovely for weddings.'

The driver said nothing but took the next hill at speed. They climbed above an icy reservoir in its girdle of pines and the strange knoll that bulges out of the first stretch of moorland like a grassy abscess.

'A Roman lookout,' said Dolly. 'Now, when we were young people, Mr Braithwaite and I used to come up here spooning, and to watch the moon rise.'

The driver still preserved his silence but the taxi met the information with a heavy and threatening clanking.

'Whatever is that?'

'Exhaust,' said the driver. 'We'll look in at a garidge.'

'What garage?' asked Toots, surveying the horizon. He was beginning to enjoy himself now, with the excitement of the event heightened by the imbecility of the taxi driver. Empty snowy acres on every side were lit by a sudden torch of sunlight.

'Now that is wonderful,' said Dolly. 'Isn't that wonderful, Toots? Do you want a hot drink? Do you want – you know – *the bottle*?'

'Landsakes, we've not been going half an hour.' Toots was cheering up no end. He was in the thick again. 'They think we're daft, you know – women,' he told the man. 'Light up, laddie. We're up in the fresh air now; we can open the window.'

The driver spurned this suggestion, pressed hard on the accelerator and the loose exhaust pipe roused itself to a crescendo of drumming and fell off in the road. The driver got out and threw it away in the snow. When he reached the bottom of Ellen's Bank he took another confident left fork and roared up the corkscrew hill to Ellen Brow, where a garage of a sort stood to the side of the road near a shuttered and barred hotel, the hotel in which Thomasina and the general had debated the pros and cons of the Seton-Fairley wedding.

The driver slammed off. They heard him round the back of the garage beating on a door.

He returned and said, 'It's gonner tek time, it's morent exhaust. Yer can get yersens a sarnie int pub,' and went off again.

Dolly said that she sometimes understood why North Country people were thought to be common. Toots said that the man was plain scum.

Dolly undid herself from the strap and managed in a moment to get out of the car. She put her feet down carefully in the sharp, crunchy snow and, holding the side of the taxi, sidestepped crabwise round to the boot, where, balancing herself, she toppled out the zimmer frame. 'I'm not having you sitting frozen here,' she said, opening Toots's door and presenting it to him.

'Hold on, now,' he said. 'Do nothing we'll regret. We could sit tight.'

'I'm going to get you in the warm. There'll be a door open to the hotel somewhere; they'd not leave it all winter empty.'

Toots grasped the handles of the frame. 'Take it easy, now,' he said. 'Stop getting hysterical.'

'I'm not uttering one word. Get your feet down.'

Toots did so, took his bearings, then gazed into the distance. He started with a few hiccuping steps very slowly towards the hotel and fell heavily on the flagstones outside its front door.

'It's all up,' he cried. 'We should never have come. Broken leg. Possibly pelvis. I'm finished.'

'I'll go and fetch someone. Don't move.'

'I can't move, you silly woman.'

'I'll get the blanket. There'll have to be an ambulance. It'll be hypothermia in no time. I never knew such a driver. This country, now . . .'

'Get yourself off inside the hotel and keep warm. Send someone out for me. Whatever's this now?'

It was the dogmatic waitress in her bulging turquoise jacket arriving in her car. The jacket she whipped off and had over Toots in thirty seconds. She fastened it round him, hauled him up to his feet and balanced him on his legs.

'What's this, then? Dead drunk at ten o'clock in the morning? Now, then, arms round me neck, we'll see you right. Whatever you doin' 'ere?'

'Get Dolly some brandy – she's a sick woman,' said Toots in the bar. 'Look at my trousers. Best suit. Feller's gone round the back of the garage. He can stay there. He can rot. If you hadn't come we'd be finished.'

'Well, I did. So what were you on with? Skiing

holiday? Sit down. We're closed, so you can have your breakfasts int' bar. Are you right? I can ring t' doctor. He's very good; he'd come. Dear oh dear, 'ere's some buns with your tea. Where you off to?'

The driver came in.

'What the hell you mean leaving them out there, yer daft soggit! Fallen int snow and yer liable. *Oh*, yes – when they're in yer care, yer liable. I'll be witness if there's a leg broke.'

'There's a car broke. It'll tek morning. I'm ringing in: where's telephone?'

'Station Taxis was always a disgrace. Get yerselluf away. I'll tek 'em on wherever.'

'It's Ellerby Priors. Our son is a clergyman there and we're visiting. Just for a very short spell.'

'A very short spell? You don't mean Jack's? Yer off for a spell wi' *Jack*?'

'Well, only an hour or so. We've come up to see our grandchild.'

'But would you ever get down that lane? Did they say it was clear?'

Toots said, looking out of the window, vaguely, 'Perfect day for the drive, we both thought.'

Dolly said, 'We didn't actually say we were coming. It was to be a surprise.'

'Git off, then, yer great lump,' said the waitress. 'I'll see to them. No distance. Get yerselluf together and be ready when we come back. You're a scandal.'

'I'm afraid there's quite a lot of things in the back of the cab,' said Dolly, 'and a chair.'

'Then he teks it all out and loads it up in my car,' she said, 'while you drink your teas and rests.'

'You are very good. I can't tell you how good.'

'Deserve a medal,' said Toots. 'Proper recognition. I'll write to *The Gazette*.'

'Write to nothing. Are you ready?'

'I'd like the cloakroom,' said Dolly, and while she was gone Toots had a go at catching hold of the waitress's hand and she had a go at slapping him off.

Outside, while the taxi driver blackly struggled with the chair on which once upon a time Jack had been held in Dolly's arms, Jack himself drove by unseen with Jocasta and Faith, heading in the direction of the estuary.

'It's all right,' Jocasta was saying. 'There's been a car up just now.'

'How is she?'

'Just lying here looking at me. She looks puzzled. Sometimes puzzled and then she screws her face up and looks amused. They've dressed her to kill. She's like a furry monkey. A mini-yeti.'

'I think we'll get something of a reception.' He smiled at Jocasta in the mirror.

Half an hour later the waitress's car nosed its way slowly and jerkily down the lane towards Ellerby Priors. Sheep stood about there, blinking their eyes, in the company of a languid girl and The Smikes, who were battling with more sheep in some pens. There was an air of emptiness, somehow.

'They've gone down to thee,' said Nick. 'They've tooken Faith to show yer. Did yer never pass them? The phone's gone down. We can't ring.'

'Is *nobody* here?' asked Dolly. 'Isn't even Philip here?'

'No, they've left him int school.'

Dolly began to cry.

– 39 –

It was a curious quartet that was proceeding up the A1 on the twenty-second of December. It was much later than Pammie had planned but she had decided that there were things that must be done about her private life if she was really contemplating leaving it behind for good. Or even perhaps only for the spring. Jack had been having many humble conversations with her now for over a fortnight, almost every evening at first but now more intermittent. Neither of them fully addressed the matter in hand, what her duties were supposed to be, her terms of employment, her accommodation, how long she would stay. They talked of the weather, the Nativity tableau, the difficulties of bereavement, of Pammie's parish church and how it would be the first time in years she would be missing its Christmas services. Jack had said, 'Perhaps you should just hop on a train and come up right away? Don't think of luggage. I don't want to beg you – what right have I? But we do miss Alice Banks.'

He did not mention Jocasta and he didn't specify exactly what it was about Alice Banks that he missed. He had found to his guilty shame that it wasn't really all that much. He thought of her angry, rusty presence over the spluttering pans and then imagined Pammie in her bright clothes and manner, talkative in shiny Surrey lipstick, catering with ease for any batch of needy souls that might present itself. Carrying little Faith about against her tweedy shoulder.

But Pammie had needed time. Her house had to be in order, her Christmas telephoning complete. No Christmas cards to send this year – the widow's privilege – but many friends who'd offered to have her for Christmas had to be placated and told she was going away, and where, and to whom. The dog had to be dumped on the long-suffering gardener, water and central heating switched off, burglar alarms pepped up and the halogen lights to the drive and the recording of a pack of Rottweilers made ready for anyone who approached the wrought-iron gates – except, of course, the postman, who knew you have to slink round the side along the wall like any self-respecting thief would do. 'Also,' said Pammie, 'how very ridiculous if Giles and Thomasina are going up there that we shouldn't all travel together.'

'Alas,' said Giles, 'Pammie – I'm afraid we've undertaken Madeleine.'

'*Madeleine*? Madeleine Seton-*Fairley*. Never! And not Puffy? Left *behind*? And what does Thomasina think of *that*, I wonder?'

'Puffy's being looked after by some woman, a Miss Banks. She's already arrived.'

'So that's where the frightful little woman went. Poor Jack. He's been very badly let down.'

'Rather a crisis going on up there, I gather. One thing and another,' said Giles. 'And very good of you to sort it out, if I may say so, Pammie. Queer sort of Christmas break for you.'

'It's probably for much longer than Christmas,' she said, looking at her nails. 'Jack may want me there with him for some time.'

'In which case,' said Thomasina, 'you'll have a mass of stuff to take and we'll need more than one car. And, after all, we'll need our own car, to come home again.'

'Oh – back on the train,' said Pammie. 'Much faster. I'll drive you to a station from The Priors. Actually, I'd like your company on the way. If you would. It might be just a bit embarrassing for me, arriving alone.' She looked coy and Thomasina looked sickened. Thomasina also looked and sounded tired.

'There will be Madeleine to transport, too,' Giles warned Pammie. 'She's immovable.'

'Oh, there'll be plenty of room. I'm only taking tweeds and woollies and boots and a present or two. Is she large? I forget.'

'No,' said Giles.

'Yes,' said Thomasina. 'Big-boned.'

The main difficulty that the journey presented was getting everyone together at the same place at the same time.

Madeleine had elected to stay all the time in London since the arrival of The Missus in Kent. She said she travelled light and had her mink with her for the cold to come and Puffy sounded to be perfectly splendid, not thinking of Christmas at all. She had a wonderful woman for Puffy. Did Giles know? Had she told him? She was growing hazier about Puffy and told Thomasina on the telephone how she had always loved him so, rather as if Puffy had already left the stage. She told Pammie that she had phoned him from the Academic Ladies one night and there had been no reply, so she had had to ring the police, who were used to her and very kind and calming and had discovered Puffy's phone had been taken off the hook. 'Probably gambling,' she said. 'People don't altogether know, Pammie, what I have had to bear.'

Then there was the general. He had had to go back to his house to see to things: excuse himself from all the drinks parties, and tell the Chaplain he couldn't take the bag round at the midnight service, and leave a present for the milkman, and countermand the two turkey steaks that he had been thinking of taking over to Thomasina on Christmas Day.

Pammie and Thomasina planned to travel from their Surrey dwellings together, side by side in Pammie's car, and pick up Madeleine and Giles in central London.

Madeleine took charge. Not stirring from one of the chintz chairs of the Academic Ladies, she arranged for the party to gather outside it and at two toots on the horn from Pammie after breakfast on the twenty-second she and Giles would step out of the door and into the car and off. Giles would of course be staying the night before with her at the Club.

'But I have my own club,' said the general.

'Mine is much more convenient.'

('I do not believe in Madeleine,' said Thomasina to Pammie. 'I think Giles has invented her to hurt me.' 'Then get rid of him,' said Pammie. 'Drop him. Drop her. Let them both melt like morning dew.' But Thomasina didn't reply.)

338

'I am not *sure*,' said Giles, 'that it is possible for me to stay at a woman's club, Maddie. I'm neither an academic nor a lady.'

Madeleine said, 'My dear, I'm not at all sure that *I* am,' and that the place was full of old generals staying with their ex-girlfriends.

This alarmed him more than anything. 'Look here, Maddie. I suppose you do realise that Thomasina and I are, well, pretty close and so on?'

But she only smiled.

He was relieved to find that he was allotted a bedroom that was decidedly single. A very nice room, virginal clean and collegiate, but a section of it had been annexed as bathroom for the room next door. An academic lady could be heard singing there in her shower. When he tiptoed with his sponge bag along the corridor in the morning he found another one making herself tea. She had ranked metal bars across her head and was reading *Sonnets from the Portuguese*. It was a world he had not met.

Madeleine had drifted mysteriously away the evening before and he'd rather wondered if it had been round the corner to the Dorchester, but there she was in the Academic Ladies foyer at a quarter to eight, waiting for the car, watching from the window. She was wearing wellingtons. Her fur coat was over a chair; her skin luminous with money and French creams. She was surrounded by luggage, enough for a cruise to Bombay.

'Edward!'

'Giles.'

'*Giles*! Did you sleep? Did the bells wake you?'

'Bells? No. There was a bit of singing.'

'Oh, I do love London at Christmas. Bells Singing. Fortnum & Mason pâté. You can often see the Queen there, you know. I've seen Charles buying his cheese at Paxton's. I do rather wonder why we're leaving it all.'

So did Giles. But then he thought how helpless and romantic and reminiscent Madeleine looked: every now and then a flicker, not exactly a smile, reminded him of what she had been. Well, still was. Somewhere. Very pretty woman. Diana Cooper type. Bloody unkind really, this crumbly wrinkly stuff they all go on about. Not on.

He sat beside her. 'I'd much rather be staying in London, if you want to know, Maddie. Some coffee?'

'You shouldn't tangle with widows,' she said. 'There's great safety in a husband about, even if it's silly old Bertie.'

'Puffy.'

'Ah yes, Puffy.'

'Coffee only in the breakfast room,' the Desk said to Giles. 'And I don't believe you're a member here.'

Madeleine said, 'Do you know, it may be nice after all to be leaving London.'

He said, 'Now – Madeleine, I want you to think very hard indeed and tell me why it is you are coming with us to Yorkshire.'

'Oh, loneliness,' she said, 'curiosity. Trying to keep ahead of my wits, or lack of them. Being with you again, Giles.'

'And Puffy?'

'Oh darling, shut up, Puffy's *gone*. Marvellous man, but he's *gone*. I always wanted to marry you. You were an awful fool.'

Outside, Pammie could be seen marching round

her small Peugeot and kicking its tyres thoughtfully, considering the hours ahead. Thomasina, in the front passenger seat, did not get out or turn her head. Giles went out, opened her door and kissed her cheek in a conjugal way and then began to arrange luggage in the boot. As well as the cases, Madeleine was transporting some large bowls of spring bulbs, bought at Harrods, that were to go in last. Giles himself was taking a gun.

'A gun, Giles?' asked Thomasina.

'Might get a bit,' he said, 'according to Maddie.'

'A gun at The Priors?' said Pammie. 'I'm afraid you're out of luck. It's a very religious place.'

'I know The Priors,' said Thomasina. 'You probably didn't notice that it's a farm. Naturally there are guns. They have sheep.'

Madeleine stood on the pavement. 'Oh, Giles won't have to shoot *sheep*, Thoms,' she said. 'We're staying with old, old friends of mine nearby with quantities of birds to shoot. Tony Faylesafe. Darling man.'

'I'm not,' said Pammie.

'No, *you're* not, of course, you're going to be cook to the parson. I hope he's paying you. They try and get away with that sort of thing, you know, parsons. Always did. I hope he isn't Catholic; they're the worst with willing women. But then I'm hopeless at religion. It all seems so unlikely. Tony Faylesafe's *very* nice. I simply rang him. "Faylesafe," I said, "I'm bringing a couple of friends with me to stay with you over Christmas," and he was absolutely thrilled.'

'Well, I hope so.'

'No doubt about it, Giles. I told him you couldn't possibly stay at that ghastly hotel where they put

341

the lights out over the cheese – yes, you told me about it, however else could I know? Do you think my memory's gone? – and I said, "We aren't religious enough for this funny fellow," and *he* said, "Well, all right, come if you like, Maddie, but tell them I'm not a great one for Christmas." '

There was a short silence.

'Perhaps he's a Buddhist,' said Pammie. 'We have some at The Priors.'

'I don't think so, darling. I think he's a misanthropist.'

The silence deepened. Thomasina, who had been thinking that Thoms was the name only Giles had ever called her, and that he must also have told Madeleine about the fiasco of the moorland hotel, said slowly, 'I shan't be staying with the Faylesafes, Madeleine.'

They were on the move now, driving down South Audley Street, the flower shops, patisseries and jewellers all awakening for a lavish day. Early in the morning the Christmas trees were lit. The huge plane tree rooted in asphalt outside the Hilton Hotel was slung with its thousand electric bulbs like moonstone drops. Hyde Park was a green haze touched with frost.

'I think I'd better warn everybody,' said the general, 'that I have to be back quite soon. Committee meetings. Thirty-first at the latest.'

Thomasina had sunk to silence beside Pammie. Aromatic Madeleine reclined beside Giles in the back. Giles's long old legs were jacknifed almost under his chin. The gun lay at their feet.

He thought, *This is a blasted awful situation*, and remembered last Christmas drowsing and boozing in a chair in Wiltshire with an old cousin; and the one before with Hilda, at the golf club. No women allowed in the bar there even on Christmas Day, but she'd never minded. Glad of a gas with the other girls.

Girls, he thought. *Good girl, Hilda. Whiskers on the chin but reliable. Herself always. Full of fight. Off round the links with the dog in those terrible trousers after lunch. Cooked Christmas dinner in the evening. No fuss. No* haute cuisine *nonsense. Turkey and sprouts – all warmed up but very nice. Couple of old friends round for Bridge afterwards. Never got tired, Hilda. Always had my old blue smoking jacket cleaned for Christmas. Good pals. Boxing Day: walked the plantations round the garrison, feet in the sand under the Wellingtonias. Wonderful trees. Planted after Waterloo to commemorate the Iron Duke.*

Pammie was rounding the bottom of Park Lane with Apsley House afloat on its island. *Tables all laid up exactly as they were for the Waterloo Ball*, thought Giles. *The Great Reception. Battalions of crystal, cartloads of porcelain, half a ton of silver. Ivory placement cards. Cream of Europe.*

Who the hell knows a thing about Waterloo now? he wondered, watching a covey of Arab ladies with slits for their eyes rolling over a pedestrian crossing by Marble Arch. *Never even heard of it.*

Glancing down Oxford Street he saw the huge, unlighted metal banners – Donald Ducks, Father Christmases – waiting for the dark, like the shredded flags in churches that commemorate old triumphs. The laden car plunged northward into the Edgware Road.

– 40 –

'Braithwaite,' said the Head, 'I suppose your parents do know, do they, that the school broke up over a week ago and that you are here only for extra coaching? Out of choice?'

Philip looked amazed. 'I thought it had been arranged.'

'I suggested it to you. You said you would enquire. You came back in here, to my office, and said that it was on.'

'Yes. I like it here now.'

'You've been doing very well. Philip, I did just wonder. Friday is Christmas Eve. Are there any arrangements to collect you?'

'Oh, I'll ring.'

'We've tried. The line is out of order at The Priors. You don't want to miss Christmas at home, do you? Do you? *Now* where are you going?'

'Oh, just out. Along—'

'You're going to wash your hands, aren't you?'

'Yes. I might.'

'Philip, could you talk about it? Do you know why you're always washing your hands?'

'They're always dirty.'

'That used not to bother you.'

344

'No.' He looked innocent. 'No, actually it didn't. Emma was saying that.'

'Does my wife allow you to call her Emma?'

'Yes. She's not exactly mad about it, but she lets me.'

'I see. She says, Braithwaite, that you've been having nightmares. She's had to wake you up a couple of times. We wonder if you really do want to stay here? Or, can you tell me, is there some trouble at home?'

'I'm not exactly mad about telling private stuff.'

'Very well. But it seems such a shame when you're beginning to get on so well otherwise. Do you want to stay on next term? Boarding?'

'Yeah, well—'

'Don't say "yeah, well". Will you answer my question. Is it the new sister? Have you had enough of her?'

'You can't get near her. She's always with Jack's Tibetans. But they're going.'

'So who will look after her then? Will your mother be in charge? Is that it, Braithwaite? Are you miserable about the baby – jealous? It's very normal if you are.'

'I don't know who's going to have her,' Philip said at last. 'There's nobody really. There's a woman coming but she's only a cook. Miss Banks left.'

'I heard something about that.'

'She doesn't write to any of us. We don't know why she went. Jack's hopeless.'

'Ah. Hopeless. Your father.'

'He's not my father. I don't know who my father is and I'm not mad about finding out. And Jocasta's not her mother. Faith's mother's dead. Jocasta has nothing to do with Faith. Well, I don't know what's going to happen.'

'Do you ask?'

'No. I don't go in for questions like that. My grandparents are great. I could really live with my grandparents and so could Faith, but they're so old and they live in a foul place on the estuary.'

'I know Toots and Dolly. Toots taught me. He must be getting on a bit now.'

'He's got more sense than Jack,' said Philip, and then shut up.

'Go off and have tea now. I'll join you all in a minute. Emma and I will drive you home for Christmas if no one turns up to fetch you, but I'll go across myself tomorrow and remind them.'

'Jocasta'll wake up all of a sudden and remember, I expect,' said Philip, 'but thanks.'

Making a Lego city on the floor with the Head's children after tea, he thought, *I wouldn't mind Jocasta forgetting, but it's supposed to be Faith's christening. I bet they've forgotten that, too.* The children crawled on him and he shook them off and they began a cheerful fight with him until he eased himself out and lay on the sofa. The family dog was on the sofa, and it rested its head on his stomach. A child tried to wheedle him back to the floor.

'It's cold ham for supper,' Emma called. 'Phil – yours with the little ones or later with us?'

'Later, please.'

'Well, well. Something new. You're growing up.'

'I'd better—'

'Where are you off to now?'

'Just washing my—'

'Phil,' she said, and stopped him. She led him into the kitchen. She took his hands and opened them

346

up and kissed each palm. 'Clean and fresh as a newborn baby's. What's up, Phil?' She put his hair out of his eyes, but he flung away.

'Nothing.'

'Come on.'

'Oh well, just Jack.'

'But Jack is the kindest man in the history of the world.'

'He may be,' said Philip, 'but he gets taken in. He doesn't understand people. Jocasta does, when she thinks, and I do, but Jack's silly. It's the sort of people he thinks he can help. He takes in rubbish.'

'They're Indian, aren't they? Artists? They sound so interesting.'

'Those ones are going. It's the next lot. He wants some down-and-outs to look after; they're off the caravan site on the salt marsh. Except he can't look after a louse.'

'Well, that's quite a good-hearted wish, isn't it?'

'He can't distinguish good people from bad. He's all set on a sod coming—'

'Thank you. Not sod, please.'

'Yes, he is. I know him. He won't come, though, because when he saw me sitting in Jack's car he disappeared fast. But Jack just *believing* he's OK! Jack's useless not to see. *Anyone* could see he was a filthy pervert.'

'You know this, do you?'

'Oh yes.'

'Could you tell me?'

'I could tell you a bit,' he said, and did.

'Oh, poor Phil,' she said. 'You should have told Jocasta. Or anyone.'

'There was no one. They're either old or mad or

347

foreign or disgusting. All of them. Everyone's disgusting.'

He began crying and she held him tight. He cried like a four-year-old, howling and gulping for some time. Her husband came in and Emma shook her head at him and waved him away.

When Philip was quieter she said, 'There's a Pink Panther video. D'you want to watch it after supper? Or I could bring you some supper to bed. You don't have to sit up with us.'

'It might be my last night here,' he said. 'I'd better sit up.'

'We could all eat now. Or d'you want your bath first?'

'No,' he said.

She scanned his face and thought how children's faces are never marred for long by tears, but other than their faces, very long. 'I hear your French is coming on,' she said. 'Maybe the school's going to France next year.'

'I mightn't be here.'

'You will,' she said. 'I promise you will. I'll not let anyone take you away – see? What's all this about? Is everyone leaving Ellerby Priors?'

'They don't know what they're doing. There's something wrong with everyone.'

'What about this baby?'

'Nobody's thinking about her. Nobody at all but me. I'm not mad about growing up, if you want to know.'

'Go and wash your hands,' she said, forgetting.

'What – now?' he said. 'I'm fine. I'll have supper.'

348

– 41 –

Jocasta and Jack stood on the doorstep. Faith was in Jocasta's arms, her eyes wide, her cheeks red, her face full of alert pleasure, her mouth a rose. There was no reply to knock or ring and the rain fell, with sleet in the wind.

'I'll look through Toots's window,' said Jocasta. Holding Faith against her shoulder, she tiptoed into the frost-painted wallflowers, to see Toots's bed inside tidily made up with its bedcover pulled smooth. The rug was turned back from the hearth although the electric fire was switched off. There was no sign of bed table, bottles, pills, zimmer frame. The daily paper lay neat and unread on a chair. The Christmas cards on the mantelpiece had been pushed back to make way for a good many white postcards and half pages of white memo paper.

'But they *never* go out,' said Jack. 'Something has happened.'

They knew that they must call on Mrs Middleditch and, putting another wrap round Faith, they walked slowly down the terrace and uneasily rang her bell.

'I'm sure I've no idea,' she said, looking over their

349

No, I haven't seen them this morning. I have my own life to see to. They know where I am if they want me.'

'Of course. We knew you would be the only one who might have—'

'Oh yes. That's what everyone says in this terrace. I've become known as the only one. When Miss Bean died, who found her? So thin you'd have thought I'd never taken her a crust. Sat up in bed at a right angle like she always was, and dead two days. I had to lay her down and she snapped. There was a crack. Like sticks under your feet. Oh yes. *And* Mr Ramshaw. *And* Mrs Scott, and her daughter never coming near in five years. They say I get left things in wills. I can tell you it's not my wish. I'd return it all if I could, half of it's rubbish, and I *don't* want your mother's tallboy, Jack. No. There's two things only I have to say to you this morning. One is that Toots was ruder to me last night than he's ever been and only because I mentioned – quite privately while Dolly was out of the room – about him fancying the woman who comes for his toenails. And also, I have to tell you, you've chosen a bad morning, my point of view. Why? Because my Bingham's left home. Just before Christmas. He's gone with an older woman in her car.'

'Oh, I am so sorry. What a troubled Christmas time for you. First Alice Banks and now—'

'If we could perhaps . . . ?' said Jocasta.

'What? Oh, step inside. Is that the baby? Well, they will be pleased, I'm sure. She's big, isn't she? Getting on now, of course. Dolly's fondest of tiny babies. New ones. Well, she won't have the pleasure of *that*, I'm afraid. I'll just get some newspaper for you to stand on. Have you rung the police?'

Emotions were at war in Mrs Middleditch. The disappearance of Toots and Dolly would have been rich meat for a year had it occurred only yesterday. The departure of Bingham infuriated her quite as much by its timing as by the fact that she had at last lost him. In her heart she had longed for a daughter-in-law for Bingham to bring home, a little fair thing who wouldn't meet your eyes. She could have been shown the perfection it is possible to achieve in a home and in a mother. Mrs Middleditch knew, as it happened, all about the absence of Toots and Dolly because she had seen the taxi go by and was furious that she hadn't been consulted, that they had hired transport of their own accord instead of letting her organise and drive them. She might naturally have had to refuse because of the trauma of Bingham, but she should have been given the opportunity for suffering and service.

The Lobster Inn, Saltburn, is where she thought they'd have gone. Turkey, stuffing, gravy, trimmings, sprouts, plum pudding, glass of red wine: three pounds twenty-five and daylight robbery. She'd offered them a Christmas dinner with her, knowing this lark to the moors was pie in the sky. That's where they'd be. Saltburn-by-the-Sea.

'D'you want to ring anybody?' she asked. 'Maybe you should contact the Social Services. I did see them going by in a taxi about half-past eight.'

'Ah!'

'To Saltburn, I'd think.'

'Saltburn at eight-thirty in the morning?'

'I'd not slept the night, what with Mr Middleditch not at all himself about Bingham. They're doing these special dinners. I'd think it was because poor Dolly has been very low lately when she thought she wouldn't be seeing the family, wouldn't you? They've had a long wait for this baby, you know. Well, isn't she pretty? I'll tell Dolly all about her. They have these bolshy fits, ordering taxis, you know, or Toots does anyway, poor Dolly. "Little gestures of independence," the doctor calls them, but I call them ugly rebellion. Ugly rebellion. It's not as if they've many friends left to go out with now, the two of them. If it's a meal, it has to be together. And wherever else have they to go to except . . . ?'

An incredulous dawning was taking place in Jocasta and Mrs Middleditch; rather more slowly in Jack.

'Unless . . .'

They eyed each other across the spotless hall.

'We must go back at once,' said Jocasta. 'It's been a very easy drive down and we'll go straight back again. We must get Faith home. At once. It was a sudden idea. We should have thought of it before. It's so easy, and she is such a very peaceful baby.'

'We used to take our Bingham everywhere,' she said. 'Up and down to Spain and once there was a typhoon.'

She shut the door on them.

On the way home, in silence, they passed the moorland hotel and the waitress's parked car. Toots and Dolly were invisible in the bar, waiting for the taxi repair, which was going on out of sight round the back of the garage. The waitress was frying bacon and eggs and supplying more hot drinks. Toots, who had refused a whisky, was sitting thoughtfully. *Half an hour, maybe three-quarters of an hour, home. We'll miss them. They'll be on their way back now unless Middleditch is in a good mood and keeps them down there. She didn't look to be in a good mood when we passed the house this morning.*

352

*

The failure of the mission drew Jack and Jocasta together a little and humbled them. The Priors seemed empty and dead when they returned and there was nobody to tell who would even begin to understand. Jocasta thought belatedly of Philip. She felt that somehow, if Philip had been there, if he'd come down with them to his grandparents, he would have known what to do. He'd have climbed in and they could have waited, made the place warm, got a meal going. Philip might have known where to find a key. Why ever hadn't they asked Middleditch for a key? Why hadn't Middleditch offered? She was sure to have one. If she'd been a normal woman she'd have seen them in, and everyone would have waited together for Dolly and Toots's return, and laughed.

Laughed. Not much laughter these days.

As Jocasta thought this Jack said, 'As time goes on I find I'm thinking such a lot about Holly Fox. You have to wonder sometimes if Faith, everyone, would be different, everything all right, if Faith still had her mother.' Then, seeing Jocasta's face, he said, 'You know what I mean. A real mother. You've been a real mother, I know.'

'No,' she said, 'I don't think I have. Phil runs me. I'm hopeless with children.'

'If he's so self-reliant, then you are a good mother.'

'I'm not sure he is. But he never notices me, Jack. He never turns to me. He never says goodbye or hello at school. I know I dragged him about the world at the start but I never, never, left him. I've never left him for a night except in hospital and our

353

honeymoon and at that funeral. I could have dumped him. It was always going on in these Communities. The children were held in common. Back home I was so clueless it's a wonder he wasn't taken into care. But I'd not have dreamed of leaving him. Yet he doesn't love me. He never touches me. I'm useless, Jack.'

All he had to say was, 'Where is Philip now? Oughtn't he to have broken up?'

'He never said the date.'

'I'd have thought that by the twenty-second of December . . . ?'

'Yes. Oh heavens, yes. He *should* be home by now. They won't have been able to telephone us. Jack, I must go over. I'll go now.'

She had taken the uncomplaining Faith back to the sheds and was getting back into her car, when a Land-Rover drove under the hospitium gatehouse with Philip's headmaster in it. Phil didn't want to come home and they would be very happy to keep him till Christmas Eve. Would Jocasta agree? Phil was no trouble at all. Doing well with his reading; French oral outstanding. And they had to say that he was being an amazing help with the children. And Emma adored him.

'But I think I'd *like* him home,' said Jocasta. 'It's Christmas time.'

The schoolmaster pointedly did not look around the chaotic kitchen: the unlit fire, Jack and Jocasta dismally muffled in outdoor clothes, not a sign of festivity. 'I'd like to talk about Phil sometime,' he said. 'It's about time for another conference. He will, of course, be staying next term? There was some doubt, I seem to remember. He said something about some of you moving south?'

354

'He said what? We've never mentioned it to him.'

'Phil picks up news as he breathes. I'd like to keep him at least another year. Preferably three. To move him now would, to my mind, be a great pity. I'd like him to board.'

'I'm not sure . . .' Jocasta walked across the room to the teapot and stroked it, looking out of the window.

'If it's the fees . . .' the Head said.

'It's not the fees,' said Jack. 'We'd manage somehow. He's our only one.'

'Let me know, then. I'll be off.'

He was back in the Land-Rover before Jocasta could think of any message for her son, shaken as she was by Jack.

'Our only one'.

'Our only one'.

Turning to Jack, she found him gone.

– 42 –

At Peterborough Madeleine announced that there was only half an hour more.

She had been engaged upon genealogical exposition, 'Billy Faylesafe being the *nephew* not the son of Tony Faylesafe, who married, if you remember, Stephanie *Besant*, that frightful woman's daughter, not altogether someone you could know, but then the *second* wife was of course Loveday *Madden*, such a pretty girl but epileptic and not altogether reliable because of that awful business with the son. Who disappeared, you know. They don't talk about it but I expect he was in the Foreign Service – Puffy always says M.I.6. He was a radio ham. Now *Bridget* Faylesafe would be Emma's cousin. *Nice* girl, Emma – it's where we're staying. Very provincial, of course, and mad about children and rather a bore if you're not that sort. Very poor clothes, but pretty and frightfully OK. Born somewhere splendid and connections in Ireland – I mean real Ireland, Low-Church, not Catholic of course, somewhere near Dublin, decent country house. Hasn't an accent, naturally, neither an Irish nor a Yorkshire one, but otherwise a bit wild and woolly. And, *need* I say, left-wing. My dear, she's married a schoolmaster, though not too bad at all – Winchester and related to the Bartram-Flites. I dare say we'll see her, unless it's the father we're staying with. I'm really not quite clear.'

'You surely know where you've invited us, Maddie.'

'Well, it's one or the other,' she said. 'Now here we are at Stamford and we can get them to carry in all the luggage. Excellent hotel.'

'We're not staying here, Madeleine,' said Pammie, 'we're stopping for lunch.'

'Of course we're staying here. I booked us all in. We can't do the journey in a day. We're far too old. Anyway, it's a chance for a fling.'

'I certainly hope you have *not* booked us all in,' said Giles. 'It's a hundred pounds a night.'

'And dinner on top,' she said. 'Wonderful dinner.'

'You live in a world of dreams,' he said.

But, as it turned out, not all the time, for three rooms had indeed been booked in the name of Seton-Fairley a week ago, and only just in time, for the hotel was very full.

'I can't possibly afford this,' said Thomasina.

'Neither can I,' said Pammie.

The general didn't like to say that neither could he, though it was true – which was more than it was for either of the other two – and it would be even truer if he had to pay for Thomasina.

'You'd be spending much more if you were in Cyprus, Thomasina,' said Madeleine, looking sharp for a moment, 'you and Pammie. And you, Giles, stodging away in the garrison. I don't know what you spend your money on. You always had stacks of it.'

Thomasina looked thoughtful. She had insisted

on Egypt being a Dutch treat.

'We can't *all* stay,' said Pammie, who had been examining the details at the desk. 'There are only three rooms booked – two single and one double.'

Neither Thomasina nor Giles could find the right words. The reception clerk waited, pen in air. The porter stood among the masses of luggage and bulb bowls, all surmounted by the general's gun.

'Well, I shall have to have one of the single rooms, obviously,' said Madeleine, 'and so will Giles. Surely you two girls can share? We all did at school, now and then.'

Giles said nothing. (*And that is* it, thought Thomasina.)

'Well,' Thomasina said, 'if we really are staying – and I think it's totally unnecessary, *I'm* quite able to drive up even to the north of Scotland in a day, but I suppose I'm that much younger than any of you – *if* we must stay, and we all have our credit cards, I don't mind sharing with Pammie. Unless it's a double bed.'

'I'm afraid it is a double bed. It is all that is left, madam. They're not popular any more. It's always the double beds that go last now. It's a sign of the times. But it is a four-poster.'

Lying side by side that night Pammie and Thomasina stared unbelievingly at the ruched satin lining of the tester above them. It had, against all the rules, been a far from unpleasant afternoon. After lunch in a conservatory full of forced spring flowers and potted palms, all but Thomasina had gone for a siesta, arranging, as they left, to meet again at tea.

Thomasina had set off for a walk through the church-lined streets of Stamford and on to the great park. She had walked fast and far, on and on, until it grew dark and she had turned back and seen the spires and towers of Rutland and Lincolnshire fading in the night as the stars came out. Back in the town she walked slowly, looking in tinselled shop windows. All the bright fruit shops. The Sally Army was singing in a square. Office workers in some tall eighteenth-century houses were looking down at them. A young woman with her children waited to cross a road. She had a baby in a sling against her stomach, a child on either hand. One child looked up and said something and the mother looked first down at her, then up at the lights across the street, and the starry sky. She laughed, and it was Holly's laugh.

It was Holly. It was five years from now. It was Holly with Faith and her younger children. They were on their way home. Andrew had a job at Stamford Hospital – '*Marvellous* luck. *Wonderful* place. Burghley *Horse* trials' – for Holly had started riding again – '*Such* nice people. You'd love it, Ma. You must come every year. Or come and live near. I shall have ten children: you'll always be wanted.'

Then the girl turned and she was plastered in make-up and chewing something. When she spoke it was broad Lincolnshire. The middle child, all of three years old, had a great dummy stuck in its mouth. Oh Holly, Holly, Holly, Holly, Holly.

They played a little Bridge after tea, until Madeleine fell asleep and Pammie disappeared to her room again.

Giles said, 'Thomasina, we must talk.'

'Not before Christmas,' she said. 'Let's let things be till then.'

359

'I'm sorry,' he said. 'That business about the room. Felt rather embarrassed, to tell you the truth. I've been thinking – were we quite ourselves, do you think, in the autumn?'

'I'm not sure. I thought you had been sent to save me.'

'I thought you were a splendid girl.'

'Yes. You kept saying so. But, you see, I began to love you, Giles.'

'Ah. Yes. I'm afraid I've treated you rather badly. Madeleine's a frightful bore. I can't get shot of her. Old times' sake, and Puffy and so on. I can't abandon her now. We should never have gone to that wedding, Thomasina. Everything was going so well before that.'

'I said not, if you remember.'

'No. *I* said not. I said you should go to see your – the baby.'

'I'm going up to change for dinner now.'

'Oh, I don't think you need to change. Very informal.'

'I think I need to change.'

After dinner she said, 'Sleep well, Giles,' and went up to the four-poster and Pammie. She heard Madeleine's voice after a time calling, 'Giles *which* is the number of my room? Oh my dear, I'm so glad you're next door. I do miss Puffy in hotels. I think I shall telephone him now. I do every night, you know, though I don't believe he notices.'

'Oh, Pammie,' said Thomasina in bed, 'oh Pammie. What a ghastly business.'

'Oh, I don't know. Makes me think of my days on the fringes of royalty, this great bed. I used to stay at Blenheim, you know. There's plenty of pillows to

360

put down the bed between us. It used to be bolsters, but you can't get bolsters now except in France.'

'Have you ever slept with a bolster down the bed?' (*I'll bet,* Thomasina thought, *she was a friend of the housekeeper.*)

'Yes. I once slept with a queer. Art student. Sweet boy.'

'I'd not have thought you'd need a bolster if he was a queer.'

They laughed.

Thomasina thought how much she liked Pammie. 'I never thought I'd be sharing a bed with you, Pammie, and Giles along the corridor.'

'You must be a bit fed up, aren't you? *I'll* be no trouble anyway. I don't suppose he was either, was he? Was he any good?'

'Pammie! Shut up. You sound sixteen.' (*And,* she thought, *I don't know you well enough for this.*)

'Oh, we're all sixteen, Thomasina, now and then.'

'You didn't understand, did you? How I could have done it?' and she thought, as she had been doing in the car, of the gulf between women with children and those who have none.

Pammie said nothing.

'You thought I was fickle to Holly, didn't you? Going off with some old man?'

'Yes.'

'Debauched?'

'Well, no. Superficial. I couldn't have done it. When Hugo died – and, of course, a husband's death must be worse – I found myself starting to get excited about doing up the house, and I stopped. It wasn't on. Not appropriate. But I think that meeting Jack has helped me so very much.'

'So what about Jack, then?' Thomasina thought,

Poor Pammie. And maybe, you know, you wouldn't have had the chance with Giles. Or with anyone, the way you strut about. You can't call Jack exactly a chance.

'Don't be silly, Thomasina. Jack's just a spiritual adviser, and I must say it was nice to be looked at affectionately after years of being thought just a jolly old thing. Death makes us self-indulgent. Mind you, men are worse. Widowers turn to *any* woman when their wives die. Searching for mother.'

'I can't remember my mother,' said Thomasina. 'Do widows go looking for father? I can't remember him either. Hardly.'

'That's probably why you got this thing about Holly. You and Holly.'

'Holly had no thing for me, Pammie, nor anyone – she never knew anything about me. She never analysed. She was uncomplicated. She trusted and it always worked. Until Faith finished her.'

'Well, she'd you to thank for being so happy. You're the one who lost out. You were smashing. We all thought you were from the start a wonderful mother – so easy and nice. I was bloody jealous. Oh, I'm so glad you're talking about her at last.' Stretching her hand across the pillows she took Thomasina's hand and squeezed it. 'Is this Giles thing over?'

'Yes. Yes, it is.'

'Well, thank God for that.'

'Why?'

'You could find a better man. If you want one.'

'There was only one,' said Thomasina, so low Pammie wondered if she'd imagined it.

The two women in their face cream, glasses of water beside them on the bedside tables, Pammie's blood-pressure pills, Thomasina's rings, both their spectacles folded near, fell side by side asleep.

Along the corridor the general stretched to answer the bedside phone and got Madeleine in mid-sentence.

'. . . playing his old seventy-eights.'

'What's this? What? Whatever time is it, Madeleine?'

'Oh, not late. Half past eleven. I've just rung Puffy and I'm afraid there's something wrong.'

'What? Wrong?'

'There's such a noise going on down there and Henry sounded quite tiddly. I couldn't speak to Puffy at all. Henry said that he and Miss Banks and Henry's friend Jerry had been playing poker, but it's very far past the time when Puffy gets put to bed. In the end I *insisted* on speaking to Miss Banks and she sounded rather tiddly, too. They'd just been having a snack and some music, she said.'

'I shouldn't worry, Maddie. We'll ring in the morning.'

'But why wouldn't they let me speak to Puffy? I don't know what staff are coming to. Do you think he didn't want to speak to me?'

'In the morning. Don't worry.'

'I do worry. They are telling lies, Edward.'

– 43 –

Andrew was getting Christmas off, maybe, he thought, out of compassion, maybe to reflect his status. After the holiday he was being promoted to a new job, as Registrar, no longer sleeping in the hospital, no longer doing three doctors' work, no longer on duty twenty-four hours a day. Knowing he'd made it at last – it had been slow: they'd thought him smug, acting above his station, condescending from a height, until Holly died, and then they'd grown sympathetic – knowing he'd made it at last and would be leaving this hospital for another, he felt not revitalised but numb. Stuck in his tracks.

On the morning of the twenty-third, Andrew was sitting on the edge of the narrow bed of his cubicle with an empty suitcase on the floor, unable to get going, get dressed, do anything. Even think.

He had bought no Christmas presents. This was the crisis grown vast in his mind. Nothing for Thomasina, nothing for Pammie, nothing for Miss Banks, to all of whom he owed so much. Nothing for the baby – though she was too young for it really to matter. Nothing for Philip, which was bad. Nothing for Jack, nothing for Toots and Dolly. He'd planned to do the lot this morning before setting off. Nip down Piccadilly to a bookshop, get some bestsellers. Ought to get Pammie something big, like a piece of jewellery. Dolly a scarf or something. Liberty's. Toots his whisky. Jocasta. Here he stopped.

Jocasta. Something small enough not to cause comment, but large enough, significant enough, for her to know he remembered what had been between them. Couldn't give her a sweater. He could have given Holly a sweater. Often had. All Holly's stuff still in the flat. His mind swooped away. Somehow he dressed and trudged out of the residential wing, but now that it was almost for the last time his feet had turned to lead. He was almost too tired to pass through the glass doors to the tired shops. Last shopping day. Oh God, he couldn't.

Last year he and Holly had packed off to Thailand, telephoned Toots and Dolly from a phone box under a coconut palm, listened to Dolly talking about Mrs Middleditch in the draughty passage with the coloured Victorian tiles, the line of coat hooks, the calendar of church services, as they watched some elephants swinging their trunks and people bathing in a dark pool afloat with lotus leaves. Holly in a white bikini, big and broad beside the Thai girls, and gorgeous. *Can't go buying diaries in Hatchards this morning. I cannot.*

A friend stopped him and said come for a drink.

'Presents,' said Andrew. 'Off north in a minute. No presents.'

'Forget them. We all know that everyone except you and me has bought their Christmas presents. Forget them. Come to lunch.'

He was having lunch with his anaesthetist wife, a

tall, silent girl with coils of dark hair, who was also exhausted, also on leave for Christmas. They were going home to Oxfordshire right after lunch. 'Come with us,' she said.

'I'm going to Yorkshire.'

'Oh, to see the baby?'

'Yes.'

'You don't look right for that journey. Are you driving?'

'Sure. Done it all my life. Home for the hols.'

'Who's got the baby now?'

'Oh, my brother. And his wife. And Thomasina's going up and the woman who looked after her when she was born. And my parents are up there. I can't not turn up. After all, she's mine.'

'She seems to have plenty of people. Why don't you ring up and tell them you can't face it and you'll come in the New Year? The baby's too young ever to remember you didn't turn up. Come back with us.'

'Or just come and stay overnight,' said the husband. 'Leave from us early in the morning.'

'These presents . . .'

'Take them later. They know you're busy.'

'That's what they don't. The only kind of work they think is work up there is slaving in the soil – they're farmers. Or creating Art.'

'Art?'

'Jack's wife's arty.' He felt huge shame. 'She's a wonderfully talented woman. Lives in a bit of another world, too. Professional. Like us.'

'I'd let her get on with it,' said William. 'Come on home with us for a goddamned sleep.'

He woke on the morning of Christmas Eve to William's wife opening his curtains, shutting his window, bringing him tea across. The room was full of light.

'Snow,' she said.

'Oh, God.'

'Nothing like so bad as up north, apparently. Andrew, I don't think you're going to make it.'

'I must.'

'Turn on the radio and listen. Don't hurry up. You'll have to leave it till tomorrow.'

'Christmas Day?'

'Why not? Leave at six in the morning. You'll walk in for dinner. They'll be thrilled.'

He stood moodily at the sitting-room window. Diamond-bright snow across the lawn. A dog prancing. Inside, a huge log fire; gold baubles hanging from oak beams; hyacinths in bowls. Laughter from the kitchen.

'I'll ring my parents.'

'Right.'

Dolly was adamant. 'Now, you're not to come. Andrew. Promise me. Freezing fog. Just think if anything should happen, we'd never forgive ourselves. We can't even get to them up there ourselves, not even on their telephone. Toots says they've forgotten to pay the bill but it's their wires down, Mrs Middleditch says. It's the worst for years. We don't mind, though. We'll see them later. We're quite resigned.'

'Have you seen Faith lately?'

'Well, no. Not lately. But we shall. And we'll see you. Very soon. Have you somewhere to go? Oh good, dear. That sounds just right for you. A jolly time. Now, have a lovely Christmas.'

'Not coming,' she said to Toots, sitting down heavy

on her chair.

'Thought not,' said he.

'He did sound tired. He's probably been up all night. He's with a nice couple near Didcot. Doctors, of course,' she said proudly.

'Won't be a lot of fun with a couple. I hope they haven't a baby.'

'I expect they mean well. Kindness to ask him. I expect it'll be a jolly party and I don't think there'll be anything much going on at The Priors. Holly's mother will never get there, for a start. She's far too delicate-looking. And Jack and Jocasta are not exactly . . . well, I shouldn't say it, especially of my Jack, but they're not all that light-hearted.'

Toots said nothing, but lay on, thinking of Didcot.

'We've Athene Price coming to dinner tonight,' said William. 'OK?'

'OK,' said Andrew, 'but she scares me stiff. Can't stand that imperious type.' (In the kitchen, out of sight, William and wife nudged each other and mouthed, 'Holly Fox!') 'OK, I'll behave. Will she be by herself?'

'With one or two more.'

It was a feast. There was a lot of wine. There was a goose. Afterwards various people lay about drowsing by the fire. Affectionately. William's wife went off to wrap presents. Other people went off home. William took the dog for a last walk in the snow. Athene Price, in her short grey velvet dress and the sexiest legs you ever saw (he thought), said to him, 'I miss Holly.'

'Oh. Yes. I didn't realise . . . ?'

'We were at baby-school together.'

'Holly seems to have been at school with

everyone. She must have kept getting expellsed, she was at so many. Or something.'

'Holly expelled? Andrew, she was perfect. Lovely friend. In a way, dying young like that and everybody thinking you wonderful, it's not bad.'

'Isn't it?'

'Andrew, what I must say is how terribly, terribly sorry I am about the baby.'

'What?'

'That you lost the baby.'

'We didn't. We didn't lose the baby, what d'you mean? She's with her grandparents. She's fine. Called Faith.'

Athene Price stared at him. 'I heard – I *did* hear. Someone said – oh God, how do things like that get around? Oh, thank goodness. Oh, I'm so sorry. They said you'd lost her. I've thought about her so often. I even dreamed about it. The other night. I dreamed about you losing the baby.' She looked so horrified by what she'd said that he went over to her and put his arms round her, thinking, *This is glacial Athene Price*.

He laid his head on her velvet dress. She was not glacial.

'I'm going up to see her crack of dawn tomorrow,' he said. 'I'll send you a lock of her hair.'

But he did neither.

Emma and Philip were making up beds. The children were screaming about. Things downstairs on oven hobs were boiling over. The headmaster was hoovering up needles around the Christmas tree. There was music blasting out from somewhere and someone calling from the kitchen. The postman, Jimmie, was sitting to his cup of tea. The dishwasher was broken, as was the tumble-drier, and in a minute Emma would have to start pegging things out on the line, where they would turn into art forms in cardboard in the frost. A dog lay chewing something precious and there were wrapping papers, ribbons and decorations afloat on every floor of the schoolhouse.

'Oh, we're nearly there,' said Emma. 'Who's flapping? All I'd like to know is how many are coming. I suppose you don't happen to know, Phil? They're your lot.'

'Coming here?'

'They were going to my father's but he said no. Grump, grump. He's coming here for Christmas Day, though he always says he won't. Somebody rang him up, someone to do with your people at The Priors, and said she was bringing a party from London for Christmas. He said no. Then she wrote to say they'd all be arriving about four o'clock and how very kind of him and so he roared at us over the phone and we said we'd have them. But he didn't know how many.'

'Maybe about a hundred,' said Philip.

'Well, there's the dormitories.'

'There's only Andrew of ours lives in London,' Philip said, 'and he'll be staying with us in the gatehouse, like he does. There's Alice, but she's disappeared and she'd come back home too if she was coming back at all.'

'Someone called Pammie? No? Someone called Thomasina?'

'Thomasina's Holly's mother. Holly's dead. She's called Thomasina Fox.'

'Holly Fox's mother? I was at school with Holly Fox.'

'She's my sister's mother.'

Emma looked thoughtfully at him.

'I think there's some man, a general,' she said, 'and this old woman called Madeleine.'

'Don't know 'em.'

'Neither does my father, but that means nothing.'

'He sounds like mine. I mean Jack. I haven't got a father. Jocasta dumped him.'

'Come on, Phil,' said Emma, 'we've heard all that. You have half a dozen fathers. Jack. Andrew in London. Toots. Nick. Ernie Smike.'

'Nick an' Ernie would be terrible fathers.'

'You never know. Pass that blanket.'

'Is it a horse blanket?'

'Yes.'

'Hope Thomasina isn't allergic.'

They laughed.

I'm going to miss this one, she thought. *Funny boy. Where does it come from? Humourless Jocasta, solemn Jack? The Indian father, I guess. He must have been one of the Marx brothers. Thomasina Fox, well, well. Wonder if Pa knows.*

'Holly Fox was quite a friend of mine,' she said. 'Then she went off with a girl called Stephanie. Girls are like that at school. Everyone was mad about Holly. I thought she was a bit of a bore actually, sometimes. Don't tell anyone. What's the baby like?'

'She's wonderful,' he said, 'when I get to see her. She's over three months now. She's almost walking.'

'*Really*! Do you play with her?'

'She's up in a hammock most of the time. The Tibetans look after her. But I read to her.'

'It must be the blind leading the blind.'

'She's not blind at all. She had a messy eye once

371

but it's better. They're all knitting eyes over there in the sheds, the Tibetans. On sort of panels.'

'Knitting eyes?'

'Yes.'

They looked at each other and started laughing again.

'Funny world,' said Emma. 'Come on down and talk while I get lunch.'

'Do I have to go home tonight, Emma? Can't I come back after Jocasta's play? Could I have Christmas here?'

'Nope. I'm not a kidnapper.'

'*Please*. I'll help you with Thomasina. She's my other granny. In a sense.'

'We'll see. We'll see if she turns up. Or anyone. The sky's heavy with snow. Look.'

At the foot of the hotel staircase the general was standing gravely. He strode a few paces forward, examined the pictures of stagecoaches and eighteenth-century travellers. He looked towards the staircase. He strode a few paces back. He examined the newspapers that were laid out upon a table. When Thomasina came down he leapt towards her, took her arm and led her into the empty dark coffee room.

'Good morning, Giles.'

'I have to speak to you.'

'There's nothing you need say. Nothing at all. Let's not get embarrassing.'

'Embarrassing?'

'About sleeping arrangements.'

He looked bewildered. 'Oh. Ha. Yes. Sleeping arrangements. No, it isn't that. That has nothing to do with anything.'

'I see.'

'No. You don't see. Well. Last night Madeleine was in a flap about a phone call she made home, and I straightened her out and sent her to bed. But I thought maybe I'd give old Puffy a ring myself, and I did. And he was dead.'

'But . . .'

'Bad business. Some sort of nonsense going on down there. I've just rung again. I asked to speak to Miss Banks, but she's left. The young man there is very upset. She's gone off on the London train, leaving her luggage. They've got Puffy away to a mortuary.'

'Madeleine?'

'I managed to stop her from telephoning. I haven't told her. I told her he'd been taken ill. I'll tell her he's dead on the train.'

'*Train*?'

'Yes. We'll go south on the Euston train from Lincoln if Pammie will drive us. Taxi to Waterloo, train down to Kent.'

'Giles, it's the day before Christmas Eve. It won't be easy. She's very old. I'm sure Pammie would lend you her car, and she and I could go on up north by train together.'

'No. no. All fixed. Here she comes.'

Breakfast in the dining room was delicious. Madeleine kept saying so. She talked of other breakfasts. Paris before the war. With Winston Churchill at Chequers. With little Jackie Bouverie in New York ('Sweet child and how she suffered'). She told the waitress that she was sure she knew her. Or her mother: Elsie Bacon who'd been parlour maid at Blackfriars Hall? No? So like her. She said goodbye at the desk with such an air of devotion to everyone that porters emerged and stood in a row for her to pass to the door ('Giles, see to it, won't you? Purse not about'). They were bowed into Pammie's car. Thomasina had passed Pammie a note on the back of the breakfast menu. 'Puffy's dead. They're off south again,' and met Pammie's outraged eyes.

On the platform Madeleine turned to Thomasina and kissed her.

'I'm so sorry, Madeleine,' said Thomasina. 'I do hope that Puffy will soon . . .'

They embraced.

'I'm sad too,' said Madeleine. 'No. Not that Puffy's dead, that's wonderful for him – yes, of course I know he's dead. Silly old Alfred's like a glass of water. I don't know how he was ever a general, you can read his face like a map. No, not sorry he's dead and he had that excellent Alice with him. No. I'm just so sorry it's Christmas. So inconvenient for the poor undertakers. And sorry – well, sorry (Yes, Miles, I'm coming), sorry, darling, for you.'

'For me?'

'For you. In a way. Though this is for the best. I do know that. You'll not miss him. He's so boring. Just right for me, though, because I can remember how sweet he was long ago. Such love untapped. The odd thing is that I didn't want him then. I thought I did, but not deep down. Now I'm landed with him.'

'Maddie, *please*.' Giles was holding the carriage door, waving the gun case. There were shouts. The train was crowded for Christmas.

'Goodbye, Giles,' said Thomasina. 'Glad you're able to go with her. And first class. You're having rather an expensive outing.'

'Yes. Thomasina, I shan't forget . . .'

'No.'

'The Mena House and the Texans. And that splendid place at Karnak.'

'The Nile,' she said, 'and the man in the pink nightshirt who wanted to clean our shoes.'

He seemed puzzled by this. 'Wasn't that—?' He looked towards Madeleine climbing aboard, smiling round the packed, carousing passengers. 'I thought that was . . . Oh yes. Of course. Goodbye, Thomasina,' and he heaved his lanky frame up the high step, turning to look back at her, stern and awkward.

He is ashamed and old, she thought. *Whatever was I doing? Poor old wooden general..*

'The party shrinks,' said Pammie. 'We'll be able to get a move on now. D'you want a tissue?'

'No. I told you last night. It's over.'

'Thank your stars you're not damaged in any way – or not more than you are. You can't see straight after a death, or you'd never have gone near him.'

'I don't agree. I won't say that.'

'You were clinging to youth.'

'For god's sake – he's seventy-two.'

'To the old order?'

'Well, maybe. Why not?'

'It's time you grew up.'

'*You* say this? For heaven's sake, what about the old man in the mountains?'

'It's what I'm telling you. One goes mad at these times. I'll recover. I think.'

'But maybe he won't recover. Dear Jack. He's very lovable.'

'What – unbridled passion for fat Mrs Jefford of Coombe? Come off it, Thomasina.'

'He's someone, Pammie. He's reckless. He's some sort of saint. I love Jack.'

'Well,' she said, 'I've never met anyone like him, I'll say that. But he's married, you know. To Madame Gloom.'

When they were well on, past Worksop, past the Doncaster bypass, boiling along towards Wetherby and the Wolds, Pammie said, 'There's something I should like to have seen and now I never shall. I'd like to have seen how Madeleine would have made out with Jack. What he'd have thought of her.'

Thomasina said, after several more miles, 'I think she would have tested his policy of universal love.'

'Where do I turn off?'

'Soon. Giles gave me directions. Oh good gracious!'

'What now?'

'His map says we're going right up the top again, near that hotel he and I went to. It's not the Faylesafe pile – it's a *school*. "The Moors School". It'll be dormitories. It's outrageous of that woman. We'll go to The Priors.'

'We might just look,' said Pammie. 'It's getting dark. They'll be expecting us. With any luck it'll be all right even if it's basic and it won't be far to turn out again for this concert thing tomorrow.'

'A Nativity play,' said Thomasina, 'and, let's hope, a christening.'

'Your granddaughter.'

'Yes. Hope she's thriving, I must say. So fearfully cold.'

'*Faith*.'

'Yes.'

'Say it.'

'Say what?'

'Faith.'

'Faith, then.'

'Wasn't there a girl called Faylesafe? Friend of Holly?'

'Was there?'

'At her school. Emma Faylesafe? Didn't you know the family?'

'Yes. I suppose there was. Madeleine told us so. For hours.'

'Say it, then. Who was she?'

'Holly's friend. At school. First term boarding. I think actually, Pammie, I'd quite like to go direct to The Priors, if you don't mind.'

'I do mind. I'm sick of people changing their mind about where they're going in this car. It's my car, I'm driving and I say where.'

'Which is here,' she said on the top of the moor. 'I say! Wuthering Heights with school dinners. Gird up your loins, dear. What's this?'

The front door opened and light stained the snow. Emma Faylesafe-as-was came out with her husband and children and Philip.

'Quickly, quickly, in you come,' she called. 'You must be dead! Only two of you? Oh dear.' She took Thomasina's hands. 'Come in, Holly's ma.'

377

And it was not so dreadful after all up on the moors on Christmas Eve.

The snow was thick on the roads up from the coast and there was no hope of Dolly and Toots reaching The Priors on Christmas Day, but the freezing fog was nowhere to be seen and the wind had dropped. The heather stuck up through the snow like prickles through a blanket – a continent of midget forest trees. The lower fields lay on the hillsides like white handkerchiefs out to dry. After dawn the sky cleared and a great sun rose through queer dragging clouds. Their trailing tentacles stroked the horizon. It was going to be warmer.

Thomasina and Pammie awoke at the school-house and wondered if they should ring Kent. Thomasina seemed not to care to. Emma said that she thought that surely the general would ring *them* up. Would he not?

Nobody knew.

So they sat over breakfast eating bacon in the dappled sunshine off the moor, Emma scrubbing potatoes and rolling them into the back of the stove for lunch, slashing up cabbages, stirring up stew. More coffee was produced. Someone was practising scales on a piano. The headmaster was in full voice, singing as he threw salt over the yard. Philip was busy somewhere with computers.

A wondrous lethargy settled upon Thomasina and Pammie. Emma talked, they listened. They watched her wading through a chaos of children about her feet, making a pudding at the far end of the kitchen table, taking tin measurefuls of flour from a sack in the corner, scattering it into the bowl from a height to get air into it. Flour hung in the sunlight. Some settled on Emma's hair and powdered her cheek.

'We're to be there by four,' she said. 'The concert thing's at five. Or so. I don't think they really know – they're like that. Phil wants to be early to find out what he's meant to be doing. There's some ceremony with the baby, isn't there? I wonder if it's Tibetan?'

'It's her christening,' said Pammie, 'and about time too.'

'I think there's to be some lovely Tibetan music. And then some carols. And then a supper. That Nick person's been over to borrow plates. I'm afraid plates are sometimes as far as they get. I'll take a big pie.'

'I don't suppose there'll be many of us,' said Thomasina. 'The snow will stop everyone. I haven't heard a word from Andrew. Are you all coming?'

'We are,' said Emma. 'Each and every one. Great honour. Never asked before. I'm dying to see the Tibetans. And the baby.'

'I should really be getting myself across there this morning,' said Pammie. 'I'm to try housekeeping for them, you know. I've been invited to be on the permanent staff.'

'Oh,' said Emma. 'Well, I wonder. It's pretty serious over there. But I'm not saying a word. I'm not very pious.'

'I *am* religious,' said Pammie, whose faith had returned during Jack's telephone calls. Thomasina looked out of the window. 'Jack and I hit it off rather well.' She turned pink.

'Yes. Everybody hits it off with Jack,' said Emma. 'He's a saint. But they're not the easiest. I suppose I shouldn't say this, but somehow, with Holly about, I feel I can. Thomasina . . . ?'

But Thomasina had left the room to find Philip.

They set off in the school Land-Rover, wrapped up warm in the near dark, at about half past three. 'I've a hip flask and some sleeping bags,' said the headmaster, but it was decidedly warmer. Big loose flakes were starting to fall. They left the Land-Rover up at the Saxon cross to be on the safe side. There was already a minibus there and the Smike motorbike covered with a tarpaulin.

'Afraid of not getting out again,' said the headmaster. 'They've brought them up. Well, nobody'll steal them tonight. Did someone say the Tibetans are leaving at Christmas?'

'Nobody can make them out,' said Philip.

'Are they nice people?'

'Pema's a bit weird. She's boring about Faith and she can't speak English. The rest are just normal, like us. The young ones. The men have gone away somewhere. Hi, Ernie.'

Ernie and Nick were walking out to the sheds.

'Gi's 'and, Philip.'

Philip ran across to them and into the studio.

*

Jocasta was sitting huddled small in a pew in the chapel. She wore a striking necklace of chunks of red amber, and when Thomasina and Pammie came in she turned, then crossed straight to them. She kissed Thomasina, smiled at Pammie and whispered, 'Do sit down, or do you want to go in and get warm? Are the school people all here?'

'Yes. I'll go over to the solar and start helping,' said Pammie.

'All done,' she said, 'but do go in. I have to stay and see to the tableau.' She smiled and said, 'It's wonderful that you've made it.'

'Whatever's happened?' wondered Thomasina, and Pammie said, 'She's quite changed. Utterly different woman. Oh, whoever's that?'

Out in the falling snow Pema, dressed in a great broadside of a coat that stood out around her like a hairy box filled the doorway of her shed and stood watching them pass. Her face was broad and dark beneath a hat like a headdress atop her scarfed head. In her arms was a bundle of heavy cloths, scarlet and orange on white. On the baby's head was a little woven cap, with ear-flaps; on her hands, red mittens decorated with amber beads. Her face was almost covered by her wrappings. She did not stir. A woven icon of an eye hung round her neck.

Thomasina saw only a glimpse of Faith's own eyes, round and faraway, all that seemed alive in the doll-like swathe in the old woman's arms.

Pema began to shout suddenly, on and on, very angry. A girl came up behind her and tried to pull her away, away inside and out of sight.

'What's she saying? What have we done?'

'She's telling you about us,' said the girl.

'What is she saying?'

Pema's voice rose to a desolate wailing and she heaved herself backwards into the dark of the shed.

'What was all that?'

'She says about exile,' said the girl, 'about you knowing nothing here. She says about walking six hundred miles to Nepal below the Mother of Earth at sixteen thousand feet. She says the Chinese kill and beat and torture. She says eighty-seven thousand exiles left Tibet, two thousand seven hundred monasteries destroyed, a hundred thousand Chinese troops walked into our country. Her baby sisters died on the journey, her grandmother died. In India her little brother later died of sickness we did not have at home. She says you all have suffered nothing. She despises you and kisses the bone of her mother which she carried next to her heart.'

'Well, I hope she doesn't let it anywhere near the baby,' said Pammie.

'How extraordinary,' said Thomasina. 'I have absolutely nothing against Tibetans, I'm very sorry for them. I am very sorry. How could we know? But please, we should like to see Faith now. I suppose three hundred miles is nothing to travel, comparatively, but we've done it for our faith too, you know, in a sense. For Faith.'

But the Tibetans had shut their door.

'Why aren't the Tibetans joining us, and where's Faith?' Thomasina asked Jack. They were in the refectory now, where everyone was drinking tea out of mugs. Some rather oily, whitish mince pies were about on trays and some small squares of cheese

382

with sticks in them. Emma had brought crackers, and her pie was warming in the stove.

'You must tell me what to do about supper,' Pammie said.

'Oh, supper,' said Jocasta. 'Are we all here?'

'So sad about Toots and Dolly,' said Thomasina, dredging up a normal remark. She felt all at once beyond hope, beyond care for anything, for anyone. That comatose bundle. That aged crone. Age and death. Deaths, deaths. Giles's stiff leg following him up into the railway carriage. That idiot Madeleine. Dead Puffy. Everyone dying. Nothing left. What about Andrew? No word. *I am the one should be dead*, she thought. *Why was it Holly? What use am I?*

'Has anyone heard from Andrew?'

Nobody had except Jocasta and she wasn't saying. The letter had been the letter she had been expecting for some time so that when she had read it she had felt it was old, dug out from some antique trunk. 'Dear Jocasta,' it had said in his tiny writing, so small that it seemed to be trying to hide its meaning; close, neat, no crossings-out. A fair copy.

Dear Jocasta,

I think that you and I have decided both together that what happened between us has been a monumental mistake. I expect that by the time you read this I shall have received a similar letter from you.

When we last saw each other after Alice Banks had gone I saw your face as it looked up at Jack. I couldn't decide what I'd seen at first. Something like utter despair of happiness in you ever again. Disillusion. And then I saw

Jack, walking so trusting beside you. He touched your neck as you both went into the refectory. You looked up at him without happiness but with such familiarity. I saw you together as a woman with her husband.

The night before you had said, 'Don't leave me.' That was when I realised that the only thing was for us to break off our life with each other.

I shall have to come at Christmas. Nothing will stop me. I know my duty to the child. But now it will be only as your brother-in-law.

I will of course always love you,
       Andrew

'I will of course always love you.' *They always end like that*, thought Jocasta. The letter had left her light and strange and she'd chucked it on the stove and gone over at once to the work sheds. There, with Ernie's help, she had spread the great canvas across the floor under the uncertain eye of the A-level girl. It had taken hours to straighten and line it with paper, and roll it right. Then they had polished the wooden crib that was to stand on the floor in front of the white space at its centre. It was lovely. Scarlet lacquered, shaped like the bowl of a lute on cross-over black legs, graced with scarlet seals.

The Smikes had come in, Nick carrying a bundle of hay. Ernie had said, 'Is Jack really wantin' live animals round the thing? They'll muct place up, sheep. And who's to go for them, as if I didn't know?'

Ernie, Nick and Jocasta had gone over to the chapel early on the morning of Christmas Eve to make space for the backcloth, fix the lights for it, and strew with hay the stone floor before it.

When all was done Jocasta said, 'Switch on.'

'Go live,' said Ernie.

The chapel fell into shadow. Through its windows the ancient buildings disappeared. The dazzle of the canvas was the only light. It seemed to drink down into itself all the colours of the world.

The life-sized painted figures of the holy family were vague. The model for the Madonna, the A-level girl, was gawky, smashed, without nationality, her arms spread towards the empty centre on the screen. Joseph, with Jack's brooding bent head, stood near her, looking down at the lighted space. On the other side were village people. One was the postman, Jimmie. Somebody, a woman in a turquoise padded jacket, was holding out a cake and thermos flask. Entangled in the painted arch of the ruined apse was a languid angel with a gold earring and black leather armour. It had the face of Ernie, watching. In opposite profile near him sat Jocasta leaning against the parapet of a bridge with a frowning face, drawing. She was drawing the light in the centre of the backcloth, drawing space, drawing her life, drawing the timeless moment. Her dark face, not dismissive, not derisive, not discontented, was concentrated on one thing only, the holiness of vision.

' 'Sgreat, Jocasta,' said Nick. 'Why int Philip in it? Where's The Missus? An' me?'

'The Missus cleared off. I left her out. Philip will be in it for real when he carries Faith up in her cradle. He stands it here, see? Centre of the blank. Two bits of flesh and blood, Faith and Phil, OK?'

'And me?'

385

'I couldn't see where you fit in, Nick. I couldn't decide whether you'd want to be in it or not. You never tell us where you stand.'

'OK,' said Ernie. 'And Nick, OK, right? It's great, though. Hey, it's . . . well, OK, Jocasta.'

'Right. Take it back across there, then, till the evening.'

Nick and Ernie carried it on their shoulders, one behind the other.

So when everyone came walking down the lane from the Land-Rover and followed the rolled-up backcloth back into the chapel, Jocasta was sitting thinking only of the tableau.

'Turn all the lights out,' Jocasta called to Ernie. 'I want this to be a sudden blaze.'

'I can't leave hold of it.'

'OK. Lay it carefully down.'

'It gonna get damaged.'

'No.' She went over to Ernie and suddenly put her arms round him and kissed him.

Then everyone came in and then out again towards the tea, and Jack arrived with his hands full of mangolds, asking if Jocasta wanted any for decorating the tableau of the stable, and he'd forgotten to get in some sheep. 'We'll manage,' said Jocasta. They went together to the solar.

'Here is Pammie, Jack,' Jocasta said.

They greeted each other with surprise and disappointment, for Jack had noticed her across at the stove already, a dumpy oldish woman bustling about in a kilt, and not recognised her. She saw a faded, tall, shabby-looking parson, far from charismatic, rather sour-looking and distant, nothing much at all. She couldn't help seeing the colour of

386

the hands holding the mangelwurzels. He couldn't help noticing her hard grey permanent wave.

He said, 'Jocasta, could I . . . ?'

'Yes, what?'

'I'm just going to put my notes together. I'll preach first, then some prayers. Then we'll have Philip coming up with the child for the tableau, and then the christening. Is that all right? No Andrew, I'm afraid, yet.'

'Quite all right.'

'It's – who now – godparents? Mrs Jefford and Philip and, well, it was to have been Alice Banks but she's not to be seen. Two will have to do.'

'Of course. What about the Tibs?'

'They are a law unto themselves, Jocasta.' They smiled at each other. 'I don't expect them.'

'They'll watch from a distance through their third eye,' she said, and for the first time since The Missus left she touched his arm.

'Oh Jocasta,' he said, 'what horrible times we've had. What things I've said to you.'

'The horrible times are over,' she said.

Soon she began to move everybody into the chapel. Nick was sent to the sheds to say that Faith should be brought across now and to ask the others to come too.

The congregation, in boots and coats and mufflers, assembled itself on the hard pews in the dark, among the plopping noises of the paraffin stoves, and as Jack appeared from behind the altar in his vestments the door opened and not only the three Tibetan women filed in but, in a flurry, Mr and Mrs Middleditch and Alice Banks.

*

Jack, unperturbed, made the sign of the cross and waited while the newcomers settled themselves, the Middleditch party well to the front, the Tibetans on the back row. Then Pema got up again and went out. Nick seemed to be arguing about something with the A-level girl and then suddenly went out too. His feet could be heard clattering over the stones of the courtyard.

Jack stood in silence for so long that Mrs Middleditch began to purse her lips and look questioningly about her. Even Jocasta looked up questioningly at him in the end. The Missus glared ahead.

At last Jack said, 'In the name of the Father and the Son and of the Holy Ghost, and in the name of God in all religions and languages, we ask Thy mercy on all of us here gathered together to grant Thy blessing on the life of this child, and remember the life of the eternal Holy Child born this night. Let us pray.

'This year has had its sorrows for most of us here tonight. Its terrors, its difficulties, doubts and temptations. We ask it to be true, oh God, that we are at least nearer to Thee than we were when the year began, that we have learned a little of Thy mercy as well as of Thy might.

'Since the death of our dear Holly Fox, it has seemed that most of us here have been bewitched in some way by our own individual daemon. We have found ourselves awash in times we don't understand any better than the eastern visitors in our midst. Yet we live in the ruins of a place which should give us strength, that has inspired the worship of God for a thousand years. The sun and the moon above us, the snow, the wind and the rain

388

are the same as those known to the people who built this holy place long ago. Why have we felt alone? Do we only now at Christmas realise that the reason is that we have forgotten the message of Christmas? It is the child. Faith came to us and we congratulated ourselves on having taken her in, but only Pema, and I think Philip, ever really considered the baby herself. Did any of us really care about *Faith*? Let us thank God that we have time to put this right. We will stand in silence now for a few moments to say our own personal prayers. Let us pray.'

As they stood, a beaky man came in and clattered forward to stand by Thomasina. Emma looked round, nudged her husband, leaned sideways and said, 'Thought you didn't keep Christmas, Pa!' The man stared ahead. Thomasina gripped the pew in front.

'Who is it? D'you know him?' asked Pammie in a loud voice. 'Is it Faylesafe?'

'Ssh.'

'Let us pray,' said Jack again.

The Thoughts of All

Thomasina thought, *Pray? Our Father which art— Dear god, have mercy on us all and hear us. I don't know where I am or what my future will be. Watch over me. Holly gone, Herbert gone, Giles gone. Garden left, must think of it. Pammie left and Les Girls and the golf club. Wish Dolly and Toots here. Tony Faylesafe. Unbelievable. Father of Hol's friend Emma. A man of long before. If he's here, why not Holly? Where is she? O Lord, I pray for beloved Holly and may she be in everlasting light, may light perpetual shine upon her. Tell me what I'm doing in*

*this place and tell me, I beseech thee, O God, how I'm to fill
up the rest of my life.*

Pammie prayed, *I thank Thee, O God, for sending me
out into this place to see if it is Thy will for me to work to
Thy glory here and serve Thee and Jack and Jocasta all my
days. All the kitchen needs is a good lime-wash and the
beams treated – say, five hundred pounds. New stove –
say, two thousand. Take up flagstones, turn and scour, not
polish. Very nice refectory table, needs treating oil and
varnish. No sign of dishwasher, absolutely necessary,
serious catering. Flowers in outer hall, visitors' book,
spring clean office: make big difference. Modern bunk beds
for groups. My bedroom, gatehouse, very romantic,
probably. Ideal conference in big retreat centre. Billy
Graham? Jack spiritual leader. I could pull strings for a
Royal visit. The south only a concept, as is the North. Use
me, O Lord, make me a channel for Thy peace. Thomasina
often here and golf at Scarborough. Who is this man? Why
isn't Andrew here? No sign of Alice the dragoness. Oh,
good Lord, who's this – it's her? It can't be! Who's the
couple she's with? Very pompous. Dreadful Dannimacs.
And may it please thee, O Lord, to look graciously upon all
of us here gathered to celebrate the birth of Thy dear Son
that we may be purged of all our sins and selfishness. Bless
my Hugo in heaven. Lighten our darkness we beseech
Thee, O Lord – and whoever is this? A troupe of gypsies?
And the queer and the hippie – well, tax-gatherers and
sinners. What a long way from Coombe Hill. Forgive my
unbelief. Yours sinc— I mean, in the name of the Father,
etc. 'Amen.'*

Emma prayed, *Dear Lord, we thank Thee for Thy great
mercy and for drawing us all together here today from
different parts of the world to celebrate Christmas. Have*

mercy on this little motherless child that she may find
some motherly arms. 'Shut up, Vanessa, you can't
hold Phil's hand. Now, leave him alone. No, Patsie,
you can*not* go up with him and carry the baby. The
baby's not even here yet. Shush!' *Oh well, yes, it looks*
as if she is. The crib's come in anyway. It's standing at the
back. And that Smike's gone out again – I hope it's not too
heavy for Phil. 'The boy has rings in his nose because
he likes to be like that, Lucy. No, you can't put a
string through it like a bull. Darling, do sit still.' *I*
thank Thee, Lord, for our creation, preservation and for all
the blessings of this life but chiefly for Thine inestimable
love, for the gift of grace and the hope of glory – and for its
continual surprises and variety. Father in church! Forgot
he knew Holly's mum. Old friend. Always met on Sports
Day. Holly always won the races . . . oh poor Holly, where
are you? Wish you were here, you great philistine. Please
bless my family and Philip. Let us be family to Philip too.
Let us have the say in his education, let no harm befall
him. Never let him believe again that he must be forever
washing his hands. 'Amen.'

Ernie thought, *I'm not getting on my knees this bloody*
floor, anyway I gotter 'old this end of t' backcloth straight
some'ow, bloody 'ell. Wherst Nick for t'other end?
Bringin' int baby, likely. Is 'e really off wi' yon lass? More
fool 'im, 'e'll be back be Friday. They'se New Age
travellers gone soft, bloody gypsies, not my type. Jack's
conned. 'E'll be conned all 'is life. Jocasta's better. Much
better. No chicken. Not a slag. Shouldn't 'ave said it.
Bloody good poster she's made. Great. Pity no Toots an'
Dolly. It a bin a great day out. Bike up the top, why not
chance a visit? Down the arcades, miss this do 'ere
afterwards wi' all the toffs. God, I wish Nick wunt go off.
London trash place, everything loose shag, no fam'ly life.

'Ostels. Pavements. Cardboard boxes. Christ save 'im. This bloody post's 'eavy. When we gant unrollt bloody thing? I's not strong enough. Need a man 'ere, where's bloody Nick t' 'elp me? 'Amen,' he added as the rest said it.

The waitress from Ellerby Moor Hotel prayed. *Our Father which art in 'eaven 'allowed be Thy name Thy kingdom come thy will be done on earth as it is in 'eaven funny how most people still know it – mind, they say not everywhere now, the streets of London they won't. These foreigners all coming in just look at them not clean all them wrappers. Is one of them got that baby under there? It's not right it's a English baby why can't it be with its granny very nice old woman and that daft old man I took to them I really did I'd've brought them up 'ere today if it'd been fit. Terrible sad when she cried, nobody 'ere, but 'im marvellous: 'Don't upset yerself now Dorothy we've had a great ride out' wish I'd sent them a card for Christmas. No picnic getting 'ere this afternoon, nice that Jocasta woman asked me. They said I was in it somewhere – some play they're putting on don't know what they mean. Said I 'ad to come, that Jocasta apologising for this place all empty that morning. Comes to see me. Not 'er fault they say she's much better. Fits in more. Used to just sit and I never like that, folks sitting when there's work to do. That look. She's got a nice face when you catch sight of it looking over at old Jack, like. Said they never got on and she was off in the heather I'd not think so. There's that woman what was with that old army cove well I never. I didn't fancy her, stuck up. Sitting next 'is lordship old-fashioned type like 'im, nice suit she's got on. Fancy all them people knowing each other. Everyone knows Jack do anything for 'im. There's that Alice Banks agen they say she was off after twenty years I'll bet they wish she was miserable old lemon*

392

can't stand 'er. Hope she didn't do the tea we're to 'ave and the peace of god which passeth all understanding keep our hearts and minds in the knowledge of the power and the glory, 'Amen.'

Mrs Middleditch said to God, *As you know Arnold and I are by birth Methodists, as so I always thought was Bingham, though Church we've come to. I'm thankful to you, God, for my Arnold seeing me through so many dangers and difficulties with Bingham – nobody knows the half but us. And Thee. And for help with Toots and Dolly. Nobody knows the trouble they are getting and who can tell the end? But Thee. I've never liked Toots. There, I'll say it, God forgive me. You can't not like Dolly, mind, but she's a very silly woman and she gives way to him every time. They think they're a cut above because of Toots being educated in London somewhere and she having something about her in her manner, though I don't see why they're any better than us, I'm sure. You should see their bathroom and the upstairs toilet – all brown stains. Well, it's her eyes. An overhead chain, fancy, these days! No upstairs carpets, only lino down since the war, and that linen basket in the corner with its lid off. It had its lid off when I started looking after them five years since and it only needs a twist of raffia. Bingham could've done it, only I didn't like to say I'd noticed, not having been asked upstairs. Officially. I don't know how they manage. He must drink all his pension. Not Dolly, mind. Very respectable woman. More than you can say for Bingham's painted thing nearly Dolly's age. God, please send Bingham home again without her. I hope they never saw us go past, Dolly and Toots. Well, they wouldn't in this snow. The cheek of this Banks. I ask you! Landing up in Station Taxis complaining and not tipping – Christmas Eve (not maybe that I blame her)! – and saying, 'Here's me*

393

auntie's gold watch and I want you to get me for Christmas to The Priors.' Well, Arnold's a good man. We didn't ask questions, didn't even speak. I can't bring myself to look in her direction here beside me. Sitting in the car back muttering, singing bits of songs. St Luke's for her, she'll not even need assessing. I'll have to complain to Dolly about it. She's their connection, not mine, and would she go to see them? Refused. Will we get back home tonight if it freezes up again? Have to sleep up here. If Bingham and that thing comes round they'll find an empty house. It's hoping they'll come round decided me on bringing this Alice. 'Arnold,' I said, 'let him come. We're never out. It'll bring him up short.' Never being out is our strength to people, but tonight we'll lock up and go. We'll miss the Midnight at St James's. They'll be lost without Arnold. Who'll carry the plate? Who's to count the money? Funny this is all the services we'll have and in a priory too, I always understood Henry VIII. In the name of thy Son our Saviour Jesus Christ, 'Amen. Arnold, you're wanted to hold the other end of the magic lantern screen.'

Jimmie the postman prayed, *Our Father which art in heaven hallowed be Thy name etc., learned it at school they don't now it's all sex education and yoga I like Prayers meself puts a shape on things. Our Father – well, fancy me being here Christmas Eve they'll be wondering. Poor old Jack, though, you don't like to disappoint him. Dear God I pray for Jack Braithwaite remembering him sitting there in the heather back to the Cross and his bottom sopping from the wet grass. 'Good morning, Post.' Looking like a child. Tears running. Heard about his brother's wife. By, she were a smasher saw her once made that Jocasta look a shadder. Jack. Well. There's a gang here tonight all right. I'd not be here if I hadn't been stopping off all day here and*

394

there taking folkses bits of shopping and papers from t'shop let's hope they don't find out you're not supposed to take anything but post now int van and three-quarters of it junk. Time was old Heart-throb at Ellerby Hotel said you could ask Post to carry chickens live with their feet tied together, and a bag of manure. It's all changed now with the deep-freezes. But I like me job, finished eleven o'clock good days. You get your interests – lonely women on t'farms asking you in for all sorts. Great. They say yon Jocasta . . . but it's all talk. Can't have been easy with that Missus. Well, nobody knows what's going to happen do they God? They say I'm in this play somewhere, there's that Ernie not able to hold up the slide-screen affair, mebbe I better give 'im an 'and, no, there's that feller with the stomach going up. Where's that Nick? Now, why's all this black lot walking out? Funny places you can fetch up Christmas Eve. Well, deliver us from evil, 'Amen.'

Jocasta closed her eyes and concentrated on the Good. She emptied her mind of images, sounds, scents, tastes, sensations. She lifted herself out of her body until she was out of the chapel. Not outside in the snow, nor above it in the icy air, but higher, higher, farther towards the moon, towards the moon, towards the sun, beyond the sun, approaching the dark that she knew would one day take her, envelop her, twist her and at last fling her out into everlasting knowledge, the presence of Truth. Beyond prayer, beyond words, Jocasta sat asking nothing, being nothing, wanting nothing, hoping nothing.

Philip, looking across at her from the pew where he sat with Emma, saw that she was no longer there with Jack, with Andrew, with him, with anyone. He didn't care. What's a mother? Faith hadn't got one. She was OK. All this was for her. All these people. Even Ernie. And Alice back again. Card games again. He wasn't mad about that. He was with Emma now. Boarding. *'I am Jocasta's son.' Oh great. Tell us another. Where's Nick? Happy Christmas, I don't think. Stupid old Jack, but Emma says it's just because he's so holy. He doesn't see what's under his nose. I love Emma. I love Emma. Who wants a mother?*

'Did you say Amen?' asked Emma of Susannah. 'Say Amen, Philip.'

'Oh, all right,' said Philip and under his breath: 'Ah bloody men.' *Alice looks awful. I wonder what's up.*

'Salley, Salleeeeee, Pride of our Alleeeee,' shouted the great and glorious voice of Gracie Fields in Alice's ears. **Alice** turned her collar up and shrank into it, her pointed face lined and drawn, her eyes tight shut, her knobbed hands clasped in prayer. Jack was strong on that. *You pray properly, not lolling about like that postman or that great tussock in the turquoise-blue bomber jacket from the pub, bossing them all about — wonder they get any customers at all. Now then, tired, yes, but let's get to grips. Dear god, thank you for all the experiences of these past days, particularly the opportunity of seeing Thy works in other places, and so that I can pray for all them stuck in London on the trains and in the streets, bundled in plastic bags, God help them. Also I pray for that gorilla feller and that fat lass with the trolley never able to get up and down in the lift for water owing to the wastage of electricity. God bless that fond Madeleine in her trouble she'll come through, being so good at acting. God bless the general. Very kind of him coming out so early to get me off that bus. Very good manners, poor old soul, with his little moustache. Paid the taxi and would*

have paid the fare down, I'm not a pauper. God bless Henry Jones and his friend Jerry. You meet some funny people, but we had some laughs. 'Come back,' says Henry. 'Plenty of work down here. They're in their dotage. It's an old folks home, this place, but they've plenty of money and they understand service. They're very nice, and many with titles.' I took to Henry Jones and I'll flatter myself he took to me. Dozy place, though, nothing going on, not like a farm or here or back in Lancashire. God bless Mother and Father and that cat. God rest their souls, all of them. Yes. And God bless our Philip and I didn't like not saying goodbye. He's looking peaky – we'll have a hand of cards on Boxing Day. Who's all these people he's in among? It's that Emma at the school. Like the Ovaltine girl. Reminds me of that Holly. Well, no Dolly and Toots. And no Andrew. No loss. No general. No loss either. That general's down with Madeleine, seeing to her. In her grief. They can't be together in the house with his chair still in the sitting room, it'll be a hotel. Expensive. Best of luck. Well, Puffy. He's out of his chains. Gone. God bless him. It wasn't the sausages. Last thing he said was, 'Don't blame yourself, Alice.' Perfect gentleman. I liked that man, God. I'd have stayed with him. Noticed me more than Jack ever did. Funny so damaged. So deep, deep sick, so pinned down hand and foot and neck – like that Gulliver. My Puffy. My Puffy. Made me put on that gramophone. Damn near forced me. Threatened me till I put it on. 'Salleeeee in our Alleeee'. 'A grand Lancashire lass,' he said. 'You remind me of her, Alice,' and he laughs, wheeze, wheeze, while I carries on and on. 'You love her really,' he says. 'All that sound coming out. All that life. You would have liked to be Gracie Fields, Alice Banks.' Then he'd call out, 'Where are you, Gracie?' He'd laugh till the tears came. Dear God, I'm missing the funeral, but no odds. He was mine for a while. I loved him. And he loved me, so

397

there. Forgive me, dear God, for loving another woman's
husband. I've nothing against her. She's South, that's all.
South and posh and daft. God bless us all. 'Amen.'

'Amen,' said Jack. 'Will you all please sit. Philip, will
you go now to the cradle and be ready. Nick? Where
is he? Disappeared. Well, perhaps you, Ernie, then,
would be ready with the lighting. Jimmie – how
good to see you – could you hold the other end of
the, er, backcloth, and be ready to unroll it?'

Mr Middleditch and Jimmie unrolled the backcloth. Philip, after a couple of nudges and 'Go on,
you'll be fine,' from Emma, walked to the back of
the chapel, towards the cradle in the semidark.

'All lights out, please,' said Jocasta. Now only the
light of the snow shone blue at the windows. The
tiny flames of the paraffin heaters spluttered. 'Right,
switch on.'

The great, blazing, triumphant celebration of birth
burst over the tatty chapel. Everyone gasped. In a
moment, whispers. 'Look at that. It's Ernie.' 'Look,
it's her – the woman up at the ridge hotel. Look,
that's the postman. Isn't Jocasta terrific? She's a
genius. Look at the background. Look at the moors
spread behind.' 'No. It's not moors. It's real high
mountains. It's the Himalayas. Look, that space in
the middle, it's like a great eye.'

'Philip,' Jack called. 'Right? Bring her up, boy,
come along.'

Philip was standing behind the crib at the back of
the chapel aisle. He was looking down into the
lute-shaped nest. He was rubbing one leg against
the other, his arms hanging down, his hair over his
eyes. Everyone was turning to watch him. Behind
his glasses he was staring steadily, deeply,

thoughtfully, into the cot. Then he ran back down the aisle and pushed himself along a pew and in beside Jocasta. He flung himself at her, held her tight with both arms and placed his head in her bosom. A sob, then a great yell of pain, came from him.

Emma quickly ran up from her pew to the cot-cradle and looked in, then looked desperately towards her husband. Alice Banks stood black-eyed, grim, beside the electrified Middleditches, facing Jack and the altar, not looking round. It was Thomasina who pushed Emma aside.

'Jack,' she called. 'Faith's not here. The crib is empty.'

Christmas Eve
– and –
Christmas Morning

On the late afternoon of Christmas Eve Toots and
Dolly were watching television. They had not closed
the curtains over the big Victorian windows of
Toots's room and the night shone blackly in. If they
switched off the main light – which they seldom did,
Toots saying that he liked to see what he was doing
even if it was nothing at all – the white patches on
the grass could be seen outside and snowflakes still
falling thickly all the time. Each had been thinking
to draw the curtains but somehow had gone on
watching the coloured square, the glitter of a
leg-show, a comedian with the face of a horse,
advertisements for cars, autumn leaves falling in
Spain, Father Christmases dancing in line in Rome.
Then the news at six, then the soap that they both
enjoyed because there was no unpleasantness in it,
not like *EastEnders*. The programmes for the rest of
the evening went up.

'Christmas Eve. No better than any other night,'
said Toots. 'Same stuff, only worse.'

'Now, we had the wireless carols at three o'clock.
They never let you down, King's College Chapel.'

'It's because you can't see them. It puts you off,
seeing them. I've seen a lot of boys. I can see

through ruffs and cassocks.'

'They sing like angels.'

'I never saw an angel.'

'It's heavenly. There's nothing like it.'

'I can't get to grips with heavenly. Shut the curtains, Dorothy.'

'Dorothy – well I never! What do you want for supper, *Tom*?'

They sat on, watching a newsflash about the weather.

'Well, there was no two ways about it in the end,' she said. 'Andrew couldn't possibly have come up in this today. I dare say nobody else will have come, either. If they're there, they'll be stuck. They'll be stuck for all the holiday. Thank goodness I was firm with him. It would have been sheer bravado.'

'Aye. We're fine our two selves.'

'I think, mind you, Toots, it'll be Mrs Middleditch's tomorrow. Be ready for it. Don't create. She'll cook a lovely dinner. You're not to complain.'

'I'll not complain. I never complain. She's a good woman. Just a bit close to home. I'll take them a bottle of sherry.'

'Yes. At least. All she does for us.'

'One bottle's about right. I thought I saw her today in that car going off with Arnold somewhere.'

'They'd never go out in this.'

'It was her. About four o'clock. Have you tried Jack again?'

'They're still out of order. Did you say eggs?'

'No, I'll not bother.'

'Now you must eat, Toots.'

'Well, a bit of bread and butter. I wonder if Holly's mother got north? Not very likely.'

401

'No. It'll be a bad time for her this year. Toots?'

'Yes.'

'I could do with Holly walking in.'

'It seems early for it, but I think I might just as well go to bed. There'll be nobody coming tonight. Not many at the Midnight; there'll be no calling in before or after.'

'No stockings to fill now,' said Dolly.

'Not for thirty years. They used to give us one.'

'Andrew did. Jack always forgot, bless him.' They thought of all the years with Jack in his wilderness, then of Andrew going, then Andrew's triumphant return with Holly.

'I always made up a stocking for Holly, even last year when she was away,' said Dolly. 'Sellotape and sticky labels and writing paper and a book of stamps. I posted it. A tube of Glymiel jelly for her hands. Hard to find. You'd have thought it was diamonds.'

'She'd have brought Faith up right,' said Toots. 'Thank-you letters and that. Like her own mother did her. By God, Dolly, it's a bloody awful condition, humanity. Everyone dying except the ones you'd never miss, and not a body coming in to see you.'

'There's someone coming now. I heard the gate.'

'Well, I hope the door's locked. It's a terrible night. One thing, there'll be no criminals out. By heaven, what a racket! They're going to break the door down. Don't open it, Dolly. Just ask through the vestibule.'

Dolly first drew a shawl round her and then all the curtains across, leaving no cracks. The beating on the door increased; the bell pealed. She opened Toots's door, unlocked the inner vestibule door,

402

glazed red and blue and white, and stood in the icy space between it and the front door and called, 'Yes?'

'Let us in, Dolly, Chrissake, it's Nick.'

'Nick? Wait a minute.'

'Don't open it, now, unless you're sure,' Toots shouted. 'We're sitting ducks here.'

Dolly undid the bolts and then turned the key of the mortice lock and found it troublesome. 'We should have had this seen to. I don't know. I'm getting so woolly-minded, I forgot. Just a minute, the sneck's sticking.'

'*Dolly*! Will yer hoory oop!'

'I can't. I'm sorry, Nick. Could you go round the back? No – wait a minute. Yes, it's coming. Here we are. Oh, the snow. Whatever's all this you've got? Now, you needn't have bothered with presents, we didn't expect . . .'

Nick pushed past her, all snow and wet leather, carrying Faith's old carrycot by its two handles. He dumped it on the carpet.

'Whatever – Nick!'

'I brung 'er. They was all over t' place messing wi' magic lanterns and that Pema's gone barmy. The others is OK but they're scared of that one. I was goin' off wi' them tonight but I didn't. They're away int van now. I was bringin' Faith ower t' chapel and this Pema starts carryin' on, wanted her away wi' them int van, so I took off and brung 'er down 'ere. Put her int sidecar an' brung 'er. It was 'er christening but they left that Pema to get 'er ready, never thought of 'er. Backcloths and tea. They get yer down, oop there. S'long, I'm goin' to t' pub.'

'Nick. Nick. You can't go. Whatever – they don't know where she is. Nick—'

403

The door slammed. In a moment they heard the bike start up. The cot lay on the floor between Toots's bed and Dolly's saggy chair. Toots was upright in the bed, wild-eyed.

'Get Mrs Middleditch. Get on that phone now. We can't have this. What do we do? She may be dead.'

Dolly got slowly down on her knees and looked into the carrycot, which seemed to be packed tight with a bale of coarse coloured cloth. She removed the plastic cover off the cot.

'It's wet through,' she said, 'but this carpet stuff is dry. I'll have to ease her out.'

'Now be careful. Use your senses. Don't do anything. Maybe we should tell the police.'

'Here we are,' said Dolly. '*Here* we are.' She got her fingers beneath the bundle and lifted it out and began to undo it. 'Whatever've they dressed her in? Whatever is this? She's in somebody's old curtains and I sent up that robe of your mother's a month ago. She's got something hung on her front. It's a bit of knitting on a card. Looks like a big eye. *Here* we are.'

Faith emerged from her wrappings. She was wearing a pale-blue plastic spacesuit with a hood. Her round eyes were wide. She stared at Dolly attentively.

'Toots, look at her. What eyes! Nothing wrong there. Let's get her out of this common thing. She's a big baby. However'd he squeeze her into this? She's that solid.'

'I tell you Dolly, get the police.'

'*Now* then. *Here* we are. Look at this hair – it's getting to curl. Toots, d'you see? You can see the marks of the waves coming. I think she's losing a bit round the back. They rub it off first thing and then there's more comes, beautiful. Isn't she good? There now! That's better, without all this clobber, far too hot. Look at those arms. And the hands. Toots, they're your hands, I'd know them anywhere. Hello! *Hello*! Aren't you lovely? Aren't you beautiful, Faith. *Faith*. Just look at that mouth, Toots.'

'Faith?' said Toots climbing off the bed, hanging his legs down the side of it, with some dignity. 'Faith? Faithy? Cock-a-doodle-doo.'

'I must get her a feed. She'll need a feed. I've got the milk powder and all the paraphernalia. I knew I should. Here, Toots, you'll have to take her. And I had some nappies.'

'You'll never do it, Dolly. I tell you, ring someone up. We're old people.'

'I said take her. Here, sit in your chair and for goodness' sake don't stir. Here's your frame in front of you. Now hold her.'

'Well,' he said. 'By Gad, what happens now? Yes, I've got her. Cock-a-doodle-doo.'

Faith beheld her grandfather and frowned. A deep line appeared between the eyes. She looked away in disdain. Then she swung an arm up at him and biffed his jaw. Then she opened her mouth. The top lip was the apex of an isosceles triangle. Up it went, the mouth, opening, opening. Faith yawned.

'She yawned, Dolly.'

'She's tired.'

'I think she's just waking up. By, she's got big eyes. What's happening now?'

Faith's mouth stayed open but she turned dark red, then purplish. Her eyes she shut tight. Her arms began to work up and down like creations on springs. From the mouth came a roar.

'Here, Dolly, she's crying. I can't manage.'

'You'll have to manage. Hold on to her and don't panic, I'm sterilising bottles. Rock her. She'll never have been held in a chair like a Christian.'

At nine o'clock Faith was still roaring and Dolly was pacing with her up and down. Toots was in torment. Though Dolly had shouted 'No!' he had rung Mrs Middleditch. To no avail. He had rung the vicar, who was about his Christmas duties and on an answer machine. Toots left a wild and incomprehensible message.

'There's nothing wrong with her.'

'How do you know there's nothing wrong with her?'

'I know,' said Dolly, the baby's frantic small face contorted beneath her grandmother's chin. 'I know. I know a cry when it's a pain and this is not a pain.'

'What is it, then? They said she never cried. They said she was a quiet baby, the quietest anyone had ever known. Always half asleep.'

Faith began to flail her fists. Dolly lifted her higher on her shoulder and Faith flung herself at Dolly's chin and began to suck it. Dolly shouted with joy.

'She's just hungry. It's the different sort of milk, I expect. They'll have her on cows' milk up there. I'll try her with another bottle, but I'll change her first.'

'I'm getting out of here,' said Toots. 'This noise going on. You'll never manage.'

'No, you're not. You can just help me. I'm lying her down on your bed while I go for some Harringtons I have somewhere and some talcum like they say they never use now – ridiculous! I've a baby-bath upstairs somewhere but I won't risk it tonight with my legs. Hush now. Hush now.'

'Great Scot, anyone passing will be thinking it's child abuse.'

'Don't be silly, nobody's passing. *Here* we are. *There* we are. Now then, she's taking the bottle. Look, she was ravenous again.'

Faith's furious rolling eyes fixed themselves on Toots as she sucked. She sucked and sucked and, as she sucked, one hand opened and closed, opened and closed, over Dolly's finger. But she kept her gaze on Toots. When Dolly rearranged herself more comfortably in her chair, Faith still sucked and sucked, her gaze swivelling again towards the rosy Toots with his tufts of fluffy hair. The milk in the antique bottle went down and down, to the last drop, and she detached herself milkily and belched. She lay replete, still staring, staring, at Toots. She blinked.

'She can't take her eyes off you, Tom.' Dolly was all composure, lifting the child to her shoulder, patting her back, rearranging a little blanket she'd made into a shawl. '*There* we are. Now I'll put her down.'

But as soon as Faith was in the cot she turned purple and began to bellow. As soon as Dolly lifted her out she stopped, and stared at Toots.

'We can't go on like this all night,' said Dolly. 'With my two I just put them down and let them cry and in five minutes they were asleep. Go to the phone, Toots, just see if we can get them. They'll be frantic; they'll be out all over the snow. They'll be wild. That Nick!'

But when Toots left the room Faith began to roar and he had to come back. Dolly laid Faith on the bed and went to phone them herself but there was still no reply. When she came back into the room again

Toots was sitting with his chair drawn up near his bed where Faith lay, his eyes at Faith's level, his head leaning against the quilt, and Faith had turned her face towards him. But Faith had gone to sleep.

'There'll be no bed for us, Dolly, tonight. I'll just sit in this chair.'

'Don't be so silly. That's bad training. You'll go back in your bed and she in her cot.'

Dolly looked young. She hurried about the room, reorganising small blankets. Shaking them. She picked up the tapestry eye and set it on the mantelpiece among the Christmas cards and brass candlesticks and the photograph of Andrew and Holly at their wedding, Holly looking regal in a great white hat.

'It's watching us,' said Toots, 'that eye, whatever it is. We've to keep a watch on that thing. You won't see me sleeping tonight.'

He did sleep at last. Faith slept, too. But Dolly sat up all night beside the cot. She set the reading lamp on the floor with a screen of books round it and moved back the electric fire into the hearth so that if she slept everything would be safe. She watched over Faith, who now slept so deep that her eyes almost disappeared, far away back in her head. She lay with a remote air, confident, proud, unconquerable. Sometimes her lips chewed, as if she dreamed of milk. Sometimes her eyes moved beneath the veined, tight lids. She lay closely wrapped, still as a small yule log inside Dolly's old blankets, and when Dolly put a hand down inside the cot to see if she needed a hot-bottle or another cover she found her warm as an animal in straw, as fruit beneath a foreign sun.

*

'Dolly? Hello?'

'Shush. She's just gone off again.'

'We dreamed it.'

'Be quiet. I'll get you your tea.'

'Where is she?'

'Well, she's here of course. Here in her bed on the floor.'

'She cried all night?'

'She did no such thing.'

'You're worn out?'

'I am not worn out, so be quiet. A happy Christmas. I'll pull back the curtains.'

'I want to look at her again.'

'All in good time.'

'I couldn't stand many nights like last night. I don't know how we did it.'

'Don't be so soft. We were only awake an hour. She's a wonderful baby.'

'Why's she looking at me like that?'

'She's not, she's sleeping. Oh – yes she is, she's awake. You've woken her.'

'Goosie-goosie-gander.Cock-a-doodle-doo.Yacker-pusser. Tweet tweet. Here, Dolly, look at this.'

Faith's arrogant stare was softening. Her head was rearing up off its blanket. Her mouth was opening in the triangle again and suddenly a hoot came out from it. Then a crow. Then a crazy noise like whooping cough.

'She's laughing. I've made her laugh. By God, Dolly, it's half past seven. We've not done badly.'

'They'll be down soon. It'll be over soon,' said Dolly, drinking tea.

Faith made a noise like a new lamb, lair-lair-lair, and began to squirm about.

'Just wait till I've finished my tea,' Dolly said. 'Which of them will it be, Toots? Which one will twig she mightn't have been kidnapped? Which of them'll think of us?'

'They'll be scouring after those foreigners. The one that comes down for her will be the one who knows. The one that understands her. The one to take her and keep her. You'll see.'

When the bell rang it was still dark. 'Want to bet?' said Toots.

'Oh, I hope it isn't Mrs Middleditch,' said Dolly.

'No. It'll be Thomasina.'

And he called to her, as Dolly opened the door and he heard Holly's mother's voice: 'Come on in, Apple Green. She's all yours.'